An Amish Home

Four Stories

Beth Wiseman, Amy Clipston,

Ruth Reid, and Kathleen Fuller

ZONDERVAN

An Amish Home

A Cup Half Full copyright © 2017 by Elizabeth Wiseman Mackey
Home Sweet Home copyright © 2017 Amy Clipston
A Flicker of Hope copyright © 2017 Ruth Reid
Building Faith copyright © 2017 Kathleen Fuller

This title is also available as an e-book.

Requests for information should be addressed to:
Zondervan, 3900 Sparks Dr. SE, Grand Rapids, Michigan 49546

ISBN: 978-0-529-11869-1 (trade paper)
ISBN: 978-0-310-35438-3 (mass market)

Library of Congress Cataloging-in-Publication Data

CIP data is available upon request.

Printed in the United States of America

19 20 21 22 23 24 QG 6 5 4 3 2 1

Contents

A Cup Half Full

Beth Wiseman

To: Ann and Bill Rogers

ken the hardest hit from the blue car. She
ber much about that day, but she remem-
e car.

ily should be at the house when we get
come you home." Abram brushed back a
h's red hair that had fallen from her *kapp*.
er entire life getting used to the fact that
nly one in their district with red hair and
she'd be the only person, as far as she
eelchair.

other and parents had come to the hospi-
. They'd all been witness to her tantrums,
nd anger at her new situation. She'd prom-
hat she would tuck away those emotions
grateful that God had spared her life, and
ept Abram from serious injury.

ttled on about more modifications he'd
home. Sarah had heard it all before. Her
shared every detail throughout the pro-
gged on Sarah's eighteen-year-old brother,
had come every day to lend a hand. Sarah
een close to her brother. They were five
maybe that was why. But, interestingly,
een the most comfortable at the hospital
just her and Johnny. He didn't fuss over
as there if she needed anything. Mostly, he
e. And that was what she needed. Time to
had happened to her.

still in the van while Abram paid the
trieved the wheelchair from the back. An
hospital had worked with Sarah, showing

GLOSSARY

ach—oh
bruder—brother
daed—dad
danki—thank you
Englisch /-er—a non-Amish person
fraa—wife
gut—good
haus—house
kapp—prayer covering or cap
lieb—love
maedel—girl
mamm—mom
mammi—grandmother
mei—my
mudder—mother
nee—no
rumschpringe—running-around period when a teenager
    turns sixteen years old
sohn—son
Wei bischt?—How are you? or Hi there.
ya—yes

* The German dialect spoken by the Amish is not a written language
and varies depending on the location and origin of the settlement.
These spellings are approximations. Most Amish children learn
English after they start school. They also learn High German, which
is used in their Sunday services.

buggy ha
didn't rer
bered the
"Your
there, to
strand of
She'd spe
she was th
freckles. I
knew, in a
Sarah's
tal most d
depressio
ised herse
today and
that He ha
Abram
made to th
husband h
cess, and b
how Johnn
had never
years apar
Sarah had
when it wa
her, but he
just let her
process wh
Sarah s
driver and
intern at th

CHA

Sarah sat next to Abr
while their hired dri
in the rear compartment
would need to get used
that she'd never walk ag
"Wait until you see
Abram latched onto Sa
he'd done a luxurious r
he'd turned it into a ha
Sarah could get around
chair ramp leading to tl
She forced a smile a
hospital parking lot, a
past month.
"Johnny helped me
and we have handrail
them." Abram's dark ey
hadn't been able to ide
Was it pity? Empathy? F
Abram that the acciden
fully, her husband had
scratches and a bump

her the easiest ways to get in and out of the wheelchair. But despite what she'd learned, Abram insisted on picking her up and putting her in the chair that would be a part of her world forever, like a child being put in a booster seat.

Abram had placed wide panels of plywood in areas of their muddy yard, including a pathway toward the porch that would accommodate a wheelchair following rainy weather. She could see her parents on the porch, both smiling, but she barely gave them a glance. Her focus was on the slowly ascending plank that stretched before her like a bridge between her old life and her new one. A railing wrapped around the porch, upon which were two white wooden rocking chairs. Sarah wondered if she'd ever rock again. Her legs would just rest on the wooden slats with no way to kick herself into motion. It had always been her favorite place to be, sitting on the porch, sipping meadow tea, and watching her husband work in the fields. Especially this time of year, in the spring, with her flowerbeds filled with colorful blooms. She'd usually knit as she rocked. At least she could still do that. Playing volleyball on Sunday afternoons with the young folks wouldn't be an option ever again. And she was certain that list would grow over time.

"I've made a roast, potatoes, and carrots for dinner." Her mother clasped her hands in front of her, smiling as Abram pushed Sarah's wheelchair up the ramp. "And a red velvet cake for dessert."

Sarah suspected there was a much larger display of food awaiting them inside. Mary Stoltzfus believed that food cured all things. But being permanently handicapped wasn't an ailment that Sarah's mother could mend.

"*Danki*," Sarah said as she looked up at her mother, then her brother, and lastly at her father, who was looking at the ground. He'd visited her in the hospital the least and had very little to say. Unusual for a man who almost always voiced his thoughts. Sometimes when he shouldn't. "I appreciate everything you've all done."

Sarah's father opened the door, and Sarah breathed in the aroma of supper. She welcomed the familiarity of her mother's cooking. But when she crossed the threshold of the front door, she gasped.

"You don't like it?" Abram stepped in front of her as the lines in his forehead creased. More lines than she remembered. "I can change it." A muscle quivered at his jaw.

"*Nee, nee*," she said before swallowing hard. "It is fine. Very *gut*." She'd known this was coming, but seeing the counters a foot shorter shocked her anyway. And all of the cabinets above the counters were gone. A long row of locker-style cupboards on the floor now housed her kitchenware against a wall, which used to have racks for hanging hats and capes.

"I can change anything." Abram walked to the sink, where he towered over it like a giant who had wandered into the wrong home.

"*Nee*, it's fine. Really." Sarah knew the hours her husband had put in to transform their home. And between working outside and putting in his thirty hours per week at the hardware store, she suspected he had lost a good bit of sleep completing the task. But he'd still found time to visit her daily at the hospital. That added the expense of hiring a driver since it was too far to travel by buggy. Her parents and brother had also incurred that cost. Sarah had become a burden before she'd set one foot inside her house. A knot formed in her throat, knowing she'd never actually set her feet anywhere again.

. . .

Abram told his mother-in-law how wonderful the food was, thanked her for preparing the meal, and thanked Johnny again for all his help. As Sarah stayed quiet and picked at her food, Abram and Sarah's father settled into a conversation about the bishop. A topic Abram would have chosen to avoid since Saul never had anything nice to say about the man. Especially lately.

"If my roots weren't firmly grounded in Lancaster County, I'd pick up and move," Saul said, frowning. "Lloyd Yoder has no business being bishop."

Mary sighed heavily. "Saul, this is not a conversation for the supper table." She narrowed her eyebrows at her husband, nodding slightly toward Sarah, whose head was down. "Especially not today."

Saul raised a bushy gray eyebrow. "I think the Lord made a mistake when He saw fit for Lloyd to become bishop."

"The Lord doesn't make mistakes," Mary said as she shook her head. "Now, eat your supper." She turned to

Sarah. "How's the roast? I bet you're glad to have a home-cooked meal, *ya*?"

Sarah nodded, but continued to move her food around on her plate. Mary would faint if she knew about all the fast-food Abram had picked up on the way to see his wife. Halfway into Sarah's stay at the hospital, their driver—Lucas—would ask, "Where to today?" Sometimes it was burgers and fries. Other times, they'd grab a pizza or deli sandwich to take to Sarah. The expense had added up, but there wasn't anything Abram wouldn't do for Sarah. And the only thing that seemed to bring an inkling of joy to her was fast-food, something they hadn't grown up on and rarely splurged on. His wife was particularly fond of Chick-fil-A and Taco Bell.

"You've done a fine job on the *haus*, Abram." Saul glanced around the room at Abram and Johnny's handiwork. Abram's father-in-law had offered to help, but everyone knew Saul had a bad back. And Abram could only take his father-in-law in small doses. He loved the man for his good heart, but he was opinionated and outspoken. And it had gotten worse since Saul and Bishop Yoder had a heated argument about fertilizer a couple of months ago following a worship service. The bishop was trying to get more folks to grow organically, and Saul wasn't having any part of it. That conversation had led into another discussion about the proper way to erect a barn, a subject that was argued quite often among the men in the district. And if Saul and Bishop Yoder hadn't already bumped heads enough, the bishop tried to tell Saul that any renovations to Abram and Sarah's house needed to be approved by him. Saul had gone bonkers and hadn't been to church since the argument.

That had been one time that Abram had agreed with his father-in-law. He'd made the modifications to their home without detailing it out for the bishop. Abram had enough problems. Specifically, he wasn't sure how he was going to pay the bills he'd run up over the past month. He hadn't mentioned to Sarah or anyone else that he only worked ten hours per week at the hardware store during Sarah's hospital stay. And the revisions to the house had far exceeded his budget. For the first time in his life, he had credit card debt.

Abram thanked his father-in-law for the compliment, but as he looked upon his wife, there was no mistaking the tears she was holding back as she kept her head down, occasionally taking a small bite of roast. Abram was not going to burden her with anything. His sole purpose was to make a good life for Sarah. He hadn't had much of a chance since they'd only been married one week prior to the accident.

They had their entire lives ahead of them, they'd made plans and shared dreams. Abram still had those same dreams, but Sarah's spirit seemed broken. As her husband, it was his job to take care of her, to help her heal, and as such, he needed to carry the weight of his burdens alone for now. It wasn't just his job. He loved Sarah with his heart and soul. But he'd done this to her, put her in a wheelchair for the rest of her life. Folks could shout his innocence to the moon and back. But Abram knew the truth.

CHAPTER 2

Sarah faced off with her new bathtub, a modern contraption that looked like it belonged in the sci-fi movie she'd seen during her *rumschpringe*. She and Abram had dated longer than most couples in their district, probably pushing the acceptable time for courtship and running around. They'd also watched more movies than the bishop might have approved of, if he'd known. Neither of them had been baptized until they were twenty and twenty-one, and it still took another three years before they got married. They'd justified the long courtship because Abram's mother was ill and later died.

"Everything okay in there?"

Sarah pulled her eyes from the tub and glanced at the closed bathroom door. "*Ya*, I'm fine. Just taking my time and being careful."

The bathtub had a door that opened from the side, and inside was a seat. She'd positioned her wheelchair right next to the entrance and dropped one armrest, hoping she could just scooch into the tub seat, similar to what she'd learned at the hospital about how to get in a vehicle. But after two attempts, she was taking a break. Her legs were like dead weight, baggage that she'd have to heave from one place to another for the rest of her life. Just taking a bath in her new tub was proving to be more troublesome than she'd imagined. She glanced at the shower stall in the corner, where Abram would be showering. Another modern convenience with glass walls. All these new amenities had replaced the claw-foot tub that had been in the house since her grandparents lived here prior to their passing.

Sarah took a deep breath, her body trembling as she lifted herself onto the bathtub seat, then she curled her arms under her legs and brought them in front of her, shutting the bathtub door. Abram had already warned her that she couldn't fill the tub until the door was shut, which was obvious now that Sarah saw the setup. She sat naked on the seat, cold water pooling at her feet, another downside to her new situation. She would never again climb into a warm, steaming bath. But maybe she should be glad that she trembled from the coldness of the water, that she could even feel it. She used the opportunity to let the flowing water drown out the sobs she'd been holding in all day.

. . .

Abram readied the bed in the same manner he'd seen Sarah do for the first week of their marriage. He folded back the light yellow and blue quilt that covered their full-sized bed, then lay the white sheet back as well, fluffing both their pillows afterward. He'd already opened the window, and a cool spring breeze filled the room as crickets chirped in the distance. The lantern was lit on the nightstand by Sarah's side of the bed, along with the book she'd been reading before the accident. Abram had offered to take her books in the hospital, particularly the one she'd been in the middle of at the time of the accident, but Sarah hadn't been interested. He glanced at the book, something he was sure Bishop Yoder wouldn't approve of. On the cover, a beautiful *Englisch* woman gazed into a man's eyes, and the title—*For the Love of June*—hinted there might be some intimacy within the pages. Something Abram had high hopes for this evening.

"Everything still okay?" He held his breath, hoping he wasn't being overprotective. Sarah had been irritated when people fussed over her in the hospital. Abram cringed when he recalled Sarah's reaction to the news that she'd never walk again. It had started out with tears, then angry comments directed at God, and finally . . . she'd said she wanted to die. The next day, she'd said she didn't mean any of it, but the first week was especially hard for her. He asked again when she didn't respond. "Sarah, you okay?"

"*Ya*, Abram. I'm fine."

It sounded like she was gritting her teeth, so he needed to back off, give her time, and be patient. But as he climbed into bed wearing only a pair of boxers, patience wasn't on his mind. He was anxious to show his wife how much he loved her, show her that nothing had changed between them, and that making a baby was still part of the plans they'd made. The doctors had assured them both that the accident hadn't affected Sarah's ability to conceive and carry a child.

Abram locked his hands behind his head, waiting for the love of his life to join him. As the lantern flickered, shadows danced throughout the room. Earlier he'd lit two lavender-scented candles and placed them on top of their dresser, which not only added to the flickering shadows in the room, but also filled the cool air with the floral fragrance.

It was a perfect night. Sarah was home, and things were going to be okay. Abram wasn't going to let his financial woes or guilt affect this evening. God would provide, as always. God had forgiven Abram for the accident, but Abram quickly asked the Lord again to help him forgive himself. His shoulders were burdened. He was carrying enough worry. Continuing to haul guilt around would only hurt him and Sarah in the long run.

. . .

Sarah managed to get herself back into the wheelchair, but she'd dripped water all over the floor in the process—their new tile floor, which replaced the wood floors that had been original to the house. The tile was modest, a cool-gray color speckled with white. Although, right away, it reminded her of the bathroom floors at the hospital. Once she'd worked her way into her nightclothes, she rolled herself the two feet to the sink, which had also been lowered. After she brushed her teeth, she opened the bathroom door and rolled through the widened doorway. The smell of lavender assaulted her from the bedroom. It was a scent she used to love, but now it reminded her of the intimacy she and Abram had shared on their wedding night and the nights that followed. Before everything changed.

Abram sat up in bed. "Need some help?"

Sarah took a deep breath and reminded herself not to take offense. Abram loved her, and he just wanted to take care of her. But was this how it would be for the rest of her life? Everyone always trying to help her?

Abram slid his legs over the side of the bed and started toward her. She held up a palm. "I've got it. I don't need help." She'd allowed him to help her in and out of the wheelchair during her stay at the hospital, but Abram would head off to work in the morning, and Sarah needed to learn to get by on her own. As she rolled the wheelchair to the side of the bed—which she noticed was lower now—she positioned herself in the way she'd learned at the hospital, then tried to heave herself onto the bed, her legs not participating in the effort, as they hung lifeless, like they belonged to someone else. All the while, the fragrant lavender made her want to throw up.

"Here, Sarah, let me—"

Abram was rounding the corner of the bed when Sarah yelled, "Stop! I can do this myself." She lifted herself onto the bed as Abram froze beside her, probably praying for his old wife to return, the one who could walk, who wasn't bitter, whom he didn't have to overhaul his home for. It was a wicked thought. They'd grown up together, dated for an eternity, and Sarah had always believed they were soul mates, an *Englisch* term she'd heard used in more than one of the movies they'd watched. But as she spit her words at him, there was no denying—the Sarah she used to be was gone, replaced by someone who couldn't seem to capture the hope she'd once carried around like a precious gift. But the Lord giveth, and the Lord taketh away. Any hope for the future they'd planned had been snatched away.

She was a smart woman, though, and she would settle into her new life. But it was a life that wouldn't include children. Sarah was worried about just being able to take care of herself. How could she possibly take care of a child now? She'd had a recurring dream in the hospital. She'd fallen out of the wheelchair. A little girl—a toddler—was walking toward the stove, which had been lowered even in her dream. Steam rose from a pot of boiling water as her baby girl reached for it. Sarah tried to crawl across the living room floor, dragging her dead legs behind her. But she couldn't get to the child, who pulled the pot off the stove each time. Sarah always woke up, sweating, consumed with anxiety. If she had a child, that's how it would always be.

Abram stood perfectly still until Sarah had tucked herself in, then he walked to his side of the bed and got underneath the covers. He snuggled up next to her, his head resting on her shoulder as he kissed her on the neck.

"It's raining again," she said softly as she lay still and closed her eyes, recalling the time a couple of years ago when she and Abram tried to rustle up three of Abram's goats that had gotten loose. Abram's mother was sick, and it was just Sarah and Abram running around the yard trying to get the goats penned. And it had started pouring. Abram was so mad that Sarah had thought he might curse. That's when she'd broken out laughing, and eventually Abram laughed, too, and they'd danced around in the rain like children. They eventually got the goats back in the pen, but it was well after dark. It seemed funny to Sarah that she'd think of that now. A day running around in the rain, something she'd totally taken for granted at the time. What she wouldn't give now to run around in the rain like a silly child.

"I missed you so much," Abram whispered as he continued kissing her on the neck.

Sarah stiffened, unwillingly and unintentionally, as if in an automatic reaction to his touch. "I missed you too," she breathed in a whisper, forcing herself to relax. The doctor had said there was no reason for them not to carry on as husband and wife in the bedroom. Sarah hadn't lost the feeling in her legs, only the ability to move them due to muscle damage. But Abram wanted to start a family, and even during Sarah's time in the hospital, he'd never veered from his desire for this. "We will have plenty of time to make babies when you are well and at home," he'd told her. And she'd never argued.

Her husband had walked into her hospital room every day, trying to hide the bags beneath his eyes, and he'd always stayed cheerful and hopeful. She wanted to fall into the safeness of his embrace, to feel him love her. But her new fear about getting pregnant had put up an invisible shield around her, a barrier she hadn't even known was present until now. She eased away and put a hand on his chest, wishing her heart could just speak to his without any words, but the sorrow in her husband's eyes deserved a verbal response.

"I don't feel well." It was all she could come up with. Even though she felt all right physically, she didn't feel well emotionally at all, so she decided it was a justified tiny white lie.

Abram cupped her chin as he leaned forward and kissed her gently on the lips. Then he smoothed her red hair back from her face and said, "What can I get for you? Do you want some hot tea? Or maybe something else?"

Sarah gazed into her husband's eyes, knowing he'd do anything for her. And as much as she wanted to make him happy, she couldn't. Not tonight.

Abram smiled sweetly. "What can I do for you?" he asked again.

Can you pray that I'll walk again? It was a hollow prayer that would never be answered. Sarah had already gone through that with the doctors, told them miracles happen, that maybe she'd walk again. They'd all been adamant that Sarah would never take another step. It had seemed cruel at first, to so despondently write off the power of the Lord. But deep down, God had chosen not to fix her. He'd taken from her, and it was her duty to accept His will.

She stared at Abram for a while before she said, "Can you blow out the candles?"

Abram's expression dropped, like she'd kicked him

in the teeth. But he recovered quickly and lifted his jaw, offering her another smile. "*Ya*. Sure."

She extinguished the lantern while Abram blew out the candles, then he got back in bed beside her and found her hand. He brought it to his mouth and kissed her fingers, then they both lay quietly, lost in their thoughts. Sarah wondered what it would be like to be lost in Abram's thoughts.

It was quiet. The rain had stopped. The crickets and frogs had put themselves to bed, and there wasn't a breeze anymore, no rustling of leaves outside their bedroom window. Just darkness and silence.

Sarah closed her eyes, even though she doubted sleep would come. It was only nine thirty, and that was their normal bedtime prior to the accident. But during Sarah's time in the hospital, her sleep schedule was anything but routine, and now she found herself wide-awake as Abram started to snore.

A few minutes later, she heard her husband's cell phone ringing in the kitchen. Sarah had never owned a mobile phone. They had a phone in the barn for emergencies, and it was easy enough to hear from the house when the windows were open. But Abram had gotten a cell phone while Sarah was in the hospital so that he could call and check on her throughout the day. Her first instinct was to run to answer it, but she quickly ruled that out as an option. If it was an emergency, the caller would try the barn phone, and Sarah would hear it. She reasoned that a call coming in on Abram's new phone must have something to do with work, so she opted not to wake her husband.

But when Abram's phone rang again in the other room, she nudged him. Then the phone in the barn started to ring.

"Abram." She nudged him harder until he moaned. "Wake up. Your phone in the kitchen is ringing, and the phone in the barn is ringing too." Her heart thumped wildly in her chest. "Something is wrong."

CHAPTER 3

Abram closed the barn door behind him and walked toward the house, shining the flashlight in front of him as he tried to sidestep the standing water still in the yard. Once he hit the sheets of plywood leading to the ramp, he picked up the pace as he neared the porch, but paused at the front door. He didn't want to lie to his wife. But he also wasn't going to burden her with the truth. Abram was surprised that the creditor man was calling so late, but he was even more startled by the way the man had spoken to him.

When Abram had hit his credit limit on the only credit card he had, he'd gone to a place in town that loaned people money. He'd been so grateful to the man who'd helped him and thanked the *Englischer* repeatedly. But now the same fellow was calling because Abram was a week late making a payment. Abram had explained that he hadn't been able to work much, that his wife had been in the hospital, and that he would make the payment when he got paid the following week. The man told Abram that was unacceptable and that if Abram didn't pay on time, they'd take him to court. Abram had never owed anyone money, so he explained to the man that he promised not to be late again if he could just give him some extra time this once. The man had grumbled but eventually said that would be okay.

He opened the screen door and walked inside, deciding to head toward the kitchen. He shined the flashlight toward the refrigerator and took out a pitcher of orange juice, freshly squeezed and left at the house by Sarah's mother. Abram's mother-in-law had kept the refrigerator stocked while Sarah had been away. He drank from the pitcher, knowing Sarah didn't like it when he did that, but hoping that she'd be asleep when he got through stalling. But she was sitting up in bed with the lantern lit when he shuffled back into the bedroom.

"What's wrong?" She tucked strands of long red hair behind her ears.

Abram wanted to lie, but he decided on a version of the truth that he hoped both God and his wife would be okay with. "I borrowed some money while you were in the hospital. It was a man at the company calling to talk about payments."

Sarah stared blankly at him for a few moments. "How much money?"

Abram swallowed hard, avoided her gaze, and got back in bed. "Not much." He cringed, reckoning that *not much* could mean different things to different people. To Abram, twelve thousand dollars was a lot. He'd only had a five-thousand-dollar credit limit on his credit card, and he'd hit that amount when he purchased his first round of supplies for the remodel.

"How much is *not much*?" Sarah turned her head toward him, frowning.

Abram shrugged. "Just enough to finish up the

modifications on the house." He rolled onto his side and faced away from her, squeezing his eyes closed, hoping she wouldn't ask any more questions. Abram had already asked Mr. Hinkle at the hardware store if he could work extra hours for the next few months, and the older man had said he could.

"I could have made do, Abram," Sarah said softly in a trembling voice.

Abram rolled over to face his wife. She was still sitting up in bed, the lantern on beside her. "I don't want you to make do, Sarah. I love you, and I want things to be as easy as possible for you. The house needs to be accessible, especially when we have *kinner*. Don't worry about the money. It's my job to worry about that." *And I'm a little worried.* But not only was it his job to take care of his family, he owed Sarah—for the rest of his life—for putting her in a wheelchair.

"We decided when we got married that we were a team." Sarah folded her arms across her chest. "Did that change?"

"*Nee*, of course not. But as the head of the household, I'll handle the money." Abram waited for the argument he suspected was coming. He closed his eyes, hoping she'd let it go.

"You sound like *mei daed* and the elders, pulling that card—head of the household. I thought we were going to be different, a team."

Abram kept his eyes closed. "We *are* a team. Let's go to sleep. We've got worship service in the morning."

• • •

Sarah stared at her husband, tempted to push the issue, but she reminded herself that she wasn't the only one adjusting to changes. She extinguished the lantern and scrunched herself down into the covers, moving her legs with her arms. For the past few weeks, her legs had become more and more foreign to her, like she needed to introduce herself to her own limbs. *Hello, I'm Sarah. You must be my legs. I can feel you, but you're useless to me.*

She rolled onto her side and snuggled against her husband, surprised that he was still mentioning children. How did Abram think she would take care of a child? And surely he didn't still want four *kinner* like they'd talked about.

As good as it felt to be in her own bed with her husband, she was still having trouble falling asleep. But when she finally did, she dreamed she was running. Through a field. But then suddenly she stopped at the edge of a cliff. A little voice in her head screamed, "Jump." When she turned around, she was back in her house, pulling herself along the living room floor toward the stove. She woke up crying.

After a few brief naps during the night, she decided to get up early and familiarize herself with her new kitchen. Maybe she'd surprise her husband by having breakfast ready when he woke up, showing him—and herself—that she could function effectively, even from a wheelchair. In the darkness, she reached for her wheelchair and pulled it as close to the bed as she could. The wheels swiveled, allowing the chair to be pulled in any direction. Glancing at Abram, she considered waking him for help, if only because her arms were sore from lifting her weight, but she decided to make the attempt on her own.

She surprised herself by getting into the seat without making too much noise. She wheeled herself to the bathroom, then turned on her flashlight. After she'd brushed her teeth, she shed her nightgown and eased on a freshly pressed dress that was folded over a hanger, noticing the hook in the bathroom had been lowered. It took forever to get the dress on, but she felt a sense of accomplishment once it was done, and she quietly left the bathroom. The flashlight didn't offer as much light as a lantern would have, but everyone was in agreement that it wouldn't be safe for Sarah to balance a lantern in her lap as she used both arms to wheel herself around.

When she got to the kitchen, she found some matches and lit the lantern in the middle of the dining room table, happy that she could sit comfortably at the table, and that Abram hadn't felt the need to shave some height off the legs. Then she rolled to the lowered cabinets and lit two more lanterns, brightening the room enough to start breakfast. She raised the green blinds on the two windows in the kitchen so she'd be able to see the sun rise, then rolled herself to the refrigerator. Surely over time her arms wouldn't be so sore. She pulled the refrigerator door open, but had to stretch to reach the eggs, which were pushed toward the back on the top shelf. For all her husband's planning, he hadn't thought about the challenge of reaching into a full-sized refrigerator.

But as she glanced around her modified kitchen, she couldn't complain. Abram and Johnny had worked hard to make her life easier, and she was going to do her best to stay positive. She latched onto the carton of eggs and placed it in her lap, then found a package of store-bought bacon. Her father wouldn't like that, but Sarah was thankful her mother had stashed some in the refrigerator. Most of the meat Sarah and Abram had was kept in a frozen storage locker in town, the way it had been done for generations. Many of their people had opted to run small deep freezers using propane, like it was done with the refrigerators, but Abram and Sarah wanted to keep some things the way they had been done by generations before them. As she glanced at her legs, she realized she and Abram might need to rethink that. Hitching the horse for travel wouldn't be easy for her, maybe impossible. But for today, she decided to take baby steps. She moved a stack of cookbooks, clearing a space on the counter to prepare the eggs.

"Look who's up early." Abram walked into the kitchen, wearing a pair of boxers and a white T-shirt, rubbing his eyes. "Need some help?"

"*Nee.* You go get ready for worship service. I'll have breakfast ready soon."

Abram yawned, but she caught a hint of a smile. "*Ya,* okay." He nodded at the cookbooks Sarah had put together before the accident. "I bet you'll sell a lot of those."

Sarah shrugged. "Maybe." She'd enjoyed designing the covers and gathering her favorite recipes, but there were a lot of Amish cookbooks for tourists to choose from.

. . .

Abram dried off after his shower and breathed in the smell of bacon cooking. Smiling, he slipped into his Sunday slacks and a long-sleeved white shirt, then took a wet rag and wiped down his black shoes, which were dirty from the recent rains and mud. He tossed the rag into the basket in the laundry room before heading to the kitchen, but when he rounded the corner, he stopped abruptly. Sarah's face was in her hands, her shoulders shaking. In her lap sat a half carton of eggs, most of them broken. On the floor were two or three in a pile of yellow mess. She didn't say anything, but took one hand and pointed to the spill. Abram took a few slow steps toward her and squatted down, gently putting a hand on her leg.

"It's okay, Sarah." He paused when she still didn't look up. "It's just eggs. There will be at least a dozen more in the barn when I go out to collect them."

She slowly lifted her head, her face wet with tears. "It's not your job to collect the eggs. It's mine." Her voice was barely above a shaky whisper. "I cleaned up as best I could, but I couldn't get them all. I can barely reach the floor to wipe up the mess."

Abram hurried to the counter and found a roll of paper towels. "Everyone drops eggs sometimes." He hurried to sop up the mess, collecting the shells in one hand, wiping with the other. "And you know how much I like bacon. I can make a meal on just that." He smiled as he looked up at her. "No crying over spilt milk, so no crying over dropped eggs either."

Sarah's lips curved upward a tiny bit and she sniffled.

"See, there's my beautiful girl." Abram tossed the

eggs into the trash can, then took the carton from her lap. "Four unbroken. And that's all we need for a fine breakfast." He set the eggs on the counter, wet a kitchen towel, and handed it to her. She wiped the egg from her dark green dress. Abram wet another towel and cleaned the floor, then stood up. "*Gut* as new, *mei lieb.*"

Sarah wheeled herself to the stove where a pan was already waiting with a dab of butter, and she cracked the four eggs into the skillet while Abram poured himself a cup of coffee and sat down at the kitchen table. He'd considered offering to finish cooking breakfast, but he sensed Sarah wanted to master the task since she'd gotten up early.

A few minutes later, his wife set a plate with two fried eggs and four slices of bacon in front of him, then made a plate for herself. After they said the blessing, Abram allowed himself a moment to soak in the beauty of the woman he'd married.

"Dark green is your best color, and you look beautiful this morning." He'd told her that same thing a hundred times, but she'd never looked prettier than at this moment. "That color makes your eyes look even greener than normal." He shoveled a bite of egg into his mouth, and he was happy to see her eating as well, a hint of a smile on her face for a second time this morning, despite her earlier upset.

A cool breeze swirled through the house, and as the sun came up, Abram felt a sense of peace. God would provide, and he was anxious for worship service so he could give thanks and praise that Sarah was home. He forced away the recollection of the accident, promising

himself to focus on the blessings to be thankful for. In
time, he would find a way to forgive himself for not
being more alert that day, for not keeping his wife safe
the way he should have.

Abram stood up and offered to help Sarah clean the
kitchen, something he'd done the first week of their
married life, but she shook her head. "*Nee*, I'll do it." She
put their plates in her lap and wheeled herself to the sink.

"I don't mind." He picked up the butter and stowed
it in the refrigerator, noticing Sarah didn't have her
socks and shoes on yet. "I can finish cleaning up while
you get ready for worship service."

Sarah filled the sink with soapy water with her back
to him. Abram was still getting used to everything
being lower, but his wife was scrubbing the dishes with
ease, so he felt good about the job he and Johnny had
done. Now, he'd just have to find a way to pay for it.

"I'm not going to worship service," she said without
looking at him.

Abram stroked the fuzz on his chin, barely enough
to call a beard yet. "Are you sick?"

"*Nee*, I'm not sick." Sarah scrubbed egg from one
of the plates, then rinsed it and put it in the drying
rack. Abram could only recall one time that Sarah had
missed worship service. She'd had the flu. "But you
should go," she said as she washed the other plate.

"Is—is something else wrong?"

She shook her head.

Abram thought for a few moments and shrugged. "I
don't think the Lord would fault me for staying home to
play hooky with *mei fraa*, just this once." He chuckled, but

stopped quickly when she spun that wheelchair around in a way he didn't know she was capable of, her eyes blazing.

"I *want* you to go, Abram. Go to worship service."

He swallowed back his anger at her tone of voice, but mostly he was hurt. He'd known from day one that they'd face a lot of challenges in their lives, but maybe he'd underestimated the time it would take for them to settle into their new married lives in a way they hadn't planned for.

Abram fought the urge to tell her she didn't have to be so snappy, but instead he pointed out the window. "We've had so much rain, the chicken coops are filled with mud, and so is the yard. I've got time to collect eggs before I go."

"I thought that's why you made a ramp, so I could go up and down." Her green eyes were stone-cold as she spoke. "And you have wooden slats in the yard for me to cross over to the chicken coops. I'll get the eggs." She straightened her back and raised her chin. "Please tell everyone I'm just not up to going today."

Sarah hadn't been alone since all of this had happened. *Maybe she just needs some time to herself.*

"*Ya*, okay," he said softly after she'd turned back around and plunged her hands back into the dishwater.

Abram walked up behind her, put his hands on her shoulders, and kissed her on the cheek. There was no mistaking the way she tensed up and held her breath, her hands becoming perfectly still in the dishwater until he eased away. He stared at her back for a few seconds before he left the room. No matter what she'd said . . .

She blames me too.

CHAPTER 4

Sarah stared out the living room window from her wheelchair, watching the rain pound against the earth as it clanked against the metal roof of the house. Small puddles were beginning to connect, and she feared the yard would be a lake by the time Abram returned from church service. She knew better than to collect eggs in this weather. She'd missed the opportunity to master that task earlier, but by now, even the plywood ramps would not keep her wheelchair from getting stuck near the chicken coops.

She regretted the way she'd spoken to Abram. There wasn't a better man in the world, and her husband had moved mountains to try and make everything perfect for her. A burst of light lit the living room, followed by a loud rumble that shook the floors. The rain poured in thick sheets across the fields. Someone should have canceled worship service today. The landscape would surely fill with colorful blooms after all the rain, but such weather made driving the buggies hazardous. She stared out the window for a few more minutes and said a quick prayer that Abram and the others would have safe travels on the way home later. But now she was

going to set out to do what she'd wanted to do since
being released from the hospital.

She moved to the middle of the living room, leaned
forward, and moved the platform out from under her
bare feet. When she did, her feet flopped around like
fish out of water for a couple of seconds until they
landed on the floor the way normal feet were supposed
to. Lifting her dress to her thighs, she eyed the scars
that ran up each leg; unsightly, red lines still visible
from the stiches she'd had. She put her dress back down
and knew she was going to fall, but no one had even
allowed her to try to stand up on her own. How would
she ever know for sure if she didn't try? She could feel
her clammy feet against the cool floor.

*Please, God. I'm begging You. I'm asking for the miracle
the doctors said wasn't possible. But You can do anything.
Please, Lord . . .*

She'd played volleyball since she was old enough to
walk, and she'd always been fairly athletic. But as she
pushed herself up from the chair using only her arms,
they trembled from the weight of her body. She waited for
her legs to do something, instinctively, partially, to lend
any sort of support. *I need hope.* But they were as lifeless
as she felt most days. When she tried to put any weight
on her feet, they turned inward. She'd surely break her
ankles if she gave all of her weight to her powerless lower
limbs. She fell back into the chair, deciding she would let
herself cry and get it out of her system before Abram got
home. *He deserves so much better than me.*

Her tears and anger mixed with pity, and the trio
of emotions melded into something she didn't know

how to identify. *Wretched* came to mind. But somehow, she was going to have to feel better. *Be* better. Abram deserved that. She just didn't know how to get to that place. Maybe she wouldn't. But she was going to need to start doing her best to fake it. She got her feet resituated on the platforms, spun the chair around, and went to the kitchen. Pineapple upside-down cake was her husband's favorite dessert, and she was going to have one waiting for him when he got home. Then she remembered she didn't have any eggs, and it was only a few moments later when that annoyance was enough to make the tears come after all. But she sucked them back when she heard an unfamiliar sound coming from outside.

. . .

Abram got his horse in the stall and ran across a river of water flooding his front yard. He'd worried all through worship service about Sarah. He burst through the front door, dripping water on the living room floor, and relief consumed him when she rolled across the room carrying a bath towel. "I was getting worried," she said when she handed it to him.

He wiped his face and dabbed at his wet clothes. "We won't be going out in the buggy for a while. Your *daed* said this rain is supposed to keep up for another couple of days. I don't remember the last time I saw rain like this in Lancaster County. Lots of places are already flooded."

"What did—did people say about me not being at church?" Sarah looked away as she lowered her chin.

"No one asked why you weren't there, they just wanted to know how you were doing." He took his hat off and ran the towel across his head and over his face again. "*Ach*, except your *mamm* and your *bruder*. They wanted to know why you didn't go. I told them you needed some time to yourself and weren't up to getting out." He nodded toward the window. "Probably just as well. It's miserable out there. Lots of folks didn't even stay for the meal afterward, worried about not being able to get home. And your *daed* wasn't at worship again."

"I wish *Daed* would get right with the bishop." Sarah smiled for a brief second. "*Danki* for understanding that I just needed some time alone."

Abram felt like the waters had parted, and he dashed to her side and squatted down. "I want to do whatever you want me to do, Sarah. Just tell me. I'll do anything. I want you to be happy."

His heart hammered against his chest as he waited for any sign of hope. *Just tell me we're going to be okay. Tell me that you don't hate me or blame me.*

She grimaced, and Abram thought his pounding heart might shatter his chest wall.

"I heard an odd noise while you were gone."

It wasn't what he'd hoped for, but at least they were talking, having a normal conversation. "What kind of odd noise?"

She shook her head. "I'm not sure."

"A person? An animal?" He wrapped the towel around his shoulders, still soaked and shivering, but not about to walk away to dress in dry clothes. "Something with the weather, like a branch snapping?"

She sighed. "*Nee*, it was like a wailing sound. At first, it scared me because it almost sounded like a child. But then I heard it again, and I don't think that's what it was." She glanced toward the window. "I would have gone to check, but . . . all that water."

"*Nee, nee.* I was worried you might try to go feed the chickens and get stuck out there."

Silence.

He'd lost her again. That's how it had been since the accident. She'd act like his Sarah, then seemed to remember her situation and retreat to whatever dark place she'd created in her mind. But he waited. She stared into space over his shoulder.

"I'm going to get out of these wet clothes." He stood up, kissed her on the forehead, and felt her tense up at his touch.

By the time he'd put on dry clothes and returned to the living room, she'd started reading a book, but she was still in the wheelchair. He thought she'd be more comfortable on the couch, but he decided to stay quiet. It was safer that way.

For the first time that he could recall, he was actually looking forward to going to work tomorrow, to a place where eggshells didn't line the floors.

. . .

Monday morning, Sarah sat in the middle of her living room, her mother standing by her side, both of them staring at the contraption her mother had brought her.

"It's an electronic gadget that will clean your floors,"

Mamm said. "I charged it at Myrna Chapman's house, the *Englisch* woman you've heard me talk about before." She and her mother both bent to have a closer look.

"It looks like a flying saucer." Sarah frowned. "And it uses electricity. The bishop wouldn't approve."

Mamm tapped a finger to her chin. "*Ya*, well, the bishop doesn't approve of a lot of things, and without an electric wheelchair, it would be difficult to sweep your floors the usual way. I can come and do them once a week, but—"

"*Nee*, I don't want you doing that." Sarah sighed as she studied the round disk on the floor, not much bigger than a kitchen plate. "You just push the button and it sweeps the floors?" *That seems too good to be true.*

"*Ya*." Her mother clapped her hands, grinning. "Try it. It says on the box that it will run for hours. So, when it runs out of energy, I will take it to recharge. At least you can sweep the floors easily once a week or so."

Sarah shook her head. "I don't know about this, *Mamm*."

"This is a small and efficient tool. Or so I've heard." *Mamm* was still smiling, like a child with a new toy.

"Your father wants you to have an electric wheelchair, but it—"

"*Nee, Mamm, nee.* That requires electricity, too, and it's much too expensive." Sarah sighed. "I want *Daed* to get right with the bishop and start going to worship service again."

Mamm folded her hands in front of her and locked eyes with Sarah. "Speaking of . . . why weren't you at church yesterday?"

"I just needed some time to myself. At the hospital, everyone hovered, and Abram hovers, and I just wanted to be alone." Mostly true. Her father might not be going to church because he wasn't right with the bishop. Sarah didn't feel right with God.

"*Ya*, I can understand that," her mother said softly, then her face lit up again. "Push the button."

Sarah grinned, leaned down, and hit Start. Her mother jumped when the gadget played a little tune, spun in a circle, then took off across the living room. "Isn't that something?" Her mother shook her head, smiling.

After a few minutes of watching the mechanical robot bounce into the walls and furniture in an effort to get around, Sarah's mother put a casserole in the refrigerator and said she was leaving. "More rain coming today. Some of the fields still look like lakes, so I better get home." She stood staring at Sarah for a few moments, then put a hand on her daughter's shoulder. "Everything is going to be all right. It's a new way of life, a challenge. But God is with you every step of the way."

"I won't be taking any steps, *Mamm*."

Her mother bit her bottom lip. "You know what I mean. Stay strong in your faith, Sarah. The Lord tests those He believes in the most, those who can endure and prevail. You might not understand why this happened, but stay close to Him."

Sarah nodded, but she didn't have much to say to God at the moment as she watched her mechanical cleaning machine banging into everything she owned. Awhile later, when the thing found her knitting basket and latched on to a thread hanging over the side, she had to chase it down in her wheelchair while she watched the pair of pink booties she'd been knitting unfurl. She slowed down and then came to a stop. Did it really matter if the booties were destroyed? She'd started making them before she knew she wouldn't be having children.

As she let that soak in, she heard a noise outside, the same wailing she'd heard the day before, only louder. And it sounded like it was coming from the porch.

CHAPTER 5

Sarah rolled herself out the door and onto the porch, a spray of rain misting her as she studied the two rocking chairs to her left. But as her eyes drifted to what was underneath one of the chairs, she brought a hand to her chest. *A duck?*

She edged herself closer as the source of the wailing began again, but slowed her movement when the bird fluttered its wings and tried to run, falling twice, shaking, and making a horrible noise. He—or she—had blood matted to its white feathers and was covered in mud. As she examined the animal, she saw that one of its webbed feet was missing, only a nub remained. Lying on one side, the duck had exhausted its efforts, its eyes barely open.

"*Wie bischt*, big fellow." Sarah brought a hand to her forehead, trying to block the spray of water blowing beneath the porch rafters. When the bird's eyes closed, Sarah wondered if it would be for the last time. She'd been around chickens her entire life, but she didn't know anything about ducks. But one thing she *did* know was that this was no baby duck.

After a while, she went inside and peeled an apple, then cut it into small pieces. By the time she rolled back onto the porch, the duck was gone, and in the distance, she could see it limping away. She cringed when the poor fellow fell again, then disappeared into the thick, rainy fog. She tossed the chunks of apple on the ramp leading to the porch and went back inside.

· · ·

Abram cashed his paycheck at the bank and walked the short distance to the loan center, glad it wasn't raining and hoping he'd still have time to eat his dinner—or lunch, as the *Englisch* called it—before his break was over. Personal Loans, Bad Credit Okay was printed in red on the glass door. Below that was a red suitcase filled with money etched into the glass. He pulled the door open and walked inside. It was a small place with two desks, each with a man sitting behind it. He recognized the *Englisch* man who had helped him before, so he took off his hat and walked that way, slowing his steps when the fellow reached into a bag and pulled out a French fry.

"I'm sorry to bother you during dinner time, but I wanted to make a payment on my loan." He reached into his pocket and pulled out a hundred dollar bill, offering it to the heavyset, older man. Abram remembered his name was Bill.

"You owe two hundred," the man said as he reached for another fry and stuffed it into his mouth. Bill had a round face with patches of dark whiskers scattered about, like he was trying to grow a beard and couldn't. Abram could sympathize.

"*Ya*, I know. But this is all I can pay right now. My wife was in an accident, and—"

"Yeah, yeah. I know. You told me." Bill pulled a hamburger from the bag and started unwrapping it. "And I'm really sorry about your wife. That's a horrible thing to have happen. You'd think that people around here would be more careful with all the buggies on the roads."

Abram still stood with the money in his hand, unsure whether to place it on the desk or not. "*Ya*, I know." He swallowed hard. "I—I can pay you the other hundred next week."

Bill finished a bite of his burger and nodded. "I know you're good for it, kid, but . . ." He sighed. "The interest rate goes up when you don't make your payments on time. You understand that, right?"

Abram nodded, glad that Bill didn't seem as nasty today as he had on the phone. "*Ya, ya*. I know."

"So, next week when you come, you need to bring a hundred and fifty."

Abram realized that he didn't understand how this worked after all.

By the time he walked back to the hardware store, he had about ten minutes to eat before he needed to get back to work. He pulled his pail from the refrigerator in the back room and sat down at the table, then dove in to a ham sandwich that he'd slapped together that morning. He thought about the first week he and Sarah were married and how she'd packed him a lunch for work each day. Usually, there was a sandwich, chips or nuts, an apple or orange, and always a note. He remembered one that read, *I love you* and another, *Can't wait to see you tonight.* But lately, it had just been a lone sandwich that he'd hurriedly made before leaving the house. He took the last bite and glanced at the pail, wishing an apple or bag of chips would appear. But not even a napkin.

"How's your wife doing?"

Abram looked up when Brenda pulled out the chair across from him. He'd worked with her for almost four years. Mr. Hinkle had six employees, and Abram and Brenda had been there the longest. But up until recently, Brenda had worked the cash register and Abram had stocked shelves, placed orders, and kept up with the inventory. Now, Brenda worked in the back office answering the phone and doing the bookkeeping so Abram ran into her more often. "She's adjusting, I think." *I hope.*

Brenda flung her long blond hair over her shoulders, pulled a container from the refrigerator, and placed it in the microwave. She turned to face him, leaning against the counter as she crossed one ankle over the other. Her short blue jeans were cuffed below her knees, and her shoes were the flip-flop kind that lots of *Englisch* girls wore. Her green eyes matched her green shirt today.

"It's bound to be hard for her to get used to being in a wheelchair." Brenda hung her head for a few moments before she looked back at him. "I feel bad for her."

Abram gulped from a glass of water in front of him as he fought the urge to tell Brenda that pity wasn't what they needed right now. Everyone had the best of intentions, but Sarah was still the same strong, beautiful woman he'd married. He just nodded as he glanced at the clock on the wall. He'd inhaled his food with five minutes to spare, but his stomach growled at him for not bringing more.

When Brenda opened the microwave, a wonderful aroma filled the air in the small break room. After she sat down, Abram saw that it was soup, maybe chicken noodle.

"You're staring at my soup as if it might sprout wings and take flight." She laughed, then blew on her spoon before taking a bite.

"It smells *gut*," he said, grinning.

"It is *gut*," she said, attempting to imitate him. She pushed back her chair, got up, and returned with a bowl. "And it's way too much for me." She poured a generous amount and pushed the bowl toward Abram, then got him a spoon. "I used to send any leftovers with David for lunch, but . . ." She shrugged. "He's out of luck now since we broke up."

Abram had met David lots of times picking up Brenda after work, at Christmas parties Mr. Hinkle had at the shop, and sometimes when he just stopped in. "I didn't know you'd broken up." He blew on his spoon and took a bite of soup, closing his eyes and allowing the flavor to settle on his palate. He'd always thought his mother made the best chicken soup ever, but Brenda might have just earned the first-place ranking.

"Yeah, we broke up a few weeks ago."

Abram thought for a few moments, realizing he hadn't seen David around. "I'm sorry."

She shrugged again. "It needed to happen, and it had been a long time coming." She smiled. "You like the soup?"

Abram nodded, smiling. "*Mei mamm* wouldn't want to hear this, but it's the best chicken noodle soup I've ever had."

"I love to cook. And I always make enough for lunch leftovers." She glanced at his lunch pail, then at him. "I can bring you some too."

Abram shook his head. "*Nee, née* . . . I wouldn't want you to do that."

"It's no big deal. I see you eating sandwiches most of the time." She blew on her spoon and took another bite.

Abram's had cooled to the point that he was shoveling it in as if he hadn't eaten in a month of Sundays. He recalled the leftovers that his mother used to send with him when he lived at home. Sarah sent sandwiches that first week they were married, but Abram couldn't have cared less what she sent him. His wife's sandwiches tasted way better than what he'd been making. When he would tell her how good they were, she'd just say, *It's because they were made with love.* Abram was pretty sure it was because she mixed the mayonnaise and mustard together and sprinkled on salt and pepper. *I need to remember to do that.* Although there wasn't a sandwich on the planet that could compare to Brenda's soup. "Well, if you had any leftovers, I wouldn't be opposed to helping you finish them off." He grinned before he took the last bite, glancing at the clock again.

"Consider it done." Brenda smiled as Abram stood up to leave. Then she winked at him.

. . .

Sarah stared at her new pantry, the one Abram had worked so hard to construct. Everything was at eye level and easy to reach. Her mother had stocked it before Sarah got home from the hospital. But as she looked at bags of rice and pasta, jams and jellies, and even some canned foods, she couldn't get excited about cooking. Closing her eyes, she recalled the way she used to run down the porch steps and jump into Abram's arms the moment he stepped out of his buggy in the evenings. She jumped when she heard someone open the front door and close it, heavy steps pounding across the living room.

"Don't you know how to knock?" she asked Johnny when he walked into the kitchen.

"It's almost suppertime, and *Mamm* is making meat loaf. She knows I don't like it. Does she think that after seventeen years that I'll suddenly grow fond of it?" He sniffed the air. "I was going to see what you had, but I don't smell anything."

Sarah closed the door to her handicap-accessible pantry. "I haven't started anything." She shrugged. "Maybe I won't cook."

Johnny took off his hat and started to put it in the spot where the coatracks used to be, but then put it on the table.

"Can you get your hat off the table, please? We eat there." She grimaced at her brother. Johnny was tall and lanky, but he seemed to stay hungry. Their mother always said he had a hole in his stomach.

Johnny picked up his hat and frowned. "So, you're not going to cook anything for Abram after he's worked all day?"

Sarah pointed to the wheelchair. "I think I'm entitled to skip a day."

"Why? Just because you can't walk?"

Sarah narrowed her eyes at him, opened her mouth to tell him to shut up, then snapped it closed as she remembered how much Johnny had helped Abram transform their home. And Johnny had been awfully good to her while she was in the hospital. But he'd known how to keep his mouth shut then and just let her be. "Well . . ." she said, stretching out the word. "Things have changed a little bit."

Johnny shrugged. "I'm glad I'm not the one married to you. I'd starve if I lived here."

Sarah blinked her eyes a few times and stared at him as her mouth dropped open a little.

Her brother's hat slipped from his hand. He picked it up from the floor, then stared at her. "What? Why are you looking at me like that?"

"Because you are being cruel."

"How is saying I'm hungry and that I'd starve if I lived here being cruel?"

"You said you're glad you're not the person married to me." She spat the words at him. "I'm sure Abram would walk away if he could. He doesn't deserve to be with someone who can't function like a normal person."

Johnny put his hat on his head, then pointed a finger at her. "Everyone let you get away with your little temper tantrums in the hospital, but it ain't like you're dead. You need to quit feeling sorry for yourself."

Sarah's jaw fell open even more as she blinked back tears. "How can you talk to me like that?"

Johnny took a step closer. "There are a lot of miserable couples in our district, and it's easy to see. But you and Abram have always given me hope that I can be as happy as the two of you are someday. I ain't ever seen two people love each other as much as you two." He paused. "Except maybe *Mamm* and *Daed*. I just don't want to see you mess it up." He let his eyes roam the room and pointed. "He did all of this for you. He loves you. He's grateful his *fraa* is alive." He pointed his finger at her. "And you can still have *kinner* and have a *gut* life."

I'm not having any kinner.

"I love you, Sarah. And you're a strong woman. I don't want that to slip away. That's all. It must seem real unfair to you, that God chose this path for you. But it's His will." He paused, sighing. "So, be that strong person for the man that loves you." He grinned. "And make the poor fellow some supper."

Sarah waited until she heard his buggy pulling away before she opened the pantry and pulled out a bag of rice, then she stretched her arm into the refrigerator and found a hen.

CHAPTER 6

Abram walked across the front yard, missing the few times in his short married life that Sarah had crossed the yard and jumped into his arms, but he was determined to be joyful and grateful. He said a quick prayer that his wife had a good day, and he felt encouraged when he walked into the living room and smelled . . . something. It didn't take long to recognize that whatever had been cooking was now burnt. He found her in the kitchen staring at a pile of pots and pans stacked in the sink. But no food on the table. She spun the wheelchair around, her face streaked with tears.

"I—I was going to make you chicken and rice. Your mother's recipe, the one she shared with me before she passed." She lifted her shoulders and slowly lowered them, still crying. "But I fell in the bathroom and—"

Abram rushed over and squatted beside her. "Are you hurt? What happened?"

"I'm fine." She covered her face with her hands, sobbing. "It took forever to get back into the wheelchair, and I could smell the hen burning. The rice was ruined too."

"Sarah, don't cry, *mei lieb*." He leaned over and brushed his lips against hers, thankful she didn't tense up or pull away. "It's been a long time since we went out to eat in town, and look . . ." He waved toward the window. "The sun is shining and there is still plenty of daylight for traveling. Do you want to go out to eat?"

Sarah's color drained from her face, and Abram realized that she hadn't been back in a buggy since the accident. "I—I don't know," she whispered.

Abram cupped her cheeks and drew her face to his, kissing her again, slower this time, lingering. "We don't have to go anywhere at all," he said with all the hopefulness of a man who missed his wife. He gazed into her eyes, trying to read her thoughts, and before he could define what she was thinking or feeling, she drew him to her and kissed him with all the passion he remembered. And for the first time in weeks, their hearts were beating as one, and in a single swoop, he lifted her into his arms and carried her to the bedroom, his mouth never leaving hers.

He gently eased her onto the bed, lay down beside her, and pulled her closer to him. "I love you so much," he said in a breathless whisper.

She touched his shoulders and gently pushed him back. "I think I *would* like to go out to eat. Somewhere close, and only if we can get home before dark."

It was over. She'd retreated again.

Abram forced a smile, helped her to sit up, and went to get her wheelchair.

. . .

Sarah wasn't comfortable in the restaurant Abram had chosen. They'd had difficulty getting the wheelchair over a high threshold, Abram had slammed her into the back of someone's chair on the way to their table, and she'd had to make small talk with two women she knew. Her heart had pumped viciously against her chest during the ride in the buggy. It was the lesser of the two evils presented to her this evening. But Abram was her husband, and she owed him something— probably more than she'd ever be able to give him.

"I'm sorry about earlier," she said in a whisper, even though there wasn't anyone nearby.

"*Nee, nee.* I'm sorry. I know you had a bad day and . . ." He opened his menu and didn't look at her.

"It's not that I didn't want to. I just, um . . ." How could she explain to the man she loved that she was terrified of getting pregnant, scared of the one thing they'd dreamed about for years?

"*Nee,* it's fine. Really." He raised his eyes above his menu and smiled at her. "I haven't had a *gut* burger in a long time."

Sarah wasn't hungry, and she could see her husband heading to the place he retreated to when he didn't want to talk about something. Sarah had a similar place she visited, and she wondered if Abram's retreat felt as dark as hers. When would they meet back at the place where their souls had first been introduced, a place with light and love and hope?

She thought about what Johnny told her. It was mean and cruel. And true. Sarah did need to stop feeling sorry for herself, if for no other reason than her love for Abram. She slapped her menu closed and put it on the table.

"I'm getting a burger too." She smiled, then reached over and touched his hand. "I love you."

Abram blinked a few times, and for a moment, Sarah thought he might cry. Had she been so awful that a simple and truthful statement could cause him such emotion? "Things are going to be different," she said, smiling again. "Soon."

Sarah was at her most fertile right now according to her calculations. In a few days, it would be safe to work her way back into her husband's arms, to see if there was any way she'd feel whole again, knowing her plans of their future looked much different than his.

. . .

Sarah awoke the next morning to an empty bed. Once again she'd overslept, not prepared breakfast for Abram, or packed him a lunch. A burnt smell hung in the air from the night before, but when she rolled into the kitchen, she saw that Abram had cleaned the dishes that had been stacked in the sink.

She looked at the clock on the wall. It had taken her thirty minutes to get in the wheelchair, wash her face, brush her teeth, get dressed, and secure her *kapp*. Fifteen minutes faster than the day before.

She opened the pantry and began taking inventory of what she had, what she needed, and then planned her day. A couple of hours later, she had two loaves of bread rising on the counter and a cherry streusel baking in the oven. She was getting ready to start washing clothes in the wringer when she heard movement on the porch. She'd noticed yesterday that the apple pieces were no longer on the porch, but she'd spotted a stray cat recently and assumed the feline or some other animal had eaten the fruit.

As she wheeled herself onto the porch, she was surprised to see her feathery visitor behind the rocking chair again. "I see you've cleaned yourself up."

There was only a hint of mud and dried blood on the duck's tail feathers. He looked up, flapped his wings, and tried to stand up, but fell. He lay there for a few moments, then tried again, and toppled over again. When Sarah was a young girl, her family had had a chicken with one leg, and he got around on just that one leg, but this fellow was trying to walk with both legs when one was several inches shorter than the other. "You need to just hop on your one leg," she said. "I'd show you if I could." She rolled her eyes. *Now I'm talking to a duck.*

She waited for him to scurry off again, but when he didn't, she went inside and brought back more chunks of apple. She tossed a few his direction, but he didn't move. She set the rest down and went back inside, thinking maybe he'd eat if she wasn't watching him.

After she pulled the cherry streusel from the oven, she rolled to the window. All of the apple was gone, and her feathery friend was back underneath the rocker. He was a big bird, a mallard, she thought. Probably displaced by all the rain. She could recall a heavy flood from when she was younger, and when it was all over, she'd watched a mother duck and her ducklings cross their front yard. Her father had said all the rain had upset the ecosystem and that the birds were most likely displaced or lost.

She filled a plate with sunflower seeds, more apple, and torn-up pieces of lettuce. Her chickens ate most anything. She wasn't sure about ducks. She set the plate on the porch and went back inside. The next time she looked out the window, the duck was eating. Smiling, she set to making a casserole for supper.

. . .

Abram bit into another ham sandwich the next day in the break room. When Brenda walked in, she grunted and put her hands on her hips.

"Why'd you bring your lunch? I told you I'd feed you." She smiled before she walked to the microwave.

Abram swallowed the bite in his mouth. "*Ach*, I didn't figure you cooked every night, so I didn't know if you'd have leftovers, and I surely don't want you to bring me food every day."

She placed a white container—a rather large one—in the microwave and set the timer. If there were one modern appliance Abram was allowed to have, it would be a microwave. The thought of hot food in two minutes sounded heavenly. He was waiting for someone to invent a microwave that ran on batteries.

"I cook most every night." She got two paper plates out of the cabinet above the small sink and placed one in front of Abram and one for herself, then she retrieved the white dish from the microwave. "This is a beef-and-cheese casserole I came up with one day. It doesn't have an official name."

"*Ya*, well, it smells *gut*." Abram pushed his sandwich aside.

"Dig in." She spooned some onto her plate and took a bite right away. Abram put a large spoonful on his plate, then bowed in prayer. Brenda was staring at him when he looked up.

"Oops," she said. "I forgot you people pray before meals. I really need to be better about that."

Abram wasn't sure how to respond. Mr. Hinkle's other four employees ate out every day, and occasionally Mr. Hinkle would eat in the break room, but he mostly went home to eat lunch with his wife. Abram would do that if he lived closer.

"You know . . ." Brenda tapped her fingernail against the table, her head tilted to one side. "I take back what I said. There are a few nights I don't cook. I don't have much of a life now that David and I aren't seeing each other, but sometimes I go out to eat with friends or something unexpected comes up. Why don't you just give me your phone number and I can text you on the days you need to bring a lunch, which will most likely be few and far between."

"Uh . . ." He rubbed his chin.

"I know you people have cell phones. I see Amish talking on them all the time."

"*Ya*, it's just supposed to be for emergencies."

She laughed. "As much as you like to eat, I'm guessing it would be an emergency if you didn't have a lunch one day." She shrugged. "Or I guess you could just grab a burger or something."

That costs money. And that thought sent him to another point. "It costs money to cook something like this." He nodded at his plate, which was nearly empty. "I don't feel right about you bringing me lunches very often."

She sighed heavily. "It's no biggie. I hate to eat alone." She snapped a finger. "Is your wife a good baker?"

"The best," Abram said with a mouthful. Although, there hadn't been much proof of that lately.

"I love sweets, and I rarely bake. Just bring me a dessert every now and then, and we'll call it even."

He smiled. "I'm not sure if that's fair or not, but okay."

Brenda reached for a pen that was on the table, then ripped her napkin in half. "What's your phone number?" When Abram hesitated, she blew out an exaggerated puff of air. "I'll only text if I'm not bringing lunch. And we already established that it would be an emergency for you to miss a meal." She giggled.

Abram gave her his phone number, finished his beef-and-cheddar casserole, and thanked her for the meal.

"No problem." She winked at him. Again.

CHAPTER 7

Sarah smoothed the wrinkles from her dress as best she could, and when she heard Abram coming up the driveway, she slipped on her kitchen mitts, opened the oven, and pulled out a chicken casserole. She set it on a thick towel in her lap and then carried it to the table, placing it next to a loaf of bread and bowls of chowchow and rhubarb jam. If she couldn't give her husband what he longed for in the bedroom, she was going to double her efforts in the kitchen. She glanced at the cherry streusel on top of the stove and smiled.

"Something smells mighty *gut* in here," Abram said as he crossed the living room and met her in the kitchen. It seemed odd that such a small accomplishment filled her with pride, whether such an emotion was forbidden or not.

"*Danki*. I'm sure you're tired of scrounging for food and taking sandwiches that you had to make for lunch." She waved a hand across the table. "I made plenty so that you'll have something to take for lunch tomorrow. You might as well take advantage of the microwave at your work."

"Uh, *ya*. I reckon I should." Abram took off his hat

and hung it on the back of a kitchen chair. "It looks great." He walked toward her, leaned down, and kissed her. "But even better is how beautiful *mei fraa* looks."

Sarah was proud of herself for learning to function in her new environment. But as Abram leaned in to kiss her again, she leaned back a little, not wanting to lead him in a direction she wasn't ready to go. "Let's eat while it's hot."

Abram straightened and walked around to his side of the table, and after they'd bowed their heads in prayer, Sarah spooned some casserole onto his plate and asked about his day.

. . .

"Just another day," Abram said as he avoided his wife's eyes. No need to mention the phone call he got from Bill, reminding Abram about his loan payment, which was now fifty dollars higher this week. And he wasn't sure Sarah would take kindly to Brenda bringing him lunches at work. Since Sarah seemed like she was adapting to her new way of life, hopefully these meals would become a regular thing and he'd take his own leftovers to work. And if not, he was okay with that too. But the more he'd thought about it, it didn't really seem right for Brenda to bring him lunches on most days, whether he brought dessert or not.

Abram slathered butter on a slice of the warm bread. "Did you know there is a duck on the porch?" he asked when she'd finished serving him.

His wife nodded. "*Ya.* I think he must be lost or something. Maybe from all the rain."

"Seems odd that he'd take up residence on our porch." Abram finished off his bread and reached for another slice.

"He only has part of one leg, so he doesn't get around very good." She paused, taking a sip of iced tea. "And he's hungry."

"How's he getting up on the porch with one leg?"

Sarah shrugged, her fork halfway to her mouth. "I'm not sure. But ducks fly, so maybe he flies up there." She sighed. "I wish I could fly."

Abram grinned as he visualized his wife with wings, soaring through the air. "Well, that would be something."

Sarah smiled a little, too, and they were quiet as droplets of rain clinked against the metal roof. "More rain," she whispered.

Abram nodded. "More rain," he echoed. As the clouds moved in, darkness fell outside, and inside only the lanterns shone, enough that he could see the pain etched across his wife's face.

He wondered if she would ever be truly happy again.

. . .

Sarah wheeled herself onto the porch the next morning as the sun struggled to shed light through the gray clouds. The steady rain that had started at suppertime kept up through the night. Her visiting duck was underneath the rocker, his eyes wide as he stared at her.

"No worries, my friend. I brought you breakfast." She set the plate of leftover bacon, more lettuce, sunflower seeds, and apple chunks next to her on the porch. Smiling, she watched him hop toward her. "You are learning to get around much better," she said as the duck took a final hop her way, putting him less than a foot from her, the closest he'd ever come. She reached down to attempt to pet the bird, but he fell backward, so she withdrew her hand and stayed still. He managed to get back up, glancing at her several times before he began to nibble from the plate.

"If you're going to hang around, I suppose you need a name." She poured from a bag of sunflower seeds in her lap, filling her palm. Slowly, she lowered her hand, and when her new feathery friend ate from it, she smiled again. She hand-fed him several more times before he retreated back to his spot behind the rocking chair.

Sarah watched the rain as the dark clouds took over, leaving no hope for even a ray of sunshine to peek through. "I'm going to call you Henry." She coaxed her new pet from behind the rocker and was still trying to feed him when her father turned in to her driveway, his buggy and horse covered in mud.

"I'm not staying long," he said as he rushed up the ramp and onto the porch, blocking his face with a paper bag he was holding. His quick actions sent Henry fluttering back to his spot behind the rocker. Her father lowered the bag, peering at the bird. "What is a duck doing on your porch?"

"He's missing part of a leg," Sarah said as she watched

the bird grow calm, nestled beneath the rocker as if safe from the world.

"But what's he doing on your porch?"

Sarah shrugged. "I don't know. Displaced by all the rain?"

"*Ya, ya.* Probably." Her father handed Sarah the bag. "Your *mamm* said to drop this off. It's your share from the bake sale, uh . . . that you had with your *mudder* . . . before the accident. She keeps forgetting to give it to you." He took off his straw hat and ran a sleeve along his wet forehead. "There's a hundred dollars, give or take, in there."

"*Danki.* But you didn't have to bring it in this weather." Sarah opened the bag and saw loose bills. "We had a *gut* sale that day."

Her father didn't seem to hear her as he moved closer to where the duck sat. "His name is Henry."

Daed inched closer, until the bird's feathers ruffled, then he backed up. "It's a shame about his leg."

"But he can fly," Sarah quickly said. "And I've been feeding him—lettuce, apples, and nuts mostly."

"No nuts." Her father straightened and walked to where Sarah was sitting. "Not *gut* for Pekin ducks, or any ducks for that matter."

"*Ach*, I didn't know that. He's not a mallard?"

Her father waved his arms a few times, shaking beads of water from his sleeves. "*Nee.* Mallards are filled with color, not white like this fellow." He waved an arm toward the door, then headed in that direction. "I could use a cup of coffee."

Sarah followed her father, and once inside, he

pushed her wheelchair to the kitchen table, and he poured them each a cup of coffee and sat down across from her.

"So . . ." *Daed* took a sip of coffee. "Why weren't you at worship service Sunday?"

"Same reason as you, I suppose." Sarah threw the comment out there as a fishing venture, curious if her father had been completely truthful about his reason for not attending church.

"You're mad at the bishop too?" He raised a dark, bushy eyebrow, then stroked his beard.

Sarah raised her shoulders and lowered them slowly, sighing. "*Nee.* I'm not mad at the bishop. But is that really why you aren't going to worship?"

Her father frowned, narrowing his eyebrows. "I didn't come here to talk about me. I came here to make sure you were all right."

"I'm fine." Sarah brought her cup to her lips, keeping her eyes on her father.

"That's *gut* to know." Her father reached for a peanut butter cookie on a nearby plate, took a bite, and put it back. "Store-bought." Sarah rolled her eyes, but before she could tell him they weren't from the store, he said, "I was worried that maybe you'd taken issue with the Lord about your accident. God always has a plan, although sometimes we don't understand it."

Sarah forced herself calm by taking a deep breath. If one more person told her God always has a plan, she might explode. "I know. But is your issue with the bishop reason enough for you to stop going to church?"

Her father huffed. "Quit turning this around and

making it about me." He blew out a long breath of frustration. "You women must learn how to do that at an early age, like you train for it or something."

Sarah grinned. "*Ya*, we meet weekly and conjure up ways to trick the men in our lives."

"Ha, ha," her *daed* grumbled as he changed his mind and reached for the half-eaten cookie.

"Don't you think it's time for you to make up with the bishop? And if not, your anger at Bishop Yoder shouldn't keep you from church."

"My business with the bishop and the Lord is my business."

"Such is the case with me." Sarah sat taller in her wheelchair as she folded her hands in her lap.

Her father pushed his chair back from the table, grabbed another cookie, then pointed a finger at her. "Don't fall into a pit of despair, *mei maedel*. You can't blame God for what has happened to you."

"I never said I did."

Daed stared at her for a while, squinting one eye. "You never said you *didn't* either."

Sarah swallowed hard. Parents had a keen instinct that seemed borrowed from God, a knowingness that was on loan while they raised their children.

"I'm going home. And report back to your *mamm* that you're okay. But I'd like to hear that you are in church Sunday after next."

"Maybe I'll see you there?" Sarah offered up a challenging tight-lipped smile while lifting one of her eyebrows.

Her father grunted as he turned his back and made

his way through the living room and to the front door.
"And quit feeding that duck nuts," he said over his
shoulder before he walked onto the porch.

Sarah waited until he was gone before she wheeled
herself onto the porch. Henry was curled up in his spot
with one wing halfway covering his face. When she
leaned down to touch the bird, he uncovered his face and
locked eyes with her. "We are both damaged," she whispered. "And if God wanted to, He could fix both of us."

. . .

Abram opened the refrigerator and eyed the leftover
chicken casserole Sarah had packed for lunch. Then his
eyes drifted over to a large container nearby.

"Oh my, what a conundrum you have. Two lunches
to choose from."

He turned quickly when he felt Brenda's breath on
his neck. "Uh . . . *ya*. I guess."

She leaned around him and pulled out her blue
Tupperware box, her blond hair brushing against his
arm. Her hair, normally straight, was curled today. He
was tempted to tell her he liked it that way, that it looked
pretty. But he wasn't sure if that would be flirting.

"So . . ." Brenda put the container in the microwave
and set the timer for two minutes. "I see your wife
packed you a lunch. What is it?"

"Chicken casserole." He inhaled the aroma of whatever was in the microwave. "What did you bring?"

"Smothered steaks with mushroom gravy and a generous side of mashed potatoes."

Abram's mouth watered as he weighed his options. "I guess we could each have a little of both?"

Brenda chuckled. "Well, that seems like the diplomatic thing to do. If you choose my steaks over your wife's chicken, that wouldn't be good. And you're surely afraid that if you don't eat my steak, that you'll hurt my feelings."

"Are you always so honest and forthright about things?"

She laughed again. "That sounds odd coming from one of you religious types. Isn't honesty always the best policy?"

"I reckon," he said softly as she took her steaks from the microwave, then retrieved the casserole from the refrigerator to heat up.

"So, no more sandwiches? Your wife is cooking for you now?" Brenda leaned against the counter and picked at one of her pink fingernails.

"Well, she cooked last night." Abram didn't know what to expect from one day to the next.

When the microwave dinged, Brenda pulled out the casserole and set it on the table alongside the smothered steaks, then she fetched them each a plate and silverware.

"I need a guy's point of view about something," she said as she sat down.

Abram lowered his head and said the blessing as fast as he could, anxious to eat. When he looked up, she was spooning casserole onto her plate. "Uh, okay," he said as he stabbed one of the steaks and brought it to his plate, noticing her hair again.

"James asked me out." Brenda took a big bite of Sarah's chicken casserole. "Oh, wow. This is great." She chewed for a while before swallowing. "Anyway, I'm not sure whether I should go out with him or not. You know . . . the whole don't eat where you . . ." She paused and cleared her throat. "You get what I mean, right?"

"Our James? The guy who runs the register up front?"

"That would be the one. I'm not sure if dating someone that I work with is a good idea."

Abram felt a wave of relief wash over him, and he felt silly to think that Brenda might have been flirting with him. Apparently, she was just a nice girl. "Do you like him? I mean, as a boyfriend prospect?"

Smiling while she chewed, she shrugged. "I don't know. He's nice enough. And he's kind of cute. But we work together, so that's setting off some alarms in my head. And . . ." She paused. "I see him talking to Mr. Hinkle a lot—and laughing. He seems like he's brown-nosing to me."

Abram wasn't sure what the color of someone's nose had to do with anything, and he wasn't sure what was proper in a situation like this. "I guess whether or not you date him depends how much you like him."

"Exactly." She pointed her fork at him. "We could start dating, then break up, then it could affect our jobs. I'm not sure it's worth the risk."

"This steak is great," Abram said as he stuffed another piece into his mouth.

Brenda grunted, but grinned. "Glad you like it, but, uh . . . what should I do about James?"

Abram shrugged. "I already told you. Depends how much you like him."

"You're not much help."

They both turned when they heard footsteps.

"No help about what?" James grinned as he rounded the table and leaned against the counter, folding his arms across his chest.

Brenda cleared her throat again. "Well, as a matter of fact, I was just asking Abram if he thought it was a good idea to date someone you work with."

Abram almost choked on a bite of steak. *Doesn't this woman have any kind of filter?* She was young. Maybe nineteen or twenty. But Abram couldn't help but think she'd make a good wife someday, knowing how to cook so well.

"Really?" James's mouth lifted up on one side as he arched an eyebrow. "And what words of wisdom does our Amish friend have regarding this?"

Abram didn't think James had ever called him by his actual name.

Brenda scraped the last bite of chicken casserole from her plate, then stood up and carried her paper plate to the trash can. She spun around, faced James, and said, "He hasn't answered yet." They both turned to Abram, and Brenda asked, "So, what's the good word? Go out with him or not?"

Abram swallowed his bite. "Uh . . . I guess . . . go out with him?" He posed his answer as a question, hoping to get let off the hook.

Brenda faced James and tapped a finger to her chin. "Nah, I think not."

Then she left.

James scowled at Abram before he followed Brenda out of the room.

Sighing, Abram wasn't sure what had just happened. More confirmation that the *Englisch* were just odd, a fact that didn't really require any more proof than he'd seen over the years.

He finished his steak, then dove in to Sarah's chicken casserole. Brenda and James could work out their own problems. Abram had enough of his own.

After he was finished eating, he made his way to the door, but he bumped into his boss. Mr. Hinkle frowned as he moved past Abram and toward the coffeepot.

Abram excused himself and was heading to the time clock when Mr. Hinkle said, "Abram, you got a minute? We need to have a chat."

Something about the way his boss spoke left an unsettled feeling in the pit of Abram's stomach.

CHAPTER 8

Friday after supper, Sarah rolled onto the porch and fed Henry some lettuce, leftover green beans, and a slice of bread. She'd quit giving the bird sunflower seeds, even though she wasn't clear what a balanced diet for a duck should be. She rolled her wheelchair into the living room. Abram had been quiet the past couple of days, and Sarah suspected why. She'd already checked the calendar, and while she might not want a baby, she did want to show her husband how much she loved him.

Her stomach swirled with anticipation and fear. Would Abram still find her desirable with legs that lay limp? She wasn't sure she'd done things right the first week they were together as husband and wife, and now there seemed even more reasons to be nervous. He lowered the book he was reading as she came closer to him.

Sarah reached out her hand, and her husband took hold. "Are you ready for bed?" She fought the shakiness in her voice by clearing her throat. "I'm ready." She smiled, determined to make life feel as normal as possible, even though she didn't think she'd ever feel normal again.

"Um . . ." Abram set the book on the couch next to him. "I need to feed the horses."

"Oh. I thought you did that earlier." Sarah held her breath, unsure what to do or say. She'd expected her husband to whisk her away to the bedroom without any hesitation.

"*Nee*, it was sprinkling a little, so I just came on in the house." He stood up, kissed her on the cheek, and went to the porch. "I'll go tend to them now."

Sarah nodded, even though something felt amiss. Abram had been leaving earlier than usual in the morning, sometimes before breakfast. And he'd been getting home later in the evenings. When she'd questioned him about it, he'd just said, "Busy day."

She jumped when his mobile phone buzzed on the coffee table. Abram had said he planned to give up the device now that she was home from the hospital—or at least pack it away for emergencies only. Leaning her head as far to the left as she could, she saw a green box. She knew that to be a text message. From someone named Brenda.

> Hey, I don't know what's going on, but call me. I miss our lunches!

Sarah stared at the phone until the screen went dark. Like her heart.

• • •

Abram fed the horses for a second time, vowing to confess his lie to the Lord later, when he didn't feel so bad about himself. Sarah was ready to resume their life as husband and wife, it seemed, and Abram didn't see how he'd fake his way happy in the bedroom. He'd done his best during supper, but nothing leaves a man feeling less manly than losing his job.

He shoveled manure, brushed both of their horses for a while, filled up the water trough until it was overflowing, and when there was nothing else to do, he trudged through the muddy puddles back to the house. Maybe making a baby with his wife would distract his thoughts and give him something to look forward to. But how would he afford a baby now? How was he going to pay Bill the loan man his money back, recover from his credit card debt, and find another job? Mr. Hinkle had been nice about it, but something didn't add up in Abram's mind. He'd been at the company longer than anyone else, except maybe Brenda. If a reduction in staff was necessary, as Mr. Hinkle had said, why didn't he choose an employee who hadn't been there as long?

Sarah was sitting in her wheelchair in the same spot as when he'd left, although she had her head hung and didn't look up when he walked in. He was letting his wife down. Again. "I—I guess I'm ready for bed." He swallowed back the lump in his throat as he thought about all the times he'd looked forward to this moment, and he feared Sarah could sense his lack of enthusiasm. She finally looked at him, her expression unreadable. Flat. Was she back in her dark place?

"I'm going to read for a while," she said as she reached for a magazine on the coffee table. A magazine about plows, tools, and farming. As she flipped through it, Abram wondered if she realized that she had it upside down.

"*Ya*, okay." He went to take a bath, the weight of his worries almost too much to bear.

When he was done, he towel-dried his hair, then wrapped the towel around his waist. Sarah was in bed, covered to her shoulders, which were bare. He forced all of his troubles from his mind and climbed in beside her, pulling her close. He owed her a display of his love. He hoped she wouldn't be disappointed.

. . .

Sarah lay on her back, wondering if this was how intimacy would be from now on; void of much emotion and over with nearly as soon as it started. Her husband no longer found her desirable. She was an invalid with limbs attached to a body that no longer functioned the way she wanted it to. As tears pooled in the corners of her eyes, she took a deep breath. Abram would never cheat on her. He'd stay true to her because it was the right thing to do. But as she slowly turned to face him, she still dreaded having to ask him why Brenda would be texting him. Sarah only knew of one Brenda, the girl he worked with. A beautiful, young *Englisch* woman with long blond hair and eyes as green as Sarah's, only bigger. Brenda was curvy in all the right places, and there wasn't a crooked tooth in her radiant smile.

Questioning Abram was now a missed opportunity, as he snored lightly next to her. She extinguished the lantern and wondered how long she could hold off going to the bathroom. The simplest of tasks were now a challenge. That's what she had in her life—challenges. Big ones and little ones. Nothing was easy anymore. She closed her eyes and let the tears come. Somewhere in the midst of her crying, she thought she heard the Lord reaching out to her, longing to take her pain away. Maybe the heavy swell of hope was wishful thinking, but when relief didn't come, she closed her ears. And she closed her heart. God had forsaken her.

. . .

Abram left the house shortly after breakfast Saturday morning. Facing Sarah was like looking his lie right in the face, and it burned and ached and scratched at his conscience. He'd have to tell her that he'd lost his job, but he was hoping to do so once he'd found another one. Farming wasn't enough to sustain most of the folks in their district, and Abram was no exception. He'd needed an outside income even before the house renovations. Their district's community health fund had covered Sarah's medical expenses, thankfully. But he had credit card debt—and Bill—to contend with. He'd just parked outside the farmers' market to see if they might have any jobs available, when his phone rang. It was Brenda.

"I'm sorry I didn't text or call you back," he said right after he answered.

"What happened? No one at work is talking. I asked Mr. Hinkle, and he said that he'd had to make some reductions in staff. But the only reduction seems to be your job. What gives?"

Abram finished tethering his horse to the hitching post, then sat down on the seat in his buggy and shrugged. "I don't know. I thought I'd always done a good job, and I was hardly ever late or missed work."

"Well, it just seems bizarre. I don't get it either. And I miss my lunch buddy."

Abram thought about Sarah and how things were at home. "It's nice to be missed," he said.

"Well, I went out with James, only once. What a disaster. He's definitely not the guy for me, and I wish Mr. Hinkle had let him go, instead of you. I feel like James is stalking me at work now. He even asked why I didn't bring him lunch, the way I used to bring leftovers for you. Ugh. He can get, bring, or buy his own lunch. I know better than this, to go out with someone I work with." She sighed heavily into the phone. "Live and learn, I guess. But anyway, I just wanted to check on you, and I was curious if Mr. Hinkle had given you a reason he let you go."

"Not really. I was as surprised as you. More so."

She was quiet for a few moments. "How's your wife doing?"

Abram braced himself for another lie. "*Gut.* She's doing *gut.*"

"Well, I'm glad to hear that. In the grand scheme of things, that's what is most important. When I was younger, I had a cousin who had some rare disease. I can't even remember what it was, but it left her in a wheelchair until she died when we were teenagers. I remember how hard it was for her to get used to not being able to walk. I'm so glad your wife is settling in and doing well. And I want you to keep in touch, okay?"

"*Ya, ya.*" Brenda was as nice an *Englisch* person as he'd ever known, but he knew they were both just exchanging pleasantries, that there wouldn't be any reason for them to stay in touch.

After they hung up, Abram went inside the farmers' market. He'd take any job he could get right now. His phone buzzed again. *Bill.* He hit End and realized he'd promised Bill a hundred and fifty dollars yesterday.

. . .

Sarah tried to focus on something besides her marriage. She'd cleaned the kitchen, done her best to tidy up the bathroom, and now she set her mechanical floor cleaner into motion. When the robot wasn't smashing into her furniture, it did manage to pick up dirt and dust, and there was a lot of both following the rains and Abram's traipsing in and out, not always remembering to shed his shoes at the door.

She wasn't sure why Abram was working on a Saturday, but she reckoned it was better than being at home with a substandard wife. Or maybe he just wanted to spend time with Brenda? That thought sent a wave of adrenaline coursing through her body.

After she threw together a vegetable stew, she checked the porch again. She hadn't seen her feathery friend all day. But she recognized Johnny's buggy coming up the driveway. She waited outside for him.

He rushed up the porch steps with a wad of cash in

his hands. "*Mamm* said twelve of your cookbooks sold at the co-op market where your stuff is. Apparently, a few *Englisch* ladies have been talking them up. They like the cooking tips you offer and the hand-drawn covers." He pushed the money at her. "I gotta go, but it's a hundred and twenty dollars."

"*Danki.*" She watched her brother pull out and waved, then she went to her bedroom and put the cash with the other money she'd started saving before the accident. She was up to five hundred and forty dollars. She'd planned to buy Abram a set of pneumatic tools he'd been eyeing since before they were married. Her husband wouldn't buy the expensive, air-powered gadgets for himself, and she'd wanted to surprise him. She was pretty sure she had enough money now. He'd worked hard to make life easier for her, and she wanted to make any future projects he took on easier for him. She wished he'd had the tools before he made all the renovations to the house, but Abram was always tinkering with something so she knew he would use them.

She'd just tucked the money in the back of her drawer, behind her nightgowns, when she heard a loud noise on the porch. "You're back, Henry," she whispered before she made her way outside.

Stroking the bird's feathery backside, Henry eased closer to Sarah until she was able to lift him into her lap. She'd read that certain ducks made excellent pets and often bonded with humans when there weren't any other fowl around. Sarah wondered why Henry didn't spend time near the chicken coop, but she was thankful for the company he provided. After a few minutes, she set him back down. She smiled when he hopped back to his spot behind the rocker, happy he'd adapted to his handicap. Sarah wondered if she'd ever be able to do the same.

. . .

It was early afternoon when Abram returned home, and he fought to control the anger that had been simmering all day. He'd spent his life serving God. He was a good worker. He was a loving husband who wanted to please his wife. So how was it that now he was in debt, jobless, and allowing hopelessness to fester in his heart?

As he walked up the porch steps, he eyed the amount of bird poop all over the freshly painted wood, and he recalled the time he and Sarah had treated themselves to roasted duck at a fancy restaurant in Lancaster. He rushed the duck, grabbed it by the neck, and held it at arms' length. All the while, the feathery creature flapped his wings, twisted and fought. Abram was just about to snap his neck when something came flying through the window, shattering the glass, and landing with a thud onto the porch. He lost his grip on the duck, who flew away, then he eyed a hardback copy of the Bible laying amid shards of broken glass.

As he stared at the Good Book, trying to figure out what had just happened, Sarah wheeled herself onto the porch. Her green eyes blazed with hardened shades of jade as she shot daggers his way.

"Are you out of your mind?" she screamed, clutching

the wheels of the chair and rolling herself forward, glass crunching beneath her. Her bottom lip trembled as she stopped in front of him.

Abram threw up his hands, then pointed to the Bible. "Am I out of *my* mind? You just threw the Bible through our window." Abram was already calculating how much a new pane of glass would cost.

"It looked like you were about to snap Henry's neck!" She stretched taller in the chair and gritted her teeth. "What kind of person does that?"

Abram leaned against the railing of the porch and stared at her. Some girls and women looked cute when they were mad. Sarah wasn't one of them. Her lips puckered, and it looked like she was sucking her cheeks in, which left her face looking drawn and old. He was about to tell her so when she released whatever air she'd taken in, her cheeks returning to normal.

"I thought it might be nice to have roast duck. Remember, we ate duck at that restaurant one time?" He paused as her jaw dropped. "What? Why are you looking at me like that? You said you loved the roasted duck that day."

Sarah was still as a statue, and Abram didn't think she was breathing. He waited. Something bad was coming.

"Henry. Is. A. *Pet*. We don't *eat* our pets." His wife's eyes bulged as she spoke, her face turned red as the barn.

Abram glanced at the broken window again. Then at the Bible. When his phone buzzed in his pocket, he knew it was Bill. The man had been calling him all day. He pulled the phone from his pocket, raised his arm over his head, and heaved the phone into the yard. Then he took a deep breath and went inside.

. . .

Sarah searched for Henry for three days. She'd wheeled herself to the barn, the chicken coops, and even circled the house. The ground was damp, but not soaked, and even though it had taken effort, she'd managed all right. But Henry seemed to have flown the coop. She was working her way up the ramp to the porch when she heard a car coming. Once she'd mastered the task, she turned and watched a large, burly man step out of a white van, then he marched toward her and stopped at the end of the ramp.

"I'm looking for Abram."

Sarah sat taller. "And you are . . . who?"

"Bill. And I'm guessing you are Abram's wife?" Bill needed to shave, and he had a large stomach that hung slightly over his blue jean pants.

"*Ya*, I'm Sarah. *Mei* husband isn't here right now. Is there something I can help you with?"

"Not unless you have two hundred dollars." The man chewed on a toothpick as he spoke. "I'm willing to work with just about anyone, but I don't take kindly to being ignored."

Sarah saw a sliver of glass she'd missed when she'd swept up the mess on Saturday. Glancing at the boarded-up window, she pushed the recollections of the day away. She and Abram hadn't said much to each other since Saturday, but they'd been kind to each other. "*Mei* husband owes you money?" she finally asked.

"Yeah. He owes me money. A lot of money. And he knows that when he's late on a payment, the interest rate goes up. You able to help with this? Or do you know where I can find him?"

Sarah swallowed hard. "I—I am guessing he is at work."

The *Englisch* man grunted. "I assure you he ain't at work. That's the first place I checked." He folded his arms across a broad chest. "I try not to come out to folks' homes, but since he got fired from his job, I didn't really have a choice."

Sarah froze. Where had Abram been going every day? Thoughts of Brenda's text swirled in her head and sent her stomach to churning. "I—I don't know where he is."

Bill shifted the toothpick to the other side of his mouth. "I want my money." He pointed a finger at Sarah. "I thought you Amish were decent, honest people."

We are. Sarah forced herself to breathe as confusion buzzed in her head. Like a hive of bees trying to make honey, Sarah was trying to organize her thoughts. "I—I have some money." She swallowed back the knot in her throat. "How much does he owe you?"

"In total? Or today?" Bill spit the toothpick out in the grass. "Today, I'd settle for two hundred dollars."

"I'll be right back." She fumbled with the screen door, trying to fling it open, and within seconds, Bill had hold of the screen and held it for her. She briefly wondered if he was going to follow her into the house.

But he remained on the porch. Sarah returned with ten twenties and handed it to him.

Bill took the money, then pointed a finger at Sarah again. "Tell your man that I don't want to have to track him down every week. Tell him to at least have the decency to take my phone calls."

Sarah watched him peel away in the white van, then she just sat there, staring into space.

Abram, what have you gotten yourself into?

CHAPTER 9

Sarah searched the yard again, calling for Henry. Her efforts exhausted, she busied herself inside the rest of the day, all the while wondering where Abram was since he apparently didn't have a job anymore. To her knowledge, she and Abram had never kept anything from each other. Until now.

She pulled a peach cobbler from the oven and set it on a cooling rack at the same time she heard a car coming up the driveway. Her heart thumped against her chest so hard she almost lost her grip on the cobbler. She hoped it wasn't that awful *Englisch* man again. But when she got to the window and saw who was visiting, she thought she might prefer the *Englisch* man.

She opened the front door and forced a smile. "Hello, Brenda." Sarah had seen the woman many times—at work parties and when she'd had a reason to visit Abram at the store. She was certain Brenda got prettier each time she saw her.

"Hey, Sarah." Brenda turned to her right and frowned. "Geez, what happened to your window?"

"Uh . . . it broke." Sarah pushed the screen open so Brenda could come in. "What brings you here? If you're looking for Abram, he isn't home." She heard the clip

Sarah regretted the outburst as soon as the words slipped out.

"Another oops." Brenda covered her face with her hands.

"*Nee, nee*," Sarah said. "That cat was already out of the bag. A man came by earlier saying Abram owed him money. A man named Bill."

"Oh, good grief. Do you mean Bill from that place next to the bank?"

"I have no idea."

Brenda shook her head. "That guy is a crook. Unfortunately, he's also my uncle. I'll see what I can do to help Abram. Uncle Bill probably charged Abram a ridiculous amount of interest at a time when Abram needed help, not more problems."

Sarah bit her bottom lip, wondering if she was the source of all Abram's troubles. *Of course I am.* She nodded as the events of the day pressed down on her.

Brenda cleared her throat and pointed to the floor near Sarah's bedroom. "Hey, did you know there is a twenty-dollar bill on the floor?"

Sarah snapped her neck in that direction and spied the bill. "I probably dropped it when I went to fetch Bill some cash. I'd been saving money to buy Abram some tools, so the money was hidden in my bedroom." She shrugged. "I've been selling cookbooks, jams, and various homemade items since right before we got married."

Brenda chuckled. "We outsiders love all the stuff you Amish make. The food is better, the quality of workmanship shines, and of course, we're all intrigued about your lifestyle."

Sarah smiled, knowing that to be true. This was the most she'd ever talked to Brenda. She was finding the woman to be friendly, helpful, and pleasant to be around in general, though she seemed to share whatever thought she had the moment she had it. "You know, when I saw your text . . ." Sarah took a deep breath and blew it out slowly. "I thought maybe you . . . maybe you and Abram, um . . ."

"What!" Brenda slammed a hand to her chest. "Oh, heavens. You thought there was something going on between us?"

Sarah avoided her eyes as she nodded. "I'm so sorry. Things haven't been . . . very *gut* lately with me and Abram. I didn't know what was going on, so when I saw your text, I guess my mind wandered to a bad place."

Brenda's eyebrows furrowed as she pressed her lips together. "I'm sorry you thought that."

"I'm embarrassed about it now. But I guess Abram has been working hard to keep things from me."

"I'm sure he doesn't want to worry you. But I will definitely have a talk with my uncle. I'll get him to make this right and to set Abram up on a reasonable repayment schedule, which I'm sure he doesn't have right now." She paused. "I can talk to Mr. Hinkle, too, if you or Abram want me to. Maybe I can find out if James said anything to cast Abram in a bad light."

Sarah shook her head. "*Nee.* I think I should wait and talk to Abram. Sometimes the Lord closes a door, but there is usually a window opening somewhere else." She realized she'd let God into her thoughts for the first time in a while.

"So, do you have any of your cookbooks here for sale? I'm a maniac in the kitchen, and I'm a cookbook junkie."

Sarah nodded. "*Ya*, I'll go get you one." She spun the wheelchair in the direction of the laundry room.

"How much are they?" Brenda called after her.

"Ten dollars."

Sarah returned a minute later and handed Brenda the book. "Just keep it, as a gift."

Brenda flipped through the pages, then shook her head. "No, I'm going to pay for it." She looked at Sarah. "This is a big cookbook for ten dollars, and it's cool the way you've drawn the cover and signed it. Can I have two more, one each for my sister and mom?"

"*Ya*, of course. But please just pay me twenty dollars and keep the third one for yourself." Sarah turned to leave, returning again with two more cookbooks.

"Who prints these?" Brenda was still turning pages.

"The print shop in town, the one down Lincoln Highway closer to Lancaster. I'd have to look at a receipt for the exact name." Sarah set the other two cookbooks beside Brenda on the couch.

"What do they charge you?"

Sarah tapped a finger to her chin. "Um . . . I believe it's four dollars each."

"Wow. You've got a six-dollar profit. You should sell these on eBay." She grinned. "Or is that allowed?"

Sarah thought about all the computers, fax machines, cell phones, and other forbidden equipment that was being used by those in her district. "I don't think the bishop would approve."

"Well, since money seems like an issue for you and Abram, I think I'd consider bending the rules a bit. What else can you sell?"

"Huh?" Sarah wasn't following. "I—I don't think I should sell things on a computer. Isn't that what eBay is?"

Brenda stood up. "Show me your stash."

Sarah raised an eyebrow, but moved toward the laundry room, Brenda on her heels. "Wow. You've got tons of stuff."

"*Ya. Mei mamm* takes it to town and some *Englisch* ladies there sell it for me."

"And I bet they take a chunk of change off the top too." Brenda picked up a homemade candle, lifted the lid, and sniffed. "I love lavender," she said dreamily. "I could sell this stuff on eBay for you."

"*Nee*, that sounds like a lot of work."

Brenda chuckled. "I didn't say I'd do it for free. I think a dollar per sale would be fair. On the cookbooks, you'd still make five dollars." She waved an arm over Sarah's other homemade items. "As for the candles, knitted hot pads, and other stuff, I'm sure I can sell those too. Gotta love eBay."

"You mean, like our own business?" Something sparked in Sarah. A sense of usefulness.

Brenda laughed again. "I doubt we'll get rich, but it would be something fun to do that would put a little money in our pockets."

"I would like that. I'm going to talk to Abram about this too." Sarah smiled. "I'm so glad you stopped by today."

• • •

Abram stared at the tall glass of beer on the bar. A bar he'd never been in before. He'd heard all about the *Englisch* drinking their problems away. He'd yet to take a sip of the beverage, but he was already wondering how many beers he would need to make his own troubles go away. He'd driven his buggy carelessly, which had landed his wife in a wheelchair. He'd made bad financial choices and owed people a lot of money now. He didn't have a job anymore, for reasons he didn't understand. Sarah was unhappy most of the time. And he'd almost snapped the neck of her pet duck and roasted him for supper.

He wrapped his hand around the glass handle on the beer mug, and he might have chugged it down in one gulp if someone hadn't cleared their throat behind him. He glanced over his shoulder. *Oh great.*

"I wasn't going to drink it." Abram eased his hand from the icy, cold mug and looked up at his father-in-law. "How'd you find me here?"

Saul pointed to the far corner of the bar, then waved at an older man sitting alone. "Larry Parks. He's a regular in here. He was at your wedding, if you'll recall. One of the few *Englischers* there. He got word to Sally at the farmers' market, who got hold of Mary Lapp, who found your mother-in-law, who asked me to come check on you. So, here I am."

Abram hung his head and sighed. Saul inched a barstool toward him and sat down. Then to Abram's surprise, his father-in-law ordered a beer. "It gives the *Englisch* something to talk about," Saul said when a beer was placed in front of him. "So, what woes in your life have driven you to drink? Is Sarah doing okay?"

"*Ya*, I guess. Maybe." He circled the icy rim of his mug as the foam from the beer dissolved.

"Hmm . . ." Saul took a big swig from his glass, then nodded at Abram's glass. "It isn't going to drink itself."

Abram had a glass of wine at a wedding once, but that's the only alcohol he'd ever had. He lifted the drink to his lips, but put it down without taking a sip. He met eyes with his father-in-law, a man he sometimes barely tolerated, but whom he loved immensely. Abram's father had died when he was a young boy. Despite sometimes being opinionated about things, Saul had easily slipped into a fatherly role when Abram had begun to date Sarah.

"The accident was my fault." Abram lifted the glass to his lips and took a drink, then scowled, knowing he wasn't going to drink the rest, if for no other reason than it didn't taste good.

"*Nee, sohn*. The accident was not your fault. And if that's what's eating you up, you need to let it go. That blue car came out of nowhere, and I don't know a man alive who could have prevented that collision."

Abram wanted to believe that. "I was distracted, and I didn't see the car until it was too late."

"Abram, you listen to me *gut*, you hear? Even if you would have seen the car, it wouldn't have made a bit of difference. The car would have hit you no matter what. Even the police said that. You were in the wrong place at the exact moment that car ran the red light. You must let that go."

Logically, Abram knew Saul was right, but he wasn't

going to be able to forgive himself overnight. And he wasn't sure whether or not to share his other problems with his father-in-law, specifically, his money troubles.

"So bury that dead horse," Saul added before he took another drink from his frosted glass. Then he cleared his throat. "How much money do you owe, and is it just credit cards?"

Abram stopped breathing. "Uh . . ."

"Don't look so shocked. No one could have accomplished all that work on the house, even with Johnny's help, and still worked a full-time job and visit the hospital too. I figured you probably cut back on your hours at the hardware store and ran your credit cards up." He paused, frowning a little. "And someone left a message on our mobile phone, said he was from a credit card company and was trying to reach you."

Abram's cheeks grew warm. "*Ya*. And I borrowed money from a company that's charging me a lot of interest now."

"I waited for you to come to me. It was a burden we should have all shared, but I also recognize a man's need to handle things on his own."

They were both quiet for a while. "And then I almost snapped the neck of Sarah's pet duck and roasted him for supper."

Saul's eyes grew round as he stroked his beard. "Mercy me. I couldn't have saved you from Sarah's wrath over that one." He chuckled, chugged the rest of the beer, then stood up. "Come on."

Abram stood up, considered taking another sip of the beer, if for no other reason than he hated to waste the money, but then thought better of it. "Where are we going?"

"We're going to the bank to get your finances squared away." He started walking, but cut his eyes toward Abram and paused. "And I don't want to hear that you went to the awful loan company by the bank. I think they set up shop there as a way to lure all the people who couldn't get loans in the traditional way. A horrible place, it is, almost criminal." He slowed his step. "You didn't do that, did you?"

Abram lowered his head, nodding. "And I sort of don't have a job anymore either."

"Well, you've sure made a mess of things." Saul slapped Abram on the back and chuckled. And for the first time in a while, Abram's stomach stopped churning, and he was almost certain he heard the Lord say, "We all need help from time to time." Or had Saul said it?

Abram sent up a prayer of thanks to his heavenly Father, and he lifted Saul up in prayer as well.

CHAPTER 10

Sarah quietly listened as Abram told her about how he'd lost his job, hadn't been able to find another one, and about all the money he owed on his credit card. He wrapped it up by telling her that her father had helped him reorganize his finances in a way that made it easier for him to handle.

"When it was all said and done, somehow things didn't look nearly as bad," he said. "I think your father took on some of the debt, even though he wouldn't admit to it."

Sarah didn't say anything until Abram told her about how he felt responsible for the accident. She'd been so wrapped up in her own self-pity, she hadn't stopped to consider how Abram was feeling. In her mind, he was just pushing to get things back to normal. She'd been so excited to tell him about her plans to sell some of her cookbooks and homemade items, but now didn't seem the right time.

"The accident wasn't your fault, Abram. I wish you would have shared all of this with me."

"I didn't want to burden you."

"Brenda stopped by earlier." Sarah folded her hands

in her lap, choosing not to tell Abram about her earlier suspicions. It would only upset him further, and Sarah had worked through that. "She thinks maybe you got fired over something James said to Mr. Hinkle. Maybe you can talk to him and get your job back."

"*Nee*, I don't think so." Abram glanced at the boarded-up window behind the couch, then at Sarah. "Did your duck come back?"

Sarah gazed into her husband's eyes, seeing herself through his vision of her. If the situation were reversed, she would have been doing everything Abram was doing to make him happy and to keep him safe. "I'm sure he will show up soon," she said with so much tenderness, she almost didn't recognize her own voice. She wasn't going to make him feel worse than he already did.

Finally, he smiled a little. "You know how they say that when God closes a door, He opens a window?"

Sarah nodded. "*Ya*." She'd tell him about the ways she planned to make extra money later, but right now, she wanted the conversation to be about Abram.

"A window opened," he said softly. "A big window."

Sarah smiled. "And?"

"Your *daed* and me are going to make furniture. Lots and lots of furniture. He has all kinds of equipment in his garage, but before he ever got a business off the ground, he hurt his back. He asked me to be his partner."

Sarah's smile grew, and for the first time in a long while, she thanked the Lord for showing them both a way to pry windows open when doors were closed. "I think that is a wonderful idea."

He hurried to her and threw his arms around her. "I love you so much."

"I love you, too, Abram. With all my heart."

Her husband picked her up and carried her to the bedroom. While things were much better overall, one thing hadn't changed for Sarah. She still didn't want to have a child for fear she couldn't properly take care of one.

But she'd already checked the calendar, and all was well. Maybe with truths coming to light, she and Abram could enjoy each other the way a married couple could.

. . .

It was a few weeks later when her mother pulled in the driveway carting the familiar brown bag. Brenda was selling lots of cookbooks, hot pads, and candles on eBay, but Sarah's mother was also selling an abundance of their items at the farmers' co-op market.

"It is much too loud at my house," *Mamm* said as she walked up the ramp to the porch. She handed the bag to Sarah. "Your father and husband are busy building things, and while they both seem happy as little larks, there are generators running, saws grinding, and . . . what was I thinking when I gave them a bell to ring when they needed something?" *Mamm* chuckled, but Sarah was fighting to hold back tears. "There is almost two hundred dollars in that bag. With your friend selling things on the computer, you must be building a nice little nest egg."

It was actually going to help pay off debt for the

renovations to the house, but Sarah was happy to be able to help. Just when she'd thought she and Abram were adjusting to a new way of life, trouble landed in her lap again.

"What's wrong?" *Mamm* sat down in the rocking chair closest to Sarah's wheelchair, putting a hand on her leg. "*Mei maedel*, what is it?"

"I—I . . ." Sarah choked back tears. "I'm pregnant."

Mamm gasped. "I'm going to be a *mammi*!" She clapped her hands several times as tears gathered in her eyes. "This is the happiest news ever. When are you due?"

Sarah turned to face her mother as a tear slipped down her cheek. "I don't know for sure."

Mamm's expression fell. "What's wrong, *mei lieb*? This is such a blessing."

"How can you say that?" Sarah lifted her palms up as she raised her shoulders. "How can I take care of a baby?"

"What do you mean?" *Mamm*'s lines on her forehead creased as she squinted her eyes at Sarah, genuinely seeming not to know what Sarah was talking about.

"This!" She pointed to the wheelchair. "I can't walk, *Mamm*."

"Sweetheart, you don't have to be able to walk to nurse, feed, love, and care for a child."

"I can't do it." She shook her head as sobs took over. "I just can't." She told her mother about the reoccurring dream. "And every time, I can't get to the baby before he pulls himself up and reaches for the pot." For the first time, she realized that the child in the dream was a boy.

Her mother gazed into her eyes for a long time until a smile filled her face. "Sarah . . . *all* mothers are scared. This is not an emotion that is exclusive to you. If you weren't in a wheelchair, you would find other things about being a mother that scare you just as much." Her mother sighed and blew out a heavy, exaggerated breath. Then she shook her head. "I didn't think I'd ever tell anyone this, but since you are having these worries, I will."

Sarah waited as her mother twirled the string on her *kapp*, tapping her foot nervously against the wooden slats on the porch as she avoided Sarah's gaze. She cleared her throat. "Okay, *ya*. Well. Um . . ."

"Goodness, *Mamm*, what is it?"

"I was always afraid of dropping you or Johnny. Especially Johnny because he was so tiny when he was born, since he was a month early and all. But I'd successfully gotten you out of diapers, potty trained, and into school without any issues, so I had to assume that I would do just as well with Johnny."

"I guess all mothers have fears, but my situation is different, *Mamm*. I will someday have a toddler running around that I can't keep up with."

"Then you don't cook unless you are right there by the stove. Or you put a baby gate up to block the *boppli* from going somewhere unsafe. There are many things you can do to curb that fear, and I'll help you. This is a blessing, Sarah. A wonderful gift from God. And I bet Abram is thrilled."

Sarah looked away as she pressed her lips together.

"You haven't told him?" *Mamm* brought a hand to her chest.

"*Nee.* I've just been so scared."

Sarah's mother stood up and paced the porch, swinging her arms at her sides. "So, you know how folks sometimes joke about Johnny being dropped on his head?"

Grinning, Sarah said, "*Ya . . .*"

"I cringe every time someone jokingly says that." She rolled her eyes and sighed, stilling her hands at her sides. "I dropped Johnny on his head when he was a baby."

Sarah covered her mouth with her hands, trying to stifle a smile, but failing miserably. "That explains a lot," she finally said, laughing.

"He was fine. He really was. I took him to the doctor, asked them to X-ray him, and prayed I wouldn't get hauled to jail for child abuse."

Sarah lowered her hands, smiling, then laughing. "It's not funny. But it is."

Mamm finally smiled. "I'm only telling you this because anything can happen whether you are in a wheelchair . . . or"—she shrugged nonchalantly—"or reaching for a platter high in the cabinet when your baby boy suddenly slings himself backward out of your arms . . ." She paused, sighing. "And lands on his head."

Sarah's mother kissed her on the forehead and said, "Share this *gut* news with Abram." She brushed away a strand of Sarah's hair that had blown across her face. "Fear is the enemy's way of separating us from God. With the Lord, there is nothing to fear. Each and every moment in our life is defined by God's love, and *mei maedel . . .*" *Mamm* smiled. "This is your moment."

Sarah nodded, knowing she needed to stay close to the Lord if she wanted to admonish her fears. She pointed to the yard. "Look! It's Henry." She stared in awe. "With six babies waddling along behind him."

"Isn't that something?" *Mamm* held a hand to her forehead, blocking the sun. "I think your Henry is going to have to be renamed Henrietta."

They both laughed. "I guess so," Sarah said. "Look, she hops on one leg now instead of trying to walk and falling over. She's figured it out for herself."

Mamm gazed at Sarah. "And you will too."

Henry—Henrietta—continued across the yard as Sarah's mother unhitched her buggy and left. The bird was almost to the edge of the front yard when she stopped and looked at Sarah. Her fuzzy yellow ducklings halted as well. Sarah smiled. *This is your moment, Henrietta.*

• • •

Sarah was sitting on the porch when Abram pulled the buggy in. The clouds had parted and the Lord had blessed them with much welcomed sunshine following all the rain. Doors had slammed shut. Windows were opened wide. Sarah had been quiet lately, but they were working their way back into a life that they were both still adjusting to.

"How was work today?" Sarah's emerald eyes sparkled with flecks of gold as she squinted against the sun's glare.

"It was a *gut* day. We finished the hutch we've been working on, and we planned out the rest of the week.

Your *daed* said he might even go to worship service on Sunday."

Neither Sarah nor her father had attended church the past couple of months.

"I'm going to attend worship on Sunday also."

Abram closed his eyes for a moment and silently thanked God for guiding everyone onto paths they seemed destined to travel. The journey wouldn't always be smooth. There would be potholes, ruts, and wrong turns. But with God's guidance, Abram knew that each step would be a coordinated effort toward doing His will.

"*Mamm* and I decided to change Henry's name to Henrietta. It turns out my duck is female."

Abram took off his hat, pulled a handkerchief from his pocket, and dabbed at his forehead. "How do you know it's a girl?"

"She crossed the yard today with six ducklings behind her. She's learned to hop on one leg and has been blessed with the gift of motherhood." Sarah smiled. "I guess you could say it's her moment."

Abram wasn't sure exactly what that meant, but he was happy to see Sarah smiling. And as her smile filled her face even more, Abram found himself smiling too. "You look like you have something on your mind," he said.

"Abram . . ." She brought both hands to her chest, blinking her eyes, still smiling. "It's *our* moment."

His wife seemed to be talking in code, but when she lowered both hands to her stomach and rubbed her belly, Abram's heart pounded wildly in his chest. So many things had gone wrong, but could it be . . . ? "Are you with child?"

Sarah nodded, and Abram rushed to her side, laying a gentle hand on her stomach. "We're going to be parents?"

His beautiful wife nodded again. "I can't promise I won't drop the baby on his head, but I'm going to be a wonderful mother." Sarah laughed.

Abram gazed into her eyes, unsure what she was referring to, but he didn't care. "You are going to be the best *mudder* ever." He lay his head in her lap, and as she ran a hand through his hair, Abram felt the Lord on their porch, in their lives.

"And you are going to be the best father ever."

Abram swallowed back the knot in his throat. *Thank You, God.*

HOME SWEET HOME

Amy Clipston

With love and appreciation for my friends at Morning Star Lutheran Church in Matthews, North Carolina

GLOSSARY

Ach—Oh!
aenti—aunt
boppli—baby
daadi—grandpa
daadihaus—grandparents' house
dat—dad
English—non-Amish person
freind—friend
freinden—friends
gut—good
haus—house
mamm—mom
mammi—grandma
mei—my
ya—yes

CHAPTER 1

The cold air seemed to seep into the marrow of Mia O'Conner's bones, and her teeth chattered as her husband steered their pickup past a large white farmhouse. Rain splashed against the windshield and beat a steady cadence on the roof of the old Chevy truck as the tires crunched on the rock driveway beside two large barns. She held her hand over the vent and shivered. Only brisk February air whooshed through. If only they had the money to fix the heater . . .

That was the least of their worries. She glanced down at their five-month-old daughter bundled under a blanket in her car seat between them.

"Well, this is it," Chace said as the truck came to a stop. The headlights sliced through the dark and illuminated the front door of a rustic, one-story cabin. "Welcome to our new home in Bird-in-Hand."

Mia blinked twice as she studied the building. It featured a small front porch and two windows. She shivered again, hoping the tiny house was warm.

"What do you think?" Chace shifted the truck into Park. "It's not much, but it's more than reasonable. Isaac is charging us next to nothing." He paused. "Isaac Allgyer is the best boss I've ever had."

Mia turned toward her husband, and his handsome face and Caribbean-blue eyes focused on her. "Well, it's not—"

Kaitlyn's sudden screech interrupted Mia's response.

Mia unbuckled Kaitlyn and pulled the sobbing baby into her arms. "Mommy is right here, sweet pea." She snuggled Kaitlyn closer to her chest, wrapping the blanket around her little body. "I guess she'll have to sleep with us until we scrape together the money for a crib."

Chace's lips formed a thin line. "We'll figure it out."

Mia swallowed a sigh as Kaitlyn's sobs subsided.

Chace pushed his door open, and a blast of frigid air filled the cab of the truck. Mia gasped and held Kaitlyn even closer. She longed to be able to afford the warm snowsuit she'd seen at a department store after all the snowsuits had been snatched up from her favorite consignment shop. Surely her baby was cold, and the guilt that had haunted her since Kaitlyn's birth flooded her once again.

Chace pulled up the hood on his navy blue sweatshirt to cover his sandy-blond hair as he stood by the open truck door. Rain beat down on him, drenching his sweatshirt and worn jeans, and no doubt his work boots too.

"Why don't you get her inside?" he called over the rain. "It has to be warmer in there than it is in here. I'll help you, and then I'll handle emptying out the bed of the truck."

Mia nodded before Chace shut the driver side door and ran to her side of the truck.

She retrieved a blanket from the diaper bag she'd

bought at Goodwill before Kaitlyn was born. After draping the extra blanket over Kaitlyn's head, Mia shouldered the diaper bag and her purse, then leapt out of the truck when Chace opened the door. She hustled through the icy rain and up the front steps of the cabin, where Chace had run ahead to hold the door open for her. It must not have been locked.

Mia stepped through the door and shivered once more as the chilly air from inside the cabin seeped through her damp jeans. She caressed Kaitlyn's head. "I think it's colder in here than in the truck."

"We just need to get the coal stove going."

Coal?

By the light of the truck's headlights shining into the cabin, Chace found a Coleman lantern that sat on a small table by the door. He flipped it on, then shut the door against the wind.

The bright yellow light allowed Mia to take in their new home. Her heart sank when she realized it was only slightly bigger than their apartment had been. She had hoped for more. A tiny kitchen with a small refrigerator, a stove, a sink, a few cabinets, and a short counter spilled into an area with a table and four chairs. Off to her right, a worn brown sofa and dark green wing chair served as a family room. Beyond the sofa were two doorways.

"How many bedrooms are there?" she asked.

"One."

"Oh." Mia adjusted Kaitlyn in her arms. Their apartment had only one bedroom. They could make do.

Chace crossed the room to a large black stove in the

kitchen. He placed the lantern on top and began examining it.

Mia balanced Kaitlyn with one of her arms and ran her free hand over the wall. "Where are the light switches?"

Chace chuckled and shook his head. Normally, the warm sound of his laugh would make her smile, but tonight she frowned.

"What's so funny?" Her sense of humor waned with every passing moment.

"I've told you Isaac and his family are Amish, Mee." He leaned back on the kitchen counter behind him and held up his arms as if to gesture around the cabin. "There's no electricity."

"What?" Mia snapped, louder than she'd meant to.

Kaitlyn gasped and then began to cry again, her wails echoing throughout the cabin.

"There's no electricity?" Mia crossed the small room and stood in front of Chace. She ignored Kaitlyn's screaming as she gaped at him.

"What did you expect me to find with our income and credit?" His eyes narrowed to slits. "I'm sorry it's not the Hilton."

Mia ground her teeth as fury boiled through her veins, exacerbated by the combination of Kaitlyn's unrelenting screams and her husband's caustic remark. She opened her mouth to deliver a biting retort just as someone knocked on the front door and called out. "Chace?"

When Chace opened the door, a tall man with dark brown hair and a matching beard that fell past his chin stood in the doorway. He was dressed in black broadfall trousers, a plain black coat, and a black hat. He looked to be in his midforties. "Chace! You made it."

"Isaac." Chace's face brightened as he greeted the man and invited him in with a nod. A woman and four children, two girls and two boys, filed into the cabin behind him. The woman and girls wore long, solid-color dresses and black coats, and their heads were covered with black bonnets. The woman, who looked to be in her early forties, had an amicable smile.

"This is my family." Isaac pointed to each one as he introduced them. "My wife, Vera, and our children, Rhoda, Susannah, Adam, and Joel." All the children had dark hair and eyes, like their parents.

Chace shook Isaac's hand and then Vera's. He gestured toward Mia and then raised his voice over Kaitlyn's howling. "This is my wife, Mia, and my daughter, Kaitlyn."

The couple both spoke, but Kaitlyn's keening drowned out their words. Mia bounced the baby in her arms as a migraine brewed behind her eyes. Could Kaitlyn sense her frustration? Mia moved Kaitlyn's fine blond hair to one side and kissed her little head. Kaitlyn continued to sob as large tears streamed from her bright blue eyes and down her pink cheeks.

"May I hold her?"

Mia looked up at who she thought must be the eldest Allgyer daughter. She had stepped closer and was smiling. Since she had already removed her black coat and bonnet, Mia could see her purple dress was plain and that a white, gauzy cap covered her hair. Her face was free of any makeup, but she had a natural beauty with flawless ivory skin.

"I'm Rhoda. I don't mean to sound prideful, but I'm *gut* with babies."

"*Ya*, she is." Her sister appeared at her side. "I'm Susannah." She was a couple of inches shorter than Rhoda, but she could nearly pass for her twin. She wore a green dress made in the same plain pattern as her sister's, and she also had a white cap over her hair.

"All right." Mia handed the baby to Rhoda, and her aching arms were grateful for the rest.

"Kaitlyn is a pretty name." Rhoda adjusted the baby in her arms.

"Thank you," Mia said.

Kaitlyn took a deep breath and then yawned before resting her cheek on Rhoda's shoulder and placing her thumb in her mouth. Her expression transformed from agitated to content in less than a minute. Mia gasped.

"I told you." Susannah grinned. "My sister is great with babies."

Rhoda pointed to the diaper bag hanging over Mia's shoulder. "Would you like me to see if she needs a change?"

"That would be wonderful. Thank you."

Rhoda and Susannah headed toward one of the doorways beyond the family room. Mia followed them to a small bedroom. Inside were a double bed, two nightstands, a lamp, and a small bureau. Mia lingered in the doorway as Susannah flipped on the lamp on one of the nightstands, and Rhoda spread the baby blanket on the bare mattress before setting Kaitlyn down on it. Kaitlyn sputtered noises at the girls, and they laughed as Rhoda checked her diaper.

"Mia," Vera said as she sidled up to her. "It's nice to meet you."

"Hi." Mia shook her hand and noted that Vera was a few inches taller than she was, possibly close to five-eight. "Thank you so much for renting us the cabin."

"You're welcome." Vera looked toward her daughters and smiled. "They enjoy taking care of babies."

"They're experts." Mia removed her damp coat and hung it on a hook by the door before coming to stand with Vera once again. "I'm thankful for the help. I wasn't sure what to do for Katie since I had breastfed just before we headed over here. I thought maybe it was the cold, but I guess she wanted to spend some time with someone else."

"Isaac checked the stove, and it should warm up soon."

"Who used to live here? Other renters?"

"No, Isaac's parents. This is what's called the *daadihaus*, which means the grandfather's house. His parents lived here until they both passed away. My father-in-law has been gone for two years." She gestured for Mia to follow her. "Let me show you around. The bathroom is right here."

Mia followed her to the next doorway and opened it. The bathroom was small but functional, with an ordinary sink, a vanity, a commode, and a bathtub with shower. Although the fixtures showed their age, the bathroom was clean. A small window provided the only light in the room.

"Did you see the propane lamps?" Vera asked as they walked to the kitchen area.

Mia shook her head. "I saw the Coleman."

Vera stopped in the family room and turned on the lamp on the table beside the wing chair. The lamp came to life, sending a bright glow throughout the cabin. "It will get warm, so it's another way to heat the cabin. The lamp in the bedroom is propane too. Do you know how to use a coal stove?"

"No. The only heating system I've ever known how to use had a thermostat."

"Let me show you." Vera gestured for Mia to follow her.

The front door opened and closed as Chace, Isaac, and Isaac's sons lugged Chace and Mia's belongings into the house. A pile of suitcases and black trash bags already clogged the small family room. Vera's youngest son dragged in a heavy bag with his tongue sticking out of his mouth. He dropped the bag with a loud *thunk* before rushing back outside and into the rain for another.

Mia turned toward Vera. "Your sons are hard workers."

Vera shrugged. "It's our culture."

"How old are your children?" Mia leaned against the kitchen counter.

Vera nodded in the direction of the bedroom. "Rhoda is eighteen and Susannah is seventeen. Adam is twelve and Joel is ten. Are you from a large family?"

"No, I'm an only child." Mia traced her finger over the worn Formica. "I'd always longed for siblings, but my mother felt children were too much of an inconvenience. She was more interested in meeting her friends at the country club."

Vera tilted her head and frowned.

"Never mind." Mia pointed to the black potbelly stove in a corner of the kitchen. "Is that the coal stove?"

"*Ya*, it is. Isaac came over earlier today and started it." Vera pointed to a bucket full of coal beside it. "You have to check it twice every day, and you'll soon figure out how much coal you need to keep it warm overnight. If we had known you were coming yesterday, we could have started it for you then. But I understand this was a last-minute situation."

Mia's throat dried as she recalled their landlord appearing at their furnished apartment earlier that day. He had previously issued a Notice to Quit, which started the clock ticking on a ten-day deadline for Mia and Chace to pay their overdue rent before they would be evicted. Ten days, however, was not enough time for Chace to gather up the money, and the deadline arrived at lightning speed. When Mr. Newman knocked on their door that morning with an eviction notice in hand, Chace begged him for an extension. But their cantankerous landlord refused, insisting they pack their things and get out by nightfall.

Mia had never felt so distraught and humiliated. She'd dissolved in tears as Chace read the eviction notice aloud to her. He promised he would take care of them. Mia was thankful that when Chace called his boss to ask for help, Isaac offered the cabin as a quick solution.

"There's a coal bin in the mudroom back here behind the kitchen." Vera pointed toward the doorway beside them. "That's also where the wringer washer is."

"Wringer washer?" Mia's eyes widened.

"I can show you how to use it another day." Vera gestured toward the cookstove. "The stove and refrigerator run on propane. I started the refrigerator earlier today. I can help you unpack your food."

Mia's eyes stung with threatening tears. *Hold it together, Mia. This woman probably has no interest in, or time for, your sob story. Besides, this is so humiliating.*

Then again, she might as well be honest. Isaac had probably already told his wife everything Chace told him about their problems. "We don't have much food." She paused to clear her throat against a lump swelling there. "We put most of Chace's paychecks this month toward our hospital bills from when Kaitlyn was born, which is why we couldn't get caught up on the rent. And that's why we wound up . . . homeless." Her voice quavered and she sniffed.

Vera placed her hand on Mia's arm and gave her a sympathetic smile. "It's okay. Have you eaten tonight? Do you need some supper?"

"We've eaten," Mia whispered before clearing her throat again. "Thank you."

"I'll have my sons bring over a basket of food before they go to school tomorrow morning."

Mia fought the urge to gape at Vera. Why would she offer to feed Mia and her family when she'd only just met them?

"Mia," Susannah said, walking out to the kitchen. "Do you have sheets? I'll make the bed for you."

Rhoda stood behind her with Kaitlyn happily balanced on her hip. "Do you want me to give her a bottle for you?"

Mia blinked. Were all Amish people this giving and helpful? She shook herself from her momentary stupor. "I breastfed her before we came, but thank you for offering."

"Okay." Rhoda sat down in the wing chair with Kaitlyn in her arms.

"Can I put linens out for you?" Susannah asked.

Mia nodded. "Oh. That would be great. Thank you." She pointed to a nearby suitcase. "I think the linens are in there."

"You're welcome." Susannah opened the suitcase and pulled out a set of mint-green sheets, along with a set of towels. "I'll make your bed and then put the towels in the bathroom for you." She walked back toward the bedroom.

"Do you have a crib?" Vera asked. "Isaac can help Chace set it up before we go home."

Mia frowned. "We've never had enough money to buy a crib. We only had a used portable crib I bought at a consignment shop, but we lost it during the move today. We left some of our baby things in the truck while we were packing up the apartment, and when we came back, they were gone."

Vera gasped. "Someone stole your things?"

Mia nodded. "They took our portable crib, baby seat, and baby swing."

"*Ach*, that's terrible."

The door opened and closed and they turned to see Chace with Isaac, Adam, and Joel, all dripping wet.

"That's everything." Chace shucked his soaked sweatshirt. His damp hair was sticking up in all directions. When he pushed his hand through it, it continued to stand up, making him look younger, closer to eighteen than twenty-four. "Thank you so much for your help."

"Isaac," Vera said. "Is that *boppli* portable crib of your sister's still in our attic?"

Mia raised her eyebrows with surprise. Was Vera offering her baby supplies along with food? This family seemed too good to be true.

Isaac rubbed his bearded chin and shrugged. "It should be. She asked us to keep all her *boppli* supplies up there for her."

"Adam, Joel," Vera began, "please go up into the attic and bring down the portable crib." Then she turned to Mia. "We'll bring you the crib that's up there tomorrow."

"Vera, you don't need to do that."

"Don't be silly. It's not doing anyone any *gut* up in our attic, is it?" Vera challenged before turning back to her sons. "Hurry over there so you can get to bed. You have to be up early for school tomorrow."

Adam and Joel grabbed their lanterns and rushed out the door.

"Thank you." Mia looked over at Chace to see his reaction to Vera's generosity, but he was leaning over Kaitlyn as Rhoda held her. He whispered to her and tickled her chin, and she gurgled as she smiled up at him. Mia's heart warmed at the sight. She relished watching Chace interact with their daughter.

"I made the bed and put the towels in the bathroom," Susannah said as she reentered the family room. "Do you have a quilt or blanket? The bedroom is pretty cold." She rubbed her arms over the sleeves of her green dress.

Chace stood, breaking free from the trance of

staring at his baby. "Yeah, we have a couple of blankets." He studied the sea of black trash bags. "They're in one of these."

"I'll help you find them." Mia joined him by the pile of bags and suitcases containing everything they owned in the world. She met his intense stare, and her heart pounded. Was he still angry with her for her negative comments about the cabin? Did he truly believe she would be willing to live only in a home with the luxury of the Hilton?

When a smile turned up the corner of his lips, she released the breath she hadn't realized she'd been holding. They were still a team, still a *family*, despite all the hardship they'd endured since Mia had learned she was pregnant.

"I think the blankets are in this one." Chace ripped open a bag, revealing a threadbare, blue-plaid comforter he had owned since before he and Mia met. "Here's this." He pulled it out and handed it to Mia before digging deeper in the bag. "And there's a blanket too. And here's one of Katie's blankets."

"I'll take them to the bedroom." Vera held out her hands. "Susannah and I will finish making the bed for you."

"Thank you." Mia handed off the blankets. Then she helped Chace search through a few more bags until they found two more blankets for Katie.

Soon Adam and Joel returned with the portable crib. Chace set it up in the bedroom as Mia and Vera located sheets for it.

"Thank you for everything," Mia told the Allgyer

family as they stood by the front door to leave. "I can't thank you enough for your help and generosity."

Vera squeezed Mia's hand. "We're happy to help you. I'll send my boys over early tomorrow morning with that basket of food for you."

"I'll drive you to work tomorrow," Chace told Isaac. "That way you don't have to pay for a driver. I want to do something to thank you for the affordable rent."

"I don't expect a ride for free." Isaac shook Chace's hand.

Chace grinned. "Let's argue about it in the morning, all right?"

"That sounds *gut*." Isaac turned to Mia. "*Gut* night."

"Good night, Isaac. Thank you again."

As the family filed out through the front door, Rhoda and Susannah gave Mia a little wave. Then the door shut behind them.

Chace locked the door and turned off the propane lamp by the wing chair.

"I'm going to feed Katie and put her to bed." Mia slipped into the bedroom and breastfed Katie before putting her down. Then she returned to the family room. "Katie went right to sleep when I put her in the portable crib. I put her warmest pajamas on her and covered her with a few blankets."

"That's good." Chace opened another trash bag and rifled through its contents before moving on to another. "I think my clothes are in here somewhere."

Mia took in their pile of possessions and the stark cabin. She hugged her arms to her middle, shivering once more in the cold. Would the cabin ever warm up?

Suddenly, a memory hit Mia, nearly knocking her off balance. It was last February, and Mia sat in her parents' family room, surrounded by their expensive furniture and her mother's vast collection of priceless paintings and prized figurines. A roaring fire in the brick fireplace warmed her body under the pink cashmere sweater Mom had given her for her birthday a month earlier.

Mia's hands shook and her stomach pitched. "I have something to tell you." Her voice trembled with anxiety.

"What is it, dear?" Mom's perfectly manicured, dark eyebrows careened toward her hairline.

"I'm pregnant." Mia's voice sounded strange to her—small and unsure, like a child's.

"What?" Mom's voice pitched higher than usual. "You're pregnant? How could you let this happen? I thought you were smarter than that."

"It wasn't planned, but Chace loves me, and I love him. I'm going to drop out of school and marry him."

Her parents studied her as their eyes widened. Her words seemed to hang in the air as the ticking of the antique mantel clock and the intermittent pop and hiss of the fire were the only noises echoing throughout the large room. Mia held her breath, awaiting her mother's response. Her father, she knew, would let his wife speak for both of them. He always had. She folded her shaking hands in her lap.

"Mia, you can't possibly be serious. You'll be a horrible mother." Mom's face twisted into a deep scowl. "You're too young to even consider becoming a mother. You have no idea what it takes to raise a child."

"I'll learn." Mia sat a little taller in the chair. "I'll work hard and be the best mother I can be."

Mom clicked her tongue. "You have your entire future ahead of you. You don't need an unplanned pregnancy to ruin your life."

"Ruin my life? How can a child ruin my life? I've thought long and hard about this, and I want this baby. This child is a part of both Chace and me, and we're in love."

"You believe you're in love, but life isn't that simple. You *think* you want this baby, but you haven't truly weighed all the consequences of having a child at a young age. This doesn't just affect you, Mia. It will reflect on our entire family."

Mom's expression hardened. "Can you imagine the scandal when our friends at church and the club find out you're pregnant? It will ruin our family's name. I can't believe you let this happen. I'm very disappointed in you."

"It was an accident, but I'm going to make things right." Mia hated the quaver in her voice. She was stronger than this. "I'm going to have this baby."

"Now, wait a minute." Mom wagged her finger at Mia as if she were a petulant child. "There's only one way to make this right." She shifted on her chair and crossed one long leg over her opposite knee. "You should live with your aunt Briana in San Diego until after the baby is born. Then you can give it up for adoption. No one will ever know of your mistake. Then you can go back to college and get on with your life like it never happened, and you'll be much happier."

"You want me to just give up my child?" Mia gasped and turned to her father. Surely, he would understand.

Dad nodded. "Sweetie, your mom is right. Don't let an unplanned pregnancy ruin your good name or your future."

"All your friends from high school are getting their degrees and heading toward a bright future," Mom chimed in. "Don't you want to be like them? I'm certain they won't want to associate with you when they find out you're pregnant out of wedlock."

A surge of fury mixed with confidence bubbled up from somewhere deep inside her. "I'm going to marry Chace and have this baby with or without your blessing."

Mia didn't want to think about the rest of their conversation that day. She had stuck to her decision and marched out of her parents' house without their blessing or approval.

But now, as Mia stood in the middle of the cold cabin, her mother's hurtful words echoed through her mind. *Was Mom right? Maybe I'm not capable of being a good mother.*

Without warning, a sob escaped from Mia's throat. She covered her face with her hands as tears spilled down her cheeks.

Strong arms encircled her as Chace pulled her to his muscular chest. She inhaled the comforting scent of his spicy aftershave as she buried her face in his collarbone. She relaxed against him, pulling strength from the sound of his heartbeat.

"Everything is going to be fine, Mee," he whispered into her hair before kissing the top of her head. "I promise I'll take care of us. This is temporary. As soon as we pay off all the hospital bills and save up some money, I'll build us a house. Does that sound good?" He placed his fingertip under her chin and angled her face so she looked up into his eyes.

"Yeah."

He wiped away her tears with his fingers and then smiled before kissing her. As Chace pulled her close for another hug, Mia closed her eyes and prayed she and Chace could give Kaitlyn everything she needed.

CHAPTER 2

Anguish covered Chace like a lead blanket as he folded one arm behind his head and stared up at the bedroom ceiling through the dark. Mia's stricken expression after Isaac and his family left the cabin filled Chace's mind. Each tear that slipped down her pink cheeks had chipped away at his heart. He was grateful he was able to calm her down and convince her to go to bed since they both were exhausted after the stressful day they had endured.

All Chace wanted was to be the husband she deserved and the father Kaitlyn needed, but no matter how hard he worked, the rug had been repeatedly yanked out from under him. He had been mortified when he received the Notice to Quit, but he was certain he could find a way to get a loan to pay the past-due rent and keep their apartment. He had tried to explain their situation to the landlord and convince Mr. Newman to give them an extension, but Mr. Newman insisted he was forced to evict them. Chace had hoped to find them a place to go before today's deadline, but there weren't any decent apartments in their price range. Also, the medical bills they had incurred with

Kaitlyn's birth had destroyed their chances of finding a nice apartment in a safe neighborhood.

Mia sighed in her sleep beside him and nestled deeper under the pile of blankets. Chace touched the long, thick, dark-brown hair fanning over her pillow. He smiled as the moment he'd first seen her two years ago took over his thoughts.

Chace hadn't wanted to go to the party since he wasn't a student at the college where it was held, but his coworker at the construction company had insisted he go. He felt out of place surrounded by young people who were getting an education and would ultimately make something of themselves—unlike Chace, who had ricocheted from foster home to foster home and barely managed to graduate from high school. While his friend flirted with a sorority girl, Chace leaned against a far wall and sipped a can of soda.

But everything changed when Chace spotted Mia across the crowded room. It had been love at first sight, just like one of those sappy movies Mia loved to watch. She was breathtakingly dressed in a short black skirt and an emerald green sweater. When her milk-chocolate eyes met his gaze, he was certain she'd dismiss him with a haughty glare, but she didn't. Instead, she smiled and raised her diet soda can in a silent toast. He mustered all his confidence and crossed the room to ask her name. They spent the rest of the evening talking in a quiet corner, and she allowed him to call her the next day. They'd been inseparable ever since.

A quiet snore sounded from the portable crib next to his side of the bed. Chace leaned over and smiled.

How he adored his baby girl. Kaitlyn was the greatest blessing in his life, his greatest accomplishment. He often felt the urge to pinch himself to make certain he hadn't dreamed his family.

When his thoughts turned to Mia's parents, Chace's shoulders tightened. Why didn't they want to meet their only grandchild? How could they so easily throw away their only child and her baby? Guilt filled him as he recalled the biting remark he'd made to Mia earlier, accusing her of wanting to live at the Hilton. That was a low blow since Mia was nothing like her elitist parents, but sometimes his insecurities got the best of him. He had to work harder at curbing his temper. His job was to cherish Mia, not cut her down.

Chace moved under the blankets and shifted closer to Mia, his leg resting against hers. Closing his eyes, he listened to the soft sound of his wife's breathing until sleep found him.

. . .

Mia woke at the sound of Kaitlyn's first whimper. She glanced at the battery-operated clock on the nightstand. It was six thirty. Since Chace had fifteen minutes more to sleep, she gingerly climbed from the bed, shivering as she pulled on her pink terrycloth robe and pushed her socked feet into slippers. She tiptoed around the bed and lifted Kaitlyn from the portable crib, holding her close to her body for warmth. Did this little cabin have any insulation at all? She scooped up one of the blankets from the portable crib.

Standing in the doorway, Mia peered over at her husband, snuggled under the blankets as he snored into his pillow. Even with spittle at the corner of his mouth, Chace O'Conner remained the most handsome man she'd ever seen. She grinned as she pulled the door closed.

"Did you sleep well, sweet pea?" Mia carried her baby to the sofa.

Kaitlyn gurgled a response as Mia began to change her diaper. When she was done, she lifted her daughter into her arms.

She balanced Kaitlyn on her hip before heading to the kitchen. She glanced at the coal stove, trying in vain to remember Vera's instructions for adding more coal to increase the heat in the house. She had no business touching the stove.

Then she turned toward the cookstove and examined it, wondering how she'd ever figure it out so she could cook for Chace. She bit her lip as confusion settled over her. She'd cooked easy meals and warmed bottles with the help of a pot of water when they lived in their apartment, but the stove there had been electric. What if she made a mistake when she tried to light the burner?

Visions of an exploding stove filled her mind as Kaitlyn's whine transformed into a steady cry. Mia examined the knobs and dials on the stove for a moment longer, but her lack of confidence in her domestic skills won out over her determination. She would figure out how to work the stove later. Right now, she needed to worry about feeding her baby.

She returned to the sofa, covered Kaitlyn with the blanket for warmth, and began to breastfeed her.

A short while later Mia supported Kaitlyn on her shoulder and rubbed her back in an attempt to burp her. The bedroom door opened with a whoosh, revealing Chace clad in worn navy blue sweatpants and a faded, long-sleeved T-shirt featuring a muscle car. Clean clothes were draped over his arm, and he yawned and rubbed his eyes as he crossed the small space to the sofa.

"How are my two favorite girls this morning?" He planted a soft kiss on Mia's lips before kissing Kaitlyn's shock of blond hair.

"We're fine, Daddy," Mia simpered. "How are you, sleepyhead?"

He shrugged, but she observed dark circles under his eyes as he gave her a crooked grin. "I slept okay." He jammed a thumb toward the kitchen. "Did you see if the stove needed more coal?"

Mia continued to caress Kaitlyn's back. "I didn't feel comfortable touching it. I couldn't remember exactly what Vera told me about adding coal."

"I'll take a look." Chace touched Kaitlyn's back, and she responded with a loud belch. "That's my girl." He snickered as he walked toward the kitchen. He reappeared a few moments later, rubbing his hands together. "I added some coal. Maybe we'll finally get some heat in here. I'm going to shower."

Mia resumed feeding Kaitlyn, and just as she had finished burping her, a knock sounded on the front door. She covered Kaitlyn with the blanket again and walked to the door. Peering out the glass, she saw Adam and Joel standing on the steps.

Mia unlocked the door and opened it. "Good morning."

"Hi. Our *mamm* asked us to bring these to you." Adam held up a basket. "I can set this on the counter for you if you'd like."

"She also said she thought you could use this." Joel held up a baby seat. "We cleaned it up for you."

Mia beamed. A baby seat! This is just what she needed since someone had taken their baby seat from the truck.

Adam put the basket on the counter as Joel put the seat on the kitchen table.

"Please tell your mother I said thank you so much. I'll try to stop by to see her later," Mia told the boys before they left.

After securing Kaitlyn in the seat and giving her a pacifier, Mia investigated the basket and found a homemade coffee cake and butter tucked inside. Tears stung her eyes.

Mia was setting two plates with coffee cake on the table when Chace reappeared wearing jeans and a gray Henley shirt. His hair was damp, and his chin was clean-shaven. He was adorable.

"Wow." He approached the table. "Is that homemade?"

"Yes, it is."

"Where did you get it?"

"Joel and Adam brought it and the butter, along with this seat." Mia touched the seat as Kaitlyn gazed up at Chace. "I think the Allgyers are our guardian angels."

Chace nodded. "I think you're right."

As they sat down across from each other to eat, Mia smiled. *Mom was wrong. Chace, Kaitlyn, and I are going to be fine.*

. . .

Chace cast Isaac a sideways glance as he steered his pickup onto the main road. "Thank you for everything you've done for my family and me."

"You're welcome." Isaac nodded with his usual pleasant but not overly emotional expression. "Are you comfortable in the cabin?"

"Yes, we are." Chace refocused on the road ahead. "It's a little cold, but I think we'll get used to the coal stove. I added more coal before I left this morning."

"I can take a look at it later if you'd like. It does take a little getting used to." After a moment he said, "We want to lend you more of my sister's baby supplies from our attic. No one in the family needs them right now."

"We appreciate it. We don't have much." Chace stole another glance at Isaac, who was now peering out the passenger side window. He had the overwhelming urge to explain why he and Mia were in such dire straits. "I was working for a construction firm when I asked Mia to marry me. I was making a fairly good salary, and I had health insurance. But I was laid off shortly before Katie was born, and when she came she wound up in the neonatal intensive care unit for five days before we could bring her home. Katie is fine, but we found ourselves drowning in debt. We sold everything we could, but it still didn't get us caught up."

Chace slowed the truck to a stop at a red light, and when Isaac didn't say anything, he continued. "Like I told you yesterday, I never imagined I'd wind up homeless, and I'm embarrassed to admit how bad things became for Mia and me. I'm just so grateful you offered us a place to live. You've been so generous to me. You're the reason my family and I haven't wound up in a homeless shelter. You gave me a job when I had hardly any experience with cabinetry."

The light turned green, and Chace accelerated through the intersection as a horse and buggy moved along in the shoulder beside the truck.

"I didn't do much," Isaac said. "You're a fast learner, and you told me you'd learned woodworking in high school. It only made sense for me to offer you the cabin when it's sat empty since *mei dat* passed away."

In the three months Chace had worked for Isaac he'd noticed how humble and self-deprecating the man was. It was just like Isaac to not acknowledge how generous he was. He smacked the blinker as the sign for Allgyer's Custom Cabinets came into view and then steered into the lot. He parked his truck in his usual spot at the far end of the parking lot, leaving the closer spaces for the customers.

"Don't be so hard on yourself." Isaac wrenched open the passenger side door. "Vera and I struggled when we were young. Every couple endures tough times, and you and Mia will come through this stronger. Vera and I will do all we can to help you." With a quick nod, he hopped out of the truck and started toward the front door of the store.

Chace pulled his keys from the ignition and then leaned back in the seat as Isaac crossed the parking lot. He was so thankful he'd taken a chance and walked into Isaac's store the day he'd seen the Help Wanted sign. Mia was right—Isaac and Vera Allgyer were their guardian angels. Maybe, just maybe, with their help he and Mia would be okay.

. . .

Mia gritted her teeth as she paced back and forth from the small family room to the kitchen, bouncing Kaitlyn as she wailed. Kaitlyn had been screaming for nearly twenty minutes and none of Mia's usual soothing techniques had been successful. Mia had tried changing her diaper, singing to her, feeding her, and rocking her as they walked, but Kaitlyn continued her tirade.

Mia looked from the kitchen to the family room, where the sea of boxes, suitcases, and bags waited patiently to be unpacked. She had so much to do, but she couldn't accomplish any of it if Kaitlyn continued to fuss.

Mia thought she heard a knock on the door, but she ignored it, certain she had misheard the noise because of Kaitlyn's sobs. When the knock sounded again, Mia opened the door to find Rhoda and Susannah.

"Hi," Mia said, speaking loudly over Kaitlyn's moans. "How are you?"

"Our *mamm* sent us over to help you," Rhoda explained as they stepped into the cabin. She removed her coat and hung it on a peg by the door before holding out her arms to Kaitlyn. "May I hold her?"

"She's really fussy today, but you can try." Mia handed the baby over to her.

Rhoda whispered something to Kaitlyn and then held her close. When Kaitlyn continued to cry, Rhoda looked up at Mia. "Would it be all right if I took her for a walk?"

Mia grimaced. "I don't know. It's so cold out."

"My youngest brother loved to go for walks when he was little," Rhoda explained, moving her body back and forth to rock the unhappy baby. "Walks seemed to be the only thing that would calm him, even when it was cold out."

"I remember that." Susannah cupped her hand to the back of Kaitlyn's head and murmured something in her ear.

Mia hugged her arms to her chest and glanced around the cabin. She was too embarrassed to admit she didn't have a stroller either. That was something else that had been swiped from the truck while they were packing up their apartment. She just hadn't mentioned every item stolen to Vera the night before. Who leaves belongings unattended like that? But they'd been so upset and in such a rush to get out of there.

"We have a stroller," Susannah offered as if reading Mia's thoughts. "We have a snowsuit about Kaitlyn's size too. I can go get them." She still had her coat on.

Mia sighed. "You are too generous."

"It's no problem. Do you need anything else?" Susannah stepped toward the door.

Mia rubbed her arms, recalling how cold she'd been all night. Had Chace added enough coal to the stove?

"It's so cold in here. Do you have any spare blankets? I'll return them when the cabin warms up."

Susannah nodded. "I'm sure we have extra quilts. I'll be right back."

"Thank you." Mia turned toward Rhoda, who spoke softly to Kaitlyn while continuing to move her body back and forth. Kaitlyn stopped crying. "You certainly are an expert. You look so comfortable with her."

"I just have a lot of experience taking care of my siblings and my cousins." Rhoda shrugged as she lowered herself into the wing chair. "Does she take a bottle? Do you want me to feed her?"

Mia grimaced and pointed toward the cookstove. "I'm breastfeeding, and I'm getting her used to formula in a bottle too. But I can't figure out how to turn on the burner so I can warm up a bottle."

"I can show you how to do it."

While holding Kaitlyn close to her chest, Rhoda followed Mia to the kitchen area and explained how to use the stove. Mia warmed a bottle and then gave it to Rhoda to feed Kaitlyn, giving Mia the chance to unpack kitchen supplies.

Mia had the kitchen organized and was starting on the boxes in the family room when Vera and Susannah knocked, then entered the cabin. Vera held an armload of quilts and Susannah steered a stroller filled with a snowsuit, quilts, and toys.

"Thank you so much." A lump clogged Mia's throat as she took the quilts from Vera. "This is too much." She walked to the bedroom and set the quilts on the bed.

"No, it's not." Vera stood behind her. "By the way,

the changing table we have is nothing fancy, but it has room for storage." She pointed to a corner of the room. "It would fit there, and you can put the crib next to it."

"Changing table? Crib?" Mia asked.

"*Ya*, I thought I told you we have a crib you can use too. I'll have Adam and Joel bring everything over later when they get home from school." Vera placed her hands on her hips. "I think it would all fit over there nicely."

Mia blinked against threatening tears. She had the urge to laugh and cry at the same time. Why was she so emotional today? "Thank you."

"You're welcome." Vera touched her shoulder. "Susannah and I are here to help you unpack if you'd like the help. We're caught up with our morning chores."

"Thank you," Mia repeated. This woman had met Mia for the first time last night but was offering to help her unpack.

Vera chuckled. "You don't have to keep thanking me. Let's get to work."

Mia, Vera, and Susannah spent the next couple of hours unpacking all of Mia and Chace's belongings and organizing the cabin. By the time they finished, the bedroom closet and bureau were full of clothes, and some of Mia's books and photos were displayed on the small bookcase near the front door.

Rhoda put Kaitlyn down for a nap in the portable crib and soon returned to the family area. "She's already fast asleep." She eased the bedroom door shut.

"Thank you." Mia placed her favorite photo on top of the bookcase. It featured Mia, Kaitlyn, and Chace posing together in their former apartment the day

Kaitlyn came home from the hospital. It was their first family photo. Mia held Kaitlyn in her arms and Chace had his arms wrapped around Mia, sporting his happy grin. They were so happy that day, so certain everything would be okay.

She scanned the small cabin and sighed. This was their home now, but why didn't it feel like a home? It just felt like a temporary place—a temporary and *cold* place—like a cheap hotel room someone would stay in overnight while on a journey to a more permanent and important location.

Vera surveyed their work. "The cabin looks *gut*."

"*Ya*." Susannah sat down on the wing chair. "It reminds me of when *Mammi* and *Daadi* lived here."

"I agree." Vera set a pile of empty boxes near the door. "It's *gut* to have someone in this *haus* again."

"How long did they live here?" Mia asked, still standing by the bookcase.

Vera was silent for a moment. "I think they were here for almost twenty years. Isaac's *mamm* passed away five years ago, and then his *dat* passed away two years ago."

"I miss them." Rhoda walked over to her mother.

"I do too," Susannah said. "I loved coming out here to visit them."

"I know you did," Vera responded. "I miss them too."

A pang of envy took Mia by surprise, and she frowned. Why didn't her parents want to be a part of their granddaughter's life like Isaac's parents had been? She dismissed the thought.

"Do you have anything to eat for supper?" Vera asked. "If not, I can bring something over for you."

Mia gnawed her lower lip while debating her response. She didn't want to lie about the meager choices she had, but they were better than nothing. "We have peanut butter, some bread, macaroni and cheese, ramen noodles, a little fruit, and a few cans of vegetables and soup. I can throw something together. We'll be fine." She was too humiliated to admit she had to save the peanut butter and bread for Chace to take to work for lunch.

Vera gave her a knowing expression. "I'll have Susannah and Rhoda bring over some food. We have plenty."

"I appreciate the offer, but you don't have to do that," Mia insisted. "I plan to go grocery shopping on Friday when Chace gets paid."

"We're happy to share our meal with you." Vera pulled on her coat. "I need to get home to finish a sewing project I started yesterday, but we will be back. Let us know if you need anything else."

Susannah and Rhoda followed suit, buttoning their coats.

"Thank you." Mia suddenly remembered a question she had. "Would you show me how to use the wringer washer sometime?"

"Oh, *ya*," Rhoda said as she stepped out to the small porch. "I can show you later when I bring over supper."

Mia waved as her new friends descended the steps and walked down the rock path leading to their large farmhouse. Then she closed the door and leaned against it. Would this tiny, dreary house ever feel like a home?

CHAPTER 3

Chace felt as if he'd been run over by his own truck. His arms, legs, and back were sore as he climbed the front steps later that evening. He'd spent all day helping Isaac build cabinets for a kitchen remodel at a huge home not far from their small cabin. Would he be able to build a similar home for Mia someday?

As he pulled open the front door, the aroma of baked chicken wafted over him and his stomach gurgled with delight. He turned toward the kitchen where Mia carried plates and utensils to the table. Her dark hair was pulled up in a messy ponytail with loose tendrils framing her face. She wore one of his old gray sweatshirts, which hung to the thighs of her jeans. Although she rarely wore makeup, she was the most beautiful woman he'd ever met.

"Hello." He hung his coat on a peg by the door. "How are my two favorite girls?"

Mia mumbled something inaudible as she placed a large bowl of noodles in the center of the small table.

He scanned the cabin. The suitcases, boxes, and trash bags were gone from the family room floor and the room was tidy. Turning to his right, he saw the small bookcase cluttered with Mia's favorite framed photos and a few books. He smiled. Mia had made the cabin a home.

"How are you?" Chace crossed to the kitchen and opened his arms in the hopes she would step into his hug. Instead, she slipped past him, her face twisted into a scowl. His stomach tightened. Something was wrong. "Where's Katie?"

"She's sleeping." Mia filled a glass with water from a pitcher. "Have a seat."

"I need to wash my hands first." Chace scrubbed his hands at the kitchen sink and then sat down across from her. A bowl of chicken and noodles and a bowl of green beans sat in the middle of the table, and his stomach growled again. He looked up to where Mia studied her plate while frowning.

"Everything looks delicious." He gave her a hesitant smile. "Thank you."

She speared him with an accusing look. "I didn't make it. Vera did."

"Oh." He paused, uncertain of how to respond to her biting tone. "Okay."

They were silent as they filled their plates and began to eat. She took small bites while studying her glass of water as if it were an intricate book she was studying for a college exam.

The reticence between them weighed heavily on Chace's shoulders. He longed to ask her about her day and share the details of his. Instead, he kept quiet, hoping Mia's fury would subside. He'd been on the receiving end of her simmering anger more than once during their two-year relationship, and he dreaded the explosion that threatened to come soon.

"This is delicious," he finally said, treading carefully. "It was nice of Vera to share their supper with us." He lifted his glass of water to take a sip.

"She insisted. She felt sorry for us when I admitted we won't have much food until you get paid on Friday."

He held the glass frozen in midair and watched his wife, trying to understand what was bothering her. "What's wrong?"

She set her fork down next to her plate and studied him. "I have never in my life been on the receiving end of handouts." She pointed toward the bowl of green beans. "This meal isn't the only thing she's given us." She began counting items off on her fingers. "She also gave us a crib, a changing table, a snowsuit, a stroller, and baby toys." Then she pointed toward the coal stove. "And she gave us quilts so we don't freeze to death. I wasn't this cold when I was living in the dorm and the windows wouldn't close all the way."

Mia lanced him with another murderous expression. "Do you have any idea how embarrassing it was to admit to her that we didn't have any food for supper other than some boxed mac and cheese and canned soup?"

Chace placed the glass on the table as his hands began to shake. He took slow, deep breaths in an attempt to calm down before he said something he'd regret.

"How can you expect us to live here? It's so cold that I'm surprised Katie isn't already sick. There's no electricity so I can't even plug in a small heater to try to warm our bedroom up for her naps. There's no phone, and I'm completely cut off from the world since we couldn't afford to keep our cell phones. What am I supposed to do if there's an emergency? Am I expected to run to the nearest hospital since I sold my car in an effort to pay some of the bills?"

"There is a phone," Chace muttered as angry heat crept up his neck.

"There is?" She fixed him with an incredulous stare. "Where?"

"By the barn. The Amish have phones. They just aren't in their houses."

"Well, you've fixed one of my four-dozen problems. How do we fix the rest of them?"

"I'm doing the best I can." He kneaded the tense muscles in his neck with his fingers. "I don't know what else I can do."

Just then Kaitlyn started to wail. With a sigh, Mia pushed back her chair and left the kitchen.

Chace stared down at his empty plate, the food souring in his stomach. Guilt and dread clawed up his sore back as Mia's hateful words echoed through his mind. He felt as if he were sixteen years old again and standing in front of Buck Richards, the most callous and critical foster father Chace had endured since his mother died and he was hurled into the foster care system when he was four.

"You'll never amount to anything, Chace, because you have no ambition. You'll just look for the easy way out. I'd bet you'll rob convenience stores, shoot the

clerks, and then wind up in jail for life, just like your worthless father."

Chace had promised himself he'd prove Buck wrong, but it seemed an impossible feat. Pressing his fingers to his eyes, Chace swallowed against the emotion lodging in his throat.

The sound of Kaitlyn's gurgle brought him back to the present as Mia returned to the kitchen with her balanced on one hip.

"Hi, baby girl." He forced a smile as Kaitlyn gnawed on her thumb and blew happy spit bubbles. "How was your day, Katie-Bug?"

"Feel her leg." She angled the baby toward him. "Feel how cold she is."

Chace pressed his lips together as he touched the leg of Kaitlyn's sleeper. It was cold.

"I don't see how this can be healthy. She's going to wind up sick one of these days." Mia lifted the baby seat with one hand and placed it on the table. She set Kaitlyn in the seat and buckled the straps. Kaitlyn responded with a happy gurgle.

"So then why don't you call your parents and ask for help?" The question leaped from Chace's lips before he could stop it. He held his breath, awaiting her eruption. The subject of her parents always sent Mia over the edge. She hadn't spoken to her parents since the day Kaitlyn was born, and from what little Mia had divulged, the conversation hadn't made any strides toward changing their decision to disown Mia.

"You know the answer to that question." She ground out the words.

He stood as renewed frustration grabbed him by the throat. "Maybe your parents would change their minds if they saw their beautiful grandchild." He pointed at Kaitlyn. "How could they possibly resist her?"

"It won't work." She gestured wildly with her hands as her brown eyes sparkled with tears. "I could send them a portfolio of professional photos of Kaitlyn and they still would refuse to help us."

"Well, I don't know what to tell you." He folded his arms over his chest. "Maybe it's time for you to let go of your pride for the sake of our child and ask your father to give us a loan until we're back on our feet."

"Let go of my pride?" Her voice quavered and her eyes narrowed to slits. "My pride has nothing to do with how my parents feel about my decisions."

A single tear trickled down her cheek, and his chest constricted. He'd done it again. He'd lost his temper and made her cry.

"Mee, I'm sorry." He reached for her, but she stepped back and out of his reach. "Why don't you sit down and finish your supper with me? I want to hear about your day."

"I have nothing else to say to you." Mia shook her head and stomped off to the bedroom, leaving Chace staring down at Kaitlyn as she kicked her feet and blew bubbles.

Chace touched Kaitlyn's toe as Buck's words reverberated in his mind again. His shoulders slumped. He wasn't worthy of Mia or this beautiful baby.

He handed Kaitlyn the pacifier that hung on a clip attached to her sleeper and then carried the dishes to the sink. As it filled with hot water, Chace peered out the small window and stared toward Isaac's house. *Will I ever be the husband Mia deserves?*

. . .

Mia sat on the edge of the bed and buried her face in her hands as angry tears splattered down her hot cheeks. She took deep, slow breaths. *Be strong, Mia! Calm down!* Soon her tears stopped, and she hugged her arms to her waist.

Her gaze moved across the room to a framed photograph sitting on top of the small bureau. In the photo, Mia and Chace stood arm in arm on the beach, their smiles wide as waves crashed behind them and the sunset bathed the sky in vivid streaks of orange, pink, and yellow. Her heart thumped as she recalled that beach trip. It was Memorial Day weekend, and she and Chace had been dating for a month. Shortly after that photo was taken, Chace told her he loved her for the first time. Back then life was simple. Mia was in college studying to become a teacher, and Chace was working for a construction company. Their future was bright with endless possibilities.

So much had changed in a matter of almost two years. Now their future was uncertain and bleak. She'd spent the day trying to convince herself she was doing the best she could as a mother, but that voice at the back of her mind kept taunting her with her mother's words: *"You'll be a horrible mother."* She had to prove her mother wrong. But how?

Her conversation with Chace replayed in her mind,

and her body shuddered with a mixture of frustration and guilt. She could feel the pain in Chace's eyes when she yelled at him, listing everything wrong with the cabin and their lives. She longed for Chace to under-stand her parents weren't going to help them.

Mia's painful conversation with her mother after Kaitlyn's birth was still fresh in her mind. She called to tell her the baby had been born and asked her if she was ready to be the grandmother Kaitlyn needed and deserved. Her mother's response was, "I'll be ready to be her grandmother when you're ready to face the fact that Chace can't give you and your baby the life you both deserve."

When her mother refused to acknowledge Kaitlyn or accept Chace as her husband, Mia burst into tears, tell-ing her mom she was still the cold, superficial woman she'd always been, and then Mia disconnected the call.

Squeezing her eyes shut, Mia pressed her fingers to her forehead. She was just as self-centered as her mother when she blamed Chace for their current situa-tion. She and Chace were in this together. They were a team. More important, they were a *family*. Chace had been telling her the truth when he said he was doing the best he could. She had to apologize to him.

Shoving herself off the bed, Mia wiped her hands down her cheeks and hurried out of the bedroom. Chace was washing dishes at the kitchen sink. Without much forethought, she lunged forward and wrapped her arms around him, squeezing him and burying her face into his back.

He gasped and then his body relaxed.

"I'm sorry," she whispered, her voice wavering. "I'm so sorry."

"Hey, it's okay." He spun and gathered her in his arms as soon as he rinsed and dried his hands. "I'm sorry too, Mee."

Mia smiled at the sound of the nickname he'd given her when they first started dating. She looked up at him and her lower lip trembled. "I'm sorry for dumping on you after you worked hard all day for Katie and me. I didn't mean it." She looped her arms around his neck.

"It's all right." He trailed a fingertip down her cheek. "No more tears."

She cleared her throat. "We're in this together, right?"

"Always. And I will do everything in my power to take care of you and Katie." Dipping his chin, he brushed his lips over hers, sending shivers of electricity dancing down her spine. "I love you."

"I love you too." Closing her eyes, she hoped they would make it somehow.

• • •

Chace perched on a stool and sipped a bottle of water as the sweet smell of new wood and stain wafted over him. He'd spent all morning sanding cabinets. Although he listened to music on his ancient iPod while he worked, he couldn't stop his brain from focusing on Mia's parents. Could he talk to Mia's father man-to-man and somehow convince him to loan Chace money? He didn't want a handout from Mia's parents; he only wanted a little help getting back on his feet.

He studied the cabinet on his workbench as the idea filtered through his thoughts. It seemed a reasonable enough request, but a tiny twinge of warning rang through his head. *Mia would be furious if she found out I spoke to her father.*

Chace blew out a resigned sigh in agreement with his inner voice. Yes, she would be, but it was his responsibility to take care of his family.

My very own family.

He'd dreamt of having his own family since he was a child, and now that he had one, he would do anything in his power to preserve it. If that meant begging Mia's father for help, then he would do it.

When the other workers in the shop left for lunch, Chace approached the front office.

"Isaac." Chace leaned his shoulder against the door-frame. "I was wondering if I could use your phone book and phone for a few minutes."

"Of course." Isaac pulled a phone book out of one of the bottom drawers and set it on the desk. "Take your time. I'll be in the break room."

"Thanks," Chace said as Isaac moved past him, disappearing into the hallway. He appreciated how Isaac respected his privacy. Isaac had never pressed Chace to share why he had needed a place to live. He never accused or admonished Chace about the dire situation. Instead, he'd offered the cabin, asking how much Chace could comfortably afford to pay for rent.

Chace sat down at the desk, opened the phone book, located the phone number for Whitfield, Price & Morgan

Attorneys at Law, and dialed. His heart was in his throat when a woman answered.

"Thank you for calling Whitfield, Price and Morgan. How may I direct your call?"

"May I please speak to Walter Whitfield?" Chace hoped he sounded confident despite the anxiety threading through him.

The woman paused. "May I ask who is calling?"

"Chace O'Conner." He worried his lower lip.

"And what is the nature of your call, Mr. O'Conner?"

"I'm his son-in-law. It's an urgent family matter."

"Oh. I will transfer you right away. Just a moment, please, Mr. O'Conner."

"Thank you." Chace kneaded one temple and mentally rehearsed what he would say to Walter. He'd met Walter a few times while he and Mia dated. Walter had been polite, but he radiated a palpable air of arrogance and disapproval.

"This is Walter Whitfield." Walter's deep, no-nonsense voice rang over the line.

Chace froze, doubt stealing his courage. *Hang up now before you ruin Mia's chances of ever reconciling with her parents!*

"Chace?" Walter sighed. "Are you there?"

"Yes, I am." Chace cleared his throat. "Thank you for taking my call."

"Is something wrong with Mia?"

For a brief moment, Chace was impressed. *So Mia's father has a conscience?*

"Mia is fine, and so is our daughter." Chace ground

out the words as anger replaced his surprise. "Did you know your granddaughter's name is Kaitlyn Leanne? Leanne is after my mother. She died when I was four." When Walter didn't respond, Chace continued. "Our baby is five months old now. She has blue eyes and blond hair. I thought she'd have dark hair and eyes like Mia, but she actually has my coloring. But she definitely has Mia's smile. She's the prettiest baby I've ever seen. I suppose I'm biased since I'm her father. You should understand that."

Chace wound the phone cord around his finger. "I'd love to send photos to you and Mrs. Whitfield." He could ask one of his coworkers to take a photo and text it to Walter since Chace no longer had a cell phone. "Would you like to see photos of the granddaughter you've never met?"

"What do you want?"

"I want to talk to you man-to-man."

"Look, my wife and I feel it's best if we stay out of Mia's life."

"I know that, and I didn't expect this phone call to change that."

"So what do you want then? Is it money?"

Chace grimaced. He hated how that sounded. "Not exactly," he said, hedging. "I want to ask for a loan. I just need some help getting back on my feet, and I will repay you with interest. When Kaitlyn was born she spent five days in the NICU. The bills on top of her delivery itself have been daunting, but if I could just get—"

"Are you saying you can't support my daughter on your construction-worker salary?"

Walter's sneer radiated through the phone. Chace silently counted to ten, keeping his thoughts focused on Mia and Kaitlyn instead of allowing his anger to destroy any chance of convincing Walter to help them.

"I'm only asking you for a loan," Chace repeated, the receiver trembling in his hand.

"I'm sorry, but I can't help you. Give Mia my love."

Before Chace could respond, the line went dead. Chace slammed the receiver onto the cradle and heaved the phone book across the room. The heavy book smacked the wall before landing in a heap by the door.

He leaned over the desk, folded his arms, and rested his forehead on them as he fought back his embittered tears. He'd reached a new low. Not only had he betrayed Mia by going against her wishes, but he'd failed to help his family. No matter what Chace tried to do, he failed. How was he going to face Mia tonight? And what would she say when she learned he had called her father?

Renewed worry and frustration surged through Chace. How could things get any worse?

CHAPTER 4

M ia sucked in a deep breath and plastered a smile on her face as hope and determination coursed through her. "This is my first attempt at meat loaf." She brought a loaf pan to the table and set it on a trivet beside a bowl with leftover green beans. Chace kept his stormy blue eyes focused on his glass of water.

Since he'd arrived home nearly thirty minutes ago, Chace hadn't said anything other than his customary, "How are my favorite girls?" After kissing Kaitlyn's head, he'd washed his hands and then dropped into his seat at the table, staring at the plate and scowling. Mia tried to coax him into a conversation by asking about his day and even asking if he was upset with her. He, however, remained reticent.

Although worry had her stomach tied in knots, Mia kept smiling as she cut a piece of meat loaf and dropped it onto Chace's plate. Her smile dissolved as she examined the bottom of the loaf.

"It's burned." Her shoulders sagged. She'd gotten chop meat from Vera and planned to pay her for it when Chace received his next paycheck on Friday. She'd used a cookbook from Goodwill to mix up the meat loaf, but lost track of time taking care of the baby and left it in the oven too long.

Mia dropped a piece of meat loaf onto her own plate and bit her lower lip. Her plan to impress Chace with a nice meal had gone up in smoke. "It's probably not that good. I guess I have a lot to learn."

Chace studied the meat loaf. He cut off a piece and then moved it to the side of his plate. "That's no surprise since your mother never cooked. I guess she expected you to have a housekeeper like she did. Why learn to cook when you can pay someone to make the meals?"

Mia gaped at him. Had she heard him correctly? She started to deliver a cutting retort but then closed her mouth as worry pushed away her anger. Had something happened to Chace today? Had he lost his job? Her stomach roiled at the thought of facing Chace's unemployment for the second time in less than a year. She took a deep breath, steadying her nerves. She and Chace were married and had a baby. They had to face their problems together as a united force.

Instead of yelling at him, she had to ease him into a conversation. She had to offer support, not sardonic responses.

"Did you have a bad day at work?" Her tone was cautious.

He shrugged as he turned his attention to Kaitlyn in her baby seat on the table beside him. A swarm of emotions hurdled across his handsome face as he rubbed Kaitlyn's foot, watching her suck on her pacifier. Mia saw anger, disappointment, sadness, and regret brewing in his expression.

As the silence stretched like a great chasm between them, Mia twirled her fork in her fingers and searched for something to spark a conversation. "I've been thinking about what you said last night, and I realized you're right."

His eyebrows rose, but he kept his eyes focused on Kaitlyn. He rubbed her leg and then took her tiny hand in his. The tenderness in his touch and his love for their daughter stole Mia's words for a moment.

"I've already sold my car and most of my jewelry." She stared down at the thin gold band on her left ring finger. "I also sold my designer clothes and purses at that consignment shop, so I don't have anything left to sell."

"What's your point?"

She peeked up and found him watching her.

"I'm ready to contact my parents and ask for their help," she blurted. "I'll need to borrow the truck." She looked at Kaitlyn, and her voice trembled. "Maybe if they met her, they'd be more inclined to help us."

"Don't waste your time." Chace stood and carried his plate to the sink, his meal untouched.

"What do you mean?"

He faced her, leaning against the sink and crossing his arms over his wide chest. "I called your father today."

"You what?" Mia dropped the fork onto the plate with a clatter. "You called my father?"

Chace nodded.

"What did he say?" She stood. While she felt betrayed by Chace for going behind her back, another emotion emerged and squeezed at her chest—hope. Chace sounded like her father had said no, but maybe with time he could get through to him, make him realize he wanted to not only be a father to Mia, but, more important, be a grandfather to Kaitlyn. After all, Mia's parents were the only grandparents Kaitlyn would ever have the chance to know.

"It didn't go well."

"What did he say?" she repeated, her words slow and measured. When Chace rubbed his clean-shaven chin with hesitation, Mia's blood boiled and she clenched her jaw. "Tell me."

"At first he asked if you were okay." He rested his hands on the sink behind him. "I told him you were fine, and then I told him about Katie, offering to send photos. He said he and your mother had decided it was best to stay out of your life. He asked me if I wanted money, and when I asked for a loan, he made a crack about how I can't support you on my construction work salary."

Mia gasped.

"I even offered to pay interest. I explained how Katie was in the NICU and we're buried in debt now. He said he couldn't help me and he told me to give you his love. And then he hung up before I could say anything else." His face softened. "I'm sorry, Mee."

A single tear trickled down Mia's cheek, and she brushed it away. She couldn't allow her parents to hurt her again. She had to be strong for Kaitlyn.

"How could you?" She took a step toward him, balling her hands into tight fists as her whole body shook, the glimmer of hope gone. "How could you call my father after I told you it wouldn't work?"

He lifted one hand and shook his head. "I was desperate." He gestured around the cabin. "You and Katie deserve better than this. It's my job to take care of you, but I'm not doing a good job." He shoved both his hands through his thick hair, looking as though he either had a monster migraine or was fighting to keep from falling apart.

"I thought I could talk to your father man-to-man, and he would appreciate the situation I'm in." His tone was thin and reedy. "I got the impression he loves you, but if he loves you, then why won't he help you? Anyone who can jet off to Europe at a moment's notice and buy his daughter a luxury car can afford to loan his son-in-law money to get caught up on bills. Am I missing something here?" His lower lip trembled as he stared at Mia. He reminded her of a little boy, and the pain in his eyes sliced through her, trapping her words in her throat.

Chace took a step toward her. "I shouldn't have called him without discussing it with you first, but I'm at the end of my rope. Today I finally admitted to myself I'm in over my head and I have no idea what else to do."

Mia wiped her hands over her wet eyes. "He has the money to help us."

"So then what's the problem? Why are your parents so determined to treat us like strangers instead of their family?" As he stood over her, something inside of her crumbled.

"They wanted me to marry someone else."

"What are you talking about?"

Mia leaned against the kitchen counter. "The day I told my parents I was pregnant and going to marry you, they told me if I insisted on keeping the baby, they would help me until I found someone more 'worthy.' In fact, they hoped I could marry the son of one of my father's partners, someone they had already been thinking about, someone they thought would take me even though I was pregnant with your child. Someone willing to hide my—*their*—shame, with vested interest in keeping the firm and their standing in the community free from gossip."

Her voice was thick as Chace's eyes narrowed. "When I called my mom the day Kaitlyn was born, she said she would be a part of Katie's life, but only if I left you. She said you would never give Katie and me what we needed."

"Wait a minute." He held his hand up to stop her from speaking. "I thought your parents cut you off because you got pregnant. Are you telling me they actually disowned you because you chose to marry me?"

"Yes, that's correct. Once they accepted I was never going to make an adoption plan, that's what they offered." The words tasted bitter in Mia's mouth.

A muscle in Chace's jaw ticked. "Why didn't you tell me about this?"

"I didn't want to hurt you," Mia said, her words tumbling out of her mouth. "I don't care what my parents think of you. I love you, and I belong with you, despite what they think a marriage should be based on. I don't care what profession you choose. I just want to be with you and Kaitlyn. We're a family." When his brow furrowed, she added, "My parents have no part of this relationship. It's about you, Kaitlyn, and me. We don't need their blessing or their money."

"We promised there would be no secrets between us." He pointed between them. "You say we're in this together, but you never trusted me enough to tell me the truth. You still don't trust me, do you?"

"That's not true!" Tears clouded her vision.

He headed for the door and pulled on his coat.

"Where are you going?" Alarm gripped her.

"Out." He wrenched the door open and then stopped, facing her. "Your parents are right. I can't give you and Katie the life you deserve. You should go home to them so you won't have to worry about Kaitlyn's well-being."

"You don't mean that," Mia croaked between sobs.

Chace nodded. "Actually, I do." Then he disappeared out the door, slamming it behind him.

Mia pulled Kaitlyn into her arms, held her close, and sobbed.

. . .

Chace shivered and zipped up his coat as he descended the steps. He had no idea where he was going, but he had to get out of the cabin to process what Mia told him. Although he'd been aware of Mia's parents' disapproval of him, he never realized how deep their rejection ran. Hearing that the Whitfields had tried to convince Mia to marry someone else had nearly unraveled Chace.

What if Mia had agreed to dump me for the partner's son?

Chace gritted his teeth and stalked past his truck, continuing down the rock path toward Isaac's barns and house. His pulse pounded with resentment toward

Mia's parents and also with fear that Mia would leave him. But how could he blame her if he couldn't even afford an apartment with electricity and heat?

"Chace?"

He turned toward one of the barns, where Isaac and Adam stood watching him. He nodded a greeting.

"Is everything all right?" Isaac asked.

Chace paused, torn between pouring out his heart to his friend and keeping all his swarming emotions bottled up until he finally exploded.

Isaac said something to Adam, and the boy waved to Chace before scurrying up the porch steps and into the house. Then he turned to Chace. "You look like you're carrying the weight of the world on your young shoulders. Would you like to talk?"

Chace cupped his hand to the back of his neck and squeezed at the tense muscles. "I feel like I've burdened you enough with my problems."

"You're a *freind*, not a burden." Isaac pointed toward the porch. "Let's sit."

Chace dropped his hand to his side. "That would be great." He followed Isaac up the back steps of the large porch and then sat down on a rocker as Isaac sank onto a nearby swing.

"You seemed upset this afternoon at work."

"You could tell?"

Isaac chuckled. "*Ya*, it was apparent when I saw the condition of the phone book and found the scuffs on the wall. When I saw you throw a roll of masking tape at the wall in the shop later, I was able to put it all together."

Chace winced. "I'm sorry. I try to suppress my temper, but it gets the best of me sometimes."

"We're all human. I've been known to kick a barn wall a time or two." Isaac crossed his arms over his coat. "Sometimes it helps to talk about it before it eats you up inside."

Chace rested his work boot on his opposite knee and looked out toward the cabin. "Mia and I are from different backgrounds. She grew up in a wealthy family with every privilege and opportunity available to her. I, on the other hand, grew up with nothing. My father went to prison for life when I was an infant, and my mother died in a car accident when I was four. Since I didn't have any other family members, I was swallowed up by the foster care system. I bounced from home to home until I turned eighteen."

Chace moved the rocker back and forth. "I met Mia when she was in college. Her parents didn't approve of me, but she didn't let that stop her from falling in love with me." He rubbed his chin, debating how much to share about the circumstances surrounding their quick engagement and marriage. "Mia's parents disowned her when she married me."

Isaac faced Chace, his eyebrows raised. "They disowned her?"

Chace nodded.

Isaac looked baffled. "Why?"

"They wanted her to marry someone who was successful." Then Chace explained how he'd called Mia's father, detailing the conversation as Isaac shook his head. "When I told Mia about the phone call tonight, she was upset. Then she told me more about how her parents feel about me." He shared what Mia had told him earlier, his shoulders tightening with renewed ire.

Isaac adjusted his hat on his head. "Are you angry with Mia or with her parents?"

The question was simple, but it touched something deep inside of Chace. "Now that I've cooled off, I understand why Mia kept it from me, but it still hurts knowing her parents wouldn't even give me a chance. I never had a real family, and I want to be a good husband and father. I want to show the world I'm more than just a punk who got lost in the foster care system. I want to be the father I never had." He blew out a deep sigh as tears threatened in his eyes. "Sometimes I just don't feel worthy of Mia, and I feel like I'm living a dream."

"Do you feel that way because her family had more money than you?"

Chace nodded.

Isaac frowned. "The *Englisch* put too much importance on money and worldly possessions. We're all the same in God's eyes, no matter how much money we make or how many expensive things we have collected." His expression softened. "But, aside from that, if Mia had been worried about having expensive things, she wouldn't have married you. You need to stop punishing yourself for not being perfect in her parents' eyes. We all make mistakes, and we have to ask God for guidance.

"One of my favorite Scripture verses comes from Proverbs. 'Trust in the Lord with all your heart and lean not on your own understanding; in all your ways submit to him, and he will make your paths straight.'" He pointed toward the sky. "Trust in God. He is the light of the world, and he will guide you onto the right path if you follow his Word."

Isaac's words punched Chace right in the center of his chest. He cleared his throat against a swelling lump.

"Mia loves you." Isaac tapped the arm of the swing. "She's stuck by you despite her parents' attempts to bribe her into leaving you. You need to stop worrying about what they think and just concentrate on doing your best. Be a *gut freind* and a *gut* husband to her. You also need to talk to Mia. Don't run away when things get tough. Stay and work things out." He paused for a moment. "You don't need to beg Mia's parents for help. If you need anything, let me know. Vera and I can help you get back on your feet."

Chace blew out a shuddering sigh. "Thank you. I'm grateful for your generosity."

"The Lord tells us to help our neighbors. Things were tough for us when I started my business, so I understand how you feel." Isaac pointed toward the cabin. "Go home and tell Mia you love her. Before you go to sleep tonight, pray. Ask God to guide you. If you invite him into your heart, he will lead you down the right path. You're a *gut* man. I'm certain you will be fine."

"Thank you." After shaking Isaac's hand, Chace hurried down the rock path toward the cabin. As he approached his truck, he suddenly remembered the two jars of baby food he'd picked up at a convenience store during his lunch break.

Chace pulled the keys from his coat pocket, unlocked the truck, and retrieved the small bag on the floorboard. He closed and locked the truck before heading into the cabin. No one was in the family room or kitchen. Panic seized him as the cruel words he'd spat at Mia before he left echoed through his mind:

"You should go home to them so you won't have to worry about Kaitlyn's well-being."

Was she packing? Was she planning to call for a cab and flee their misery?

"Mia?" His voice was tight with worry. "Mia?"

The bedroom door opened, and Mia stood in the doorway, frowning.

"I just got her to sleep." Mia pulled the door closed behind her. "She was getting cranky." Once the door clicked shut, she studied him, folding her arms over the front of her red sweater. Her dark eyes were red-rimmed, and a pang of guilt slammed through him.

He hung his coat on the peg by the door and then closed the distance between them, holding the small grocery bag out to her. "I forgot to give this to you earlier."

"What's this?" Her brow puckered.

"Take it." He gave the bag a little shake.

She pulled out the two small jars of food. She looked at them and then back up at him. "You bought baby food?"

"Yeah." Chace took the jars of baby food and put them back into the bag and set them on the chair behind him. "After I hung up with your dad, I was so furious I walked over to the nearby convenience store and picked up a sandwich and drink. I know it's wasteful to buy lunch, but I needed to blow off some steam. When I saw the display of baby food, I remembered Katie's reaction when I gave her the pears and bananas the other day." His heart twisted with contrition. "We weren't sure how she'd react to solid food since it was our first attempt at introducing them, but she'd squealed with delight. I wanted to hear that laugh again. Actually, I would do anything to make you and Katie happy." He gripped her forearms. "I'm sorry I keep hurting you. I didn't mean it when I said I wanted you to go back to your parents. If you left me, I don't know what I'd do."

Mia's lips formed a sad smile as she cupped her hand to his cheek. "I know that."

He leaned into her touch as if it were his lifeline. "Thank you for choosing me despite your parents' objections."

"My parents are so blinded by their materialism that they don't see how amazing you are. I love you. That won't change no matter what my parents say or do."

He pulled her against him and kissed her. She looped her arms around his neck, relaxing against him. When he broke the kiss, she rested her head against his chest and he breathed in the sweet scent of her shampoo.

"I'm sorry for not eating supper," he whispered.

"You don't need to apologize. It was pretty awful." She looked up at him and scrunched her nose. "I'll ask Vera for some cooking lessons."

He tucked a long strand of her soft, dark hair behind her ear. "And I'll do everything I can to take care of you and Katie." Resting his cheek on her head, he closed his eyes and recalled Isaac's advice.

Thank you, God, for bringing Mia and Kaitlyn into my life. Please show me how to be a better husband and father. Please guide my path. Amen.

CHAPTER 5

Kaitlyn blew raspberries and yanked Mia's hair as Mia knocked on the Allgyers' back door the following morning.

"Ouch." Mia laughed, trying to untangle Kaitlyn's pudgy fingers from her hair. "I should've pulled my hair up this morning."

Kaitlyn continued to spray spit bubbles and tug Mia's hair hard enough to tip Mia's head to the side.

"You have some grip for a little one," she mumbled.

The back door swung open and Rhoda grinned. "Mia! Kaitlyn!"

Kaitlyn squealed and kicked her feet into Mia's side.

"Hi, Rhoda." Mia smiled, despite her throbbing scalp. "I was wondering if I could talk to your mom."

"Of course." Rhoda held her hands out to Kaitlyn. "May I hold her?"

"That would be fantastic." As Mia handed Kaitlyn to Rhoda, Kaitlyn released the lock of Mia's hair. Mia rubbed her head and followed Rhoda through the mudroom to the kitchen. "She enjoys trying to rip my hair out."

Rhoda chuckled.

"Kaitlyn!" Smiling, Susannah rushed over from the kitchen counter to greet her, then touched Kaitlyn's hand as she gurgled. "Hi, Mia."

"*Gut* morning." Vera smiled as she finished drying a dish.

"Good morning." Mia dropped her diaper bag onto a kitchen chair. "If you're not too busy, Kaitlyn and I thought we'd come for a visit." Her cheeks heated. "I was also wondering if I could get some cooking lessons from you."

"That sounds like fun." Vera placed the clean dish on the counter. "The girls can take care of Kaitlyn, and we'll cook and chat."

Rhoda and Susannah nodded in unison.

"We have that *boppli* swing now," Rhoda said. "We can use it here and then carry it to the cabin for Mia."

Mia's eyes widened. "You have a baby swing I can borrow?"

"*Ya*, we found it in the attic this morning, and Rhoda and I cleaned it up for you," Susannah said.

"I'm certain our *aenti* would be happy you're getting some use out of it." Rhoda smiled at Kaitlyn, who gave a sweet sigh while fingering the ribbons on Rhoda's gauzy head covering.

"Thank you so much." Mia was overwhelmed. "I've missed the swing we had before."

"We're grateful you can use it," Vera said.

"Let's take Kaitlyn into the family room and see if she likes this swing." Rhoda gestured for her sister to follow her.

"So what would you like to learn how to make

today?" Vera put a large cookbook on the table and started flipping through it.

"I'm open to learning anything. My mom never cooked, so I never learned. When I was in college, I mostly ate in the dining hall or out at restaurants."

"Your *mamm* never cooked?" Vera furrowed her brow.

Mia shook her head. "We had a housekeeper. She did the cooking and the cleaning so my mom could spend her days socializing and volunteering for charities."

Vera nodded. "I see. Would you like to try a chicken casserole?" She examined the book as she spoke. "I already have enough leftover cooked chicken. We can put it together, and then you can store it in your refrigerator until you're ready to bake it. Does that sound *gut*?"

"That sounds fantastic." Mia gnawed her lower lip. "I can pay you for the ingredients when Chace gets home."

Vera peered up at her. "I'm not concerned about that. I just want to make sure you're eating well. Let's get started." She pulled out a mixing bowl and baking dish.

As she walked over to the counter, Mia scanned the large, open kitchen, taking in the plain white walls, sparsely decorated with a single shelf that held a few candles and an antique clock. The floor was a worn tan linoleum pattern, and a long wooden table with six chairs sat in the middle of the room.

The far end of the kitchen included a propane stove and refrigerator, resembling the appliances in the cabin. This kitchen, however, had ample counter and cabinet space. A small window over the sink looked out over a yard with large, thick trees decorated with bird-houses. The kitchen was warm and homey, despite the absence of her mother's ornate decorating.

"How was the meat loaf last night?" Vera asked.

Mia groaned and rolled her eyes. "Terrible. That's why I need cooking lessons. I burned it. I put it in the oven and then Katie woke up from her nap. I changed her diaper and spent time with her, and I lost track of time. I didn't realize it had burned until I served it to Chace, but obviously the meat loaf had been in too long."

"Don't be so hard on yourself. I've done that too." Vera explained the recipe to Mia and soon they were gathering the ingredients and supplies.

"How did you meet Isaac?" Mia asked while dicing chicken.

"We met at a singing."

"What's a singing?"

"That's when the youth get together to play games and sing hymns. Isaac grew up in a neighboring church district, so we went to different schools. Our youth groups were combined that night, and we became friends." She looked over at Mia. "How about you and Chace?"

Mia wiped her hands on a paper towel. "It was sort of the same situation. I was in college and we met at a party. I didn't want to go, but my roommate insisted I studied too much and needed some fun. Chace and I saw each other across the room. He smiled, and I smiled back at him. He was the most handsome man there." She laughed. "He introduced himself to me, and we spent the rest of the night talking. He asked me for my number, and that was it. That was almost two years ago."

"What did you study in college?"

"I wanted to be a teacher, but I didn't get to finish." Mia frowned, waiting for Vera to ask why. She was too embarrassed to admit she'd gotten pregnant, but Vera didn't question her. Vera never questioned or judged her, and Mia was grateful. Besides, once she mentioned how recently they had married, Vera would know the truth.

"We met when I was nineteen and only in my second year of college," Mia continued. "When we decided to get married last March, I quit school. I hope someday I can finish up my degree. I've always wanted to be a teacher, even though my mother didn't approve."

"Why didn't your *mamm* want you to be a teacher?" Vera sliced more chicken.

"Teachers don't make enough money. My mother only cares about status. She always told me to marry well so I could enjoy a nice lifestyle. That's why she never approved of Chace either."

"Have you asked them for help? I'm sure they would want to help you."

"They disowned me."

"How can that be? You're family! Kaitlyn is their grandchild."

Mia shared what her father said when Chace called him yesterday.

Vera shook her head. "I'm so sorry for everything you've been through. I hope someday your parents will realize how wrong they've been to reject you—and your family."

"I do too." Mia's voice was thick. "I can't thank you enough for everything you've done for us. We would probably be in a shelter right now if it weren't for you and Isaac."

"I meant it when I said we know how hard times can be. Isaac's *dat* had a dairy farm, but Isaac wanted to become a cabinetmaker. We struggled when we first started his business. Our parents tried to help us, but they had fallen on hard times too. We made it through, but there were days when I wondered if we had enough food to last until Isaac finished a job. When he told me Chace needed a place to live, I wanted to help you."

Mia sniffed as tears flooded her eyes. "You are a blessing to us."

"We're happy to see a family in the little cabin." Vera turned back toward the recipe. "Now let's finish this casserole so we can figure out what we want for lunch."

"Okay." Mia smiled, grateful for her new friend.

. . .

"I can't believe how big Katie has grown during the past month." Susannah looked down at Kaitlyn, who sat on her lap and sucked on her pacifier.

Mia nodded as rain pounded on the cabin roof above them. "She's outgrowing her clothes. I need to go by the consignment shop after Chace gets paid next week." She carried four mugs to the table and then gathered tea bags and creamer. As she turned toward the table, she stepped in a puddle. She looked up at the ceiling to see water dripping. "Is the roof leaking?"

Vera turned in her chair and frowned. "*Ya*, I think it is. I'll tell Isaac."

"Chace can help him fix it." Mia brought the tea bags and cream to the table. "He has plenty of experience with roofs."

Rhoda stood. "I'll finish the tea, and you can find a pot to catch the water."

"Thanks." Mia dried the floor and then set out a large pot. They could hear water splash into it as Mia sat down at the table.

"The past month has gone by so quickly." Vera lifted her mug. "It feels like you just moved in."

"I know," Mia agreed. "Our first wedding anniversary is next week."

"Oh, that's so exciting." Susannah held Kaitlyn up to her shoulder.

"Do you want me to take her?" Mia asked.

"No, she's fine." Susannah caressed Kaitlyn's head.

Kaitlyn nuzzled closer against Susannah. Would Mia's mother be affectionate and cuddle with Kaitlyn the way Susannah and Rhoda did? Mia pressed her lips together.

"We can help you plant a garden in the spring," Rhoda said, yanking Mia from her thoughts. "My grandmother had a garden right outside the back door." She pointed toward the mudroom. "If you want, we can plant one there."

"That's a great idea," Vera chimed in. "Your *mammi* had the most beautiful vegetables."

"That sounds great." Mia cupped her mug in her hands. Would they still live in the cabin by the time the vegetables were ripe? Her heart tugged at the thought of leaving her new friends. But was it fair to raise Kaitlyn in the cold, rustic cabin with a leaky roof and no electricity? Would Mia be a terrible mother if she chose to raise her child here?

. . .

Chace rolled over in bed and yawned. His back and neck were sore from sanding and painting cabinets all day yesterday. He reached his arm to the left and expected to feel Mia beside him, but he found cold sheets instead. He rubbed his eyes and then focused his attention on the bright green numbers on the clock next to the bed. It was almost nine. He'd overslept.

Groaning, Chace rolled onto his back and stared up at the ceiling. It was Saturday, and he felt like a train had hit him. He'd worked hard all week, hoping to help Isaac get ahead on projects and also increase his paycheck. Now he had to fling himself out of bed and complete the honey-do list Mia had prepared for him all week. First on the list, he'd promised Mia he'd fix the leaky roof today after she'd complained about it last night. Now he just had to find the energy to do it.

With a moan and a grunt, he shoved himself out of bed and shuffled out to the kitchen, where Mia stood at the counter, beating an egg in a bowl. She glanced over her shoulder at him, her pink lips turning up in a breathtaking smile. She was so beautiful with her thick, dark hair falling to her lower back. What possessed Mia to pick him when she could've had any man she wanted?

"Good morning, sleepyhead." She nodded toward the bowl. "Do eggs and toast sound all right?"

"Sounds great. Thank you." He smiled down at his daughter, kicking her feet in her baby seat. "Hey, princess. How are you this morning?" He clicked open her safety belts and lifted her into his arms. He breathed in her familiar scent, baby lotion and diaper cream. "Are you going to help me fix the roof today?"

Kaitlyn babbled a response, latching a hand to his T-shirt.

"I'll take that as a yes." He leaned against the table and faced Mia. "I didn't mean to oversleep. I'm just exhausted."

"It's all right." She scraped the egg into the pan. "I suppose you deserve it after working all week."

Kaitlyn coughed, and Chace's eyes widened. "How long has she been coughing?"

"She started yesterday. I have some medicine left from her last cold." Mia adjusted the flame under the frying pan. "Hopefully that will take care of it since we can't afford to take her to a doctor."

Frowning, Chace rubbed Kaitlyn's golden hair. Someday soon he'd find a way to give his daughter everything she needed.

• • •

Mia wiped a cloth over the pane of one of Vera's kitchen windows later that afternoon. She hummed to herself while enjoying the simplicity of the work.

"You really don't need to help us clean," Vera said as she scrubbed the counter.

"I'm happy to help you. You've done so much for us." Mia peered out the window to where Chace helped Isaac and two other men carry benches into the barn. After Isaac and Chace finished fixing the roof on the cabin, Chace had offered to help Isaac prepare for the church service they would host in their barn tomorrow.

Vera chuckled a little. "You can't possibly want to clean my windows. One of the girls can do it if you'd rather do something in the cabin."

"It's no trouble at all. I'm glad to help you prepare for the service." Mia moved the cloth over another pane as she again looked out toward the barn. Chace laughed as he and Isaac stood with another Amish man. Mia admired how the sun brought out the golden hue of Chace's sandy-blond hair. He was so handsome dressed in jeans and a blue, long-sleeved T-shirt, with mirrored sunglasses shielding his eyes. He chuckled again before he and Isaac unloaded another bench from the long buggy that had delivered the benches yesterday.

Vera sidled up to Mia. "It seems as if Isaac and Chace have known each other for years. He thinks very highly of Chace. That's why Isaac sometimes slips into speaking Pennsylvania Dutch with him. He just feels that comfortable with Chace, and now we all feel comfortable with both of you. And also, your husband is a talented carpenter."

"Thank you." Mia began working on another

windowpane. "He is talented, but he often doesn't acknowledge how good he is."

Kaitlyn squealed, and Mia turned to where Rhoda sat at the table feeding Kaitlyn a jar of pears.

"Let me know if you get tired of holding her," Mia said.

"It's fine. We're having a *gut* time, right, Katie?" Rhoda smiled. "She's a *gut boppli*. She's much happier than Joel was."

"That's true," Susannah called from the family room, where she was mopping the floor. "Joel cried all the time."

"Do you two go to youth group?" Mia asked the girls as she continued to work.

"*Ya*, we do," Rhoda said. "We like seeing our friends."

"Do you have a boyfriend, Rhoda?" Mia asked.

Rhoda's cheeks turned bright red as she focused her eyes on Kaitlyn.

"Rhoda has a crush on Sam Swarey," Susannah sang.

"Be quiet," Rhoda warned through gritted teeth.

"Sam?" Vera asked. "Lydia's son?"

Rhoda nodded, her cheeks as bright red as an apple.

"I had no idea," Vera said.

"I'm sorry." Mia frowned. "I didn't mean to embarrass you."

"It's not your fault." Rhoda rested Kaitlyn on her shoulder and caressed her cheek. "Sam is nice to me. We enjoy talking to each other at youth gatherings."

"It's *gut* to start out as friends." Vera wiped down the refrigerator with a rag. "Your *dat* and I were friends before we started dating."

"We're just friends," Rhoda said.

"He likes you," Susannah insisted.

"You think so?"

Susannah nodded. "It's pretty obvious with the way he looks at you."

Rhoda sighed, and Mia and Vera exchanged knowing smiles.

"How did you know you were in love with *Dat*?" Rhoda asked Vera.

Vera smiled. "He was my best friend, and we could talk about anything. I always felt comfortable with him."

"What about you, Mia?" Rhoda asked.

Mia looked out toward the barn, where Chace helped carry another bench inside. "Chace and I clicked the first time we met. He was easy to talk to, and he treated me with respect. I just knew he was the one." She turned toward Rhoda, who grinned. "Make sure Sam treats you well. If he makes you feel bad about yourself, then he's not the one."

"Mia is right," Vera added. "Take your time and get to know him. Marriage is for life."

Rhoda nodded. "I plan to take my time and get to know him. There's no rush."

"That's right," Vera chimed in.

"We should plan a big meal together." Susannah had moved to the doorway where they could see her. "Mia, Chace, and Katie can eat at our *haus*. Maybe we can do that one night next week. What do you think, *Mamm*?"

Vera nodded. "That sounds like a great idea. What do you think, Mia?"

She smiled at Susannah. "We would love to come. What can I make that's easy? I don't want to mess it up."

"You won't mess it up," Vera said.

As Rhoda began discussing the menu for their supper, Mia glanced over at Rhoda and Susannah and smiled. What would it have been like to grow up in a warm, loving family like the Allgyers'?

Then Kaitlyn coughed in Rhoda's arms and Mia frowned.

• • •

Mia held Kaitlyn to her chest as she looked out the window Sunday morning. "Look at all those buggies. Probably two hundred people are sitting in Isaac and Vera's barn for church this morning." The rock driveway and the nearby field were clogged with buggies while horses filled the nearby pasture.

Chace came up behind her and rested his hand on her shoulder. "That's a sea of buggies."

"It is." Mia smiled up at him. "It was nice of you to help Isaac set up the benches yesterday. I heard him tell Vera you were a tremendous help."

He shrugged as he kneaded the knots in her shoulders. "I heard you were helpful inside the house too."

"It was the least I could do." Mia looked out the window again. "I think it's neat how they have church in their barns. It's a lot of work for the family that's hosting the service, but it's also special to share church in your home."

"Yeah, that would be special." Kaitlyn coughed, and

he rubbed the baby's arm. "I told Isaac I would help him load up the benches tomorrow. They aren't permitted to do it today since they don't do even that much work on Sundays."

"That sounds like a great idea." Mia turned toward the sofa. "Why don't you get comfortable and I'll make us hot chocolate. Let's just relax today."

He grinned. "That sounds amazing." He held out his hands and took Kaitlyn. "Let's snuggle, baby girl."

Mia smiled as she walked to the kitchen. She couldn't wait to spend the day with her family.

. . .

Mia sat between Rhoda and Susannah at the Allgyers' kitchen table Tuesday night. Just as Susannah had suggested, they had planned a family dinner, surprising the men when they arrived home from work. Mia smiled across the table at Chace as Joel and Adam shared stories about their day at school.

"How was work today?" Vera asked Isaac when the boys were done talking.

"It was *gut*." Isaac nodded. "Chace is doing fantastic work, and we got a contract for another new *haus*."

"That's great." Mia grinned at Chace.

"Thanks." He shrugged.

"Chace," Mia said, and he looked up at her. "I'm proud of you." Something unreadable flashed across his face.

Katie coughed from the swing they'd brought with them behind Mia, and Mia spun to face her. When

Katie coughed again, Mia pulled her from the swing and held her close to her shoulder.

"Is she okay?" Vera asked.

"I think her cough has gotten worse since the weekend." Kaitlyn coughed again, and Mia stroked her back.

"Do you want me to hold her?" Chace offered.

"No, it's fine. I'll hold her." Mia balanced Kaitlyn with one arm and ate with her free arm.

When supper was over, Chace followed Isaac, Joel, and Adam outside to take care of the animals. Mia strapped Kaitlyn into the swing and helped take the dishes, glasses, and utensils to the counter.

When Kaitlyn became fussy, Susannah rushed over to the swing. "May I change her and give her a bottle?"

"That would be wonderful," Mia said. "Her diaper bag is in the corner."

"Do you need help?" Rhoda offered.

"No." Susannah lifted Kaitlyn into her arms. "You always get to take care of Katie. Now it's my turn."

As Susannah carried Kaitlyn into the family room, Mia placed the platter of leftover chicken and dumplings on the counter and began scooping them into a large container. When she heard Kaitlyn coughing in the family room, Mia stilled, listening to the sound of the cough. Could she possibly have pneumonia?

The coughing stopped, and Mia continued to scoop the food into the container. The worry that had taken hold of her last night resurfaced as she thought about her baby's health. She needed to get Kaitlyn to a doctor. But how would they pay for it? All their credit cards were still maxed and their savings account was bare.

She had applied for medical insurance, but the deductibles were enormous. She was able to get formula and a little bit of food through government assistance, but it didn't cover much—not even diapers. She might be forced to find some cloth diapers and give the wringer washer some extra use.

Mia could ask her parents for help, but she couldn't propose the idea again without hurting Chace. Now he knew the truth about the extent of their rejection. *Still, Mom might be apt to help me if she had a chance to meet Kaitlyn.* She grimaced. She didn't want to hurt Chace, but she had to put her child's needs before hers or her husband's.

"I'm concerned about Kaitlyn. Would you like to try a couple of home remedies I've used for my children?"

Mia looked up at Vera, who was drying a dish as Rhoda washed. "Yes, that would be great."

"After we finish the dishes, I'll give you a few things that should help."

"Thank you." Mia hoped the home remedies would work as she turned her attention back to the leftovers, snapping the lid onto the container. What if the remedies didn't work? Knowing how hurt she'd been when Chace contacted her father without consulting her, she hoped she would never deliberately betray him the same way. But her concern for her child settled onto her shoulders and squeezed at her muscles.

Was Mia denying Kaitlyn the medical attention she needed by not asking her parents for help? The question rocked Mia to the core.

CHAPTER 6

Chace's shoulders slumped, and the weight of his anxiety pressed down on him as he followed Isaac out to the barn later that evening.

"Thank you for your help with the chores," Isaac said.

"You're welcome." Chace shivered and hugged his coat tighter to his chest. "I can't believe it's March already. Our first wedding anniversary is Friday."

Isaac grinned. "That's a special day."

"It is." Chace frowned.

"You have the same expression on your face you had the day you spoke to Mia's *dat*." Isaac leaned against the barn wall. "What's on your mind?"

Chace pursed his lips and glanced toward the house. Peering through the window, he saw Mia sitting at the kitchen table talking with Vera and the girls. "I didn't expect my life to turn out this way."

"What do you mean?"

Chace took a deep breath, preparing to tell Isaac the whole truth about his marriage to Mia. "When I asked Mia to marry me, she was pregnant with our child." He paused, awaiting Isaac's criticism, but instead, Isaac simply nodded. "It wasn't the best situation, but I was already deeply in love with Mia and had planned to ask her to marry me after she graduated from college. Unfortunately, she didn't get to finish. She quit her junior year, and we got married."

Chace leaned against the barn wall beside Isaac and folded his arms over the front of his coat. "I've already told you about Mia's parents. I knew we would have a rough start, but I thought I could provide for Mia and Kaitlyn. I'd hoped we'd have a house by now. At lunch today, I went by the bank to ask for a loan to consolidate all our medical bills and credit card debt, but they turned me down, saying my credit wasn't good enough." He looked up at Isaac. "I don't know how long we're going to be here. I'm just grateful we have a safe place to live."

Isaac patted Chace's shoulder. "You take all the time you need. Vera, the children, and I are enjoying having you all here. You've become like family to us. You just do your best to take care of your family, and it will all come together in God's time. You can't rush God's plan for your life."

Chace nodded as Isaac's words rolled through his mind. He understood Isaac's words—he needed to be patient. He just hoped Mia would be patient too.

. . .

Chace stared down at Kaitlyn in the crib. He reached in and touched her head before tucking the pink quilt around her little body. As he studied his precious baby,

Isaac's words echoed through his mind. He could wait for God's time. He'd found himself praying while he stained a cabinet at work, and he realized Isaac was right. Praying was the best solution. He'd attended church with one of the foster families that had hosted him during his tumultuous childhood, and church had helped him find peace during those tough times. Unfortunately, his time with that family was cut short, and he hadn't attended church since. Would Mia attend church with him? The thought of sitting in church beside her warmed his heart.

The bedroom door opened, and Mia padded into the bedroom, dressed in pink flannel pajamas with matching slipper socks. With a frown twisting her face, she placed the lantern she was holding on the nightstand by her side of the bed and then raised her eyebrows. Half of her attractive face was in shadow and the other half was lit by the soft yellow glow.

She's asleep, he mouthed.

Mia nodded and then climbed into bed, sinking under the mountain of quilts.

Chace kissed the tips of two of his fingers and placed them on Kaitlyn's head before climbing into bed beside Mia. She leaned over and flipped off the lantern. After she was settled, he circled his arms around her small waist and towed her to him in hopes of stealing a kiss. But she kept her back to him, facing the wall. His eyes adjusted to the dark room with only a dim light spilling in between the edge of the green shade and the window casing.

Why had Mia suddenly turned cold toward him?

She'd kissed his cheek when he arrived home from work, and she'd smiled at him from across the table during supper at the Allgyers' house. Her demeanor had changed, however, when they arrived home. She only gave him one-word answers to his questions, and her pretty face was fixed with a permanent frown.

"Is everything all right?" he whispered.

"Yeah." Her voice was muffled by the quilt pulled up to her chin.

Chace longed for Mia to turn toward him and kiss him, but she didn't move. His earlier thoughts about attending church as a family returned, and he opened his mouth to discuss it with her. Before he could share his idea, Kaitlyn coughed, and Mia sat up ramrod straight, worry radiating off her.

When the coughing subsided, Mia lay back down, facing the ceiling. "I'm almost out of the cold medicine I had, but it hasn't helped much anyway." She turned toward him. "I don't want to take the chance that Vera's home remedies won't work. Our baby needs to see a doctor."

Chace's shoulders tightened as frustration washed over him. So this was the source of her aloofness. "Work is getting busier, and my paychecks should improve soon." He reached for her hand, but she pulled it back, the rejection lancing through him. He bit his lower lip in an effort to assuage his temper. "Things are going to get better. It's just going to take some time. We may be here longer than I'd hoped, but you have to trust me. We'll have our own house someday."

"I understand that, but that doesn't help me right now when Kaitlyn needs medical care."

Kaitlyn coughed again, and Mia moved to the crib. Chace scooted to the edge of the bed as Mia leaned in and stroked Kaitlyn's back until the coughing ceased. Then she returned to bed, again facing the wall, and Chace crawled over to her.

"Mee." He touched her arm. "I have a couple of dollars to spare, so I'll pick up cold medicine on my way home from work tomorrow. Just tell me what you want me to get, okay? I don't know what else I can do. Let's try the cold medicine one more time."

"Fine." She pulled the quilt over her shoulder.

Chace rolled onto his back and hoped once again that Mia would have patience with him. And that more of the cold medicine and Vera's home remedies would take care of Kaitlyn's cough.

. . .

Mia kneaded her temple where a headache throbbed as she held a screaming Kaitlyn against her shoulder. Kaitlyn moaned and coughed again, the sound deep and wet in her little chest. The home remedies Vera recommended hadn't helped, and the bottle of cold medicine was empty. Mia touched Kaitlyn's head, now burning with fever. The Tylenol she'd given her had worn off and that bottle was empty too. Panic seized her stomach as she paced back and forth in the tiny kitchen. Kaitlyn had become progressively worse throughout the afternoon and needed a doctor *now*. Mia glanced at the clock on the counter and gritted her teeth. Chace should've been home an hour ago.

Where is he?

Above her, rain pounded on the roof of the cabin and droplets of water sprinkled down through the ceiling, peppering the linoleum floor with small puddles. When a drop of water splashed on her shoulder, Mia shivered, and anger shoved away her panic. She was tired of this cold cabin, tired of running out of food, and tired of not having the money to take care of her daughter the way a mother should.

Mia longed for their tiny apartment, but then a vision of the large house that had protected her during her childhood filled her mind. Didn't Kaitlyn deserve to grow up in a warm, safe home similar to Mia's childhood home? Tears stung Mia's eyes as the pain behind them flared.

Kaitlyn moaned and coughed again, and Mia patted her back.

"It's okay, sweet pea," she whispered, her voice wobbly. "Just hang in there. Mommy will take care of you."

They needed help, but could she risk destroying her relationship with Chace for the sake of their child?

Headlights bathed the family room in a soft yellow glow, and trepidation trickled down Mia's spine. She had to make Chace understand that Kaitlyn was their top priority, even it if meant living on ramen noodles for a few weeks. She couldn't let their baby suffer any longer. Chace was going to take Kaitlyn to the emergency room now or Mia was going to take Kaitlyn to her parents.

Mia's eyes widened and she swallowed a gasp. Was she going to actually do that? Was she ready to give up on Chace, leave him? Was she going to abandon him the way his father and foster parents had?

Her mouth dried and her hand trembled as she cupped the back of Kaitlyn's head. She closed her eyes and took a deep breath. *Chace, please support my decision to take our baby to a medical facility.*

If Chace didn't agree, Mia hoped she had the courage to do what she needed to do for Kaitlyn.

. . .

Chace sat alone in his truck and studied the tiny cabin in front of him. He blew out a frustrated sigh and tried to muster the emotional strength to thrust himself out of the truck and into his home. Still, he sat glued to the worn and cracked vinyl bench seat.

The old truck's engine rumbled as it idled, a fitting melody to accompany his defeated mood. He'd picked up a few essential groceries along with the new bottle of cold medicine at lunchtime and walked to find one of the truck's rear tires flat. He took the tire to a nearby shop hoping to get it plugged, but it was too far gone for an easy fix. Instead, he had to use the rest of the money in his wallet to buy a tire.

Tomorrow was their first wedding anniversary, and thanks to the new tire, Chace didn't have enough money to buy Mia flowers or even a card. And he wouldn't be able to afford anything from tomorrow's paycheck either. Mia would be crushed, convinced he'd forgotten their special day.

Chace was a failure, just as his foster father Buck had predicted.

Leaning forward, he folded his arms over the

steering wheel and rested his forehead against them. The engine continued to rumble, causing the steering wheel to vibrate. After a few moments, his inner voice came to life, elbowing its way through his self-pity.

Get it together, Chace. Be a man. Be a father. Be a husband. Go inside and tell Mia what happened.

After a few moments, he sat up straight, shut off the truck, and gathered up the bags of groceries he'd purchased, the cold medicine inside. Chace stepped into the cabin and came face-to-face with Mia, glaring at him with venom in her dark eyes. Kaitlyn was tucked into Mia's shoulder, moaning and crying between coughs. Chace opened his mouth to ask how Kaitlyn was feeling, but Mia cut him off.

"Where have you been?" She pointed to the clock on the kitchen counter. "It's after seven!"

Whoa. He blinked and clenched his teeth in an attempt to bite back the bitter, defensive words threatening to explode from his lips.

"Were you planning on sitting outside all night?" She nodded toward the front door. "Why did you have to hide in your truck instead of coming in to check on your baby? Did you forget she's been sick?"

Chace pinned his lips together as anger roared through his veins. Unable to trust his mouth with a retort, he marched over to the counter and slammed down the bags of groceries and his truck keys.

Startled, Kaitlyn jumped, and a howl escaped from her small mouth. Mia hugged her close, whispering something in her ear. Guilt washed over him for a brief moment, but then evaporated when Mia glowered at him.

"Good job," she snapped. "Now she's crying." She walked over to the kitchen area and peered down at the groceries on the counter. "What did you buy? How did we have the money for all this?"

"I only bought the things you mentioned we needed and the cold medicine." He ground out the words as he put a half gallon of milk in the refrigerator. When he turned to face her again, his foot slipped on a small puddle, and he grabbed the edge of the counter, righting himself. He looked up at the ceiling and groaned. "The roof is leaking again?"

"Again?" She gave a harsh laugh. "It never stopped leaking. And it's still cold in here." She lanced him with a furious stare. "I need to take Kaitlyn to a doctor. She's running a fever now, and her cough is worse. She needs medical attention. Did you spend all our money today?"

Chace leaned against the counter and scrubbed his hands down his face. Heat radiated from his cheeks as he scowled at Mia.

"You did!" Mia's voice rose as Kaitlyn screamed, her face as red as a cherry. "You spent all our money without discussing it with me first?"

"Please give me a second to explain," he said, holding his hands up in an effort to calm her. "When I came out of the grocery store, my truck had a flat tire. I tried to get it repaired, but it couldn't be fixed. I had to buy a tire."

"You had to buy a tire?" She waved her free hand in the air. "So our baby needs medical attention and you spend the rest of our money on a tire. That's just fantastic." She spat the words at him and then marched toward the bedroom.

"Mia!" he called, but she kept walking away. "Mia!" He shouted her name louder, and she stopped and spun toward him, her eyes shooting daggers at him. His body shook with raw fury. "I'm sorry I don't work hard enough for you. I'm sorry I don't make enough money to give you the life of privilege you were used to before you got tangled up with me."

She shook her head. "That's not what I—"

"Wait." He held his hand up to silence her, and to his surprise, she complied. "I can't work any harder than I already do. I didn't plan the flat tire, but I convinced Isaac to stay late to finish up a few things so I can make up the tire money in next week's paycheck." He pointed toward the door. "The last thing I wanted to do was spend money on that old truck, but I have to get to work every day so I can bring home money for you and Kaitlyn." He drew in a shaky breath. "I had hoped I could surprise you by getting groceries and still have enough money to buy you flowers and a card for our anniversary tomorrow. But now I can't get you anything."

"You think I'm worried about getting flowers and a card on our anniversary?" Her eyes widened. "If that's what you think, then you don't know me at all. I don't care about anniversary gifts. I just want to take my baby, *our* baby, to a doctor. She's getting sicker, and I'm terrified she has bronchitis or worse." Her eyes shimmered with tears. "I'll eat ramen noodles for a month if that's what it takes to get her to a doctor. You can keep your flowers and card. I care about our child's health."

Chace's eyes narrowed. "So you think I don't care about Katie?"

Mia lifted her chin, her expression obstinate.

Something inside of him broke apart, and Buck's words rang loud and clear in his mind for the second time this evening. The room closed in on him, and he couldn't breathe. He had to get out of that cabin and clear his head before he said something hateful to Mia that he could never take back. He stalked toward the door.

"Where are you going?"

"I need to cool off." As he wrenched the door open, he glanced over his shoulder to Mia holding Kaitlyn against her chest.

Tears streamed down Mia's face. "You're going to just walk away from us?"

"Yeah, I am," he said, his answer seething with sarcasm. "Isn't that what you and your parents expect from me? After all, I'm nothing but a piece of trash from the foster care system. I have no ambition or potential, and I could never measure up to your high-class parents or their friends. You'd have been better off if you'd married the man your parents suggested. He could've bought you a mansion in that swanky Philly neighborhood where your parents live. It would have been an improvement over this life, where you're shackled to me and a life of poverty."

Mia gaped at him as Kaitlyn cried out and then coughed.

With his pulse pounding in his ears, Chace marched out the front door, then slammed it behind him. He shivered in the cold rain and pulled up the hood on his coat as he strode past Isaac's barns toward the large pasture.

Leaning against the wooden fence, he took a deep breath in an effort to placate his shuddering body. He hated himself for spewing those cruel words at Mia before rushing outside. Why couldn't he keep his temper in check? Why did he always have to hurt her?

Chace stared across the dark pasture as ice-cold rain dripped down his face and soaked through his coat. He needed time alone to sort through his confusing emotions. After he calmed down, Chace would have a civil conversation with Mia and work things out with her. He just needed time to figure out how to fix this before it was too late.

. . .

Mia stared at the door, the slam echoing through her mind. She stood frozen in place, waiting for Chace to reappear with an apology and a warm hug, but the door remained closed. Kaitlyn whined and coughed, and the sound propelled Mia into action.

She rushed into the bedroom and changed Kaitlyn's diaper before packing a bag for Kaitlyn and one for herself. After they were bundled up in warm coats, Mia snatched the truck keys from the counter and dashed outside.

She hoped Chace would be waiting for her on the steps, ready to apologize before offering to drive Kaitlyn to the hospital, ready to beg for medical attention even though they had no way to pay for it. But the front steps were empty. Balancing Kaitlyn on her hip and their bags on her opposite shoulder, Mia scanned the area in a desperate search for Chace's tall silhouette in the dark, rainy evening.

When she didn't find him, Mia loaded Kaitlyn into her car seat and set the bags on the truck's passenger side floor. Then she started the engine and steered toward the main road, heading toward Philadelphia and her childhood home.

Mia's stomach roiled as she imagined begging her parents for help. Would Chace ever forgive her? Kaitlyn coughed again, and Mia dismissed her concerns about Chace's feelings. All that mattered right now was Kaitlyn. She just hoped Chace would someday understand her decision to put Kaitlyn before their marriage.

· · ·

Chace heard the rumble of his pickup and panic rocked him to his core. *Mia is leaving me! I have to stop her!*

He took off running toward the driveway. Sliding through the mud, he came to a stop at the bottom of the driveway just as the truck bounced onto the main road, accelerating out of his sight.

Reality slammed into him, knocking him to his knees in the muddy, rocky driveway. Chace had finally pushed Mia too far, and now she and Kaitlyn were gone.

What did you expect? You couldn't support them! Mia had no choice but to leave you. She's better off without you!

Tears burned his eyes as he tried in vain to swallow against the messy lump of despair and regret clogging his throat. His world crashed down around him. It was over. He'd lost everything he loved most in this world. He pressed at an ache in the center of his chest and tried to breathe.

Chace buried his face in his hands. He wasn't worthy of Mia or Kaitlyn, and they were better off without him.

But how could he let them go? Mia and Kaitlyn were his reason for living. He was nothing without them by his side.

As he slammed his eyes shut, Isaac's words filtered through his mind like a salve to his tortured heart: *"Trust in God. He is the light of the world, and he will guide you onto the right path if you follow his Word."*

Kneeling on the muddy driveway, Chace opened his heart. *Please, God, bring Mia and Kaitlyn back to me. Please help me be worthy of them. In Jesus' name, amen.*

Then Chace sobbed.

. . .

Mia steered the pickup into her parents' horseshoe-shaped driveway ninety minutes later. Her pulse pounded as she wiped her hands across her cheeks. She'd spent most of the trip crying and whispering to Kaitlyn, promising her they would be okay. But Mia would never be okay without Chace by her side.

She turned the key and the loud engine died, leaving the cab of the truck silent except for the tapping of the raindrops peppering the windshield. She stared up at the brick mansion, taking in the lighted, manicured landscaping and dozen large windows staring back at her. The oppression that had haunted her when she lived in that house weighed heavily on her, pressing down on her chest.

Mia looked down at Kaitlyn. She resembled a tiny angel as she slept with her pacifier plugging her mouth. Mia couldn't stomach the idea of Kaitlyn living in that same cold, contemptuous house with Mia's mother dictating to Kaitlyn what to wear, whom to choose as friends, and, ultimately, who was worthy of her love. Kaitlyn deserved a home full of love and acceptance, not judgment and price tags.

"What am I doing here?" Mia's heartbeat galloped with anxiety. She had to find help elsewhere. She couldn't run the risk of her mother manipulating her in exchange for monetary assistance.

Kaitlyn coughed, her chest rattling, and Mia turned the key. She pulled out of the driveway and drove down the street, her parents' home fading in the rearview mirror.

When she slowed at a stoplight, Mia's childhood church came into view. She slapped on the blinker and steered into the parking lot, which was half-full with cars for Wednesday night services and committee meetings. Mia parked near the front of the lot and lifted Kaitlyn into her arms, folding a blanket around her. Then she slipped in through the front door of the church, careful not to draw attention to herself.

When she entered the sanctuary, a peace settled over Mia. She glanced around, taking in the large, colorful stained glass cross and the familiar wooden altar. Memories of Easters and Christmases spent sitting between her parents in this holy house filled her mind. She sank into a pew in the back row and held Kaitlyn to her chest as renewed tears threatened to spill. Mia closed her eyes.

God, I'm lost and have no idea where to turn. I'm terrified Kaitlyn's illness is progressing, but I don't know how to find her help. I'm also terrified of losing Chace. The last thing I want to do is break his heart. Everyone he's ever loved has abandoned him. How can I find help for my baby without losing my husband? Please help me, God. Please guide me. Send me a sign. Amen.

Mia hugged Kaitlyn as tears rolled down her cheeks. She kissed the top of her head as silent pleas continued to pour from her heart. Mia's mind was suddenly flooded with images of Chace and Kaitlyn—Chace holding Kaitlyn, hugging her, whispering to her, and watching her with love in his eyes. Kaitlyn needed and deserved both of her parents, but how could they take care of her if they were living in poverty?

"Mia Whitfield? Is that you?"

Stunned, Mia craned her neck over her shoulder to see the church's pastor standing at the back of the sanctuary. "Pastor Deborah?"

Pastor Deborah Morgan approached. "I didn't mean to startle you. I was walking past the sanctuary, and I saw you sitting here alone. May I join you?"

"Yes, of course." Mia scooted over and wiped her tears.

Pastor Deborah was in her midforties and had dark

hair and warm brown eyes. She sat beside Mia and peered down at Kaitlyn. "Who is this little cherub?"

"This is Kaitlyn Leanne." She angled the baby toward her. "She just turned six months."

"She's beautiful. May I hold her?"

"Of course." Mia handed Kaitlyn to Pastor Deborah. When Kaitlyn coughed, Pastor Deborah frowned. "Has she been seen for that cough?"

Mia shook her head and sniffed. "My husband and I don't have any health insurance or any money. I live in Bird-in-Hand now, but I came here to ask my parents for help. When I got to their house, I couldn't face them because my mother told me I had to leave my husband before she'd help me." She took a trembling breath in an attempt to calm her frayed nerves. "I didn't tell my husband I was going to see my parents, and he's going to be so upset when he realizes I left. I didn't even think to leave a note. I'm so confused. I don't want to hurt Chace. I just want to be a good mom."

"Slow down." Pastor Deborah touched Mia's shoulder. "Someone here can help. She's in a committee meeting right now. Come with me, and I'll get her for you."

Mia followed Pastor Deborah out to the hallway. Deborah disappeared inside a classroom and then reappeared with someone Mia knew, Dr. Renee Simpson. She was tall with graying brown hair and bright hazel eyes. She wore a fashionable red coat and designer shoes with an expensive designer purse and matching messenger bag slung over her shoulder.

"Mia!" Dr. Simpson hugged her and then looked

down at the baby in Pastor Deborah's arms. "Is this your baby?"

Mia nodded. "Yes, she is."

"May I hold her?" Dr. Simpson asked.

Pastor Deborah handed off the baby and then nodded toward an empty classroom. "You can go in there and talk. I need to check on another meeting before I head home."

"Thank you so much, Pastor Deborah." Mia hugged her.

"I'm happy I could help you." Pastor Deborah smiled and then headed down the hallway.

After they sat down at a table in the classroom, Dr. Simpson held Kaitlyn while Mia told her about her situation. Kaitlyn coughed a few times, and Dr. Simpson's brow furrowed.

When Mia finished, Dr. Simpson shook her head. "Why didn't you call me? You know I would see Kaitlyn without charging you."

Mia blinked. That was a valid question. Dr. Simpson had been Mia's pediatrician when she was growing up, but it had never occurred to Mia to ask her to see Kaitlyn.

"I'll listen to her chest right now," Dr. Simpson said. "You can bring her to see me for a follow-up next week."

"Thank you," Mia whispered.

"But first, I want you to tell me what's going on with your parents." Dr. Simpson touched Kaitlyn's arm. "I had no idea you had a baby."

Mia shared everything, beginning when she told her parents she was pregnant and ending with her trip to their house this evening.

"I've seen your parents occasionally in church during the past several months, but your mother never mentioned your marriage or baby." Dr. Simpson clicked her tongue. "When I ask about you, she gives me a tight smile and says you're fine."

Mia leaned her arm on the table. "I'm not surprised since I'm her biggest disappointment."

Dr. Simpson frowned. "Don't say that. You're doing the best you can." Her expression softened. "Gary and I were broke when we were in medical school at the same time, but we got by. It may seem like the end of the world now, but you and Chace will be fine." She smiled. "Is Chace the handsome man who was with you at your parents' Christmas party two years ago?"

"Yes." The time of that party seemed like a decade ago.

"Gary and I talked to Chace, and we liked him." She looked down at Kaitlyn. "You have two good parents, little girl. You will be just fine." Then she peered up at Mia. "I'm sorry your parents can't see the good in Chace. They're making a huge mistake by not accepting your choices. Your mother has a darling granddaughter right here. I will have to tell her all about her." She nodded toward the messenger bag on the floor. "Would you please open that and hand me my stethoscope? We can do the exam right here."

"Thank you." Mia opened the bag.

Nearly an hour later, Mia stood outside the truck with Dr. Simpson as Kaitlyn lay asleep in her car seat.

"You get the prescription filled right away." Dr. Simpson explained where the closest all-night pharmacy was located. "Do you have money for the prescription?"

Mia shook her head. "No, I don't, but Chace will be paid tomorrow."

"That's not soon enough." Dr. Simpson pulled out her wallet and gave Mia a handful of bills. "I would have given you free samples if we were in my office, but it's late and Kaitlyn needs this medication now. Use what's left for diapers and gas."

Mia stared at the money in her hand. "Dr. Simpson, I can't accept this—"

"Don't be silly." Dr. Simpson waved her off. "Consider it a wedding and baby gift since I wasn't able to celebrate with you. And call me Renee. You're a grown woman now." She wagged a finger at her. "I know it's a long drive, but I want to see Kaitlyn in my office early next week. Call my office and tell the scheduler I'm expecting you, all right?"

"Yes." Mia hugged her. "Thank you so much."

"You're welcome, sweetheart. You'll get through this. Don't give up on Chace. He's a good man. I could tell the minute I met him." She frowned. "And I will talk to your mother when I see her at church." She tapped her pocket where she'd stowed her cell phone. "I'll show her the photos I took of her adorable granddaughter and she'll see how wrong she's been about you and Chace."

Mia held her breath as an unexpected pang of hope filled her. Could Renee be the one to convince her parents to become the loving grandparents Kaitlyn needed and deserved?

Mia tucked that hope deep inside her heart. Then she thanked Renee again before climbing into the truck and heading home to Bird-in-Hand.

• • •

Mia glanced at the clock on the dashboard as she parked the truck in front of the cabin. It was twelve fifteen in the morning—the day of their first wedding anniversary. Her stomach fluttered as she looked up at the cabin. A light glowed in the front windows. Had Chace waited up for her? Would he ever forgive her and understand why she'd driven off without an explanation?

She got out of the truck and went around to the passenger side, then gathered up the bag from the pharmacy on the seat and began working on unhooking Kaitlyn's safety belts.

"Mia?"

She jumped, dropping the bag onto the floorboard of the truck. She spun around and faced her husband. "Chace!" She wrapped her arms around him. "I'm so sorry for not telling you where I went."

"We can talk about it after we get Katie inside." He patted her back. "It's cold out here. Let me pick her up."

"Okay." Mia gathered the bag, jogged up the steps, and held the door open for Chace as he carried Kaitlyn into the cabin. Her eyes widened as she stepped inside. It was warm, toasty warm. She dropped the bag on a kitchen chair and scanned the room. Two quilts were draped over the sofa and lighted candles flickered throughout the family room, giving it a romantic glow.

She crossed to the bedroom doorway as Chace pulled off Kaitlyn's snowsuit. Mia's heart swelled with love and admiration as he kissed Kaitlyn's head before gently tucking her under the blanket in her crib. He was the daddy Kaitlyn needed.

Chace motioned for Mia to walk out to the family room. He closed the door behind him and then raked his fingers through his hair, causing it to stand up in all directions. He was so handsome her breath caught in her throat for a moment.

Mia crossed her arms over her middle as her heart pounded. "Are you ready to talk?"

"Yeah." He pointed toward the sofa. "Let's sit."

She sank onto the sofa and he sat down beside her, draping a large quilt over their laps. "I'm sorry. I shouldn't have run off, but I was afraid Kaitlyn had pneumonia and I panicked. I found out she has bronchitis, and I got her medicine. I have a follow-up appointment next week, and she's going to be just—"

"Mee, wait." He held up his hand. "Start from the beginning." He paused, frowning. "What did your parents say? Are you leaving me to move in with them?"

"My parents?" Mia shook her head. "I didn't see them."

"You didn't?" His frown softened. "But if you didn't see them, how did you see a doctor and pay for the medication?"

Mia explained what happened.

"So you didn't see your parents?"

Mia shook her head, moving closer to him. "No."

"Why not?"

She reached up and touched his face, enjoying the feel of his whiskers. "Because this is my home. This is where my heart is, and this is where Kaitlyn and I belong."

He pulled her into his arms. "I'm so grateful to hear you say that."

"I could never stay away from you," she whispered into his shoulder as she circled her arms around his neck. "Kaitlyn and I need you. I'm so sorry. I had no right to be so cruel to you earlier."

"I'm sorry too." He rested his cheek on the top of her head. "I was so worried when you left. Isaac found me in the driveway and told me to have faith in you. He helped me get the stove working properly. I wanted the place to be inviting when you got home, so I found the candles. This is the best I can do for an anniversary gift this year."

"It's perfect." She smiled up at him. "Everything is perfect if I'm with you."

"I feel the same way." He trailed a finger down her cheek. "What do you think about finding a church to attend as a family?"

"I love that idea." She smiled. "And I love you."

His eyes sparkled in the flicker of the candlelight. "I love you, Mee."

She tilted her head. "How did you know I'd be back?"

"I told you. Isaac told me to have faith in you, and I do have faith in you. Because I know you. Happy anniversary, babe."

Chace leaned down and brushed his lips against hers. Closing her eyes, Mia lost herself in his kiss and enjoyed the feel of their home sweet home.

A Flicker of Hope

Ruth Reid

Glossary

ach—oh

boppli—baby

bruder—brother

daadihaus—a smaller home on the property that the grandparents live in

daed—dad or father

danki—thank you

dochder—daughter

doktah—doctor

Englischer—anyone who is not Amish

fraa—wife

haus—house

geh—go

guder mariye—good morning

gut—good

hiya—a greeting like hello

jah—yes

kaffi—coffee

kalt—cold

kapp—a prayer covering worn by women

kinner—children

kumm—come

maedel—unmarried woman

mamm—mom or mother

mei—my

nacht—night

nau—now

nay—no

nett—not

Ordnung—the written and unwritten rules of the Amish;
the understood behavior by which the Amish are
expected to live, passed down from generation to
generation. Most Amish know the rules by heart.

Pennsylvania Deitsch—the language most commonly used
by the Amish

rumschpringe—running-around period when a teenager
turns sixteen years old

sohn—son

washhaus—an outdoor laundry area

wilkom—welcome

wunderbaar—wonderful

yummasetti—a pasta dish with meat and cheese

CHAPTER 1

A jar of peach preserves in hand, Noreen hiked up the cellar's wooden steps compiling a mental list of the other ingredients needed to make the cobbler. One cup of sugar, milk, vanilla, a dash of nutmeg . . . She opened the door leading into the kitchen and, stepping inside the room, was met with a blast of radiating heat so oppressive she immediately recoiled. Flames shot up from the stove and black smoke engulfed the kitchen. Noreen's lungs tightened. She grabbed a dish towel from the counter and swatted at the flames, only instead of putting out the fire, the blaze roared even higher. The fringed end of the dish towel caught fire, consuming the fabric and burning her hand. Panic-stricken, she flung the flaming towel toward the sink, but it hit the window and ignited the curtains.

Get out before it's too late. Disoriented by the dense smoke, she stumbled over a chair and fell against the table, displacing the dishes set for supper. A water glass rolled off the table, landed with a thud on her head, and shattered when it hit the floor. She winced at the sharp blow. Her head throbbed, but the shooting pain in her hip kept her still. Gasping a lungful of thick, hot air, she choked. Her airway sealed.

Don't panic. Think. The window? Blocked. Flames had spread from the curtains and now trellised the walls. *Stay low. Crawl out.* She snaked a few inches on her belly, taking in short gasps of air close to the floor. The consuming scent of kerosene overwhelmed her senses. The oil lamp must have fallen over when she hit the table. Now the lamp's contents were cascading down the table leg and soaking into the braided rug she was lying on. Noreen scrambled to her feet as the rug torched. Upright, the dense smoke burned her eyes, fogging her vision.

"Noreen!"

She froze.

"Noreen, where are you?" Thomas's shout carried over the crackling walls.

"Thomas!" She coughed.

A distorted outline of her husband emerged through the smoke. He thrust the handkerchief he'd been using to tent his nose and mouth at her face, then gathered her into his arms. The last image she had of the kitchen was flames licking the ceiling.

Once outside and a safe distance from the house, Thomas lowered her to the ground. His dark brown eyes scanned her body with intensity. "Are you all right?"

Coughing hard, she could only manage a nod.

"Stay here." He sprinted toward the house, covering his nose and mouth with the crook of his elbow as he disappeared back into the smoke.

"Nay!" she called, but it was too late. She clamped her teeth over her bottom lip and stared at the horrid death-trap. *Nothing's worth saving. Please* kumm *back, Thomas.* "Lord, what is he risking his life for? Please, keep him

safe. He's all I have, Lord." Tears burned her eyes. A massive amount of black smoke bellowed upward. It seemed like hours before Thomas finally stumbled from the house. He reached the bottom porch step and dropped on the ground, coughing between gasps.

She ran to her husband, then sank to her knees beside him. Noreen placed her hand on his back, feeling his muscles tighten with each raspy breath. "You had me out of *mei* mind," she said. "You could've died."

She might as well have been lecturing to the wind. He pushed off the ground, then unbuttoned one of the lower buttons of his tucked-in shirt and removed the small tin box, which he kept buried under the winter blankets in their bedroom closet.

Noreen stood. "You went back in for that?"

He shot her an *I can't believe you'd ask* glare, embedding the soot deeper into the lines on his forehead and making him look older than his thirty-nine years. Thomas shoved the tin box into her hands before running toward the equipment shed. "Put that in a safe place," he said over his shoulder.

Noreen inched her hand over the box's jagged edges. The old tin was where he kept his letters. She hadn't seen it in years. Several loud pops, which sounded like a round of ammunition, fired from inside the house and drew her attention from the box.

"Noreen, get back!" Thomas shouted. He held a shovel in one hand and several feed buckets from the barn in the other.

She met him at the water pump. "That sounded like gun shots."

"Probably *mei* deer rifle."

She went to set the tin box down so she could help fill the buckets.

"I asked you to put that away," he snapped. He cranked the pump handle, placing more thrust on the iron lever than was necessary to bring water to the surface.

"But don't you—"

"Noreen" was all he needed to say.

She spun to face the *washhaus* and darted away. Noreen placed the box on the shelf above the washtub, grabbed the two buckets from the floor, and raced back to the well.

"Take the pump handle," Thomas said, giving it another hard push. He grabbed the full buckets, two in each hand, and toted them to the fire.

Noreen cranked the pump handle and water gushed into the pail. By the time she had the next two filled, Thomas was back with the empty ones. He made a quick exchange and rushed back to the house.

Thomas's brother Jonathan and his teenage sons, Peter and Jacob, cut across the fields separating the two properties, bringing more buckets. "Patty's gone to alert the others," Jonathan said, taking over the pumping. Their rural Posen, Michigan, district stretched over miles of farmland, interspersed with copses of pines and *Englisch* farms.

A short time later, men, women, and children from their Amish district responded. Even some of their English neighbors came to offer assistance. A bucket brigade quickly formed. Noreen was in charge of placing the empty buckets under the spigot for Jonathan to fill, then passing them to the bishop's wife, Alice, who passed them along to the next person in line and ultimately to Thomas, who went dangerously close to the house each time he tossed water onto the fire.

Flames shot out the windows. Soon the roof was ablaze. The house groaned under the heat before caving in on itself, sending tiny orange and red embers soaring upward. Noreen's vision blurred. For half a second she couldn't move. Years of hard work, heartache, and joy reduced to a heap of hot embers. It all seemed unreal.

Moments later, a young boy pointed to a nearby stand of jack pines engulfed in flames. Focus shifted to the secondary fire. A flurry of men ran, water splashing over the sides of their buckets. One by one, they threw the contents of their pails on the newly spawned blaze. Suddenly everyone's homes were at risk, given how dry the silage corn fields were for late September. The warmer summer had made the drydown quicker, but if stalks caught fire it'd easily spread to the Wagner farm and from there, every house, barn, and crop in the district would be in jeopardy.

Multiple gallons of water were tossed on the fire, only it wasn't enough to stop the flames from reaching the first teepee-style bundle of corn shocks. The dried cornstalks fed the ravaging fire, driving it quickly across the field. Noreen grabbed a pail handle in each hand and carted them to the next person. Breathing hard, expanding her lungs to full capacity, carting the pails the ever-increasing distance from the pump was a challenge. *Lord, help us, please.*

Just when Noreen thought all hope was lost,

firefighters from Posen arrived, using their massive hoses to squelch the flames and saturate the area's ground.

Exactly how long it took to contain the fire, she had no idea. Her entire body was numb. With the immediate danger past, Noreen released the empty bucket, allowing it to clang to the ground. It was over. All that remained were a few standing charred wall posts still smoking. Handling so many five-gallon pails of water left her arms feeling like lumps of bread dough. When the womenfolk took turns giving her a hug, she was too weak to return the gesture. The ladies talked of plans for a sewing frolic to help replenish the loss, but Noreen stood apart, still dazed and unable to wrap her mind around all that had happened.

"I have enough material for a dress or two," Mary Beth said.

Others chimed in what extras they had to offer and the topic shifted to surplus canned goods, kitchenware, and pantry items.

Her sister-in-law Patty came up beside Noreen. "Let's continue this talk at *mei* place. We can wash up and have tea. Besides, the mosquitoes will start to swarm soon now that the fire is out."

True. Dusk in northern Michigan at this time of the year meant either dousing yourself with cedarleaf oil or having to battle an army of mosquitoes if you wanted to be outside. She didn't want to be outside. A chill settled in Noreen's bones. Between losing the heat from the blaze and the nighttime temperature dropping,

Noreen's arms prickled with goose bumps. She hugged herself as much for comfort as for warmth.

Patty twined her arm around Noreen's elbow. "Tea sounds *gut* to you, *jah*?"

A cup of tea sounded good—if she could swallow. The fire had left Noreen's throat raw. She licked her dry lips and tasted smoke. Between the burning sensation brought on by the acid rising from her stomach and inhaling too much smoke, she wasn't sure even tea would help. Then again, it would be nice to wash up. Soot caked her skin.

Noreen was about to accept Patty's offer when she spotted a firefighter in a reflective jacket, oxygen tank in hand, approach Thomas. She slipped her arm out from Patty's. "I have to check on *mei* husband." She broke free from the group of womenfolk. A new surge of adrenalin infused her veins. Thomas sat slumped against the trunk of a maple, his legs splayed out in front.

"Thomas!" Her voice cracked.

CHAPTER 2

Noreen dodged the collapsed fire hose stretched over the ground as she rushed across the yard to where Thomas was slumped against a tree. The rescue worker removed her husband's straw hat and set it aside, then positioned a clear breathing mask over the bridge of Thomas's nose and extending past his mouth. Noreen dropped to her knees at her husband's side.

"Try to take slow, deep breaths, sir," the man helping him said.

Thomas's lips pursed. His shoulders lifted as he inhaled the oxygen, his chest expanding. A bubbly crackling noise escaped his airway, sounding like a man gagging on his own fluids. He jerked the mask from his face and coughed. Spasms overtook his body.

"Wha-what's happening?" Her gaze darted between her husband struggling to catch his breath and the worker who'd trained his eyes on Thomas, but for whatever reason hadn't initiated any treatment. A few seconds later, the spasms subsided. A sheen of sweat matted Thomas's light brown hair to his forehead. He panted short, shallow breaths, and when he looked up, his eyes held a dull cast that caused her insides to shudder.

"Let's get the oxygen mask back on you." The rescuer, a tall wiry man, repositioned the mask over Thomas's face. "Try to relax your breathing." The man demonstrated several deep, even breaths and coaxed Thomas to follow.

Thomas eyed the worker with a vacant gaze.

"Let the oxygen help you," the man said, repeating the same deep cleansing breaths with an encouraging smile.

Noreen placed her hand on her husband's shoulder. Beneath the soot, his face was a blistering shade of red. Even after working all day in the open field exposed to the direct sun, he never looked this burnt. On closer evaluation, his eyebrows appeared singed, his beard a few inches shorter. "You went so close to the fire," she said, blurting her thoughts. "Are you okay?"

If he answered, she couldn't hear over the hum of the fire truck's engine. She directed her question to the worker. "Is he going to be all right?"

"He breathed in a lot of smoke, ma'am. Were you in the house as well?"

"*Jah*, but I feel fine." Noreen's eyes stung with tears recalling how Thomas had given her his handkerchief to breathe into. Even when he went back into the house, he didn't use anything but his elbow. She could have prevented this disaster. Had she not gone down to the cellar when she did . . . *Oh, Lord, I caused all of this.*

"I'd like to transport him to the hospital, but he's refused."

Of course he did. Her husband was as stubborn as a goat.

"Thomas," she said loud enough for her voice to carry over the commotion. He looked at her, a withered echo of sadness in his gaze. "You need a *doktah* to check your lungs." She tapped her hand against her chest. "Your lungs are filled with smoke."

Thomas shook his head slowly.

"Please, Thomas."

He closed his eyes and turned away from her.

Noreen clamped her mouth closed. She'd learned over the years that this gesture meant the topic was closed. Pleading wouldn't help. She'd been dismissed. Noreen glanced up at the worker. "He won't go."

"If that's his decision," the man said, "I can't force him."

Seeing the man adjust a valve on the oxygen tank, Noreen feared the worker was about to discontinue the oxygen. It made sense now that the fire was out and Thomas had turned down emergency transport that the workers wouldn't stay much longer. After all, it was getting late. Except for what light spilled over the area from the fire truck's flood lamps, it was dark.

She had half a mind to get Bishop Zook involved. Someone needed to talk some sense into her husband. She peered over to where the men milled around the base of the smoldering rubble and spied the bishop. As she set her feet to stand, Thomas caught her arm. He shook his head and she sat back down. Even in his weakened state, the man was bullheaded.

The firefighter glanced over his shoulder, then redirected his attention back to Thomas. "Is the oxygen helping?"

Between the mask shielding his voice and the inter-ference from the surrounding noises, Noreen wasn't sure if he'd muttered yes or no.

The rescuer held two fingers against Thomas's wrist and studied his watch. After a minute, he looked up and asked, "Does your chest still feel heavy?"

Thomas stared blankly at the man.

Noreen leaned closer. "Did you hear his question? He asked if your chest feels heavy."

Thomas furrowed his brows at her. After nearly fifteen years of marriage, they could communicate without words. Her husband's gaze held a warning she couldn't easily ignore. Still, he hadn't answered the res-cuer's question. A two-ton plow horse could be sitting on his chest and Thomas wouldn't admit it was heavy.

"Tell the firefighter if your chest feels heavy," she insisted.

Thomas touched his chest midsternum.

"That's where it hurts?" Noreen turned to the worker. "What does that mean?"

"He really needs to see a doctor. His heart rate is fast, his blood pressure slightly elevated. I don't like the congested sound I hear in his lungs."

Thomas removed the oxygen mask again and coughed. "*Mei* throat's . . . dry," he rasped. "Noreen—" He coughed harder.

She pushed off the ground. "I'll get you a glass of—" Her words caught in her throat. The house was gone. The water glasses, the leaky faucet that would never stop dripping, the kitchen cabinets Thomas had built . . . everything—gone. Her shoulders sagged.

Lord, I feel so helpless. I can't even get mei *husband a cup of water for his parched throat.*

Voices muffled around her and, for a moment, she had the sensation of everyone moving in slow motion. The firefighters packed equipment into compartments of the fire truck; their *Englisch* neighbors climbed into their cars. She hadn't even thanked them.

Thomas barked another mucous-laden cough and Noreen sprang into action. She hurried across the yard to the *washhaus*. Without a lantern, it was impossible to see inside the wooden shed. She blindly felt her way along the wall until she touched the washtub, then she patted the area to the right where she had hung a washrag on a peg the day before. The rag would have to do. She hurried out of the building and over to the well pump.

Shards of pain tore through her shoulder muscles as she cranked the handle. The pump felt harder to prime than usual, but she persevered. A few forceful pumps and cold water gushed from the spigot. She soaked the cloth, wrung it out, then soaked it with water again. She didn't want Thomas ingesting any soap residue left behind from cleaning. Even after she was sure the cloth was clean, she rinsed and wrung it out one more time. Her fingers stiffened and turned numb from the icy water, which should certainly soothe Thomas's throat.

Patty strode across the lawn. "How's your husband?"

"His throat's dry and his lungs are filled with smoke," she said.

"Is he going to the hospital to get checked?"

"He refused, and knowing how stubborn he is, nothing will change his mind." Noreen gave the rag a tight squeeze, more an effort to release tension than to drain any excess water from the cloth. A few steps away from the pump, she glimpsed the flicker of lanterns in the distance, the glow reminding her of fireflies. The members were making their way to the parked buggies at the end of the driveway where the horses were tied a safe distance away from the fire to prevent them from spooking. Noreen twisted the washrag, then realized she'd extracted too much water and turned back to rewet it.

Patty followed her back to the pump. "Do you want to go with us to take the *kinner* home?"

Noreen shook her head. "I'm going to stay. Thomas might decide to go into the hospital. He might need me." He wouldn't. Thomas didn't need anyone. She gave the rag a shake. "Thanks for your help. I appreciate it."

"Once the *kinner* are settled, I'll gather a few supplies. Jonathan plans to stay a little longer. I think Bishop Zook is too. Can you think of anything you'd like me to bring back?"

"A water glass would be nice. I'm wetting this rag for Thomas to suck on, but I'm sure he would appreciate more to drink."

"Absolutely." Patty placed her hand on Noreen's shoulder. "Maybe when I *kumm* back, you'll be ready to leave, *jah*?"

"We'll see." A hearty cough carried across the night air. "I imagine that's Thomas reminding me about the water."

"I'll see you in a little while." Patty headed toward her buggy.

Noreen returned to the area lit by floodlights from the fire truck. Thomas was still propped against the tree, breathing into a mask, the rescuer squatting next to him. To her untrained ears, his breathing sounded better. Less wheezy. His chest expanded and fell several times without triggering a coughing fit. That had to be good. She sat next to him and handed him the rag. "Hopefully, you can suck enough water out to help your thirst."

Thomas removed the mask and rasped, "*Danki*" as he placed the corner of the cloth into his mouth. The longer he went without the mask, the more his lungs rattled. He hadn't improved as much as she first thought.

She studied how his chest moved up and down in sync with the wheezy sounds he made. Inhaling, exhaling—it all looked exhausting for him. "Your breathing is still labored. Is the oxygen helping at all?" Her question was for the man attending him as much as for Thomas.

Thomas groaned.

Noreen noticed the worker's strained expression and asked again, "He's going to be all right, isn't he?"

"I still think he should see a doctor," the man said.

A firefighter approached, wearing a reflective jacket and pants, clipboard in hand. His yellow, oversized rubber boots had a film of ashes covering them. He glanced at the clipboard. "Are you Mr. and Mrs. King?"

"*Jah*," Noreen replied.

"I'm Lieutenant Kyle DeBoer. I was told you are the homeowners?"

Thomas withdrew the rag from his mouth. "*Jah*, that's right."

"We'll be packing up our equipment and heading out shortly, but I wanted to let you know my report will be available tomorrow. I'm sure your insurance company will request a copy and I'll file one with the county fire investigator as well."

"We don't have insurance," Thomas said.

"Then you probably won't need an investigational analysis to determine where and how the fire started."

Noreen's insides wrenched. They didn't need an investigator to tell them what she already knew. She neglected the simmering beef stew. She caused the fire.

"*Nay*, we won't need a report." Thomas turned and coughed into his fist.

Noreen picked up the oxygen mask. "Maybe you should put this back on."

"*Nay*, I'm fine." Thomas pushed off the ground and stood. "How much do we owe you?"

"I don't handle the billing." The firefighter tapped his pen against the clipboard. "The fire department will send a bill to the township and from there I'm not sure. There might not be any charge for the service." He motioned over his shoulder toward the smoldering embers. "Be careful around the ash pile. It'll stay hot several more hours. You'll also want to watch for any new hotspots that could develop. I don't think you'll have any problems, but secondary fires have been known to start even after a fire is thought to be contained."

"*Jah*," Thomas said. "I plan to keep a close eye on it all *nacht*."

The man's brows lifted and he turned to the other firefighter who had been administering the oxygen.

"Mr. King doesn't wish to be transported for treatment," the man who had been caring for him said.

"That's right." Thomas coughed.

The lieutenant eyed him a moment as if assessing Thomas's condition. "Then I guess our work here is finished." He offered a friendly smile before turning his attention to the other man. "How long do you need, Jack?"

"Five, ten minutes." The firefighter glanced at his clipboard, flipped a page, then spoke to Thomas. "If you're absolutely sure you don't want to go to the hospital, I'll need you to sign a release-of-treatment form."

"I'll sign it."

Noreen leaned closer to Thomas. "Are you sure you don't want to see the doctor?"

He shot her a *let it be* glare, turned to the worker, took the clipboard and pen, and jotted his signature on the form. "Thanks for your help," he said before walking away.

If only she could fool herself into believing his curt behavior was an oddity. But it wasn't. He wasn't the same jubilant man she'd married fifteen years ago. But life had been different then.

CHAPTER 3

"Then marry me."

Thomas's proposal stole Noreen's breath. His brown eyes pleaded for her to answer *jah*, but her mind whirled with fragmented thoughts. She turned her gaze to the sun's orange-red reflection shimmering over Sunken Lake. *A proposal.* She should feel honored. But rushing into marriage wasn't the answer.

Thomas reached for her hand. "Let's sit closer to the water." He led her around the nettle bushes and down the grassy slope to the sandy shore where they sat on a fallen log. After a gentle squeeze of her hand, he let it go. He stared at the lake, elbows propped on his knees and chin rested on his fisted hands. Within seconds, he repositioned himself so he was straddling the log, facing her. "Is your tongue twisted?" He tipped her chin up slightly with the pads of his fingers. "Open your mouth."

"What?"

"Oh, she does talk. For a minute there I thought something had caught your tongue." He slapped his hands against his thighs. "Hmm . . . wonder what she's thinking. Does she remember that only minutes ago a man proposed?"

Noreen smiled. "I'm thinking you've been breathing in too much wood glue. I only turned eighteen a few months ago. *Mei* sisters waited until they were in their midtwenties to marry. Besides—"

He stifled her words with a kiss. A kiss so complete it left her insides fluttering like a curtain on a windy day. When he lifted his lips from hers, his gaze held a determination she'd never seen before.

He cocked a grin. "You don't want to wait until you're an old maid, do you?"

"I still have a few more years before that happens. Eighteen is hardly the age to worry about growing old alone."

"I suppose," he said with a chuckle, "if you're willing to take that risk." He pulled her into a hug and kissed her forehead.

Old maid. She huffed, unsure if she should be annoyed by his statement or flattered by his persistence. Deciding she'd rather enjoy his company while they were still together, she leaned her head against his sturdy shoulder and snuggled into his warm embrace. If she could choose the ideal place to become engaged, it would be here—sharing a log next to the lakeshore at the end of a perfect day, yet the circumstances weren't as ideal as they appeared. They hadn't courted long. He'd only just recently kissed her, and up until then, she wasn't sure why he kept asking to drive her home from the singings.

Noreen smiled, recalling how he'd hardly said a word and never looked her in the eye more than a few seconds in the beginning. Then, when he finally did kiss her, he did so with such complete control. Any measure of sound reasoning she'd once possessed disappeared with the rush of new sensations. At that moment, she was his. Even now, sitting next to him, her breathing was uneven. The same giddy, unbalanced, tingling sensations rippled through her veins as they did every time she was nestled in his arms. Yes, she could marry Thomas, raise a houseful of *kinner*, and be the most content *fraa* in the district. Thoughts filled her mind how nice cooking and cleaning and sewing for her husband would be. Her heart pounded harder, faster, nearly drowning out the lulling sound of meadow crickets chirping in the distance. *Put things in perspective. Mamm* and *Daed* would never allow her to marry.

Noreen pushed off his chest, shaking her head, grounding the lofty thoughts. "I'm leaving at the end of the month." She swatted a swarm of pesky gnats. "I'm going to miss this place, the members of our district . . . you."

"You say that like I'm an afterthought. You'll miss the district and people—and oh, *jah*, you, too, Thomas."

"You most of all." If he could look inside her heart, he would understand she didn't want to move, didn't want to leave him.

"Then marry me," he repeated, this time with more conviction.

She shook her head slowly. "*Mei* moving isn't the reason we should get married."

His smile faded.

Noreen stood. "It isn't like I'm leaving Michigan," she said, stepping just out of reach of the foamy wave. "Oscoda County is—"

He bounded up from the log. "Sixty minutes away by car in *gut wedder. Mei* horse wouldn't make that trip."

"We can write." She took a step backward and the soles of her black leather shoes sank into the wet sand.

"Or we could get married." He lifted his brows as if to prompt agreement, and when she didn't respond, he slid his arm around her waist, pressed her against his chest, and captured her mouth fully.

She had known him all her life but never to be impulsive—nothing like this. A shudder washed over her as he trailed kisses from her mouth, over her cheek, and to her ear.

"I don't want to be your pen pal," he said, drawing his words in a husky breath. "I want to be your husband."

He kissed her like she was already his wife, weakening her resolve. *Yes, I'll marry you*, her mind echoed, but an inner voice of reason took over. *Take captive every thought and bring it into submission.*

Over the lake, a flash of lightning preceded a loud clap of thunder by only a few seconds.

"That was way too close." Noreen pulled away, adjusting her prayer *kapp* as she stood. Raindrops plunked in the lake, creating ripples of circles.

Thomas didn't seem concerned about the change in weather or finding shelter. "You haven't given me your answer."

"I haven't even invited you to a family supper, and you're asking me to be your *fraa*. What are *mei* parents going to think?"

Thomas tilted his face skyward as the rain came down harder. She hadn't realized he was chuckling until he made eye contact with her again. "I've worked several summers for your father. I've eaten several meals with your family. He's even asked me to—"

"To what?" Thunder rumbled in the distance.

"To make sure you get home safe."

"Then I suggest you take me home before people talk about us leaving the singing so early." She lifted the hem of her drenched dress enough that it didn't drag over the ground and took off through the meadow where he'd tied his horse.

Thomas caught up to her. "Since when have you given any merit to tittle-tattle, Noreen Trombly?"

She stopped to catch her breath. "I don't. Usually." Until tonight. Leaving the singing as early as they had would certainly provoke a host of speculation. Her father would be waiting up—upset if she didn't come home at a decent hour. Not to mention being soaked to the skin. He'd expect an explanation about that as well. "*Kumm* on." She took off sprinting.

"Hey, wait up."

She glanced over her shoulder and tripped on a slippery rock. Falling forward, the palms of her hands landed on a patch of bull thistle. "Ouch." She shook her hands, feeling like a hundred needles had stuck her at once.

Thomas helped her up. "You don't have to be in such a hurry. It's *nett* like you're going to melt in the rain."

She looked down at her dress. She'd have to scrub hard to remove the mud stains.

"What are you fretting about? Even covered in mud, you're beautiful."

She continued to the buggy. "What makes you think I'm fretting?"

He opened the passenger door, waited for her to

climb onto the bench, then untied his horse. Once he was seated beside her, he faced her. "I've known you a long time. I know when you're happy, when you're sad, and when you're irritated. I know when you're fretting over something." He brushed a raindrop away from her cheek with the back of his hand. "And I know you don't belong in Oscoda County. Your place is with me."

Despite the chilly springtime air making her shiver, warmth she'd never experienced spread to her core as his arm came around her shoulders. She leaned her head against him. If only for the moment, this was where she belonged. At his side.

As quickly as the rain came, it disappeared. The ride home was much like their first ride together. Neither of them talked. But unlike the other times he'd driven her home, when he stopped the buggy next to her porch, he set the brake and climbed out.

Lantern light from the sitting room window spilled out on the porch as Noreen climbed the steps. "I had a nice time, *danki*."

"I did too." He leaned against the banister and crossed his arms. "What time should I *kumm* for supper tomorrow?"

"I must say, you're awfully forward, Thomas King." She eyed him carefully. The light from the window illuminating his confident smile. Perhaps she didn't know him as well as she thought.

He pushed off the banister. "I don't have much time to convince you to marry me, do I?"

CHAPTER 4

PRESENT DAY

The mosquitoes hovered in vicious droves as if preparing to hibernate for the winter. Noreen slapped a mosquito biting the side of her neck while another one droned near her ear. Perhaps she should move closer to the burn pile. She'd sat next to the woodshed on the chopping block to get out of the smoke, but Thomas and the men hadn't seemed bothered by the blood-sucking pests, which was probably because they hadn't left the smoldering ashes. Thomas stood between his brothers, Jonathan and Levi, each with shovels in their hands. Noreen didn't recall seeing Levi arrive, but he was covered in soot like the others. From where she sat, she couldn't make out what Thomas was searching for, but the determined look on his face showed the object's importance.

Bishop Zook approached the men and clapped Levi's shoulder. Without the house to buffer the noise, the men's short bursts of conversation carried across the lawn along with sporadic pops and crackles in the smoldering rubble.

A glow of lamplight flickered in Noreen's peripheral

vision. Patty ambled toward her, pillows, blankets, and a large brown paper bag in hand.

"I see just about everyone cleared out," Patty said.

"*Jah. Nett* much anyone can do *nau.*"

Her sister-in-law glanced over at the men. "I'm surprised Levi is still here. You heard Rebecca gave birth to a *sohn* earlier, didn't you?"

Noreen shook her head.

"The *boppli* was, as Sadie told, a few cups shy of a ten-pound bag of sugar."

Noreen smiled. The district midwife had her own twist on newborn measurements. "He came early."

"A couple of weeks."

"Were you there to help?"

Patty shook her head. "But from what I heard, she had quite the time of it. Sadie's still with her."

Noreen understood why Rebecca hadn't asked for her assistance, but Patty was a mother of six, a champ at giving birth.

Patty motioned to the men. "So what are they doing with the shovels?"

Noreen couldn't help but wonder if her sister-in-law changed the subject for Noreen's benefit. Patty had a tendency to tiptoe around the subject of babies and giving birth. But Noreen let it go. "I have no idea what they're doing. Everything is still so hot. Even if they find something useful, it's unlikely they'd be able to save it." She sighed. In their small Amish district, they believed in living a simple lifestyle, avoiding modern conveniences, and not idolizing material belongings. It was a way of life she chose, but something told her this would be the first time she'd experience what going without really meant. Even though she and Thomas didn't have much, it was hard to lose everything.

"Well, I brought you these blankets and pillows, but I think you and Thomas should stay with us. Like you said, there isn't anything more that can be done tonight. Besides that, it might get *kalt*."

"The fireman said something about watching for the fire to restart, so I don't think Thomas will want to leave anytime soon."

Patty's face puckered. "And you?"

"I'll stay with Thomas. He inhaled a lot of smoke. I don't want to leave him alone." Noreen reached for the bedding. "I'm sure these wool blankets will keep us plenty warm." She planned to make a bed in the hayloft once everyone left.

"I brought you a *nacht* dress, a pair of heavy socks, a bar of soap, washcloths, and in *mei* buggy are a couple quart jars filled with *kaffi*, cups, and a few cheese sandwiches. I'm guessing you haven't eaten anything yet."

"*Nay*, I was in the process of preparing supper when the fire started."

"*Ach*." Her friend's eyes widened. "I didn't realize the fire started in the kitchen."

Noreen nodded. "I'm *nett* sure what happened. I was down in the cellar at the time."

"You must have been terrified." Patty rubbed her arms. "Just hearing about it makes the hair on my arms rise."

"It all happened so fast." Noreen bowed her head. "I shouldn't have been so careless."

"No one was hurt. We have a lot to be thankful for."

"*Jah.*"

"I should have brought something more than just sandwiches and *kaffi*. I could have warmed up some *yummasetti* had I known."

"Sandwiches are plenty." The smoky taste in her mouth had stolen her appetite. Noreen set the bedding on the chopping stump. "I'm sure you need to get home to the *kinner*. I'll walk to the buggy with you. I think I could use a cup of that *kaffi* you brought." She glanced over her shoulder at Thomas. Something told her this was going to be a long night.

Light from the lantern Patty was carrying splayed across the ground and kept them from stumbling over debris. It seemed odd that only a few hours ago she was trying to choose which preserves to use to make dessert.

The back end of Patty's buggy had more supplies than just the coffee and sandwiches her friend had mentioned. Patty had thought to bring an extra lantern, bug spray, toiletries, and changes of clothes for both her and Thomas. Being brothers, Jonathan and Thomas were about the same height and build, so sharing clothes wouldn't be a problem.

Noreen held the quart jars of brewed coffee close to her body, the warmth spreading through the dress to her skin.

The men lumbered toward the buggies, Thomas carrying a lantern, Jonathan and Levi supporting shovels on their shoulders, Patty's sons toting the buckets. They stopped at the bishop's buggy, parked a few feet away. Just as the womenfolk had made plans earlier for an upcoming sewing frolic, Noreen was sure the men would be talking about rebuilding the house. After a brief interchange, the bishop drove off. The brothers talked for a little longer, their muffled voices carrying over the evening air, congratulating Levi again. Levi went to his buggy, and Thomas, Jonathan, and the boys continued toward Patty and her.

Yawning, Peter and Jacob tossed their buckets in the back and climbed into the buggy.

Jonathan stood next to Patty and smiled lovingly at his wife. "Did you take Matthew and the girls home, *fraa*?"

Noreen grinned at the affectionate way Jonathan always called his wife *fraa*, *mamm*, or Mrs. King—so different than Thomas, who barely called her at all.

"*Jah*, they were worn out." Patty yawned.

Jonathan and Patty married less than a year before her and Thomas, and living next door, the four of them had always been close. Noreen had even assisted the midwife in bringing all six of Patty's children into the world, and had witnessed firsthand the immediate bond formed between mother and child.

Noreen turned to Thomas. His light brown hair was shades darker from black smoke and sweat matted to his forehead. "Patty brought us some sandwiches and *kaffi*."

Thomas smiled, forming tiny soot creases at the corners of his mouth. "*Danki*. We appreciate it."

"I told Noreen if you two wanted to *kumm* home with Jonathan and me, I'd heat up the leftover *yummasetti*."

"It was *gut*," Jonathan added, patting his belly.

"It sounds delicious," Thomas said, his voice hoarse. "But I need to stay and make sure everything is okay.

But, Noreen"—he faced her—"why don't you stay with Patty tonight? You'll be more comfortable."

"*Nay*," Noreen flared, then, recognizing the sharpness, softened her tone. "*Mei* place is with you." She shrank at Thomas's furrowed brows. She hadn't meant to upset him. He held his tongue, but he rarely said anything when tension rose between them. Sometimes his silent treatment went on for days. She hoped this wasn't one of those times.

After a few seconds of awkward silence, Jonathan spoke up. "We, ah . . . We should head home, *fraa*." He took the shovel to the back of the buggy and tossed it inside with the buckets.

Patty's gaze darted between Noreen and Thomas. "Well," she said, a hint of nervousness in her tone. "I hope you'll join us for blueberry pancakes in the morning."

Noreen smiled weakly and made a noncommitting shrug she hoped her lifelong friend understood without words. It would be up to Thomas.

Patty climbed into the buggy as Jonathan untied the horse's reins from the tree branch. "Our door is unlocked if you get *kalt* or change your mind," he said.

"*Danki*," Thomas replied. Although it was clear to Noreen that he had no intention of changing his mind, even if he got cold during the night.

Noreen clutched the jars of coffee closer to her body. Once the buggy was in motion, she turned to her husband. "Would you like a sandwich and mug of *kaffi*?"

"Maybe later." He turned and ambled toward the burn pile, shoulders slumped. Noreen suspected it wasn't just losing the house that had stolen Thomas's joy. Noreen hadn't seen a bounce in his step in a very long time.

CHAPTER 5

Noreen peered out the sitting room window, bubbling with anticipation as Thomas's buggy pulled into the yard. He was early. An hour and a half early. Apparently, he hadn't listened when she told him supper was at six. The *yummasetti* hadn't even finished baking. She planned to make fresh biscuits to go with the noodle dish and banana pudding for dessert. Noreen pressed her hands over the folds of her dingy gray dress. So much for changing into one of her Sunday dresses.

Thomas climbed out of his buggy and tied his horse to the post next to the barn. He looked toward the house and shot a wave her direction.

Noreen's face warmed. She scooted away from the window, then, unable to restrain herself, peeked around the curtain. Thomas certainly had a self-assured bounce in his step. But he wasn't heading to the house, he was going into the barn.

Mamm's voice rang out from behind her, startling Noreen. "Noreen, didn't you say you wanted to make banana pudding?"

"Oh, *jah*. I did—I mean I still do." She hurried past her mother and went into the kitchen. Her heartbeat galloped at a pace that left her winded getting the ingredients together. After Thomas's proposal last night, her mind wouldn't rest. The lack of sleep was evident today. She couldn't remember how many egg yolks to use. "Two—*nay* three."

Mamm lifted her brows. "Is everything all right?"

"I couldn't remember how many eggs. Strange, isn't it so? I just made it last week for the Sunday meal." Everything seemed strange lately. Mrs. Thomas King. Thomas's *fraa*. Her thoughts went askew as she measured the milk, then the flour and sugar and, dumping the ingredients together in a saucepan, she recited her married name. *Noreen King*. She decided the name fit her.

Mamm mixed the biscuit batter, humming cheerfully. Her mother sang whenever she was excited. Lately, she sang all the time.

"Your father thinks we should have space for a small fabric department in the new store. Isn't that exciting?"

Nay. *It's sad. Depressing. Lonely.* Her parents wanted to start a new life sixty miles away while she was trying to decide if she would start hers here in Presque Isle County with Thomas.

"Your sisters are ecstatic about the idea."

She didn't doubt that. Her two sisters married the Fisher brothers two years ago and had moved to Mio with their husbands' family. Verna and Carol Diane had tried to convince *Mamm* and *Daed* to move two years ago and hadn't stopped asking in the intervening years. After *Daed*'s accident last fall, her sisters increased pressure for the rest of the family to move. Financially, the move made sense. With her father unable to work, they weren't able to keep up with the farm. He'd already sold off the land and the plow horses. The house was bound to go next.

"We'll take turns running the shop," *Mamm* said.

Noreen frowned. Her mother and older sisters had already planned Noreen's future. She wanted to object, but this wasn't the time, nor was she prepared to tell *Mamm* about Thomas's proposal. "The *yummasetti* should be almost done, don't you think?"

"*Jah*, I'm sure it's close." Her mother removed a potholder from the drawer and used it to check the noodle dish. "A few more minutes yet." She slid the pan back into the oven. "I put some packing boxes in your room. I know we're *nett* leaving until the end of the month, but I thought you could pack your winter things."

"Do we have to talk about moving *nau*?" she snipped, then immediately regretted the tone she'd used. "I'm sorry."

"I know you don't like the idea, but this is a chance for a fresh start."

"*Jah*, I know." Noreen layered the sliced banana pieces over the pudding. Pleased with the appearance, she wiped her hands on a dishrag. "I'm going to run upstairs and change *mei* dress." Not that she cared anymore about entertaining company. Noreen tossed the rag on the counter and hurried upstairs.

. . .

Thomas rubbed his clammy hands on the sides of his pants. He'd never asked for permission to marry someone's daughter before. The words he'd rehearsed on the ride over here slipped his mind when he spotted Noreen's father dipping the old coffee can into the oat bin. Leaning over, Mr. Trombly's spine rounded near the shoulders and upper back, giving him the distorted appearance of bending over much farther than he actually was. The hunched back was the result of an injury he sustained working in the field. Hired to help reap the fields, Thomas had been working to bundle the wheat stalks while Mr. Trombly was feeding the thrasher to separate the wheat from the straw. Thomas hadn't seen the machine turn over on Mr. Trombly but he'd witnessed the spine-crushing results. His employer couldn't feel his legs. He'd recovered better than expected, although as he healed, his spine, improperly aligned, fused together.

"I heard you would be joining us for supper tonight," Mr. Trombly said without glancing up from the barrel.

"*Jah*, Noreen invited me."

The gray-bearded, fiftysomething-year-old man grimaced when he straightened. "Did she tell you we eat at six?"

Thomas nodded. "I, ah . . ." He motioned to the can of oats. "Would you like me to feed the horses?"

"I'm *nett* an invalid." He ambled toward the stalls.

"No, sir. I didn't mean to imply that you were." Thomas followed him to the buggy horse's stall, noting the empty water trough when he peeked over the gate. Before he could offer to replenish the water, Mr. Trombly grabbed the bucket. He took a few steps and paused. "Here," he said, steeling a grimace as he handed Thomas the pail. "Take this out to the pump and fill it, please."

Thomas gladly left to get water. He needed a chance to reformulate his approach. He cranked the iron handle a few times to prime the pump. "As you know, Mr. Trombly, your daughter and I have been courting for a while *nau* and we've developed feelings for one another." Clumsy wording. He needed a more direct approach. "Noreen and I are in love." Maybe. "I can't live without her." No. "I love your daughter and want to marry her." He glanced at the house. Noreen was no longer standing in front of the sitting room window. He couldn't see her in the kitchen either. Water gurgled up from the well and gushed into the bucket, filling it with one more hard thrust on the handle.

Mr. Trombly was standing at the stall, chewing a long piece of straw and staring at the mare eating oats.

Thomas emptied the bucket of water into the trough, then lowered the pail.

Mr. Trombly removed the piece of straw from his mouth and twirled it between his thumb and index finger. "I'm sure you've heard by *nau* that I found a buyer for the farm. We're moving at the end of the month." He chomped on the straw once more as if silently informing Thomas there was nothing more to say over the matter.

"That's what I wanted to talk to you about." Thomas dried his wet hands on the front of his shirt. "Noreen wants to stay here . . . with me."

Her father's eyes narrowed on Thomas. He removed

the straw and opened his mouth, but then tossed the straw and walked away.

"We love each other," Thomas said, trailing behind.

"I gathered that much from what I overheard at the pump." He kept walking.

"You heard me?"

"*Sohn*," he said, stopping at the door to face Thomas. "The pump is only a few feet from the barn. I can hear supper called from the back pasture."

Heat rushed up Thomas's neck and spread to his face. "Then you know we want to get married." Mr. Trombly glared at him a moment, then continued out the door.

Thomas crossed the lawn beside him. "You were the one who asked me to look after her after your accident."

"Because I thought I was going to die trapped under that machine." He kept walking, his gait noticeably uneven.

"I kept *mei* promise to you. *Nau* I want to take care of her the rest of *mei* life."

Noreen's father stopped. "*Nay*, you were to look after her as an older *bruder* would—I trusted you."

Thomas looked down at his boots. He'd kept a brotherly distance for most of a year. He hadn't even kissed her until he was sure he'd fallen in love.

"You're *nett* on *rumschpringe*. You're a baptized member of the church." He stopped a few feet from the porch and lowered his voice. "I should take you before the bishop and have you repent of your sins in front of the members for bringing *mei* daughter home muddy and soaking wet. Her *kapp* was practically sideways on her head." He shook his head. "I'm no fool. The rain had stopped before the singing ended."

Thomas swallowed hard. In hindsight, convincing Noreen to leave the singing early wasn't the smartest thing he'd done, nor was getting caught in the rain.

"You involved *mei* daughter's *gut* name in gossip." The older man crossed his arms. His stone-cold expression suggested he might be contemplating bringing the matter to the bishop.

"I asked Noreen last *nacht* to marry me. The talk would stop if you granted us permission."

"She's young—you're both young." He climbed the porch steps.

"I'm twenty-four," Thomas said, following him to the door. "Most of the men *mei* age are married. And plenty of *maedels* marry at eighteen."

"Because they have to," Mr. Trombly growled under his breath.

Thomas's jaw tightened. "I can assure you," he spoke slowly so that Noreen's father got the point. "That isn't the case with us." He softened his tone. "I'm the same person you trusted to look after your daughter." He huffed in frustration. "I didn't plan to fall in love with her. It just happened."

After a moment of studying Thomas, Mr. Trombly opened the door. "You're unprepared to ask for *mei* daughter's hand. Where would you live?" He jerked his head, motioning Thomas, although begrudgingly, inside.

"I own property. I'm going to build in"—Thomas's gaze traveled up the staircase and stopped on Noreen—"stages," he said, finishing his sentence without returning his attention to her father. Her cheeks turned a rosy shade as if she'd been able to read his mind. Easily embarrassed, she would cover her nose to hide her freckles any second. Although she wasn't keen on her fair skin that burned easily in the summer, or that her hair was more red than brown, she was beautiful in every way to him. His gaze followed her down the remaining stairs and when she landed on the bottom step, he greeted her with a wide smile. "*Hiya*, Noreen."

"Hello, Thomas. I hope you like *yummasetti*."

Her blue dress brought out the vibrancy in her eyes. When she looked at him, her eyes' pale blue hue almost seemed translucent. He'd once heard a person's eyes were a reflection of their soul. She was beautiful, pure—refreshing as a cold drink on a hot day.

Mr. Trombly quietly cleared his throat as if to remind them he was in the room.

Heat infused Thomas's face. Thankfully, a clatter in the kitchen drew her father's attention away.

CHAPTER 6

Thomas dragged the rake through the debris, feeling as useless as the burned rubbish he moved from one spot to another. The lantern light limited his ability to see beyond a small circumference, so he'd have to wait until daylight to thoroughly sift through the pile. But he had to do something.

Off to his right, a glow of lantern light illuminated Noreen's form as she sat perched on the chopping block, shoulders hunched and her hands wrapped around a mug. He should have insisted she go home with Jonathan and Patty. Outside was no place for her. The mosquitoes this time of the year were merciless. And admittedly, he wasn't much company. She hadn't always appreciated his need to have time alone and he had zero desire to listen to her optimistic rhetoric. Sure, he was thankful that she got out safe, that he could finally take short breaths without much pain, and that the fire didn't spread to the barn or past their corn field. But God could have prevented the fire in the first place. Had He wanted to, God could have prevented the past fifteen years of heartache. But who was he to understand the mind of God?

Thomas took a short breath without discomfort, then tested his lungs further and breathed in deeply. This air exchange triggered a cough, which produced a thick substance in the back of his throat. The time he'd had walking pneumonia, he coughed up greenish phlegm. This constant cough hours after the fire was no doubt God's way of reminding him that he wasn't out of the woods. Maybe his thankfulness had been in vain. Next, the muscles between his ribs would spasm. That had been happening sporadically since he went back into the house to retrieve the tin box.

Thomas coughed hard and spat a liquid, coal-tinted substance onto a piece of wood that used to support the tie beam. The sizzle told him the building material and household contents were still too hot to handle. Perhaps tomorrow cleanup could start.

Timorous footsteps approached from behind. He turned slightly and noticed Noreen walking stiffly, trying hard not to spill the contents in the mug she was carrying. "I poured you some *kaffi*," she said softly, eyes on the liquid sloshing over the rim of the mug. "It won't stay warm much longer and without a kettle—" Her words broke. She glanced up and offered a weak smile along with the mug. "I thought you might want to take a break."

He hadn't done any work yet, but he set the rake on the ground and accepted the mug. *"Danki."*

"Can I get you one of the cheese sandwiches Patty brought?"

"Nett nau." He took a drink. The tepid coffee was too strong to appreciate hot or cold. Thomas studied

Noreen as she stared at the smoldering mound. He couldn't help but wonder if she was rehashing memories of better times or simply pondering their losses.

She cleared her throat. "I heard Rebecca gave birth to a boy. Your *bruder* must be thrilled."

"He should be. Levi got the *sohn* he'd wanted."

"You make it sound as if he's been disappointed with his three daughters."

"Of course that isn't true," Thomas snipped. "What man wouldn't feel blessed to be a father? *Sohn* or daughter."

She turned her gaze to the ashes. "I thought I was going to die in the fire. When you showed up in the kitchen . . ."

"You were surprised." He finished her sentence. Despite using a soft, even tone, she recoiled, a wounded—or was it appalled?—look in her eyes.

"I just wanted to thank you for saving *mei* life," she snapped.

They were both tired and on edge. The Bible warns of tribulations, and this was just another trial. Either they would work through it or it would drive a deeper wedge between them. But that wasn't new. He took another swallow of bitter coffee and grimaced.

"I'm sorry," she muttered.

He lifted his mug. "You didn't make the *kaffi*." He cracked a smile, hoping it would help diffuse the tension between them.

"I'm sorry," she repeated, stiffening her back and evening out her tone, "that you felt obligated to save me."

Obligated? He didn't know any man who wouldn't

try to protect his family, rescue them, lead them to safety. It was the husband's duty—his role. He stifled the thought to set her straight and instead took a deep breath and released the tension in a sigh. "You should have gone home with Jonathan and Patty. You won't be comfortable here."

She stared at him hard, eyes watery. "You think I'm too feeble to sleep in the barn, but I'm *nett*."

"That's *nett* what I meant." He tossed the last bit of coffee on the cinders, the hissing reminding him of when water boiled over the kettle spout and hit the surface of the wood stove. Now, the cast-iron stove, with its detached stovepipe, stood by itself, its white enamel coating burned down to the primer.

She reached for his empty mug. "I'm going to make up a bed in the hayloft . . . if you care to join me."

"Later." He snatched the rake off the ground. "I need to watch to make sure the fire doesn't restart." It wouldn't, the firemen had doused it good, but he needed some excuse to avoid spending more time with his wife. She was being emotional again and he wasn't in the mood to tiptoe around her this time.

Noreen walked away, crossing the lawn in the darkness. A few moments later, lantern light flickered in a barn window.

Thomas recalled how they had once promised each other that they'd never go to bed angry, but that was years ago—things were different then.

A sharp spasm in his rib muscles stole his breath. He clasped one hand over his chest and gripped the rake handle tightly, diffusing the pain. *Lord, help me.*

CHAPTER 7

Thomas guided Noreen by the arm down the wooded path. "You're *nett* peeking, are you?"

"*Nay.*" She giggled.

He tipped his head slightly to get a better view of the blindfold placement. Her eyes were covered by his handkerchief.

She sniffed the air, her nose twitching like a rabbit. "I know we're *nett* at the lake." She sniffed again. "Damp. Mossy. Balsam."

He wasn't surprised she figured out quickly they were in the woods. He loved the woodsy scent in the spring especially after it rained. Twigs snapped under his feet.

"Where are you taking me?"

"Almost there." He spotted a fallen tree blocking the path a few feet ahead and he stepped in front of her. "Careful, there's a tree down." He reached for her hand. "Watch your step."

"How do I manage *watching mei* step wearing a blindfold?"

He chuckled. "*Gut* point. I suppose you'll have to rely on me, won't you?" He crossed the rotted log backward, keeping his eyes on Noreen. "Big step."

She followed his instructions, gingerly feeling her way with her foot over the fallen oak. Suddenly, her balance shifted, both arms teetered. "*Ach!* Thomas!"

He caught her before she tumbled to the ground. "I have you."

"I'm *nett* sure I like being led blindly anymore."

"I won't let you fall." He coaxed her forward. "Just a few more feet." He chuckled at the way she shuffled her feet along the mulched bed of pine needles. He stopped her. "Okay, you can look."

She peeled off the cloth binding and scanned the area.

He pointed to a red rag tied around a large maple. "I'm going to build a swing and attach it to that limb so we can swing as we grow old together."

She smiled weakly, confusion spilling into her gaze.

He placed his hands on her shoulders and pivoted her westward. He inched closer and drew her attention to the large oak with the blue rag tied around it. "That's one corner of the *haus*." He pointed to another blue rag tied to a tree a few feet to the left. "That's another and," he said, directing her attention to the heavier wooded area where the third and fourth marked trees were impossible to view because of the dense woods, "the other boundaries are just beyond those pines and before the stand of birch trees."

"The *haus*?"

"Our *haus*."

"And the white rags?"

"Those are the trees I'm keeping. Everything else will be taken down. We'll have a large lawn and garden area. The barn will go somewhere over there." He motioned to the right, but she wasn't following. Her face had turned ashen. He dropped his arm. "What's wrong?"

"Thomas, I can't go against *mei* father's wishes." As tears collected on her lashes, she averted her gaze. "If he knew I was with you—alone in the woods . . ."

"We're *nett* doing anything wrong."

"It doesn't matter." Her mouth trembled and a breathy sob broke loose. "I can't marry you."

• • •

A week after Thomas's proposal, Noreen cut through the woods on his property and spotted him sitting with his back against the maple tree, fiddling with a stick. "I'm glad you got *mei* message."

"You said it was important." He tossed the debarked stick and patted the mossy ground beside him.

"I can't stay long." She scanned the wooded area. Thomas's property was tucked off the main road, but someone could be out mushroom picking and stumble across them. Satisfied they were alone, she plopped down beside him. "I wasn't sure I'd be able to steal away. *Mamm* had me doing laundry all morning. I hung the bedding on the line and then told her I needed more boxes from town." Hearing movement in the foliage, she looked to her right. A squirrel sprung from the bushes and scaled a nearby tree. Blowing out a breath, she caught him studying her.

His eyes twinkling with mischief and sporting a lopsided grin, he placed his arm around her shoulders and gave her a squeeze. "Why are you so nervous?"

"I told you. I'm supposed to be packing—or going after boxes. Not spending time with you in the woods. Alone." But she had to see him.

Thomas frowned. "He's still sore about us leaving the singing early, isn't he?"

She nodded.

"I should have known better. I'm sorry I got you in trouble." He tipped her chin up. "Before supper the other *nacht*, I asked him for your hand in marriage. For his blessing."

"And he said *nay*."

"He said I was unprepared."

Until he motioned to the building site, she hadn't noticed the sawdust around a few of the trees.

"I've been cutting down trees," he said, smiling proudly. "I'm preparing the land."

Thomas cupped his hand over her shoulder and plotted aloud the house he planned to build, the square feet, the number of bedrooms, the pros and cons of building a basement, but she couldn't concentrate on anything but the weight of his arm around her and sharing this place next to him—where she belonged.

"I want a big wraparound porch," he said, lifting his hand long enough to point and remind her of the staked-out markers.

If she closed her eyes, she could visualize the white

painted banisters, the mat at the door for people to wipe their feet, and a colorful array of hanging planters filled with blooming pink petunias. She could see it all because Thomas had a way of describing every detail, bringing it all to life.

"You don't want a wraparound porch?" He broke her silence.

"I do, it's just . . ." It seemed pointless to plan a house they might never share. The distance between the districts would prohibit spending time together. Not like this.

"I'm going to ask your father to *kumm* look at the land. Maybe if he sees where I plan to build and that I've started to timber the property, he will give us his blessing. The lumber for the *haus* is already cured. These logs will be used eventually for the barn. Soon, I'll have enough money to purchase the windows and insulation, and Jonathan is giving me a wood stove that one of his *Englisch* customers no longer wants." He chuckled. "I'm getting carried away, aren't I?"

"You're excited, and I am too."

"Your father will think differently when he sees for himself that I can take care of you."

She would like nothing more than for Thomas to take care of her, to live on this plot of land, and to be his wife. But her father wasn't an easy man to convince, which was why her sisters waited until they were in their midtwenties to get married. After they move next week, Thomas might grow weary of waiting. He might find someone else to share his life. She wished her father hadn't been injured. Then they wouldn't be forced to sell the farm and move. Leaving Thomas, her childhood home, her friends, the district . . . *Cast all your care upon Him, for He cares for you. Don't worry about tomorrow* . . . And don't think about moving, she chided herself.

She reached for Thomas's hand and twined her fingers with his. "Can the kitchen windows face the barn?"

He grinned. "Of course."

"I'd like to have something to look at while I'm preparing the meals and doing dishes," she said, falling into sync with their earlier topic.

"You can have anything you want." He shifted slightly, his gaze intent. "I'm serious, Noreen." He lifted his hand to her face and caressed her cheek with the calloused pads of his fingers. "I want you to have the house of your dreams."

Her insides warmed. She lowered her head as heat reached her cheeks.

"Why are you blushing?" he teased, nudging her shoulder with his.

"Maybe our *haus* needs more bedrooms. I do want a houseful of *kinner*."

"Do I need to build a third story? Because if you want a dozen or more *kinner*, I'm all for it."

"I don't think a third story is necessary." She chuckled softly. "There's plenty of land to build an addition."

Thomas leaned closer. "I knew the first time I kissed you that I was going to marry you."

"You did? I mean—you hardly looked me in the eye for weeks." Obviously since their first kiss, he'd morphed into a man with purpose. He wasn't averting his gaze either. If she was reading his expression right, his big brown eyes had reached a whole new level of intensity.

He traced his finger around the outline of her lips. "I love you."

"I love you too." Her voice quivered as charges electrified her nerves.

He kissed her cheekbone lightly, then trailed soft kisses down the bridge of her nose and to her lips. His slow, careful movements brought her off the ground as she moved into his embrace, parting her lips, tasting a hint of coffee on his tongue. Caught up in the moment, in the tenderness of his touch, something unleashed within her. A soft moan escaped her when his hand moved to the small of her back and he pressed her harder against him. Yes, she was his. This moment would live in her mind forever.

The hardened sound of someone clearing their throat broke them apart. Peering up at her father's scowled expression, her heart pounded, the beats jumping over themselves.

Thomas bolted to his feet. "Mr. Trombly, we were just—"

"Noreen, go to the buggy. *Nau!*"

· · ·

Two days after Noreen's father found them in the woods together, Thomas answered the knock on the screen door hoping to find Noreen, but instead found Jonathan's fiancée, Patty, eyes red-rimmed and sniffling. His brother and Patty's wedding was next week; perhaps her tears had something to do with that.

"Jonathan went into town," Thomas explained.

"I came to give you this." Patty extended a letter-sized tin box toward him. "It's from Noreen. She asked me to give it to you."

"Oh?" He stepped onto the porch and inspected the box. It looked like something she would keep sewing supplies in.

"Noreen wrote you a letter and said it was inside."

"*Danki.*" He eyed Patty, who was obviously shaken. "Are you okay?"

"*Nay, nett* really." Her voice squeaked and her eyes were budding with tears. "I have to go." She twirled around, hurried off the porch, and climbed into her buggy.

His brother would have his hands full when he married that one. The woman's emotions were braided as tight as twine. Thomas closed the door and turned his attention on the tin box. Opening it, he discovered an envelope with his name scrawled on the front and removed it.

Dear Thomas,

I don't even know how to begin this letter. The guilt and shame I feel is overwhelming. I never should've snuck away to meet you in the woods. My father is furious. He still hasn't spoken to me and it's been two days. My mother just cries—a lot.

I heard my parents talking last night about me. My behavior has disgraced the family. They're sending me

to live with my sister. I don't know when. Oh, Thomas,
I shouldn't have gone against their wishes. I hate that
my *daed* looks at me with disgust, like I'm tainted
now. I hate that my mother cries all the time because
of me. But I hate not being with you. Planning our
future, our house.

I don't think I'll have a chance to sneak away again.
I'll have to settle for seeing you on Sunday (that's if I'm
not shipped off before then).

Love,
Noreen

Thomas folded the letter and placed it back in the
tin. He couldn't let Noreen's father think poorly of her.
He had to set things straight.

"Was someone at the door?" His mother set the basket of dirty laundry on the floor.

"Patty, but I told her Jonathan had gone into town."
He pointed to the basket. "I need to run an errand.
Would you like me to carry the laundry basket out to
the *washhaus*?"

"That would be great, *danki*." She followed him outside and scurried ahead of him to open the door to the
washhaus. "You can set it next to the tub."

He lowered the clothes basket.

"Are you going to be home for supper? I think
Jonathan is having his meal with Patty's family. Levi
will be home so it'll be the three of us."

Thomas shrugged. If all went well at Noreen's house,
he'd be invited for supper. "If I'm *nett* back in time, will
you save me a plate?" He'd eat twice.

"You know I will."

He hadn't said anything about asking Noreen to marry him. His mother knew they were courting and had made a few comments about liking Noreen. She even quizzed him the other day about wanting rags to stake out trees, but he didn't spill the beans. Until Noreen's father gave his blessing, what good would it do?

Thomas hitched the buggy and drove to the Trombly farm. From the driveway, he glanced at the kitchen window, then, not seeing Noreen, looked at the large sitting room window and finally lifted his gaze to the bedrooms on the second story. *Noreen, where are you?*

He climbed the porch steps. The door opened as he lifted his hand to knock.

"Noreen's gone," Mrs. Trombly said. "She decided to leave early and start getting things settled."

In order to send Noreen to Mio, they would have had to hire a driver. Why would they have gone to that extra expense when they were set to move in another week? He craned his body to see around her. Boxes lined the wall, but Noreen wasn't anywhere in sight.

Mrs. Trombly shifted her stance to obstruct his view. "I told you, Thomas. Noreen is gone. It's for the best."

For the best? The day his father passed away flashed before his eyes. Days prior to his death, a massive stroke had left him bedridden and unable to care for himself. Thomas recalled overhearing him beg God to take him. "It's for the best," his father had pleaded.

Acid coated the back of Thomas's throat. He should have prayed more for his father, but he was young. He'd never lost anyone to even understand how painful it'd be. Thomas swallowed, but it did nothing for his dry throat. "I've prayed about marrying Noreen." His declaration was as much for himself as it was for Noreen's mother. But even as the words spilled from his mouth, a sinking feeling settled in. God had taken his father—had God also taken Noreen?

"I think you should take up your concerns with *mei* husband—or better yet, talk with the bishop."

Thomas had tried to reason with Mr. Trombly two days ago with no success. After Noreen's father found the two of them kissing, he refused to acknowledge Thomas at all. He merely stood, arms crossed, and glared at Thomas while ordering Noreen to get into the buggy.

"I won't bother you anymore. I'll talk with your husband." He turned, his thoughts whirling with what he needed to say.

"Thomas, wait." Mrs. Trombly hurried down the porch steps and stopped before him. "Don't upset him. He isn't a healthy man."

"I'll try *nett* to." He plodded across the lawn and found Mr. Trombly in the equipment shed. Thomas cleared his throat. "May I speak with you a moment?"

"Noreen's gone," he replied without looking up from placing a wrench inside a crate.

"So I heard." He entered the building.

The elder man crated more tools. "We have nothing to discuss."

"I believe we do." His insides shaking, he fought to keep his voice steady. "The *nacht* I was here for supper and had asked your permission to marry your daughter, you told me I was unprepared. That I had no place for Noreen and me to live."

"I remember."

"That's what we were doing in the woods. I was showing Noreen the property where I plan to build a *haus*." He kept to himself how Noreen had sent a message to meet her there. Her father might never forgive her defiance.

"That's *nett* all you were doing," he grumbled.

"We kissed. Nothing more."

He harrumphed. "Because I stopped you."

"*Nay*. Because I love and respect Noreen."

Mr. Trombly gripped the worktable, his knuckles turning white. Making short raspy breaths, the man's complexion paled. His legs wobbled half a second and before Thomas could respond, Noreen's father crumbled to the floor, clutching his chest.

CHAPTER 8

PRESENT DAY

After a sleepless night alone in the barn, Noreen arrived at Patty's house early enough to help prepare breakfast. But Patty took one look at her disheveled appearance at the doorway and shuttled Noreen into the washroom with a clean dress, then instructed her to come to the kitchen once she'd freshened up.

Noreen splashed cold water on her face, instantly feeling more refreshed and alert. She scrubbed the soot off her hands, arms, face, and neck. Better. Except her hair still reeked of smoke, but she'd wash it later when she had more time. She slipped into the clean dress, then headed toward the commotion of clattering dishes. The scent of bacon frying wet her mouth with anticipation and prompted quicker steps.

"Do you feel better after washing up?" Patty poured coffee into two mugs.

"*Jah*, much better. *Danki* for the clean clothes."

Patty's thirteen-year-old daughter Amanda stood at the stove, spatula in hand. The two younger girls, ten-year-old Kathleen and eight-year-old Karen, were busy setting the table. All three girls had their mother's blue eyes and golden hair and worked in unison much like Noreen and her sisters had growing up.

Patty handed Noreen a mug of coffee. "Let's sit for a moment and enjoy our *kaffi*." She pulled out a chair for Noreen, then plunked down on the one opposite.

Noreen admired her friend's stamina. Patty's day started before sunrise and she was still going strong even after the rest of the household went to bed. She often said her favorite time of the day was first thing in the morning when she had a few minutes of silence and could be alone. Although Noreen had agreed, she couldn't relate. For her, she was alone most of the morning, afternoon, and evening. She had to work to fill the silence.

"You didn't sleep well," Patty said. "I see it in your eyes." She added sugar to her cup and stirred it. "I wish you would have stayed here last *nacht* instead of sleeping in that old barn."

"I slept all right." Noreen looked at her steaming beverage. "Once I fell asleep," she added, not lifting her gaze.

"And that took all *nacht*, didn't it?"

Noreen forced a smile. She couldn't admit the truth—marital problems, not the fire, had kept her awake most of the night. She glanced at the plate on the counter heaped with bacon and over to Amanda at the stove, flipping pancakes. She turned back to Patty. "Are you sure the girls don't need our help?"

Patty gazed lovingly at her daughters. "They have it under control. Amanda is turning out to be a very good cook."

Amanda looked their direction, the tight mother-daughter bond evident in the wide smile she gave Patty.

A wisp of envy tugged at Noreen. It was bad enough she was often envious of Patty's solid relationship with Jonathan, but seeing her daughter's affection left Noreen starving for something she could never have. *Sip the coffee and think of other things.*

"Noreen?"

Patty's tone caught Noreen's attention. "Did you say something?"

"I asked what your plans were today."

"I was thinking this might be a *gut* time to visit *mei* family." Noreen avoided Patty's gaze when she noticed her sister-in-law's eyebrows rise. "I haven't been to Mio for a visit in a while. *Mei* nieces and nephews are practically grown."

"And you think *nau* is the right time?"

Her sister-in-law must think it was odd to consider leaving so soon after losing the house. But Noreen couldn't stand to sleep another night alone in the barn. Besides, she would be out of Thomas's way. Before she had a chance to explain, the kitchen door opened.

Jonathan and the boys entered with the milk containers. Thomas, to Noreen's surprise, trailed in last. He'd been busy tending the livestock this morning and hadn't committed to coming for breakfast. At the same time, Thomas had insisted Noreen should go, and this time, she didn't argue about him needing to eat as well. He was a grown man.

Thomas glanced at her and smiled. "You look all cleaned up."

She nodded. He didn't look bad for not coming to bed last night. He'd changed into the set of Jonathan's clothes Patty had donated. Thomas's hands and face were not spotless, but cleaner. He must have washed up at the pump.

Patty pushed her chair back and rose. "I'll pour you two some *kaffi*." She took her youngest child, Matthew, by the shoulders and faced him toward the hallway. At the same time she signaled for her other two sons to go wash up.

Jonathan nudged Thomas's arm. "Grab a seat." He strode to the end of the table and sat.

"We sure appreciate you having us over for breakfast," Thomas said, taking the chair opposite Noreen.

"You're always welcome here," Jonathan said.

"Excuse me." Noreen slid back from the table, feeling awkward. She hadn't sat while others worked around her since she was a youngster.

Amanda set the plate of stacked pancakes on the table while Karen carried a jar of maple syrup. Kathleen picked up the plate of crispy bacon. A few slices fell off the plate and hit the counter, but Karen was there to scoop them up. She stole a nibble off one piece only to be scolded by her mother for eating before the blessing was said.

Patty handed Noreen a mug of coffee for Thomas. Noreen added a dash of cream, as he liked it, then placed it on the table in front of him.

"*Danki*," he said, interrupting the conversation he and Jonathan were having about lumber estimates.

By the time the boys returned to the kitchen and

settled into their places at the table, the meal was ready. Jonathan directed everyone to bow their heads and after a brief moment of silence, was first to start filling his plate.

The conversation about needed building materials continued between the men. Listening to Thomas explain where he planned to rebuild, Noreen noted a hint of excitement in his tone.

Patty passed the maple syrup to her husband, but directed her question to Thomas. "Do you plan on building right away?"

Thomas shrugged. "I hope to have it roughed in before snowfall."

Jonathan drizzled syrup over his pancakes, then passed the jar to Thomas. "The boys and I will help after we harvest the potatoes."

"*Danki.* Levi plans to help once he takes his pumpkins to market. His crop is twice the size as last year and with a new *boppli*, Rebecca won't be able to help him."

"I heard they found a buyer who plans to ship them all downstate," Patty interjected.

Jonathan glanced at his wife and sighed. "We should have planted a big pumpkin patch instead of putting in all those acres of potatoes." He shifted his attention back to Thomas. "The cutworms were bad despite using oak-leaf mulch and sprinkling wood ash around the base of the plants."

"Maybe pumpkins are the way to go, but do you want to spend your days rolling pumpkins to make sure they don't grow lopsided?"

"You have a point." Jonathan stabbed his fork into

the fried potatoes with vigor. "*Mei* knees couldn't handle it."

Posen had plenty of potato farms and fall was always busy, especially for the Amish farmers who harvested their crops using horse-drawn machinery.

"Noreen," Patty said. "If you're going to be out of town, I can organize the meals for the *haus* raising."

"I—ah . . ." Noreen spied Thomas with his fork paused in front of his mouth, his face pinched in a scowl. She should have mentioned going to visit her family to Thomas before saying something to Patty. Her sister-in-law shifted in her seat. *Please, don't say anything else.*

"We can talk about it another time," Patty suggested.

Thomas held Noreen's gaze several seconds before setting his fork on the plate and picking up his mug of coffee.

Jonathan and Patty exchanged glances. The girls were having their own hushed conversation at the other end of the table and the boys were too busy eating to notice the sudden tension.

"Your pancakes are really good, Amanda," Noreen said. "Did you use buttermilk?"

"*Nay*, just regular milk."

"But she's made them with buttermilk before," Patty said.

Noreen took a bite of the pancakes, even though she was no longer hungry. The food clumped in the back of her throat.

Thomas avoided eye contact the remainder of the meal. When his plate was clean, he excused himself, saying he needed to get started on the burn pile.

"I'll be home after I help clean up the kitchen," Noreen said.

Thomas donned his hat at the door. "Take your time."

Jonathan walked outside with him as the boys scurried away from the table. The girls immediately began clearing the dishes.

Noreen took the last sip of coffee, then rose from the chair. As she reached for her plate, Patty grasped her hand.

"I need you to look at some material," Patty said.

Noreen followed her sister-in-law into a small, all-purpose room, where stacked crates were labeled Rags, Mending, or Material.

"I don't know what's going on," Patty began, "but you need to go home and straighten things out with your husband."

Her sister-in-law was right. Things with Thomas had been strained for too long. Noreen's eyes moistened. She tilted her face toward the ceiling, hoping the tears wouldn't fall. "He didn't *kumm* to bed last *nacht.*"

"I'm sure he was worried about another fire starting."

"That was his excuse, but the firemen said it wasn't likely." She drew a breath and slowly released it. "He blames me for the fire."

"That's all the more reason for you to go to him *nau*. You can't let hard feelings *kumm* between you. You've been through harder times than this and you made it."

Noreen nodded, though she wasn't convinced. They had lived—or rather tiptoed—around the pain that tore them apart.

Patty handed her a cloth. "Dry your tears and go to your husband. He's hurting too."

"I know," she whispered. "I've prayed something would . . ." *Oh, Lord, this is hard to admit.*

"Would what?"

"I asked God to . . . to do something about *mei* marriage. We're like two strangers living together. Thomas isn't happy . . . It's *nett* how I thought—" She dabbed the cloth at the corners of her eyes. *Breathe.*

"Don't stop praying for him. A *fraa*'s prayers are very powerful."

"I believe that too. I was so afraid when Thomas ran back into the *haus.* I had a horrible feeling that God was answering *mei* prayer—doing something about our broken marriage. Oh, Patty, I thought I was going to lose him." Noreen trembled. She couldn't shake the feeling that things would never be the same.

. . .

The ashes had cooled enough to load the wagon to take to the county dump. Thomas scooped a shovelful of debris, then tossed the contents into the bed of the wagon, his thoughts concentrated on Noreen. Knowing she had made plans to spend time with her family in Oscoda County, he hadn't been able to think about much else.

"Thomas?"

His wife's voice stopped him from shoveling and he turned to face her. "I didn't notice you walk up," he said dryly.

"I thought you might need some help." She grabbed

the rake leaning against the side of the buckboard and began working on the opposite side of the mound, where the sitting room used to be.

The task was dirty, exhausting, something she didn't need to be doing. Yet she worked the rake swiftly, jabbing at the rubble as if she had something to prove. "Be careful you don't get cut. Some of the metal pieces are jagged."

She pulled the remnants of her home into a pile. "I'm all right."

Of course you are. He resumed shoveling. She hadn't taken his advice—hadn't needed his advice in years. He thrust the shovel under a six-foot section of tin roofing material and pried the end of it up. He reached for the tin and gave it a tug, but the metal was awkward to grip wearing the heavy leather gloves, and it slipped through his hold. With another hard pull he freed it from a section of roof joist that hadn't burned. He hauled the metal to the wagon, its tinny clang echoing as he tossed it with the other damaged material.

Thomas patted the ashes off his gloves. Removing debris piece by piece, it would take days to get this mess cleaned up. He stole a glance at Noreen swinging the rake. Her palms would be splintered and rubbed raw by noon working the rake bare-handed. He strode to the barn. The gloves he used to muck stalls reeked, but they'd do the job. Returning back to the pile, Thomas stopped before Noreen, dropped the barn gloves on the ground at his feet, and began peeling off the ones he'd been wearing. "Use these."

"Oh, I couldn't take your gloves."

"I have another pair." He held her rake so she could put the gloves on. "When were you going to tell me about your plans to visit your family?"

"I haven't had much opportunity to talk with you about anything." She shoved her tiny hand into the glove with a thrust. Lifting her gaze, her eyes pierced his. "Have I?"

He wasn't opposed to her leaving. Only that he'd heard the news from Patty. His wife should have spoken with him first.

Noreen took the rake back, brows furrowed. "You broke your promise last *nacht*."

"So that's why you're running back home." His curt tone made her flinch, though he offered no apology. He'd end up chiding himself later for his actions, he always did. The sound of buggy wheels crunching over gravel drew his attention. He recognized the bishop in the driver's seat immediately, but had to squint to see his wife, Alice, seated beside him. The buggy rolled to a stop next to the barn. Thomas swiped the gloves off the ground and headed toward the bishop's buggy. He and Alice climbed out, scanning the area.

"It looks so different in daylight," Alice said.

"*Jah*," Thomas said.

Noreen approached, smiling. "It's nice of you to stop by."

"I brought sandwiches, potato salad, and cookies for dessert." Alice signaled Noreen with a quick wave. The two women walked to the back of the buggy.

"I see you're already busy cleaning up," the bishop said.

Thomas nodded. "I wanted to get started on it as soon as possible. It won't be long before the first frost, and I'd like to be under roof by winter."

Bishop Zook removed his hat and ran his hand through his thin gray hair, then put his hat back on. "You don't plan to rebuild on the same site, do you?"

"*Nay*, I think the new *haus* will go between that stand of birch trees"—he pointed to a cluster of trees off to his right—"and the big maple." Thomas caught sight of Noreen in his peripheral vision, her lackluster expression one of profound sadness. He hadn't told her the plans or his intention of taking down the big maple that they had once sat under while planning their future. He had promised to build a swing and mount it on the low-hanging branch. But that was fifteen years ago. It wasn't like they spent much time together in the yard. His memory flashed to the time he guided her blindfolded down the wooded path to this location. He'd tied blue rags around the trees to mark this very spot.

"Once everyone finishes harvesting their crops, we'll organize a work bee. What about your winter wheat?"

"It's planted." The weather dictated planting and harvest times, understandably so. An early frost would be detrimental. "The sugar beets can wait until after the *haus* is built and the corn crop is gone. What wasn't consumed by fire was destroyed by excess water. It'll mold."

"Don't worry. I'll see that we all give fodder for your silage bin."

"*Danki.*" Thomas studied the sandy soil. He wished there was another way. He didn't like taking handouts.

"Where did you and Noreen stay last *nacht*?"

"Here. I wanted to make sure the fire didn't start again."

The bishop's gaze traveled over the destruction. "Our *daadihaus* is empty."

Thomas pretended to ponder the offer. Sleeping on a mattress rather than on a mound of hay did sound tempting.

"Alice would love the company."

Don't commit. Their lives would be an open book—his life—Noreen was leaving.

"Alice already started airing it out."

"I appreciate your offer." *But . . . but what?* Jonathan's mother-in-law lived in his *daadihaus*. Levi and Rebecca just had a new *boppli*. He and Noreen had no place to go.

"Lunch is ready," Alice called from a picnic blanket placed under the crimson canopy of the big maple.

Thomas glanced at his dirty hands. "I better wash up."

The bishop examined his own and ambled alongside Thomas to the pump.

Once cleaned up, they approached the picnic area. Noreen waited until Thomas sat down before handing him a plate with a ham-and-cheese sandwich and two scoops of potato salad.

"Danki." Thomas cracked a smile at Noreen, keenly aware the bishop and Alice were watching. He couldn't hide their strained relationship. Perhaps he shouldn't try.

"It's a little chilly today," Alice said, breaking the silence.

Shoveling debris, Thomas hadn't noticed, but he appreciated the bishop for agreeing with Alice and continuing the conversation about the soon-approaching winter season.

Every year, speculations were made if it'd be a hard winter, which in northern Michigan it almost always was. Noreen was quiet. Probably reflecting on the worst snowstorm of all time—the first winter they were married. The snow was waist high in some areas, the wind brutal, and, trapped inside, they both despised the coldness before the winter was over.

"Would you like a peanut butter cookie?" Alice held out the tin of cookies.

"*Danki.*" Thomas took one and bit into it, but his appetite was gone, thinking about that winter so long ago. He wasn't sure why the flood of memories had to appear now. Perhaps it had something to do with Noreen wanting to leave.

Once the meal ended, he and the bishop wandered over to the mound of ashes, leaving the women to continue their talk about curtains and rugs.

Bishop Zook peered over the sideboards of the wagon. "Have you found anything salvageable?"

Thomas shook his head. "I don't expect to."

"You never know." The bishop scanned the massive pile as though silently taking inventory of all that was lost.

Thomas recalled the long hours—a labor of love—it took to build the house. How proud and excited he was to hammer the last nail. The feeling of accomplishment so grand, everything else paled in comparison. *Take heed and beware of covetousness, for one's life does not consist in the abundance of the things he possesses.*

Recalling the parable of the rich fool, Thomas pushed his prideful memories to the back of his mind.

Bishop Zook cleared his throat. "I understand Noreen was in the *haus* when it caught fire. How is she doing?"

"She's fine." His matter-of-fact answer was met by Bishop Zook's disapproving frown. Thomas should have made a point to sound sincere even though what he said was true. Anytime he would ask Noreen how she was doing, she always replied *fine*. About everything. Always just fine.

Bishop Zook glanced over in the women's direction, then quirked his brow at Thomas. "You sure about that? I've known the two of you—and both your parents— for years . . ." Bishop Zook droned on unaware Thomas had tuned him out.

Thomas didn't need more sage advice. He'd be a rich man if he'd collected everyone's two cents over the years. Fatigue settled into his bones. Too many cookies. Now he needed a nap. Thomas rubbed his temples.

Bishop Zook stopped talking and, with a slightly cocked head, eyed Thomas hard. "You haven't been listening, have you?"

"Sorry. I haven't had any—" *sleep*. He went silent, averting his gaze to the debris pile. "*Nay*, I wasn't listening. I'm sorry."

"I know this can be a stressful time for both you and Noreen. Men and women don't always react or even grieve alike."

He should have known. Noreen said something this morning to Patty, and his sister-in-law felt obliged to tell her cousin, Alice, who in turn told the bishop.

"I suggest you pray."

"I do." He prayed, read the Bible, studied the Scriptures, followed the *Ordnung*. What else must he do?

"Do you and Noreen pray together?"

Thomas tugged his collarless shirt. "Sometimes."

Bishop Zook was silent a moment. "God calls us to dwell with our wives with understanding," he said, quoting from 1 Peter. "'Give honor to the wife, as to the weaker vessel, and as being heirs together of the grace of life'"—he patted Thomas's shoulder—"'that your prayers may not be hindered.'"

Thomas nodded.

"Make more of an effort and watch and see how God responds."

More effort, sure. That'll be easy. He forced a smile. "I will."

CHAPTER 9

Thomas wiped his hands along the sides of his pants and drew a deep breath before entering the hospital room. Mr. Trombly was lying on the bed, an oxygen mask covered his nose and mouth, and wires connected him to a machine beeping in tune with squiggly lines bouncing on a wall monitor. Thomas stepped closer, careful not to wake Mr. Trombly. His withered form appeared emaciated. If Thomas hadn't seen his chest rise and fall, he would have thought the man had died.

Someone cleared their throat and Thomas jolted.

"I didn't mean to startle you," Bishop Zook said.

Thomas swallowed hard. When he received news that Mr. Trombly had wanted to see him, he wasn't expecting to meet with the bishop at the same time. "How is he?"

Before the bishop could answer, Mr. Trombly's eyes opened. He lifted a trembling hand to his face and pushed the oxygen mask away from his mouth. "Thomas?"

"I'm here." The man's skin held a gray, deathly cast.

He'd aged in the month since his admission, looking now to be a man in his eighties rather than the active man in his late fifties.

"How long have I been here?" Mr. Trombly's voice strained.

"Thirty-two days." Thomas cleared his throat, unsure what else to say. He had tried to visit several times only to be turned away by Mrs. Trombly. When Thomas inquired, he was given the same abbreviated information: *"He's alive, his heart is weak."* She was holding back what she really wanted to say, that Thomas had stressed her husband—caused the heart attack.

"I'm dying," he rasped.

Thomas jerked his gaze over to Bishop Zook who, sitting quietly in the corner, nodded solemnly.

A knot formed in Thomas's throat. He hadn't meant for this to happen. He merely wanted to obtain Mr. Trombly's blessing to marry his daughter.

"After *mei* accident—"

The man's face pinched in what looked like pain.

Thomas turned to the bishop. "Should we call the nurse?"

Bishop Zook pushed off the chair and approached the bed. Standing next to the hand railing opposite Thomas, he assisted Mr. Trombly with repositioning the oxygen mask. "Would you like me to tell him, Abe?"

Mr. Trombly flicked his eyelids.

"When he was hospitalized after his accident, the doctor found a tiny mass on his kidney. Apparently it's growing," the bishop said.

"Can't they do surgery?"

He shook his head.

His breathing more controlled, Mr. Trombly removed his mask once again. "That's why we were moving—tell him, Menno."

The bishop cleared his throat. "Abe wanted to make sure Esther was taken care of. He wanted her surrounded by her daughters because when the time came"—he paused briefly—"Esther wouldn't be able to keep the farm going. In Mio, Verna and Carol Diane's husbands would take care of things. In addition, they would look after Noreen."

"I would have taken care of Noreen and Mrs. Trombly," Thomas said. "I would have made sure she kept her farm."

"It's all been taken care of *nau*. The farm has already been sold."

A combination of resentment and sorrow warred within him. After his father passed away, Mr. Trombly had given Thomas a job, even praised him for his hard work and for taking care of his mother. And yet, Mr. Trombly wouldn't consider him for his daughter.

"Do you love *mei* daughter?"

"Yes, with all *mei* heart."

"Will you promise . . . to always love her? Put . . . her needs," he rasped, the veins in his neck bulging. "Put her needs above your own?"

"Yes, I promise." Tears stung Thomas's eyes. "Do we have your blessing to get married?"

"Build your *haus*," he wheezed, then his eyes closed.

. . .

JULY, FIFTEEN YEARS AGO

"Ready?" Thomas called out to his brothers, Jonathan and Levi, who were squatting next to the framed eight-foot section of wall. "On three. One, two"—Thomas sucked in a breath—"three." In unison, they hoisted the studded wall and jimmied it into position. Sweat rivered down the creases of Thomas's face, stinging his eyes and coating his lips with saltiness as he held the wall.

"Put a level on it, Levi," Jonathan said.

"It's *gut.*"

Thomas drove the nail shank into the stud. Once toenailed to the subfloor baseplate with heavy-duty nails, Thomas stepped back and admired the work. After several weeks of flooding rain that delayed pouring the foundation, it felt good to move forward with the project. Noreen had been gone two long months and he had every intention of marrying her by the end of summer, which meant having the house built.

Levi jangled a handful of nails. "Are we standing the next wall before we break for lunch?"

Thomas wanted to keep going, but Jonathan would make the decision. His older brother had more building experience having worked for an *Englisch* construction company for several years and finishing his own house prior to marrying Patty. Of course when Jonathan was building his place, it wasn't during haying season, so he had help from most of the men in the district. Thomas couldn't wait until after harvest. Noreen had indicated in her last letter that her father's condition was failing quickly.

Jonathan removed a hankie from his pocket and

wiped the sweat from his brow. His face was red from being in the sun too long and his lips looked chapped. "I'd like to get as much done today," he said, licking his lips. "I have to work the rest of the week."

"Let's do it." Thomas measured the sixteen-inch center and pencil-marked the spot to nail the two-by-four stud, then measured another sixteen inches for the next stud. Jonathan sawed the boards and Levi nailed the steel plates. They worked well together. At one time they had even discussed forming their own construction company made up of Amish men.

Before long another wall was built and anchored in place. Thomas slid the hammer through the loop of his tool belt and patted his rumbling stomach. "Let's eat."

Levi shed his tool belt and climbed off the concrete slab. Jonathan set the handsaw down.

"*Daed* would have been pleased that you're using his hammer," Jonathan said, sitting next to Thomas under the shade of the maple tree. "His father had given it to *Daed* when he started building the farmhouse for *Mamm*."

Thomas ran his thumb over the hammer's smooth steel head. He'd never known his grandfather. Thomas was in school when his father died, but the hammer held special significance, knowing it'd been used to build his grandfather's, father's, and now his home. He unwrapped the foil from his meat-loaf sandwich and took a bite.

Jonathan jabbed his elbow into Levi's side. "I have some of *Daed*'s tools for you when you're ready to get married and build a *haus*."

Levi stretched out his long legs before him. "They'll rust before I'm ready to get hitched."

Thomas chuckled. "*Mei* thoughts exactly. That is until I started courting Noreen." He recalled his initial reaction when Mr. Trombly was trapped under the thrasher and had asked him to watch over her. She had just reached the age of courting, and watching over her meant driving her home from the Sunday singings. At first he hadn't wanted to tie up his time, not that he was interested in another girl—he wasn't. His heart was still wounded from Rachel jumping the fence and he wasn't keen on starting a new relationship. But he'd made that promise to Noreen's father and, as it turned out, she was easy to talk to. He recalled the first time he kissed her and how she'd complained he'd stolen her breath. Little did she know at the time, she'd stolen more than his breath, she'd stolen his heart.

Thomas glanced up as the sun disappeared behind a dark cloud. They didn't need more rain. Construction had already been delayed enough. He took another bite of his sandwich, washed it down with a drink of water drawn from the well, then finished the meal. He had a letter sitting in the buggy from Noreen he was anxious to read.

CHAPTER 10

"What all did you tell Patty?" Thomas said through gritted teeth as he waved good-bye to the bishop and his wife.

"Is this about me going to visit *mei* family?"

"You tell me."

"I don't have to go." She snatched the rake and headed to the pile.

He closed his eyes, started to count to ten, but only made it to three. He stormed after her. "Fine. You want to go tomorrow? I'll arrange for someone to drive you."

"It's better than sleeping in the barn by myself." She whirled the rake into a cinder pile and spiked something tinny with the prongs.

He shouldn't have to remind her, but he did. "I wanted to make sure another fire didn't start."

"The fireman said it was unlikely." She whirled the rake again.

Thomas conjured a rebuttal in his mind but chose to hold his words. Perhaps they did need time apart. At the same time, he'd rather her family not know about their strained marriage. He had promised her father before he passed away that he would take care of Noreen—love her at all times, put her needs above his own. He'd failed her.

Thomas marched over to the wagon and grabbed the shovel propped against it. The lack of sleep was wearing on him. His muscles were tight. Working a few minutes in what used to be the kitchen, he uncovered the porcelain sink. Intact. Perhaps reusable. He removed a section of drywall that had fallen into the basin and tossed it aside. Lifting the sink, he groaned under its weight, made it a few steps, then set it down.

"I'll help." Noreen dropped her rake.

"Stay there. You shouldn't be trekking through this stuff." He lifted the sink again and was able to move it to the edge of the pile. Blowing out a few quick breaths, he pointed to the shovel he'd set down. "If you would move the shovel so I don't trip, I should be able to get this." He hoisted the sink once more and carried it to the wagon where he lowered it to the ground.

"Do you need help getting it into the wagon?"

He shook his head. "I think we can reuse it."

She looked at the sink and grimaced. "But it leaked."

There she went again, reminding him of his inadequacies as a husband. Noreen had made a point of saying something every time she emptied the pail of water he'd placed under the sink to catch the drips.

"Did you forget?"

Thomas clenched his jaw. "We don't have unlimited resources to replace everything." He struggled to keep his tone even. "Besides, the leak was small."

She frowned.

"Where did you put the tin box yesterday?"

Her brows crinkled. "On the shelf in the washroom. Why?"

"Just wanted to know." He didn't want to frighten Noreen. There hadn't been an Amish home burglarized since last year when several of the homes were broken into while everyone was at the bishop's house for Sunday service. Thomas glanced at the amount of stuff in the wagon, mindful of not overloading it to where the horses wouldn't be able to pull it. He'd load a few more items, then make a run to the county dump.

"Do you want me to bring you the tin?"

"*Nay*. I don't want it lost in this mess." He glanced at the pump. "I'm going to get a drink. Do you want me to fill a cup for you?"

"*Nay danki*, but I'll get yours."

"That's okay." He lumbered to the pump. Even in their bickering, she was a dutiful wife. *Lord, I wish the relationship could be like it was when we were first married.* He cranked the handle until icy water sputtered up from the well, then cupped his hands to catch it. After several satisfying gulps, he glanced at the work yet to do. His gaze stopped on Noreen who was standing off to the side, shoulders hunched and shaking. *What happened?* He dashed across the yard. "Are you hurt?"

"*Nay*," she whimpered. Her eyes filled with tears as she held up a soiled remnant of material not much bigger than a lap cover. "Do you know what this is?" Her voice hitched.

He studied the various shades of green blocks. "It's our wedding quilt, right?"

She nodded.

"Can it be fixed?"

"Nothing is fixable. It's—it's all destroyed." Her eyes flicked with anger. She stormed over to the wagon and threw the scrap of blanket over the sideboard with the other trash. "There isn't *anything* worth salvaging, is there?"

His throat swelled. She wasn't talking about the house anymore, not even the quilt. *How can I fix it, Lord? Show me, please.*

She turned her back to him and, falling against the wagon, buried her face in the crook of her arm.

Thomas inched up behind her. "Please don't cry."

"I shouldn't have gone to the cellar."

"What are you talking about?"

"It's *mei* fault we lost the *haus*. I know that's why you're upset."

He shook his head, but she wouldn't have seen him. "I'm upset because it seems like we've had one thing after another go wrong for years. I'm mad at myself. I should have cleaned the stovepipe when I noticed creosol building up." He inched closer, placing his hand on her shoulder. "Don't blame yourself. The fire isn't your fault." When she didn't immediately respond, he gently pivoted her shoulder in order to see her face. The heaviness in her eyes told him the bishop had been right. He should have been more aware of her feelings and not so callous. "I'm sorry, Noreen—for everything."

And in that very moment, it felt as though God was removing the blinders from his eyes. Noreen was adorable with soot smudged on her nose and forehead.

Her eyes held a sadness that instantly caused his throat to tighten.

He swallowed hard. "I didn't exactly break *mei* promise last *nacht*."

Tears collected on her lashes and she lowered her head.

Wrong thing to say. He lifted her chin with his thumb and gazed into her puffy, red-rimmed eyes. "I promised I would never go to bed angry."

She stood straighter as though readying herself to respond. Her icy, blank stare could freeze fireflies midflight, but he was made of stronger stuff than a bug.

Thomas grinned, but that didn't simmer the angry hornet. "I never went to bed—*yet*," he explained.

Her shoulders went limp. When she blinked, tears spilled over her lashes, clearing a path down her soot-smeared cheeks.

He kissed her forehead despite the dirt, inhaling the smoky scent on her *kapp*. "I've been short with you lately and I'm sorry."

"It feels like we've lost each other," she whispered.

Thomas inwardly cringed. *Lord, I never meant to cause her pain.* She was right. They had lost each other . . . years ago.

Noreen squared her shoulders. "We should get back to work."

Lord, we need You. Our marriage needs You. "Wait," he said, reaching for her hand. "Let's pray."

"*Nau?*"

He nodded. Normally, they said their prayers silently at the table or before bed. They hadn't been as faithful in their devotions as when they were first married. He reached for her other hand and held them both as much for support as for leadership. He didn't wait to see if she bowed her head before closing his eyes.

"Father, we're like sheep that have lost our way," he began. "Please, help us. Restore our marriage. Show us how to rebuild what we've allowed the trials in life to erode." His voice choked as he thought about his words. "I love Noreen. I want to be a *gut* husband. Show me how to start over before it's too late. Amen."

"That was beautiful, Thomas."

His eyes moistened. These sappy emotions had sent him off-kilter. Until he held Noreen's hand and began praying, he hadn't realized how much he'd missed her. Missed the intimacy they once shared. "We're going to start praying more together. Every day."

A smile creased her lips.

He squeezed her hands reassuringly. "The fact that the quilt didn't burn completely means something. Perhaps it was God's way of getting our attention. A remnant of hope, *jah*?"

She half shrugged, then looked over her shoulder at the mound. "We should get back to work."

As she turned, he stepped in her path. "I meant those words I prayed. I want to be a *gut* husband. I love you, Noreen."

She stared at him quietly, lips trembling.

Say something. Don't give up on us. When she averted her gaze, he continued. "I was thinking about lying down for a little while."

"*Jah*, I imagine you must be tired." She flipped her

thumb over her shoulder at the ash pile. "I—um—I'll see if I can fill up the wagon and get it ready to take to the dump."

He moved closer, wrapping his arms around her small waist. "I was hoping you would *kumm* with me. *Fraa*."

. . .

AUGUST, FIFTEEN YEARS EARLIER
"*Guder mariye*, Mrs. King."

Noreen opened her eyes to find Thomas standing at the bedside, wearing only his pajama bottoms, a coffee mug in each hand. She grasped the edge of the quilt, covering herself as she scooted into an upright position. "I didn't expect *kaffi* in bed."

He set the steaming mugs on the nightstand. "I know you don't like it when it's hot. Let it cool a few minutes." He slipped under the cover and sidled up beside her.

"I still can't believe we're married," she said, her voice quivering in the same nervous pitch as last night when they climbed under their wedding quilt together for the first time.

"You don't need this blanket," he said, uncovering her bare shoulder. He kissed her exposed skin. "I love you, Mrs. King."

"I love you too." She giggled when he playfully nuzzled her cheek.

He watched her intently.

Looking him in the eye, she said, "You have to promise me something."

"Anything." He kissed her neck.

She stifled another giggle before it erupted. "I'm serious about this, Thomas. You have to look at me and promise you'll never go to bed angry—about anything."

He propped up on his elbow, his hair ruffled, and smiled. "I promise." He winked. "*Nau*, may I have a few minutes of your time this morning before I have to leave you to milk cows?"

"Uh-huh," she said, sliding completely under the quilt.

CHAPTER 11

An angelic glow of sunlight shed through the cracks of the barn planks. Noreen squinted at the flecks of hay dust floating in the golden haze of morning light and sighed. God had a marvelous way of making all things new. Beautiful. She hadn't felt this cherished in a long time.

The beam of sunlight highlighted the spot next to her—where her husband should be. The goose-down pillow still had the indent where Thomas had rested his head. Exhausted from lack of sleep, he'd fallen asleep quickly. She'd laid next to him, listening to his muffled snore and feeling blessed. God had answered her prayers.

Something clanged directly below the loft where the milking station was located. Thomas muttered something to one of the cows. Noreen tossed the cover back and scrambled to her feet. She dug through the paper bag Patty had left with her, found a clean dress and apron, and changed into her sister-in-law's garments. The freshly laundered scent wafted, making her smile. Until she took one look at the dirt caked under her fingernails and the smudges of soot on her arms. A clean dress would do little to make her presentable. Noreen adjusted her *kapp* and pulled a piece of hay from her hair. She needed a brush. Noreen searched the bag. Not finding anything, she resigned to accept her unkempt appearance.

She made her way to the wooden ladder and descended slowly. Beyond the wall partition, Thomas was milking a cow—and singing. Something Noreen hadn't heard in years, but it'd been years since she helped Thomas with the barn chores. Usually she was busy preparing breakfast while he did the morning milking. She eased around the wall divider and into the milking area. The cow munched on grain while immobilized in the milk stanchion. Thomas sat on the three-legged stool, his forehead resting against the cow's side, and his hands gently squeezing down on the front teats.

The horses needed feeding—the hogs, piglets, and chickens, too—but hearing Thomas serenade the jersey was more enticing. His mood had certainly lifted since getting some sleep. Noreen leaned against the wall. His deep baritone voice still held the same soothing quality she had longed to hear again. She rested her head against the pole, pretended it was Thomas's shoulder, and for the briefest second, she was fifteen years younger, life was growing in her belly, and she and Thomas were filled with joy.

"How long have you been standing there?"

Opening her eyes, she found him smiling, his gaze on her midsection. She dropped her hand and straightened her posture. "I haven't heard you sing in a long time."

He shrugged. "The cows are a captured audience."

"*Jah*, I seem to remember you said singing kept them calm."

His smile faded and he returned to milking.

Wrong thing to say. Noreen rubbed her hands on the sides of her dress. "What can I do to help? I haven't milked a cow . . ." *since we got married,* "in a while. But I think I can get the hang of it again."

He glanced up, a twinkle of surprise in his eyes. "Are you sure you want to?"

She nodded.

He stood. "I seem to recall you were a fast milker."

"A better singer," she said, making her way across the concrete slab to where another stool was suspended on a spike protruding from the wall.

"Let me get it." He crossed the manure gutter, which ran the length of the barn and dumped into the compost area outside. "You don't have to do this."

Unlike many men in the district, her husband had never expected her to help with the barn chores. But she had to do something. Without meals to prepare or windows to wash, she felt useless. "I'd like to help."

Thomas hesitated a moment, then reached for the stool and brought it down. He carried it over to the stanchion and placed it beside Bess. "Have a seat. I'll get the bucket of sudsy water and a rag."

"I, ah . . ." She stared at the cow chewing its cud. "Does she kick?" A wife shouldn't have to ask whether or not their cow kicked. She was her husband's helpmate, or at least that was supposed to be her role.

"Maybe you shouldn't do this." He bent down and picked up the stool.

"*Nay*, please." She grasped his forearm. "I want to help." She wanted to get over the fear of what kept her out of the barn.

"I don't want you to get hurt again," he whispered.

She smiled, finding comfort in his concern. "I should be able to—" Bess's ropy tail snapped, swatting Noreen's backside and causing her to jump and let out a high-pitched squeal, which startled the cow. Noreen squeezed her eyes closed and braced.

"*Kumm* on," Thomas said in a gentle tone. "You're *nett* ready for this." He reached for her hand and gave it a tug.

She lowered her head and followed him out of the milking parlor. She shouldn't be frightened. Thomas had sold the ill-tempered beast. Besides, the accident was years ago.

"I'm sorry," she whispered. "I thought I could handle . . ." A shudder ratcheted along her spine as she recalled the crushing weight of the cow pinning her to the cold concrete floor. She squeezed her eyes closed in an attempt to block the memory of her body tangled around cow hooves, and how in a frantic scramble to loosen itself from the stanchion, the cow panicked, stepping on Noreen's leg, arm, and finally coming down on her entire body. Noreen bore the brunt of the heifer's weight for no more than the few seconds it took for the beast to right itself, but the damage was done.

Noreen gasped a short breath, vaguely aware of Thomas dropping the stool.

He ushered her into his arms. "Don't think about it." He kissed her temple. "Please, don't think about it."

She burrowed her face into the crook of his neck, inhaled the smoky scent on his skin, and sobbed. Her husband was patient, holding her close, not rushing to return to milking. She rested her head against his chest. Feelings she had bottled up, painful memories she thought she'd buried, resurfaced from being back in the milking parlor.

Thomas cupped her face in his hands. "I'm going to take you to the bishop's *haus*. He offered his *daadihaus* to stay in until our place is built. Unless, you would rather go to visit your family."

"*Nay*," she said immediately. "I want to stay with you."

CHAPTER 12

Noreen fastened the last pair of pants on the clothesline. Five loads washed, wrung, and now flapping in the fall breeze. In addition to catching up on the laundry, she'd swept and mopped the floors, dusted, and cleaned the soot off the oil lamp chimneys.

They'd already had a few snow flurries and a hot cup of herbal tea sounded good, but she didn't want to sacrifice the freedom of being outdoors just yet. It wouldn't be long before ice and snow would keep her indoors most of the day. Besides, she'd been cooped in the house too long. Morning sickness had kept her in bed more days than she cared to count. Patty had warned her that the first trimester might be rough, but Noreen was in her fourteenth week and still was unable to eat much more than saltine crackers without getting nauseous. On top of that, the scent of brewing coffee, a favorite aroma prior to pregnancy, now caused her stomach to rebel.

Noreen inhaled deeply, letting the crisp air fill her lungs. The trees were bare, their brilliant shades of reds, oranges, and yellows gone. Now the dead leaves carpeted the brown-tinged grass. Thomas was predicting a hard winter due to the number of foggy mornings he'd counted in August. As he liked to point out, the old folktale had proven true in other years. He wanted to be prepared and have a surplus of firewood stored up. Winter didn't matter to Noreen. Springtime was much more important—the month of May in particular, when they would welcome their first child into the world.

Noreen walked the line, patting the towels and bedding she'd hung out earlier. The towels were still damp, but the quilt was dry. Reaching for the clothespin, a fluttering tickled her middle. She placed her hand on her abdomen and waited for it to happen again.

"Hey, Noreen?" Thomas called from the woodshed a few feet away.

"*Jah?*"

He leaned the axe against the chopping block and jogged toward her. Concern illuminated his face as his gaze traveled to her midsection. "Everything all right?"

"*Jah.*" She smiled, experiencing the movement again.

"What's wrong?"

"I think the *boppli* kicked." She reached for his hand and placed it on her belly.

"I don't feel anything," he said.

She frowned. "*Nay*, I don't either. Maybe it wasn't anything."

"Or maybe your body was telling you to rest." He cupped his hand over her shoulder and turned her toward the house. "Let's go inside. I'll make you a bowl of soup."

"You go ahead. I want to bring the quilt in since it's dry."

Thomas glanced up at the sky, but thankfully said nothing about the slim chance of sleet or snow. He unclipped the corner closest to him and helped her fold the blanket. "Do you want me to get the towels?"

"*Nay*, they're still damp."

He carried the quilt into the house, taking it straight to their bedroom.

"I already changed the sheets, if you want to spread out the blanket." She went to the head of the bed and caught the end as it landed. After tucking the side next to the lampstand, she leaned across the bed and adjusted the other side.

Thomas flopped on the bed and pulled her into his arms.

"Thomas King," she scolded. "Your clothes have saw-dust on them."

"Oh well, I'll have to do something about that." He rolled off the mattress and slipped his suspenders off his shoulders, then unfastened his shirt buttons, a mischievous glint in his eye.

"That's *nett* what I meant."

"But you have to admit, it's a *gut* idea." He peeled off his shirt, his arm muscles taut. "Just think," he said, flinging the shirt on the floor. "In a few months we won't have any afternoons to ourselves." He lowered her to the bed and showered her with kisses.

"When the *boppli* starts *schul* we will," she said as his hand roamed her abdomen.

"By the time the first one is old enough for *schul*, we'll have three or four more."

Feeling a flutter, she directed his hand to the spot.

His eyes widened. "Is that the *boppli*?"

She nodded.

His brows arched, then fell, and his smile faltered a little. No doubt struggling with both pride and fear over the responsibility God had entrusted to them. She placed her hand over his. This moment she would store in her memories forever.

· · ·

FEBRUARY, FOURTEEN YEARS EARLIER

Outside the kitchen window the icy February wind howled. This was the third day it snowed so hard that the whiteout conditions prevented Noreen from even being able to see the barn. Thomas had been right. This was one of the hardest winters on record. The stick he used to measure snowfall had registered over three feet and even more had drifted across the open fields and closed the roads.

Noreen was grateful she had enough supplies and didn't need to go into town to buy groceries. February was the shortest month and yet it felt like the longest. The door opened in the sitting room and the cold draft reached the kitchen. Noreen rounded the corner as Thomas pushed the door closed with his boot.

His arms loaded with wood, he stomped snow off his boots, then crossed the room and dropped the logs into the woodbox. He coughed into his gloved hand.

"You sound worse."

"*Jah*, I think the cold moved into *mei* chest." He removed his gloves and hung them on a hook behind the stove to dry.

"Let me help you with your coat," she said.

"*Nay*, please keep your distance. I don't want you getting this."

She smiled. "We share the same house. I think I'm already exposed to whatever germs you have." He'd been sick a few days, but last night was the worst. His temperature soared to 102 despite the acetaminophen she'd given him.

The faint scent of the menthol ointment she'd rubbed on his chest earlier still lingered after he shed his coat. Kicking off his boots, he coughed again, harder, and his entire body seemed to droop in fatigue.

She took his coat and hung it on the wall peg. The boots she left in front of the wood stove. "If you want to sit down, I'll bring you a cup of tea with honey." He rarely ate honey and he always preferred coffee over tea, but these last few days that he'd been under the weather, coffee had upset his stomach.

Thomas lumbered into the kitchen. His rosy cheeks were wind-chapped, his lips dry and cracked. He stood before the stove, hands spread above the heated surface. "The snow has already surpassed last year's mark on the stake. Four inches higher just since this morning."

"You said it was going to be a bad winter."

"Even *I* didn't think it'd be this bad."

Noreen readied the cups with tea bags. The water was already hot. She kept the kettle going most of the day to keep a little steam in the house. Otherwise the dry heat the wood stove put out was unbearable. As she poured hot water into the cups, the tea bags floated to the surface. She refilled the kettle with water, then returned it to the stove.

"I didn't get the new runners mounted on the buggy yet. I'm sorry." Thomas's teeth chattered. "I know how much you wanted to go to the sewing frolic."

"I wouldn't leave you home alone feeling the way you do." Noreen dunked the tea bags up and down in the water. "Besides, if this weather keeps up like you're predicting, the frolic will be postponed. And that's okay. I have plenty of time to finish making *boppli* blankets and clothes." She'd already made several nightdresses using the soft cotton material of one of her old white aprons, and in three months, she would have an entire wardrobe made, knitted socks and everything. "How much honey would you like?"

"A spoonful is *gut*."

She added the thick sweetener, then handed Thomas a mug.

"*Danki*." He clutched the mug with both hands and gently blew over the surface. He took a sip, making a pinched expression as he swallowed.

"Your throat still hurts, doesn't it?" He'd refused lunch earlier because his throat was so sore.

"*Mei* whole body aches. I feel like I've gone through that wringer washer of yours."

"You poor *boppli*." She lifted her palm to his forehead and frowned. "You need to go back to bed. You're boiling hot."

"If I lie down *nau*, I might *nett* get back up to milk the cows. And I still need to bring more firewood inside so it can dry." He crossed the room and sat at the table.

"Would you like a cookie?" She reached for the jar on the counter.

"Nay danki."

"You must be sicker than you're letting on." She sat in the chair opposite him.

"I'll feel better after I drink this." He took another sip.

Several members of their district had been sick. Patty's little one had only recently gotten over the whooping cough. When Noreen spoke with Patty yesterday, her sister-in-law wasn't sure if she was coming down with something or if she was pregnant again.

Thomas placed his elbow on the table, rested his head in his hand, and closed his eyes. Sweat beaded on his forehead.

Noreen rose from the chair and gave his arm a tug. *"Kumm* with me. You're going to bed."

He stood. "I have chores to do first."

"Later." She slipped her arm around his waist. "I'll wake you up in a couple of hours."

"Okay, maybe you're right. I am feeling a little dizzy."

Noreen helped him into bed, then went to the kitchen for a glass of water and more acetaminophen. He was already asleep when she returned, and she wasn't about to wake him. She left the medicine and water on the nightstand, then slipped out of the room.

Spying her knitting needle and the booties she'd started, Noreen scooted the rocker and her yarn basket closer to the wood stove. Three hours later, she lost window light and could no longer see her stitches now that the sun had set. She set the knitting project in the basket and crept down the hall and into the bedroom.

Thomas was snoring.

She stood beside the bed, debated half a second, then couldn't bring herself to wake him. Between the woodbox in the sitting room and the kitchen, they had plenty of dry wood. Thomas always liked to keep more on hand than they needed, but after milking the cows, she could grab an armload to bring inside.

Noreen quickly bundled up in her wool cloak, scarf, hat, and mittens. She slipped her boots on, then fought the frozen-stuck door to get outside.

The trail to the barn was slick and her feet slid across the frozen ground. It was bad enough that she couldn't see her feet, but the pregnancy waddle tipped her off-balance. If she slipped and fell, she'd have to roll off the slippery pathway to get traction under her feet to get back up. The mental image made her chuckle. As children, she and her sisters played in the snow, rolling around, flapping their arms to make angel wings.

Biscuit, the buggy horse, neighed when she entered the barn. Noreen glanced at the frozen water in the trough and frowned. As insulated as the hay kept the barn, the water still froze every winter. She grabbed the pitchfork and spiked the ice, breaking it up for the horse to drink. She did the same for the plow team, Peanut and Butter.

The two Holsteins were waiting by the back door, bawling. Thomas usually milked them much earlier. Noreen pushed the large sliding door to the left, its hardware gliding along the metal track. Patches and Buttons plodded into the barn, automatically going into their separate stanchions. She quickly gathered the supplies, a bucket of sudsy water and rag for washing the udders, a milk pail, and a stool.

Thomas sang to the cows when he milked. Noreen had heard him singing in her father's barn when Thomas had helped with chores after her father's accident. When she'd walked up on him, his face turned cranberry red. "*Cows like* mei *singing*," he'd explained. Noreen liked to sing, too, but she wasn't about to serenade a cow. Not today.

Stool in place, she sat beside Buttons, the tamer of the two, and began. Patches stomped her hoof in the next stanchion. "I'll be with you shortly, Patches," Noreen said calmly. She should have milked the cows before feeding the horses. Delays in the milking schedule, even an hour or two like tonight, increased the cows' agitation. Patches was a bit temperamental on good days, never mind the state she was in now that milking was late.

A short time later, Noreen finished milking Buttons. She moved the stool, empty bucket, and wash pail into the next milking stall. Noreen dipped the rag into the sudsy water, her wet hands stiffened from the cold. The moment she lifted the washrag to the udder, Patches kicked up her hoof and struck Noreen's hand. Dropping the rag, she jerked her hand away. Her wrist began to throb. Wiggling her fingers sent shards of pain up to her elbow. She submerged her injured hand in the cold water, but it did little to ease the pain. Patches shifted her weight and suddenly, the stool went out from under Noreen. In clambering to get up, hooves pummeled her legs, feet, and hands several times. Then without warning, the cow came down, pinning Noreen against the wall divider with its crushing weight. A flash of bright light filled her vision, and her ears rang with a piercing pitch. *Don't panic. Stay calm.*

In the process of trying to right itself, the cow kicked, striking Noreen. Shards of pain stabbed her ribs. She let out a cry, but that only startled the cow and increased its frenzied movements.

"Noreen!"

Thomas. Oh, thank God.

He eased between the cow and his wife. "Are you hurt?"

"I don't think so." She moaned.

"Don't move. I'm going to take Patches out." Thomas grabbed the cow's halter and pushed her backward.

"Patches hasn't—" A sharp pain seized her words. She puffed short breaths. *Don't talk.* Thomas would see that the cow hadn't been milked.

He was at her side, kneeling. "Where do you hurt?"

"Everywhere." She tried to push off the cement, but the hand that had been kicked couldn't bear any weight, and she flopped back down.

Thomas's arms came around her and pulled her up. *Dizzy. Everything was spinning.* She took a step but her ankle collapsed as if poked by a hot iron.

His grip tightened around her waist. Still feverish, heat radiated off him. "Lean on me."

With his assistance, she passed the horse stalls,

the grain bin, the tack room, and by the time they reached the door, she was breathing easier. The icy wind whirled around them, stinging her face, numbing her body. The wind had filled in the path to the house. Fresh snow covered the porch steps.

"Go easy," he said. "It's icy."

Noreen couldn't see her feet, let alone the steps. Her foot slipped, but Thomas was there to hold her steady. She eased up the remaining steps, entered the house, and tugged off her scarf.

Thomas came up behind her to help with her cloak. "You should have woken me up."

"I wanted to let you rest. You're sick, Thomas. I can feel how hot you are just standing next to you." Noreen cringed as a shot of pain sliced through her side.

"What's wrong?"

She doubled over. *Inhale. Exhale. Inhale.* No reprieve. The pressure tightened around her midsection.

"Noreen?"

"Something's . . . happening."

CHAPTER 13

It hurts," Noreen said, exhaling. Holding her belly with both hands, she sucked in another breath. Her face contorted, turning a deep shade of red.

"I'll hitch the buggy." Thomas lunged for the door, but she grasped his arm.

"*Nay!* Don't leave me."

"You need to see the *doktah*." He struggled to keep his tone even, but it didn't ease her panic-stricken grip. She wrenched his arm tighter.

"Noreen, calm down. I'll be back as soon as I get the buggy ready."

"*Nay!*" She doubled over. "This can't be happening. It's too"—she squeezed her eyes shut—"early. I'm only twenty-seven weeks." Suddenly, her eyes opened wide and she looked down.

He followed her gaze to the small puddle on the floor. Melted snow?

"*Mei* water broke," she said.

The pace of his galloping heart made the room spin and set alarms off in his head. *Think! Don't panic. Stay calm.*

"Thomas." Her fixed glare demanded attention. "I have to lie down."

He swept her into his arms and carried her down the hall. Inside the bedroom, he lowered her gently onto the mattress. "Please, try to relax." He paced the length of the room and stopped at the window facing the barn. Still snowing. He'd have to figure out a way to attach the runners to the buggy. Surely the snowplows had cleared the main roads by now. Hearing heavy panting, he turned away from the window.

Noreen pulled the quilt off the bed.

"Honey," he said, "please, lie down and rest."

She sat on the edge of the bed, held her belly with one hand, and pointed to the chest of drawers with her other. "I'll need a *nachtdress*, please."

"Sure." He went to the dresser and jiggled the middle drawer loose. He removed the garment. "Can I get you anything else? A glass of water? Warm milk?"

"Towels," she said, easing off her dress. The garment fell to the floor as she held the edge of the mattress, gripping it with white-knuckle force. "Several towels," she said, forcing her words through gritted teeth.

"Ah—*jah*, okay." He left the room, grabbed a stack of towels from the bathroom closet, taking a moment to wet a washcloth, then returned to find Noreen sprawled out over the bed. Bruises had already formed on her arms, ribs, and legs. She rested her hand on the purplish area of her ribs, breathing erratic. Perspiration dotted her forehead, soaking into her prayer *kapp*. This was his fault. He shouldn't have taken a nap. Now his battered wife was writhing in pain, and what could he do to ease her suffering? Nothing. Thomas swallowed. *Do something.*

He set the towels on the dresser and approached the bed with a washcloth. Easing down on the edge of the bed, he slid her prayer *kapp* off and blotted her forehead with the damp cloth. "Do you want help getting changed?"

She was still a moment, breathing easy, but as he studied her midsection, her rounded form grew lopsided as a bulge the size of his fist pushed from the inside. Her face grimaced. "The pressure is—" She pursed her lips and she blew as though blowing on a whistle. "Check for the *boppli's* head."

He moved to the end of the bed. "Nothing yet."

Seconds later, her back arched. She lifted her upper body, her face a bright shade of red. Releasing a loud cry, she dropped back against the mattress.

"I—I'll get Patty."

"*Nay*, Thomas. Stay. Don't leave me." She barely had time to recover before the next wave of contractions brought her off the mattress, hands clutching her bent knees. Lasting no more than a minute, she collapsed, exhausted and with tears streaming down her face. "I can't do this."

He sat next to her. "Yes, you can." He kissed her forehead. "You can do it, darling." Using the damp washcloth, he blotted her forehead again.

Her eyes closed. Her breathing slowed. "We should be timing the contractions," she said, her voice weary.

The only clock was hanging on the wall in the sitting room. Guessing, he'd estimate the contractions no more than three or four minutes apart. The last two, almost on top of each other, were more intense if he was to measure by the volume of her cry. They had subsided, at least for the moment. His only experience with the birthing process was with cows. Most progressed fairly rapidly and he just monitored. Only once did he have to step in and pull the distressed calf out. But assisting his wife—his baby's arrival—he needed Patty. Thomas eased off the bed.

"Don't leave," she whispered, sounding half-dazed.

"I'll only be gone a few minutes. I promise."

Her eyes shot open. "*Nay*, please. I'm afraid."

Thomas paced, torn between getting help and staying with his wife. He wanted nothing more than to stay and reassure Noreen, but in the end, his wife would need someone much more qualified than him. He had no idea what to do for her. He could deliver a calf, but not his son or daughter. Noreen needed Patty. He waited until her eyes closed once again, then slipped out of the room.

"Thomas?"

He paused half a second, her whimpers tugging on his heart, then continued down the hall. *I'll make it quick.* He grabbed the lantern from the sitting room and donned his coat and scarf on the way out the door. More snow had fallen and the freezing wind numbed his cheeks and the tip of his nose. He debated whether he should harness the horse, but there was no telling how bad the road was. He decided not to risk getting the buggy stuck, so he trudged across the field, the snow thigh-high, to reach Jonathan's house. Patty answered the door.

Without waiting for her greeting, Thomas blurted, "There's been an accident. Noreen's water broke. We need your help."

"I'll get *mei* coat."

Jonathan rounded the corner from the kitchen. "Did you say something about an accident?"

Thomas nodded. "Patches came down on Noreen while she was milking. The *boppli*'s coming early."

Patty's mother came out from the kitchen, dish towel in hand. "Don't worry about little Jacob. I'll listen for him."

Jonathan removed his coat from the hook. "I take it from the snow on your pant legs that you didn't get the runners on yet."

Thomas shook his head. He wouldn't use the excuse of being sick. A fever was nothing compared to what Noreen was going through. He should have been prepared.

"I'll hitch the sleigh." Jonathan shoved his boots on. "Do you want me to go after Sadie?"

The midwife lived five miles west of them. It'd take extra time, going in the opposite direction of town. Burning with fever, he wasn't thinking straight. The baby was early. They needed someone with experience. Thomas reached for the doorknob. "*Jah.* Let's go."

As Thomas pulled the sleigh out from under the lean-to, Jonathan harnessed his mare. Meanwhile, Patty gathered a few supplies and met them outside.

The road home wasn't as bad as Thomas had expected. The packed snow made it easy for the sleigh to glide over the surface. His brother dropped Thomas and Patty off next to the porch.

As he opened the door, Noreen's curdling scream filled his ears. He rushed into the bedroom. Soaked in sweat, Noreen was beet red and bearing down.

Patty whizzed past him in a flurry, shedding her coat at the foot of the bed. After a quick look she gave the frantic order, "Stop pushing."

"I can't," Noreen panted. A second later, her face pinched and she cried out again.

"Noreen," Patty said sternly. "The *boppli*'s in the wrong position."

Thomas caught a glimpse of what Patty was talking about and almost went faint. One of the baby's arms was exposed as well as the cord. Exchanging glances with Patty, he recognized her fear-stricken expression as someone at a loss for what to do. Acid rose to the back of his throat.

"Thomas, go rewet the washcloth," Patty said, handing him the damp cloth and shooing him toward the door. "*Kalt* water."

He'd offer to boil water if it'd help, but he'd heard that was a remedy for impatient fathers, not a necessity. Thomas gazed at his wife, lying in the center of the bed, a section of the sheets fisted in her hands, and moaning in agony. Tears pricked his eyes.

Patty nudged his arm. "Go freshen the washcloth, Thomas."

He stepped into the hall, closing the door behind him. Inside the bathroom, he tossed the washcloth in the basin and let the cold water run over it as he dropped to his knees and bowed his head. "Lord," was all he could say for several seconds as he fought back the tears. "Please, have mercy. I beg of You, Lord. Watch over Noreen and the *boppli*. Keep them safe."

"I have to push. Help me!"

Noreen's shrill cry pulled Thomas up from the bathroom floor. He whispered, "Amen" as he rushed down the hall. Opening the door, he was caught off guard by seeing Noreen lying on her left side and Patty attempting to shove a pillow under his wife's hip.

"Grab the other pillow," Patty said, motioning to him. "We need to get her hips elevated higher than her head."

He snatched two more pillows and handed them to Patty, then, at his sister-in-law's instruction, gently lifted Noreen's legs so Patty could place the pillows. Noreen gasped sharply. The new angle was awkward and looked horribly uncomfortable. But after seeing that more of the cord was now exposed, he realized that the shift in gravity would hopefully help keep the baby inside.

Noreen wept.

"Sadie will be here soon," Thomas said, dabbing her forehead with the cool cloth. It seemed like hours since Jonathan had dropped them off. He hoped the midwife was home.

"I want this"—Noreen grappled for his hand, tightening her hold as the contraction strengthened—"over."

"I know you do." He leaned down and kissed her forehead. "It won't be long before you're holding our *boppli*. You're going to make a great *mamm*. Focus on that."

CHAPTER 14

Thomas blinked a few times, his eyes slow to adjust to the morning light. It took a half second for his mind to register the surroundings even though he and Noreen had been staying at the bishop's *daadihaus* over a week. Thomas glanced at Noreen sleeping peacefully beside him. Her cheeks were a pretty pink shade, soft if he were to touch them, and the tiny lines on her forehead from years of working in the garden had vanished in the morning light.

Noreen stirred. Opening her eyes, she smiled. *"Guder mariye."*

"Morning." He rolled up on his elbow. "You look the same as the day we married."

She yawned. "You're still sleep deprived."

"Nay," he said, pulling her into his embrace. "You're beautiful."

Noreen held his gaze, studying him silently.

"I'm serious." He kissed her forehead. "And I'm truly sorry for *nett* telling you more often. I'm glad God gave me you." As he spoke, her eyes glistened. Tilting her face, he leaned in and kissed her. She was his bride. A gift from God to love and to cherish.

They were still in bed when a knock sounded at the door. Thomas pulled on his pants, grabbed the shirt he'd worn the day before, and shoved his arms into the sleeves as he made his way to the door located in the mudroom. He moved aside for Jonathan to enter.

His brother smirked. "Were you still in bed?"

"I haven't gotten much sleep since the fire." *Poor excuse. The fire had been over a week ago.* Thomas combed his hair with his fingers.

"Your plow team was out. I discovered them in *mei* field this morning."

"How in the world . . . ?" He was sure he'd stalled the horses and locked the barn after finishing the chores last night. Thomas grabbed his boots, then realized he wasn't wearing socks.

"The boys put the horses in the pasture with ours. You may have a break in your fence."

"The fence isn't the problem," he mumbled. "I'll be back in a second. I need to get socks." He tossed the boots on the floor and returned to the bedroom.

"Who was at the door?" Noreen said, adjusting the pins in her prayer *kapp*.

"Jonathan." He swiped his socks off the floor and sat on the bed.

"Everything okay?"

"*Jah*, the team got out last *nacht*." He pushed his foot into the sock. "I have to go."

"What about breakfast?"

"Maybe later." He scooted out the door before she

could ask more questions. It wasn't uncommon for livestock to get loose. Once he had to help round up his brother's cattle that busted the fence and ended up roaming a half mile away. Thomas donned his straw hat and coat at the door.

The air was crisp, the sky cloud-covered and gloomy.

Jonathan motioned to his buggy. "I'll give you a ride. Jump in."

"*Nay danki.* I'm going to be there most of the day cleaning the debris." Thomas headed to the barn.

The farm was two miles east of the bishop's place so it didn't take long to get home. The wagon was still parked next to the pile of ashes, loaded and ready to be taken to the dump. But as Thomas neared the barn, he noticed the lock had been broken. *Looters.*

Within minutes evidence of intruders marked the building. The walls to the horse stalls were spray-painted red with despicable words he'd never repeat aloud. A pit formed in his stomach. *Relax. What's done is done.* Self-talk wasn't doing much to reduce the tension, especially when the inside of the stalls were smeared with more of the same vandalism. At least the horses were safe at Jonathan's. Who knows, maybe the intruders had tried to steal them. Thomas took comfort knowing his young team was stubborn and responded to Pennsylvania Dutch.

Thomas closed the stall door and continued his investigation, making his way to the back of the barn where the four newly weened piglets were sharing a stall. The hair on Thomas's arms stood as a chill spread over him. The usual squealing sounds were absent.

He pushed the top portion of the stall door open and gasped. All four piglets were gone. The horses had made their way to Jonathan's farm, perhaps the piglets were somewhere nearby. Anger infused his veins. The piglets were too young to fend for themselves.

He stormed to the equipment room to get an empty crate. He would need something sturdy to carry the piglets back to the barn. He pushed the door open to the equipment room and froze. Everything was gone. The harness, tools, even the pitchfork. Thomas growled under his breath. He'd paid over three hundred dollars for the harness alone. But those losses paled to what he noticed next. Lying on the floor next to the grain bin sat the tin box—empty. Every dime he'd saved had been stored in the box. Money to rebuild their home— for next year's crops. He should have remembered to take the box when they moved into the bishop's *daadihaus*. Stupid! He should have expected something like this to happen.

Thomas kicked the wall, letting out a grunt. He repeated the action only harder, then kicked the wall again. Several minutes later, he was worn out, shrouded in hopelessness. His foot throbbed. How was he going to tell Noreen that he couldn't rebuild their house? It'd take years to save that much again.

. . .

Noreen peeked out the kitchen window of the *daadihaus*, but couldn't see beyond the dim lantern light on the porch. It wasn't like Thomas to be this late.

"Lord, I pray he hasn't been hurt." She paced the kitchen. Perhaps in the process of cleaning up the debris, he dropped something on himself. He could have stumbled and fallen on broken glass. She opened the oven and peered in at the pan of golden cornbread muffins. Another minute or two and they'd be done. She paced from the window in the kitchen to the one in the sitting room, which overlooked the bishop's house. Noreen went back to the stove and removed the muffins. Probably sticky but good enough.

After jotting a quick note should she and Thomas cross paths, Noreen donned her cloak. She grabbed the lantern on the porch and trekked across the yard toward the bishop's house. Perhaps if they weren't eating, she could borrow their buggy.

In the distance buggy wheels rumbled over the road in front of Bishop Zook's house. She waited for the buggy to get closer, holding her breath. "Pull in," she muttered.

A few moments later, horse hooves clapped the gravel driveway. Noreen blew out a breath.

"Whoa." Thomas stopped the horse. "Noreen?"

She lifted the lantern higher. "*Jah*, it's me. I was getting ready to *kumm* look for you."

"Sorry I worried you."

His voice sounded strained. Maybe he was just tired. It'd been a long day. "I'll reheat the chili while you're tending the horse."

"I hope you made cornbread too?"

"I just took the muffins out a few minutes ago." Noreen headed to the house, stopping once she was on the porch to glance over her shoulder. Thomas wasn't talking to Biscuit as he usually did when he removed the harness. Something was wrong.

Inside the house, Noreen fed the stove another slab of wood. Although the embers were still hot, the house was a little drafty and she wanted the chill out of the air. She placed the pot of chili on the stove, then filled the coffee kettle with water. Soon, the chili was sputtering.

Thomas entered the kitchen through the mudroom, soot embedded in his frown lines. He dropped something heavy on the table and plopped down on the chair.

"This will be ready once you wash your hands." She stirred the pot with a wooden spoon to make sure the chili was heated all the way through.

Thomas pushed off the chair and lumbered to the sink where he sudsed his hands quietly. He'd always been a deep thinker, sometimes he sat for hours without talking, but he hadn't been this quiet since they moved into the *daadihaus*.

She didn't like the silence. In losing their house, their relationship had rekindled and she wasn't about to let it go back to how it was before. It was lonely living with a man who kept to himself. She opened her mouth to ask how his day went, then decided to wait. *Don't smother him. Give him space.*

The kettle whistled.

"I'll get it." He came up beside her and grabbed the potholder off the counter.

"Danki." She dipped the ladle in the pot and filled the bowls as he poured two cups of percolated coffee. It

wasn't until she placed the bowls on the table that she noticed the hammerhead, dark with soot, lying in the center. "Can I move this?" She motioned to the tool.

"You can throw it away for all I care."

Noreen picked up the weighty piece. Instantly she understood his moodiness. This was his father's hammer. The one he'd used to build their original house. "Did you find it in the rubble?"

He nodded.

"I'm sorry," she said.

"We lost everything, Noreen."

A sadness she couldn't quite explain washed over his dirt-smudged face. She cleared her throat. "*Nett* each other."

He bowed his head. If he prayed, it was briefly. Before she took her place at the table, he was eating.

She broke the silence. "Were you able to get a lot done?"

"Three loads to the dump." He took a sip of coffee.

Noreen lifted the spoon to her mouth and blew gently on the chili. "I thought I'd help tomorrow." She took a bite.

"*Nay*, I can manage."

"But there's no sense doing it by yourself. The men won't be available to help until the harvest—"

"I said I can manage."

Noreen placed her spoon in the bowl and scooted her chair back. "I forgot the muffins." She brought the plate of cornbread muffins over to the table, but her appetite was gone. The few bites of chili that she'd eaten hadn't set well in her stomach.

After a few minutes of silence, he motioned with his spoon to her bowl. "Aren't you going to eat?"

She shook her head. "I'm *nett* feeling so well."

"Been sick all day?"

"*Nay*, it just *kumm* on me." Noreen appreciated his attempt to start a conversation, even stilted as it was. Even though Thomas rarely talked about his deceased father, he treasured his father's hammer. Finding it in the ruins would have triggered memories of his childhood.

Noreen took a sip of water, but even that didn't alleviate her queasy stomach. Had the room not started to spin, or her forehead not moistened, she would have blamed the sudden flu-like symptoms on the chili.

CHAPTER 15

PRESENT DAY

Jonathan's face paled, staring at the graffiti. "Did you report this to the police?"

"They were here earlier taking pictures and dusting for prints." Thomas tightened his jaw to the point of it hurting. "Apparently, the police responded to another call earlier where pigs' blood was used to vandalize a building."

"Do they think the crimes are connected?"

"After I told them about the missing piglets, they do." Thomas had searched the area thoroughly for the pigs but to no avail. Once the police shared about the other vandalism case, it made sense why he wasn't able to find his livestock.

Jonathan shook his head. "Disgusting, isn't it?"

"*Jah.*" Thomas moved a piece of straw with the toe of his boot.

"I have a gallon of white paint. It probably won't be enough to cover it, but you're welcome to it."

"*Danki.*" Unable to look at the hideous crime scene any longer, Thomas turned away. Now that the police had completed their inspection, he could scrub the walls. At least when the robberies had taken place in the past, no one had lost any livestock. For a while it seemed their community was being targeted. Every other Sunday, while they were all gathered for the church meeting, the burglars were helping themselves to whatever they could find. Mostly cash tucked away in sock drawers. Thomas left a few dollars in the sock drawer, but had placed the bulk of the cash in the tin box, thinking the money was safely tucked within the pages of the letters inside the envelopes.

Thomas grabbed a bucket and headed out to the pump.

Jonathan followed. "We'll load your equipment and tools and take it and the livestock to *mei* place."

"I doubt they'll be back. They've taken everything of value. The plow team's harness, tools; they dumped the grain barrel over."

"Still, you should move the livestock to *mei* place just to be safe."

"*Jah*, I agree." Thomas placed the bucket under the pump spigot.

"At least they didn't steal your team or your horse and buggy," his brother said. "And they didn't take your water bucket."

"Oh, that's a blessing for sure." His brother was doing his best to lighten the situation, and maybe if the thieves hadn't found the tin box, Thomas would have appreciated Jonathan's attempt more. But his savings was gone. He didn't feel much like celebrating a bucket being left or singing God's praises for that matter.

"What else is troubling you?"

"Isn't that enough?" Thomas hesitated a half second, then cranked the pump. Admitting he'd been stupid enough to leave the tin box in the barn wasn't easy.

"Stuff can be replaced," Jonathan said.

"*Nett* soon enough," he muttered under his breath. He released the pump handle and picked up the bucket of water. Once the walls were washed, he'd work on cleaning up the ash pile. That is, if his brother kept an extra shovel in his buggy. The bandits had taken even that.

"Are you worried about the harness for the team? I have an extra one. I have all the tools needed for building too."

"*Danki.*" Thomas opened the barn door. He added detergent to the bucket, mixing it with his hand to make it sudsy. He was silent several minutes, then, unable to hold it in any longer, he said, "They took *mei* savings. Money I had planned to build the *haus* with."

"You had it in the barn?"

"*Nett* smart, I know." He had moved it from the washhouse to the tack room. Thomas carried the bucket into the first stall. "I haven't told Noreen about any of this. The vandalism, the missing pigs . . . the money for the *haus*. She doesn't know."

Jonathan sighed. "You have to tell her."

Thomas sloshed the wall with soapy water and began to scrub. He and Noreen had just started to reconnect. What if not being able to build the house put another wedge between them?

. . .

"Where did all this stuff *kumm* from?" Thomas could hardly see over the stacked boxes in the sitting room of the bishop's *daadihaus*.

Noreen poked her head around the kitchen wall, her hands sudsy with dishwater. "They're donations."

Thomas flipped open one box, scanned the various kitchenware contents, then closed the flap. He made his way to the kitchen where more boxes cluttered every surface of counter space as well as the table. "Wow, more stuff."

"Isn't it amazing? We've been so blessed."

"Indeed." He pushed a wooden crate of pots and pans to the end of the table and sat down.

"We won't need anything for our new home," she said, her voice ringing with excitement. "Maybe a few things like linens and towels."

She rattled on though his focus drifted. A week had passed since the barn was vandalized and every day a little more of his stomach lining had eaten away having not shared the news with his wife.

"I take that back," she said, rinsing a washed plate. "I remember seeing towels in one of the crates in the sitting room." She pivoted to face him, her eyes big. "Did you want *kaffi*? I've been so busy telling you about everything we received that I forgot to ask."

He smiled, enjoying the vibrancy in her eyes. Her cheeks held a rosy glow he hadn't seen in a long time. He wasn't about to hamper her mood with bad news. Not today.

Noreen's nose scrunched. "What are you looking at?"

"You." He stood.

"Should I put the kettle on?"

"*Nay.*" He took her into his arms. "I have to tell you something."

Noreen pulled back, her forehead creased. "You look serious."

"And you look beautiful." He smiled, which seem to put her at ease again.

She leaned her head against his chest. "Is it bad to say that I'm happy here?"

"Why would you ask that? I want you to be happy."

"Sometimes our big farmhouse felt lonely . . . just the two of us."

"I understand." The farm's empty rooms represented unfulfilled dreams of a big family. A sad reminder of how empty their lives had become. He understood that all too well. Thomas squeezed her a little tighter. "I'm sure the bishop wouldn't mind if we stay longer."

"*Ach*, no." She lifted her head. "I'm looking forward to our new home—starting over. Besides," she said, motioning to the stacked boxes, "it's going to get cramped quickly when the members start donating furniture."

He forced a smile, hoping it'd mask his disappointment. It would have been much easier to tell her a few minutes ago about having to put the rebuilding on hold. "I should go. I promised Levi I would help pick pumpkins."

"Oh, okay." She stepped out of his embrace and swiped her hand at a wrinkle on her dress. "Is that what you wanted to tell me?"

He opened his mouth, but lost his nerve. "Did you

want to ride along and visit Rebecca and their new *boppli*?"

"*Nay*, I was hoping to consolidate some of these boxes today. At least clear a pathway to the bedroom."

He wouldn't rush her. Lately, she avoided newborns. Noreen probably didn't even realize she was doing it. The older she became, the more she found excuses not to visit new *mamm*s and babies. Her biological clock wasn't ready to expire, but Noreen thought so, and even though she never complained, he sensed her pain.

"I'll be back by supper." Thomas weaved around the boxes in the sitting room and grabbed his hat at the door. Before going over to Levi's, he planned to finish the tree swing he'd promised Noreen he would build when they first were married. Fifteen years was a long time to wait to sit together under the big old maple. With all that had happened, he hoped the surprise would spark a new hope.

"I have errands to run, so will you leave me some money before you go?"

Thomas pretended not to hear the question and slipped out the door. He didn't have any money to leave. The errands would have to wait.

CHAPTER 16

PRESENT DAY

Lively chatter filled Alice's sitting room as the women's sewing bee continued into the late November afternoon. Noreen always enjoyed participating in the frolics, especially when they were all gathered together to help a family in need, but she wasn't used to this much attention and the experience was humbling.

"The most yardage of material is green," Sadie announced, kneeling on the floor with the measuring tape. "I hope you don't mind your curtains green."

"I'll be just happy to have *mei* windows covered," Noreen replied.

The womenfolk laughed, awakening little Eli from his nap. Rebecca lifted him up from the wicker basket and checked his cloth diaper.

"It's hard to believe he's already two months old," Noreen said.

"I can't wait until he sleeps through the *nacht*," Rebecca said, yawning.

"Even better is when they're able to feed and dress themselves," Patty chimed. "I was beginning to think

I'd never get Matthew out of diapers. I'm so glad those days are over."

A pang of regret stabbed at Noreen's heart. If only she had something to add to the conversation—in the experience of motherhood. The women's voices blended together as Noreen's thoughts drifted to the time when she and Thomas had first learned she was pregnant. Had their son survived, he would be thirteen. Seemed like yesterday. Then again, so did the two miscarriages in the years following. "Nothing is impossible for God," Patty used to say, encouraging her to remain hopeful. But over the years, Noreen learned to discard any bud of hope before it bloomed.

"Is he still feverish?" Sadie asked.

"It finally broke Sunday *nacht*," Rebecca said. "I didn't like missing service, but I didn't want to risk anyone else getting sick either." She gazed fondly at her infant. "Levi wasn't thrilled about Eli and I being home alone. Hearing about the vandalism and stolen livestock had him rattled."

"Did anyone else hear that the police have connected the slaughtered livestock with another crime?" Sadie asked.

"Slaughtered livestock!" Noreen stuck her fingertip with the needle and jerked her hand away. "I never heard about any of this," she said, examining her finger. "When did it happen?" The finger stick began to bleed so she shoved her finger into her mouth, her gaze traveling around the room, unsure what to make of the women's blank stares.

Alice jumped to her feet. "Who would like more *kaffi*?"

Noreen set aside the shirt she'd been working on for

Thomas and stood. She didn't want more coffee, but she could use a break. Focusing all afternoon on tiny stitches had made her stomach queasy. "I'll help."

Patty rose. "I'll join you." She leaned closer as they exited the room. "Are you okay?"

"I'm a little tired. Alice and I peeled, cored, and mashed three bushels of apples into applesauce yesterday." Noreen wasn't complaining. The past couple weeks canning with Alice had been a joy.

"I was talking about the stolen pigs and vandalism," Patty said.

Alice clanged the kettle holding it up to the faucet. "Patty," Alice said, narrowing her eyes. "Will you get the bowl of sugar down from the cabinet?"

"How many places were broken into?" Noreen continued the conversation.

Patty glanced at Alice. "I only heard of one." She faced the cabinet.

Noreen reached in front of her and removed the glass sugar bowl. "What are you *nett* telling me?"

Again Alice and Patty exchanged glances.

"Your complexion looks a little washed out. I thought maybe you were coming down with something," Patty explained.

This wasn't about how washed out she looked. Sure, when the robberies had occurred in so many Amish homes in their community, she'd been fearful. But so had all the womenfolk.

"I thought you were a little pale when we were doing apples yesterday," Alice added, her attention focused on pouring coffee into the mugs.

"I might need glasses," Noreen admitted. "Yesterday focusing on peeling apples and today *mei* eyes are giving me fits trying to sew. It's made me nauseated."

"When *mei* vision started to change, I used to get headaches." Alice set the kettle on the stove.

"I get them when I'm feeling stressed," Patty said.

Perhaps stress was the reason. Not knowing if their new house would be finished by winter was stressful. Nay, *it isn't about the house.* She and Thomas were spending more time together like they had when they were newlyweds. If anything, the house fire, losing everything, had brought them happiness.

Noreen caught a glimpse out the window of a buggy. Excitement fluttered her insides as her husband's buggy rolled to a stop next to the *daadihaus*. Thomas had finished early, which meant if the debris pile was cleaned up, they could start building soon. Perhaps they would be moved in before winter after all. She could hardly wait to be in their own home again.

"Someone *kumm* in the driveway?" Alice rose to her tiptoes and peered out the window over the sink.

"Thomas. He's home early."

Her husband climbed out of the buggy slowly. His posture hunched, something was wrong. "He's limping."

"You better go to him." Alice made a shooing gesture with her hand.

Noreen grabbed her wool cloak from the coatrack and hurried outside. She rushed across the yard and came up beside Thomas, who was hobbling on one foot. "What happened?" She placed her arm around his waist.

"I stepped on a nail and it shot through the sole of my boot and into my foot." He cupped her shoulder. "How's the frolic going?"

"*Gut*. We've been busy sewing all morning."

He grimaced, taking a step.

"You'll probably need a tetanus shot."

"*Jah*, but I'll worry about that later." He hobbled inside with her assistance and plopped down onto a wooden chair.

Noreen knelt beside him and unlaced his boot. The way he winced as she removed his boot indicated he hurt worse than what he was letting on. Blood had soaked through his wool sock and marked the bottom of his foot. Even though the puncture wound had stopped bleeding on its own, the skin was red with jagged edges. No telling how deep the nail had penetrated. "What size nail?"

"A rafter spike."

"No wonder you're limping." Noreen stood. "I'll make a salted foot bath." She filled the kettle with water, placed it on the stove to heat, then prepared a soapy rag to clean the wound.

The wound already looked bruised around the puncture. "How deep do you think it went?"

He shrugged. "It felt like I was passing a kidney stone when Jonathan removed it."

"You for sure are going to need a tetanus shot."

"I'll soak it in kerosene and salt."

She shuddered, recalling the time she had spilled lamp oil on a paper cut and how much it burned. The water was heated by the time she cleaned his foot.

Noreen added a large amount of salt, then placed the basin on the floor in front of him.

Dipping his toes in, he flinched.

"Is it too hot?" She bent down and touched the water. Warm.

He submerged his entire foot, gritting his teeth and clenching the edge of the chair with a white-knuckle grip. "Don't you want to get back to the frolic?"

She glanced up and frowned. "Thomas King, are you trying to get rid of me?"

He tapped the tip of her nose with his finger. "*Nay*, silly."

Noreen pushed off the floor. "Be right back. I'm going to get supplies." On a mission, she grabbed a towel from the linen closet, a clean pair of socks from the bedroom, then hunting through a small tote of first-aid products, found a Band-Aid. Living out of boxes with everything in disarray was tedious. She liked things in their place. Noreen's thoughts skipped to the women's conversation about the vandalized home. She returned to the sitting room. "Why didn't you tell me about the break-in?"

Shock registered on his face. "Wh-what did you hear?"

"That livestock were stolen, possibly slaughtered, and . . ." Noreen cocked her head. "Whose place was it?"

Thomas closed his eyes briefly.

"Ours?" Unease trickled down her spine.

He nodded. "I didn't know how to tell you."

Apparently Patty and the others didn't know how to break the news either.

"The piglets were . . . stolen."

Or slaughtered? Noreen's stomach roiled. As an acidic taste landed on her tongue, she clamped her hand over her mouth and rushed out of the room. She was vomiting when Thomas appeared at the bathroom door.

He leaned against the doorframe, water puddling at his foot. "I'm sorry. I didn't want to upset you."

"You shouldn't be on your foot." She leaned over the basin and vomited again.

Instead of leaving, he hobbled to the linen closet, removed a washcloth and hand towel, and handed them to her.

"*Danki.*" She wet the cloth with cold water.

"There's something else I need to tell you," he said, sheepishly bowing his head. "The money I'd been saving—the money for building the *haus*—was stolen."

She dropped the washcloth in the sink. "When?"

"Last month, when the barn was vandalized. I should have remembered to bring the tin box when we moved in here."

"The tin box our letters were stored in?" The tin box he went back into the flaming house to get.

Thomas nodded. "When the robberies started a year ago, I put our savings into the envelopes with the letters, assuming the money would be safe." He slapped his thighs. "We lost everything."

Things were making sense. "So that's why you hurried out of the *haus* when I asked for spending money?"

"I have some to give you *nau*. I was able to sell scrap metal I found in the fire waste."

"I don't need it *nau*." Noreen moved past him and down the hall. She needed air. Vomiting had left a foul taste in her mouth, or maybe the bitterness was from being the last one to know that it was their place that had been vandalized. She grabbed her cloak hanging on the hook by the door and slipped outside.

Voices trailed across the yard as the women's frolic let out. The dozen or more women and children flocked to their buggies, going home to prepare the evening meal. Noreen should be getting supper ready too. Instead, she ducked under the pasture fence, too nervous to look behind her, worried someone might spot her and want to talk. She needed a few minutes alone.

The first heavy snow flurries of the season came down sideways in the wind. She grasped the neck opening of the cape to keep the draft from entering. Had she not asked Thomas about the robbery, would he have blamed the frozen ground for why they couldn't build?

Noreen followed the cow path down to the creek. The irony-orange current was swift, washing over the shallow rocky bottom. This was a popular place for the neighboring children in the district to play after helping in the garden on a hot summer day. Noreen especially loved the sound of rushing water. She sat under a nearby tree, trying hard to concentrate on something other than the house, but it was no use.

It isn't about the house, she insisted. She'd been perfectly content these past weeks living in the bishop's *daadihaus*. Up until a few minutes ago, she and Thomas had gotten along well, or so she thought. Now she wasn't so sure his attentiveness wasn't a wild attempt to keep her from finding out the truth. A horse snorted and she whirled around.

Thomas climbed off Biscuit, favoring his injured foot, and ambled toward her. "I should have told you."

"I don't understand why you didn't. And don't say you wanted to spare me from the gruesomeness because the womenfolk knew. It was a matter of time before one of them slipped."

"I was wrong." He sat beside her and leaned against the tree. "I messed up everything." Thomas positioned himself to face her. "I'm sorry I failed you."

Noreen's heart grew heavy. "You didn't fail me."

"I promised your father I would take care of you always."

She reached for his hand. "And you have."

"But I don't know when we'll be able to rebuild. I spoke with Bishop Zook about us staying through the winter, but we might need to stay even longer."

He tilted his face up, but his watery eyes still gave him away. She hadn't seen him this torn up in years. Not since she miscarried and he blamed himself. For a while she had blamed him too. For owning an ill-tempered cow, for leaving her alone when he went for help. She could have prevented the heartache from lingering. The accident wasn't his fault. Neither was the house fire or the thieves stealing their savings. She wasn't about to let guilt consume him or what remnant remained of their marriage.

Noreen lifted her head. "I'm happy living in the bishop's *daadihaus*. We've had a chance to grow closer . . . It feels like home."

He rubbed his eyes and smiled. "I think so too. But I want you to have *your* home."

"I love you, Thomas."

He leaned over and kissed her forehead. "I love you too." He pulled her into a hug and after a moment of holding her tight, he released her. "Do you want a ride home?"

"You go ahead," she said. "I'll be there shortly."

The lines on his forehead deepened. "Are you sure everything is all right?"

Noreen nodded. "I need a few minutes alone to pray about something." *Please don't ask what it's about.*

Thomas hesitated briefly, then stood. "I'll see you in a few minutes then?"

"*Jah.*" She waited until he mounted the horse and rode away before bowing her head. "Lord, I don't understand why *mei* stomach is so queasy. I've had this flicker of hope before and . . . and for whatever reason, You didn't find me fit for motherhood at the time. Please, have mercy. If I'm with child, please help me accept the outcome. And if this is just a flu bug"—her throat tightened—"I'll accept Your will."

Noreen leaned her head against the tree, eyes closed, and relaxed to the sound of the babbling creek. Within minutes, the nausea was gone, replaced by an indescribable sensation of peace. Noreen remained seated several minutes, not wanting to lose this sense of wellness in her soul.

The sun was close to the horizon when she finally trekked back to the house. Several buggies lined the bishop's driveway. Surely the women hadn't decided to stay longer. Perhaps Bishop Zook had called a meeting. She climbed the porch steps and opened the door to the *daadihaus*. The room was flooded with men and multiple pockets of conversation going on at once.

She scanned the room, surprised so many could fit in the cramped space.

Thomas weaved through the crowd. "Noreen," he said, smiling wide. "Bishop Zook has offered to give us the *daadihaus*. We can move it to our property."

"What? Really, it's moveable?"

"It won't be easy, and it'll take multiple teams to pull it." Excitement bubbled over him as he turned to Jonathan. "But we can do it, *jah*?"

His brother nodded. "I don't see why *nett*. The horses pulled big loads of logs without much problem. Of course that was in the winter using sleigh runners."

"That's *wunderbaar*," Noreen said.

Thomas agreed, but was quickly pulled into another conversation about how they would dig under the foundation to secure the straps. The bishop suggested detaching the porch and if necessary, the back bedroom, and hauling them separate.

Noreen caught a glimpse of Alice leaning against the kitchen's entry wall, arms folded and smiling. Noreen made her way through the crowd. "Are you sure you're all right with this?"

"Other than missing you in *mei* backyard, I'm thrilled the old place has a purpose again." She bobbed her head toward the kitchen. "I've put the kettle on. Let's have a cup of tea while the men plan the move."

Noreen's stomach rumbled. "A cup of tea sounds *gut*."

CHAPTER 17

"Looks like the men have the chains in position," Noreen announced to the women. She, along with the other women and children, had been waiting patiently in the bishop's warm kitchen as the men prepared the *daadihaus* for the move. Noreen slipped on her cloak and went outside, anxious to see the six-horse draft team in action.

Puffs of white fog billowed out from the horses' nostrils as they tossed their heads and snorted.

"I think they chose the coldest day," Patty said, sidling up to Noreen.

Alice joined them, hugging herself, teeth chattering.

"Jonathan said the more packed the snow, the better the sleigh will glide." Patty burrowed her neck and half her face under her wool cloak.

Noreen tapped the ground with the heel of her boot. "It's frozen *gut*." So were her fingers and toes since she ran out of the house without grabbing her mittens. But she wouldn't be outside long. Once the horses pulled the house off the property, she and the other women would go back inside and begin preparing the meal.

January wasn't an ideal time for this type of work. Her husband was bundled in heavy clothing, a scarf around his neck. Still, the brutal weather had turned the tip of his nose red in a short time. Thomas glanced Noreen's direction and smiled. He would certainly be cold and hungry by the time the house was moved and positioned over the foundation.

Noreen touched her cheeks. Numb. "Maybe we should send some jars of *kaffi* with the men. I'm sure they'll want something hot to drink before long."

"Too late." Patty pointed at Jonathan and Thomas climbing aboard the makeshift sleigh.

Noreen sucked in a sharp breath as Jonathan snapped the reins and called out for the team to pull.

Despite having detached the front porch, back stoop, and bedroom, the structure didn't move.

Thomas jumped down from the sleigh and walked beside the team.

Jonathan signaled the horses once more and this time they jerked forward.

"*Kumm* on Turbo, pull," Jonathan called in a frustrated tone.

The front two horses went first to the left, then to the right, digging their hooves into the snow to find traction. The steel runners sank down. Another lunge and the house inched forward. The men, women, and children cheered.

Noreen studied her husband's determined expression. The tip of his nose looked raw. No doubt the wool socks and insulated boots weren't enough to keep his toes from going stiff.

After a difficult start, the horses found their rhythm. Her new house moved down the driveway. *Such a glorious sight.*

Alice nudged Noreen's arm. "We better get the chicken and dumplings on the stove."

Noreen trailed the women back into the house, but Patty stopped her from going into the kitchen with the others.

Her sister-in-law crossed her arms. "Have you told Thomas about the *boppli*?"

Noreen raised her brows. "How did you—?"

"I'm the mother of six." Patty studied Noreen head to toe. "Four months?"

Noreen placed her hand on her midsection. "Three."

"And you never breathed a word." Patty shook her head.

"I wanted to tell Thomas first but he's been preoccupied with preparing the *haus*." She shrugged. "I'm trying *nett* to get *mei* hopes too high. I might miscarry again."

"There's a season for all things," Patty said, reaching for Noreen's hand. "You've waited a long time and I believe God will bless you with a healthy *kinner*. You're going to make a *gut* mother."

"I wish I had your faith," Noreen said softly.

"It's easy for me to tell you *nett* to fret, but please don't." Patty squeezed her hand. "And tell Thomas."

Alice came around the corner holding a small box. "I forgot to give this to you yesterday when it arrived."

Noreen noticed her sister's address and tore open the box. She lifted the hammer from the brown paper wrapping, admiring the new wooden handle. "I was hoping Carol Diane's husband would be able to finish the handle in time." She batted a tear from her lashes. "Thomas had used this when he built our first *haus*."

Alice smiled. "I think it'd only be fitting for him to use it *nau*."

Noreen ran her finger over the hammer's smooth wooden handle. "*Jah*, I agree."

"I'll hitch the buggy." Patty headed to the door.

"And I'll get a few jars of *kaffi* ready." Alice disappeared into the kitchen, returning a few minutes later with a basket of canning jars filled with coffee.

Noreen could hardly wait to see her husband's expression when she gave him the hammer. She scooted outside and down the porch steps. "*Danki*, I won't be too long," she told Patty, taking the reins.

A short time later, she veered the horse down Leer Road. Trees had been taken down to widen the driveway in order for the house to fit. Thomas glanced up as she entered the yard and began walking her direction.

"It isn't ready," he said.

"I have something for you." Climbing out of the buggy, Noreen presented him with the box.

"What's this?" He glanced over his shoulder at the men, whose arms were waving at Jonathan who was directing the team.

"I'm sorry. I should have waited." She started to climb into the buggy, but stopped when his hand caught her arm.

"Stay. Please." He waited until she nodded before he turned and jogged back to the men.

Noreen watched as the men worked together to get

the house lined up with the foundation. Then Thomas unlatched the horses from the structure, led them to the other side, and reattached the chains. The building wasn't much bigger than the woodshed and *washhaus* combined, but the tedious task of lining it up just right took precision. Noreen watched as the men leveled first one side, then the others.

Thomas wiped his gloved hands on the sides of his pants and approached her. "Sorry. That took longer than I thought."

"Understandably so. That was impressive to watch."

"Jonathan deserves the credit," he said.

"You all did a fine job." She handed him the box.

"What's this?"

"Open it," she said, excitement bubbling up within her.

Thomas pulled back the box flaps, then lifted his gaze to meet hers.

"It's your hammer," she said. "I had it fixed. That's why I . . ." She stopped talking. He didn't need to know that was why she'd asked for money. Alice had paid the shipping to send it to her sister's place in Mio.

Thomas was studying the hammer in silence, turning it over and running his hand over the wooden handle. When he looked up, his eyes were watery. "This is a nice surprise, *fraa. Danki.*"

"I couldn't throw it away."

He smiled. "I'm glad you didn't."

"I have another surprise for you," she said.

"*Jah*, I see you brought us *kaffi*." Thomas motioned to the men to come over. "This hot *kaffi* will hit the spot."

She couldn't tell him she was pregnant now. Not

with the men walking toward them. "How soon will you be ready to eat?"

He glanced upward. "It must be close to two *nau*."

"*Jah*."

Jonathan handed out jars to the men.

"What time do you want to stop to eat?" Thomas asked his brother.

"Depends if you want that back bedroom attached before dark."

Thomas chuckled. "We don't want to sleep under the stars, that's for certain."

Noreen's face heated. She and Thomas had been married over fifteen years and she still blushed over personal things like discussions about their bedroom. "I'll leave you alone so you can get back to work." She turned to climb into the buggy when she caught sight of the swing hanging from the maple tree. "Thomas." She pointed to the swing. "When did you put that up?"

Thomas frowned. "You weren't supposed to see that until tonight."

"I'm sorry I spoiled your surprise." She covered her eyes and turned toward the buggy. "I'll pretend I didn't see it."

He helped her into the buggy. "*Danki* again for the hammer."

"You're *welkum*."

"I have another surprise for you, but I'll have to give that one to you later." He winked.

Noreen smiled. Her surprise would have to wait too.

. . .

The temperature plummeted along with the sunlight. Any minute the sun's pink hues reflecting off the snow would fade completely and make it impossible to work any longer. Thomas scaled the ladder, taking position on the top rung. "Can you see the level?"

"It's *gut*." Jonathan signaled to Levi who set the anchoring nail in place.

Hammers soon echoed as Bishop Zook and Jonathan's eldest son secured the opposite wall.

Thomas fastened the wall header. As it turned out, detaching the building went much faster this morning. Without the extra footage, moving the house was easier for the horses, but rejoining the two sections had proved challenging as, in the move, the walls jimmied off-kilter. On top of that, everyone was tired. Daylight was fading quickly, and they were all ready to call it a day. Thomas moved down a rung on the ladder. Having to lean awkwardly in order to drive the nail, he stretched his achy muscles to the point of them cramping.

"Done," Levi announced.

"Us too," Bishop Zook said.

Thomas sank the last nail, then shimmied down the ladder filled with a satisfied sense of accomplishment. He placed his hammer into the loop of his tool belt. "I can't see anything but shadows or I'd thank you individually. I couldn't have done this without all your help. *Danki*." His eyes moistened unexpectedly. Thankfully the men wouldn't notice in the dim light.

"We're happy to help," Jonathan said, and the others agreed.

"I'd say we finished just in time." Levi touched

a match to the lantern wick, illuminating the area. Shortly after, other lanterns were lit so that the men could gather the tools.

In all the barn raisings Thomas had taken part in, they never worked this late. Of course during the summertime the days were longer. It couldn't be much past six o'clock, yet it felt like midnight.

Thomas began collecting tools, placing them in a large wooden crate. He wasn't going to mention the missing shingles that still needed to be replaced. He planned to wait until the others left before mending the roof. Thomas picked up a handsaw, but paused when the jangling sound of a horse's harness drew closer. A buggy rambled up the drive.

"Whoa," Noreen said.

Thomas set the saw in the crate and went to meet his wife. "We just finished."

"I was beginning to worry something might have happened."

He should have thought to send one of his nephews back to the house to update the women. Usually the women attended the barn raisings or other building events and could see for themselves when the building was finished. But with the weather so cold, it only made sense for them to stay inside.

"I brought fresh *kaffi*," she said.

"Sounds *gut*." He turned toward the lantern lights. "Anyone want *kaffi*?"

Not surprisingly there were no takers. The men still had barn chores waiting for them at home. Thomas too. Only his livestock were at Jonathan's.

Jonathan came up beside them, lantern in hand. "You two are *welkum* to *kumm* for supper."

"I packed sandwiches," Noreen was quick to say.

Thomas reached for her hand.

"Unless you'd rather have something hot," she added.

He was cold from being outdoors all day. But something had prompted her fast response. Did it have something to do with why her hand was shaky? Thomas studied her a moment, but her face was too shadowy to see her expression. He'd eaten a hardy dish of chicken and dumplings earlier, so he wasn't too hungry. "A sandwich sounds *gut* to me."

"*Nett* me. *Mei* stomach's been growling for a hot meal." Jonathan lifted the lantern higher, aiming it toward the house. "*Nau*, if I could just round up the boys."

Jacob and Peter lumbered out of the house toting equipment, tired expressions on their faces.

Thomas handed Noreen the lantern. "I'll be back in a minute." He joined Jonathan as he headed to his buggy. "I'll be over later to help with chores."

"Don't worry about it." His brother placed his tool belt inside the buggy. "The boys and I can handle it."

"Are you sure?"

"*Jah*, I'll see you in the morning." Jonathan boarded his buggy.

"*Danki* again." Thomas shot a quick wave, then turned. Catching a glimmer of lantern light under the maple tree, he smiled. Noreen was waiting for him on the swing.

He sat down next to her and placed his arm around her shoulders. "What do you think?"

"Definitely worth waiting for," she said, lowering her head to his shoulder.

He twined his gloved fingers with hers. If the weather weren't so cold, the gentle gliding motion of the swing would lull him to sleep. "You *kalt*?" he asked when the wind picked up.

"A little."

He stood and reached for her hand. "You ready to see your other surprise?" Without giving her time to answer, he swept her into his arms and carried her to the house. "As you can see by the missing boards, the porch steps need repair." He entered the house. "*Welkum* home, *fraa*."

"It feels like we've never left."

"Other than the furniture being all pushed to one end of the room."

"That's simple to fix."

Without putting her down, he continued toward the bedroom.

Noreen giggled. "I thought you were hungry."

"We can eat later." He lowered her to the edge of the bed, then went to the closet where he had stashed the present he'd been waiting to give her. He handed her the box wrapped with brown paper and tied with twine.

"What's this?"

"Open it and see."

She pulled the twine off and ripped open the paper. "Oh, Thomas." Her voice squeaked. Tears brimming her eyes, she lifted their wedding quilt out of the box.

Thomas gasped. It wasn't any bigger than a baby quilt. Oh, Lord, now she was crying. Thomas dropped to his knees at the side of the bed. "I'm sorry, Noreen. I thought Patty understood I wanted her to *add* to the blanket."

"You saved it."

"*Jah*, but . . ." He didn't want it to remind her of a painful topic. He should have opened the box and looked at it before giving it to her. Thomas reached for the quilt. "Let me put it away."

"*Nay*." She dried her eyes with the ball of her hand.

"Do you want to make it into a pillow? I think if you sew the sides together and with a little stuffing . . ."

"It's perfect just the way it is." She gazed at the quilt. "I can't believe you saved it from the trash pile."

"Are you sure this won't . . . upset you?"

"Because it's the size for a *boppli*—it won't fit our bed." Her eyes welled with tears again.

"Noreen, I'm sorry."

"I have a surprise for you as well," she said, smiling. "We're going to have a *boppli*—Lord willing."

"What?"

She nodded. "July."

His jaw went slack. "July," he repeated.

"Are you happy?"

"Of course I am." He bound to his feet and whisked her into his arms. "I love you, Noreen."

"I love you too."

He kissed her lightly on the lips, then pulled back. "You know what this means, don't you?"

She shook her head.

"We're going to have to add another bedroom."

BUILDING FAITH

Kathleen Fuller

To James. I love you.

GLOSSARY

ab im kopp—crazy, crazy in the head
daag/daags—day/days
daed—dad
danki—thank you
dawdi haus—small house used for in-laws/parents/
    grandparents
familye—family
geh—go
grossdaadi—grandfather
gut—good
gute nacht—good night
haus—house
kaffee—coffee
kapp—white hat worn by Amish women
maed—girls
mamm—mom
mei—my
nee—no
sehr—very
sohn—son
ya—yes
yer—your
yers—yours
yerself—yourself

CHAPTER 1

Faith Miller ran her palm across the smooth, cherry wood surface of the bread box, then blew sawdust off the top. The cherry was fancy for something as simple as a box to hold bread, but the wood had belonged to her grandfather, and she wanted to use it. Fine particles of dust floated in front of her, dancing in the air of her grandfather's woodshop. This was her sanctuary. She had loved being here as a small child, helping *Grossdaadi* with his various woodworking projects. It had been a hobby for him, a serious one. He would have rather been a carpenter than a farmer.

Like her grandfather she loved the smell of the wood, the feel of the sawdust on her hands, the precision of measuring to one fifteenth of an inch. She stood back and inspected the bread box, a birthday gift for her mother. A little more light sanding, a few coats of varnish, then a clear coat, and the box would be finished.

She ran her fingers across the sleek, soft wood again and listened. Her grandfather used to tell her the wood talked. Not in words, of course, but it spoke to him on a soul level. Wood had never spoken to her, but she didn't have the deep connection with carpentry and woodcrafting her grandfather had. She yearned for it and spent as much of her spare time as she could increasing and perfecting her skills.

She stood up and stretched. It was late—very late. She should've gone to bed hours ago. She had to get up early in the morning to go to her job at Schlabach's Bulk Food store with her younger sister, Grace. But as each hour had passed, she kept telling herself just a little bit longer, a little bit more work, and then she would stop. She needed to sand down the top of the bread box until it was glass-like smooth. She eyed it critically. The surface still wasn't perfect but it would have to do, at least for tonight.

Faith pushed back the stray strand of hair that refused to stay in her *kapp* and glanced out the shop window at the inky darkness. She didn't accomplish everything she had wanted to, but she was tired, a feeling she'd been increasingly familiar with. It had always seemed that way lately—so much to do, but not enough time to do it. At twenty-two she'd learned the hard lesson that life was precious and time was short. She didn't want to waste a single minute.

She turned off the lantern and walked out the door, stepping into the night air, cicadas and bullfrogs punctuating the dark silence. The house where she lived with her sisters and parents was a few yards away. Everyone would be asleep by now. *Like I should be.* She could barely make out her footsteps as she stumbled to the back door, but she didn't dare turn on her flashlight. If her father knew she was out so late, she'd get another lecture, another reminder that "early to bed, early to rise makes a man wise." Perhaps working on a bread box well past midnight wasn't the wisest decision, but it was worth it.

She crept into the house and slipped off her shoes, then carefully made her way up the stairs and opened the door to the bedroom she shared with her twenty-year-old sister, Grace. Her other sisters, Charity and Patience, were in their bedroom down the hall. They were still in school, and in the morning the family would be bustling to get to their jobs and to the schoolhouse, all under the supervision of her mother.

As soon as Faith shut the door, Grace turned on the battery-operated lamp. Faith jumped. "Grace," she hissed, squinting her eyes in the bright light. "What are you doing up?"

Grace folded her arms and leaned back against the pillow, her ash-blond hair in a long braid that hung over her shoulder. "You woke me up."

"Sorry. I was trying to be quiet."

"Not quiet enough. Where have you been?"

Faith unpinned her *kapp* and set it on the dresser. "I was out in the woodshop."

Grace glanced at the small clock on the bedstand. "It's almost one a.m." Her grin turned sly. "If I didn't know any better, I would have thought you snuck off to *geh* visit somebody."

Faith grimaced. "I would never do that."

Grace arched a dark-blond eyebrow. "Never?"

Faith's cheeks heated but she didn't look at her sister. "That only happened one time. Now, turn off the light so I can put on *mei* nightgown."

Grace chuckled. "Guess I hit a nerve," she said before turning out the light.

Faith heard the rustling of covers as her sister settled in bed. She quickly changed into her nightgown and got into the twin bed on the opposite side of the room. She closed her weary eyes to say a quick prayer.

"I was worried about you." Grace's soft voice lilted in the darkness.

Faith's eyes opened, even though she couldn't see her sister. "Why would you be worried about me?"

"You're spending a lot of time in *Grossdaadi*'s woodshop. More time than you used to."

Faith closed her eyes again. "I have work to do."

"You have work to do during the *daag*. Work you get paid for. That should be *yer* priority."

Holding in a sigh, Faith bit her tongue before she said something she would regret. *Nothing like getting a lecture from my little sister.* "I take *mei* job at Schlabach's seriously. So far there hasn't been a problem."

"Then why did I have to wake you up yesterday morning to get ready for work?"

Oh. Faith had forgotten about that. "So I slept in a bit. Usually I'm up before you. Now, quit talking so I can get some sleep or you will have to wake me up again come sunrise."

"See, you're already crabby."

"*Gute nacht*, Grace."

"'Night, Faith."

Faith closed her eyes again, but she wasn't near sleep like she'd been moments ago. Her sister was right. She had been spending a lot of time in the woodshop. But Grace didn't understand. Nobody understood. She needed to be out there. She needed to work on her projects. They gave her purpose, much more purpose than working in a bulk food store, cashing out customers and straightening shelves of flour and salt and baking supplies. If she knew there was a way she could sell the small projects she made so she could do woodworking full time, she would. But no one in her church district took her work seriously. The one time she had suggested taking a small birdhouse to Schlabach's to see if it would sell, her father had given her a look that could melt ice cubes. "You have a job," he'd said. "One that is appropriate for a woman." Then he'd gone back to reading his paper. End of subject.

This time Faith couldn't keep herself from sighing. She flipped over on her side. There was something else nagging at her. Or rather *someone* else intruding on her thoughts. She blamed Grace for bringing him up. Thanks to her sister, Faith couldn't stop thinking about the time she actually *had* snuck out of the house to meet someone. Silas Graber.

They had just started courting, and one Saturday evening last fall he came over after everyone had gone to bed. It had been pitch-dark outside, much like tonight. He'd tossed pebbles at her window until she met him in the backyard.

"You're going to get us in trouble," she'd snapped. "It's a miracle you didn't wake up Grace."

"*Kumme* on." He put his hands on her waist. "Nothing wrong with having a little fun."

"This isn't fun." But her heart thrummed with excitement. "It's risky."

"I'll take the blame. If *yer daed* discovers us, I'll tell him you found me irresistible."

"Ooh." She lightly batted his shoulder with her fingers. "What am I going to do with you?"

"You can kiss me, for starters."

She'd found out later that Grace had only pretended to be asleep and knew exactly what Faith was doing. She should have known then that her relationship with Silas wouldn't work. She'd always followed the rules—with the exception of that night—and Silas played by his own rules.

She pressed her lips inward, forcing the memory out of her mind. Which wasn't easy. She had been willing to marry him at one time. Thankfully she had realized the kind of man he really was. Irresponsible. Selfish. Undependable. She'd come so close to making the biggest mistake of her life almost a year ago when she'd become engaged to him. Then tragedy had struck, revealing his real character. Breaking up with Silas had been the best decision she'd ever made.

Still, she felt a pinch in her heart. Like her memories, she tried to ignore it. She was over him—for good.

• • •

Silas ran his hand through his hair and pulled on the ends. He looked at the paperwork on the kitchen table. A stack of bills to the right and the accounting book to the left. It was late, nearly one in the morning, and his brain was swimming with numbers that didn't make sense. He didn't have much of a head for figures. Never had. It had taken him years to learn how to measure accurately, which was a necessary skill for his job. He'd been happy to eyeball things, but that always ended up ruining whatever project he was working on. At first his father had been patient in teaching him. But eventually he accused Silas of not paying attention. There had been a nugget of truth in that, especially when he was younger. Silas would eventually take over his *daed*'s carpentry business at some point. Unfortunately, that time had come sooner than either of them had imagined.

He stared at the bills again. They needed to be paid. Some were even overdue. He had work lined up for the next couple of weeks, but no new orders after that. Normally he would be happy for the break, which would give him a chance to go fishing. He hadn't been near a creek or river in weeks, and he missed the quiet peace he always found when casting his line into the water. But fishing didn't pay the bills and he needed more work. It didn't help that a new carpentry shop had opened up a few miles away, further diluting what was already slow business.

He needed to go to bed. He had to open up the shop in the morning, and he'd already worked four hours after closing today. For the past two months he'd been handling most of the work himself. His father helped out when he could, but for the most part Silas had the responsibility of running the shop, filling orders, taking care of accounts, and making sure the business—and their family—didn't go under.

All that required organization—and he had never been organized. Another one of his downfalls, one that used to drive his father crazy. But now his *daed* didn't say anything about Silas's lack of focus, which had improved recently out of necessity. He didn't say much lately, not since *Mamm* . . .

Silas pushed away from the table and stood. He arched his back, then went to his room upstairs. He was tired. Bone weary, really. But he wouldn't let his father down. He'd done that before. He'd let too many people down, Faith most of all.

He shook his head. He needed to stop thinking about her, stop nursing the pain that had been in his heart since she ended things between them. They had been apart for nearly half a year after dating for two, and he needed to move on. Some days he thought he had. But when he was tired or lonely or . . . anything . . . he missed her.

Yet how could he move on when they lived in the same church district and saw each other every other Sunday? They didn't speak, but just seeing her was enough to remind him of the good times . . . and the bad. Near the end the bad had outweighed the good.

He fell into bed, closed his eyes, and was instantly asleep. The next morning he rose early, fixed coffee, and started on breakfast. He'd finished cooking the sausage links by the time his father came into the kitchen, bleary-eyed.

"Rough night?" Silas asked, his tone heavy.

"*Ya.*" *Daed* sat down.

Silas nodded and took a sip of his coffee. Then he

poured a cup for his dad and set it in front of him. "Breakfast?"

"*Kaffee* will be fine. Make *yer mamm* a plate, though. I'll take it to her."

He did as he was told, adding one sausage link to the scrambled eggs and toast he had at the ready. He set the plate in front of his father. Giving Silas an appreciative smile, *Daed* said, "I'll be out later this morning to help you in the shop."

"I've got it under control." Silas ignored *Daed*'s skeptical look. "Really, I do."

"I need to work, at least when I can."

Silas nodded, relenting. But he knew his father may or may not be able to work today. And Silas needed to be prepared for that. It was time for him to grow up, to be responsible. He was twenty-two years old but he'd spent his entire life acting like a kid. Then the diagnosis came, changing his life and his parents' lives forever.

His father picked up the plate. "I'll see you in a little while."

Silas nodded as his father left. He downed his coffee, inhaled the eggs and toast, washed and dried the dishes, then went out to open up the shop. He started mixing up the mahogany wood stain he would apply to a china hutch that needed to be ready for a Yankee customer by tomorrow afternoon. He'd barely finished preparing the stain when the bell above the door jingled. He turned to see his friend Melvin Weaver walk in.

"Hey," he said, putting down the container of stain. "What brings you here so early this morning? I figured you'd be at the harness shop already."

"I'm on *mei* way. I've been meaning to come by before, but we've been so busy with the *haus*, time got away from me."

"I know how that is." Silas put his hands on his hips. "What can I do for you?"

"We've got the kitchen framed in and drywalled," Melvin said. "I'd like to hire you to build the cabinets and do the flooring."

Silas had to keep his jaw from hitting the floor. Melvin was getting married in a couple of months, and he was working hard to get his future home ready. Silas mentally calculated how much money he'd profit from making and installing cabinets and installing flooring in the spacious house. The cash would go a long way toward paying the bills. He couldn't believe his luck. No, not luck. God was answering his prayers. Maybe that's why business had slowed. God knew Melvin would need a carpenter, and the Lord was dropping the opportunity on Silas's doorstep. "Wow," he finally said, at a loss for more words.

"I know it's a big project, but you do great work, Silas. I want these cabinets to be perfect for Martha. You're the best there is, next to *yer daed*."

"He taught me everything I know." Silas was pleased by the compliment. He did have natural skill, an intuition about how to create something beautiful out of raw materials. His father had admitted that several years ago, which had only added to *Daed*'s frustration with him. "You're wasting the talent God gave you," he'd said more than once. "You need to focus instead of daydreaming."

But his father hadn't realized that daydreaming and

imagining were part of the process for him. In *Daed*'s defense, Silas hadn't realized how important focus and discipline were. He was learning that lesson now. "Martha will have the best cabinets in Middlefield," he promised.

"*Gut.*" Melvin grinned. "I'll pay top dollar too."

Silas almost leaned against the counter with relief. The Lord provided the opportunity. All Silas had to do was not mess up. "I'll have to work on the installation during the evenings and weekends though, for the next couple of weeks. *Mamm* . . . she hasn't been feeling well. I've been taking care of things here at the shop while *Daed* is . . . helping her." *Daed* insisted on keeping *Mamm*'s condition a secret as long as possible. The man could be so stubborn. They could use the community's help. But he wouldn't argue with him. *Daed* was suffering as much as *Mamm*, and Silas would let his father deal with the pain in his own way.

Fortunately, Melvin didn't pry. "Can you get the work done before the wedding?"

Silas did a few calculations in his head. Then he redid them just to make sure they were right. "*Ya*," he said. He'd get it done. "I'll stop by and take some measurements after work today."

"Sounds *gut.*" Melvin looked at the clock on the carpentry shop wall. "Speaking of work, I need to get to the harness shop. Martha's *daed* doesn't abide lateness." He turned to leave, then paused. "The *haus* is unlocked," he said over his shoulder, "so feel free to go right on in."

"I will." Once his friend was gone, Silas let out a whoop of joy. Finally, some good news. Now he was seeing—and feeling—some hope. *God, You are good.*

CHAPTER 2

A few hours after she arrived at Schlabach's, Faith was surprised to see her cousin Martha walk into the store. She smiled, happy to see her. "It's the middle of the *daag*," Faith said. "Are you off work already?"

"I'm on lunch break." Martha's smile brightened her pretty face. She and Melvin Weaver were engaged to be married, and even though they hadn't announced their engagement at church yet, it wasn't a secret. The entire district knew the wedding would be soon.

Martha was not only Faith's cousin, but one of her closest friends. Yet this past year they hadn't spent much time together. Faith could blame Melvin for that, since Martha did spend a lot of time with her fiancé. But to be fair, Faith hadn't exactly made herself available to Martha either, not when she spent all her free time in her grandfather's shop. But now that Martha was here, Faith realized how much she had missed her friend.

"Do you have some time for a bite to eat?" Martha asked. "I brought us lunch."

"Definitely." She gestured to the empty store. "We haven't been very busy today. Let me tell Grace that I'll be back in a bit."

A short while later Faith and Martha were sitting behind the store at a small picnic table the owner of the store, a Yankee named Mr. Furlong, had put outside for the employees. Early spring days like this were the perfect time to enjoy the warmer weather. Martha pulled out a paper sack from her large tote bag and put it on the table. "Roast beef sandwiches okay?"

"Sounds delicious."

Martha took out the sandwiches and two apples, then handed one sandwich and an apple to Faith. They bowed their heads in silent prayer before they started eating.

"How's business at the harness store?" Faith asked, glancing at her sandwich. She usually cut her sandwiches in two equal pieces, but since she didn't have a knife—

"Here." Martha handed Faith a small knife.

Faith beamed as she took it. "You remembered."

"Of course. You're the only person I know who insists on cutting her sandwiches."

"They're easier to eat that way."

Martha picked up her whole sandwich. "Work at the shop is fine, although *Daed* is wondering who's going to take *mei* place in the office after Melvin and I get married."

Carefully cutting her sandwich, Faith said, "I guess he'll have to look outside the *familye* to find someone."

"*Ya*, although he said every time he hires someone new they end up marrying one of us." Martha tore off a small piece of crust from her bread. "You know Jonah is single now."

"He and Rachel broke up?"

"A couple of weeks ago. *Daed*'s keeping a close eye on him now. He's the only person at the shop other than Melvin who's not related to us, and Fanny is marrying age. I guess *Daed*'s not ready to see his youngest daughter tie the knot anytime soon. Not that he has anything to worry about. Jonah's been working with us for so long, he's like the brother we never had. But he would be a *gut* catch for someone else."

Faith wasn't sure if Martha was making small talk or if she was hinting at something. "Doing a little matchmaking, are you?"

Martha's eyes grew round with fake innocence. "Me? Of course not." Her expression turned serious. "That didn't turn out too well the last time."

Another heart pinch. Again, Faith ignored it. "It's not *yer* fault Silas and I didn't work out."

"I really thought you would," Martha said in a soft voice.

Faith took a bite of her sandwich so she wouldn't have to respond. She tried to enjoy the juicy roast beef and spicy horseradish, but she couldn't, not while Silas was fresh on her mind. Again. She swallowed. "How are the wedding plans going?" she asked, desperate to change the subject.

"*Gut. Sehr gut*, actually. I've had a lot on *mei* mind lately, though."

"I imagine getting ready for a wedding is a lot of work when you're the bride." She tried not to think about how close she came to finding out firsthand how much work was involved.

"But on the subject of the wedding," Martha said, "I have a question for you."

Faith prepared herself for what she knew was coming. She would love to be one of Martha's wedding attendants. Or even her maid of honor. She opened her mouth to say so, when Martha surprised her for the second time that day.

"I would be so happy if you would make the cabinets for our kitchen."

Faith shut her mouth. Surely she heard her wrong. "What?"

"I know how much you enjoy woodworking and you're really *gut* at it. I would love to have something of *yers* in *mei haus*. I thought the cabinets would be perfect, and I know you would do an excellent job."

"I'm not sure what to say."

"Say *ya*." Martha frowned. "Unless you can't. If you're too busy with work, I'd understand—"

"*Nee*. I'm not too busy." Faith clasped her hands together. She couldn't believe this was actually happening. She would be able to make something bigger than a bread box. This was a real job, one that was complex and challenging. The fact that she was making something for her dear friend and cousin was a bonus. "I'm so pleased you asked me."

"Of course I'll pay you."

Faith shook her head. "I won't hear of it. This is *mei* gift to you and Melvin."

"That's a generous gift," Martha said.

"*Grossdaadi* has a lot of wood in the shop. He was always doing different projects."

"I remember. It will be nice to have something of his in our *haus*."

Faith looked at Martha intently. Martha hadn't been as close to *Grossdaadi* as she had, but they had both loved their grandfather. "You know he would have wanted the wood to be used for a *gut* purpose. So if you're okay with oak cabinets, then they will be my wedding present. I can stain them any color you like."

"You can decide on the stain. I trust *yer* judgment."

Excitement bloomed inside Faith. "I'll have to come by and take some measurements. Would tonight be okay?"

"*Ya*. The *haus* is unlocked since there's nothing in it. Melvin will be putting in the plumbing soon, but right now it's basically rooms and walls." She looked at Faith, her brows knitting. "Are you sure I can't pay you at least for *yer* time?"

Faith held up her hand. "*Nee*. I want to do this for you."

Martha's eyes grew soft. "*Danki*, Faith." She paused. "I've missed you. I don't want us to grow apart after Melvin and I get married."

"We won't." She wanted the words to be true, but she wasn't so sure. Once Martha and Melvin married, they'd have their own house and their own lives. They'd still be part of the church and Faith would still see them, but they wouldn't have much in common anymore. And once they had children, Martha would be busy and become closer with the other young mothers in their community. The thought saddened her. She didn't want to lose her friend. *I'm so tired of losing people I love.*

But she wasn't going to mourn, not when she finally

had a project that was not only challenging, but meaningful. "I can't wait to come up with the plans," she said.

"And I can't wait to see what you come up with."

"I won't let you down, Martha," Faith said, smiling. "I promise."

. . .

That evening Faith was so eager to get to Martha's new house she didn't want to bother eating supper. As her mother was putting the meal on the table, Faith slipped on her light jacket. The warmth of the day had turned cool. "Where are you going?" *Mamm* asked. "Supper is almost ready."

"To see Martha." A little lie, which could turn into the truth if Martha happened to be at her future home tonight.

"Now?" *Mamm* set a bowl of cabbage salad on the table. "I'm sure her *familye* is starting supper too."

"I won't be gone long."

Mamm lifted one eyebrow. "All right. Tell her parents I said hello."

Faith walked out the door as Grace, Charity, and Patience came into the kitchen. When Faith was outside, she blew out a long breath. She didn't want to explain to her mother what she was doing for Martha. *Mamm* didn't approve of her spending so much time in her grandfather's workshop, either.

She did have to get her measuring tape and possibly some tools, so she darted inside the shop, found the items, then went to hitch up her buggy.

Thirty minutes later she arrived at Martha's house. She went to the front door and opened it. Martha was right; it was little more than a shell. The layout of the house was simple and she found the kitchen right away. It was empty, too, and the floor was still plywood. A single window was on the south-facing wall, the perfect height for a sink to be placed under it. It was a fairly large space, which didn't surprise Faith. Martha had always wanted a lot of kids. She said a quick prayer that the Lord would bless Martha and Melvin with as many children as their hearts desired. Then she went to work measuring, thinking about the type of cabinets Martha would like.

"What are you doing here?"

She turned at the familiar voice, her heart stopping in her chest. Then it skipped a beat when she saw Silas standing there. She immediately put her heart in check, although she wished it didn't need so many reminders.

But her heart had other ideas, because her pulse started to hammer as she and Silas stood in the same room alone for the first time since their breakup. It was one thing to see him at church. Among the community they could avoid each other. Here, there was nowhere to hide.

He tilted his head, then crossed his arms over his chest. "I didn't realize you were giving me the silent treatment."

She frowned, confused, then realized she hadn't answered his question. She lifted her chin and stared him down, determined for him to know he didn't affect her. "I'm measuring," she said.

"I can see that." He put his hands on his hips.

She saw the tool belt around his waist, and a knot formed in the pit of her stomach. "Why are *you* here?" Although by the sinking sensation in her stomach she suspected she already knew the answer.

He paused, looking at her with equal intensity. "Measuring."

They continued the standoff, their gazes locked. He was still gorgeous. He always had been, with chestnut-colored hair that curled at the ends, thick eyebrows above brown eyes that always held warmth and a twinkle of mischief. Faith tried not to think about the two years they'd spent together. The plans they had made. The plans she had made, to be a wife and a mother. He had ruined all that. "What, you ran out of fish to catch?"

His gaze narrowed. "Why are you here?" Silas asked again, this time slowly, as if she didn't understand what he was saying. He also didn't respond to her cutting remark. Then again, he didn't have to. They both knew she had always come in second to stupid fish. Sometimes third . . . or not at all.

Dread formed in her stomach as realization dawned. Martha was her cousin, but Melvin was Silas's good friend. Surely, no . . . "Martha asked me to build their kitchen cabinets."

Silas scoffed. "Martha must have made a mistake, because Melvin asked me to make the cabinets and put in the kitchen flooring."

"She didn't make a mistake. Martha asked me a few hours ago."

"Melvin asked me this morning."

They stared at each other, and Faith wasn't sure what to do. "This must be a miscommunication."

"Must be."

"We'll have to talk to them about it."

"Might as well do it now," Silas said, turning to leave. "I'll *geh* talk to Melvin."

"I'll *geh* talk to Martha." Clearly he didn't want to be around her. Which shouldn't bother her, but it did . . . a little. Okay, a lot. Yet she should have known he had moved on from her.

Silas stopped. He looked at her again, and she searched his eyes for the softness, the love she used to see there. Instead she saw something rare for Silas. Seriousness. "Just to let you know," he said, his voice stronger and more confident than she'd ever heard it, "this job is mine. Melvin wants a proper carpenter to do the work."

That made Faith's blood boil. "I *am* a proper carpenter."

"You're a hobbyist. There's a big difference."

"You never respected the fact that I am as *gut* a carpenter as any man."

"That's not true." He paused. "I know you're *gut*."

She ignored the tiny bit of satisfaction his remark gave her. "Don't think I don't know what you're doing, trying to put me off guard with sweet talk."

Silas huffed. "Think what you want. You always do. I was just letting you know I am *not* giving up on this job."

Faith looked at him. "I'm not giving up on it either. Martha is *mei* cousin—"

"Melvin is *mei* friend—"

"And she asked me to do this and I will do it."

"We'll see about that."

She watched Silas walk out the door, held her breath, then exhaled when she saw him disappear. She turned off both lanterns and heard the sound of Silas's horse and buggy leave. How had she not heard his buggy approach? Then again, she always became engrossed in her tasks, enough to block out everything around her.

A stab of grief hit her. It always did at unexpected times, often the worst times. She had been so focused that day in the woodshop, using a bevel-edged chisel to practice her carving skills on an old piece of wood. If she had paid more attention, maybe she would have heard her grandfather cry for help just outside the door of the shop. She would have been there in time—

She drove the thought away. She wasn't about to let Silas take this opportunity from her. It wasn't as if he needed the extra work. He and his father had their own carpentry shop. Why would Silas need to take on an extra job? Faith thought about that for a moment as she got into her buggy, then shook her head. It wasn't any of her business what Silas did anymore.

That was how she had to live her life now. Not get involved, not entangle herself, not risk her heart.

CHAPTER 3

"Silas, I don't know what to say." Melvin held out his hands and shrugged his shoulders as they stood in the living room of Melvin's parents' house. "I had no idea Martha was going to ask Faith to make those cabinets. We've been so busy dealing with work and wedding plans and other things that have to be done to the *haus*, I guess we didn't talk about it."

"It's okay, Melvin. I just want to get everything cleared up." *And to set Faith straight.* She hadn't changed a bit since she'd broken their engagement—and his heart. She was still hard, still brittle, still jumping to conclusions . . . and still hurting. He could see the pain in her eyes, hidden behind a mask of pride. Although she was an Amish woman and in good standing with the church, she was the most prideful woman he knew. But she didn't have to be. He hoped she'd realize that someday.

He gave himself a mental shake. Faith wasn't his concern anymore. She had made that clear six months ago. But this job was his concern, and he wasn't going to let her, or anyone else, take it from him.

"I'll have to talk to Martha about it," Melvin said, derailing Silas's train of thought.

At first Silas wondered what there was to talk about. Wasn't Melvin in charge of building the house? Then again, while he knew marrying Faith would have been the biggest mistake of his life, if they were married, would he make a decision like this without her input? Even if she wasn't so stubborn and headstrong, he would never decide something so important without involving her. Which made him understand why Melvin wouldn't do that to Martha either. "That's fine," Silas said. "Just let me know." *And let Faith know too.*

That brought about a twinge of guilt. More than a twinge. Faith was a good carpenter. Her grandfather had taught her well. But she wasn't experienced. She'd never done a project as big as a whole kitchen. She only helped her grandfather in his woodshop.

"How about Martha and I meet you at the *haus* tomorrow evening? That will give us time to straighten this out."

"I appreciate it, Melvin."

"*Nee* problem. I'm sorry for the mix-up."

"I'm sure you and Martha will work this out." Silas left, confident that by this time tomorrow the kitchen job would be his, and his alone.

. . .

"Faith, I had *nee* idea," Martha said when Faith stopped by her house on the way home. "Melvin and I . . . I guess we talked about the kitchen. I can't remember." Martha put her fingers to her forehead. "Things have been so busy."

"I understand," Faith said as Martha sat down on the couch. "And it's okay."

"*Nee*, it's not." Martha looked distressed. "Of all the people in Middlefield Melvin had to ask, it had to be—"

"Silas." Faith sighed. "But I understand why he did it. I'm sure he wants the best for you and Silas is very *gut*." She had to admit that. It wouldn't be fair to him not to. He was really talented. But he was also irresponsible and so lackadaisical about work and life that he drove her *ab im kopp*.

At first his carefree attitude appealed to her. He was spontaneous, like the night he'd come over and they'd kissed under the stars. He'd made her feel special, even loved. But love was more than midnight kisses and charming smiles. Love was putting the other person first. Choosing to honor a commitment—like a relationship—instead of treating it as an afterthought. Love was about being there during the worst time of her life. Which he hadn't been.

"I'll tell you what," Martha said, her face brightening. "I know Melvin and I can work this out. We'll discuss it and come to a decision. I'm sure he'll see *mei* point of view and how much I want you to be involved in this. Melvin and I will talk tonight and then I'll meet you tomorrow at the *haus*. Does that sound *gut*?"

"Perfect," Faith said. She was sure Melvin would see Martha's side.

As she drove home, she couldn't stop wondering why Silas was taking on extra work. Was there something wrong at his father's carpentry business? She hadn't heard anything. Then again, she always tuned out any mention of Silas. No, this was a simple mis-understanding. Melvin and Silas were friends, and it would be like Silas to want to do the work as a favor to Melvin. Just like Faith wanted to do for Martha. Silas was kind like that. He was the kindest man she knew.

She straightened in her seat, lifting her chin and steeling her resolve. Blood was thicker than water, at least in this situation. She had no doubt that Martha and Melvin would make the right decision, and that by this time tomorrow, Faith would be able to start work-ing on making the most beautiful kitchen cabinets anyone in Middlefield had ever seen.

. . .

When Faith arrived at Martha's new house the next evening after work, she was more tired than usual. She'd spent last night in the woodshop drawing dia-grams and searching through the large stash of her grandfather's wood. Just as she had told Martha she would, she found a lot of beautiful oak, and after some quick calculations, she realized that if she was careful and didn't make any mistakes, she'd have just enough to build the cabinets.

Once again she'd stayed out in the shop longer than she should, and when she finally went to bed, she couldn't fall asleep. Not because she was excited, but because for the first time, she started to have doubts. She'd never worked on a project this extensive before. She'd helped her grandfather repair a few cabinets, but she'd never planned an entire kitchen. Silas was right. She was a hobbyist. She couldn't deny that. He was a professional. She couldn't deny that either.

But she also couldn't spend energy doubting herself. For years she had wanted to prove herself to someone other than her grandfather. Now she had that opportunity, and she wouldn't let self-doubt eat away at her. She could do this. Martha had confidence in her. More important, she had to maintain confidence in herself.

Faith parked next to Martha's buggy, then tethered her horse. The April air was a little chilly tonight, and a stiff breeze blew the skirt of her dress around her knees. She tucked her chin farther into her lightweight jacket and went inside. As she crossed the threshold, she froze. Martha wasn't there, but Silas was. "Oh *nee*," she said before she could stop the words from coming out of her mouth.

"Glad to see you, too, Faith," he said.

"*Yer* sarcasm is not appreciated." She looked around the empty room. "Where's Martha?"

"She and Melvin left a few minutes ago. They had more to talk about."

Faith frowned. "I thought this was already settled."

"So did I." He was still wearing his coat, and she realized she hadn't seen his buggy outside.

"How did you get here?" she asked.

"I walked."

Her frown deepened. The distance between this house and Silas's wasn't that far, but it made for a fairly long walk. And she knew what it meant when Silas took walks. She noticed tiny lines of strain at the corners of his dusty brown eyes. "What's—" She stopped herself.

It wasn't her business what was wrong with him. Not anymore. She lifted her chin. "You made a wasted trip," she said. "I'm telling you right now that I'm the one who has the job."

"We'll see about that." He nodded toward the door.

Faith heard the sound of horses' hooves outside on the driveway. She gave Silas a cool look before folding her hands together.

The door opened and Martha walked in. Faith started to smile but her smile slipped as soon as she saw her cousin's solemn expression. Melvin was right behind her, looking just as grim.

"This can't be *gut*," Silas muttered behind Faith.

"Hi, Faith." Martha's smile was forced. Melvin kept his gaze on the crude floor.

Silas stepped forward. "Have you come to a decision?"

Faith looked at him, her brow wrinkling. Again, there was something different about Silas. He'd always been so laid back. Too laid back, in her opinion, although he was the one person she could fully relax around, who with one look or word could make her smile. At least he had been. Now he was serious. Determined.

Melvin and Martha exchanged a look. "We've been talking," Melvin said hesitantly.

"We know," she and Silas said at the same time.

"And we're having a bit of a problem," Martha added.

"What kind of problem?" Silas asked.

"Well . . ." Melvin looked at Silas, then at Faith, then back at Silas again. "We can't choose between the two of you."

Silas folded his arms over his chest much like Faith had her arms crossed over hers. "What do you mean you can't choose?"

"We both agree that each one of you would be good for the job," Melvin said, sounding a little more settled now. "We want to hire you both."

Faith shook her head. "*Nee*—"

"Nope," Silas said.

Faith nodded. At least she and Silas could agree on something. "That would be a disaster."

"Bigger than a disaster."

"Now wait a minute." Melvin held up his hand. "Look, I know you two have a . . ."

"Past," Martha said gently.

"And I realize Martha and I made a mistake by not being on the same page about this. But building a kitchen is a big project. Both of you work during the *daag*. Martha and I think the job would go faster and be easier on you two if you cooperated and did the work together."

This was ridiculous. How could they even think she and Silas could work together? They could barely stand to be in the same room with each other. She also wondered if Melvin and Martha were telling the whole truth. "Can I talk to you for a minute?" she asked her cousin. Then she glanced at Melvin and Silas. "Privately?"

Martha nodded, the grim look on her face returning. She headed out the door and Faith followed her.

A blast of cold air swirled around them. Spring was always so unpredictable. It wasn't much warmer inside the house but at least there they had protection from the howling wind. "I can't work with Silas," Faith said, seeing no reason to be tactful. "You know why. Besides, I thought you had confidence in me."

"Oh, Faith, I do. So does Melvin. But we also know Silas does good work. Melvin and I would like to get the *haus* finished as soon as possible. It only makes sense to hire two carpenters." Her expression turned stern. "I understand if you can't work with Silas. But we aren't changing our minds. If you and Silas can't come to an agreement on this, we'll hire someone else. I'm sorry."

Faith's teeth started to chatter. What was she going to do now? She was tempted to tell Martha to forget it, but reined in her thoughts. She still wanted to do something special for her cousin. Wasn't that one of the main reasons she wanted to work on the kitchen? She could do that, and still prove herself while working with Silas. Then another thought came to her. "What if he doesn't agree to work with me?" Which was a likely possibility.

"Then we will hire another carpenter to work with you." Martha tucked her hands into her coat. "Faith, it's cold out here and frankly I'm tired. Melvin's tired. We've both been a little stressed."

Faith became concerned. "Is everything okay between the two of you?"

"Oh, *ya*, everything is fine. It's just that he and I have different ways of doing things, and if we don't consult each other on the important stuff, then misunderstandings happen. Like this one."

Faith could relate to what her cousin was saying.

Wasn't that one of the problems she and Silas had? They were different people. Polar opposites.

"But Melvin and I also complement each other," Martha said. "That's the beauty of our relationship. He's strong where I'm weak, and vice versa. Plus," she said with a grin, "we love each other and we always work things out. That's what couples do."

Resisting a frown, Faith nodded. In the past she and Silas couldn't work out their issues. And now they were both expected to come to an agreement about collaborating on the kitchen. She didn't know if that was possible.

"Now can we go inside?" Martha asked.

Faith nodded and followed her cousin. While she was glad Martha and Melvin had a strong relationship, they had what Faith and Silas lacked. They had love.

CHAPTER 4

Silas, I'm really sorry," Melvin said, shuffling his feet against the plywood floor.

Silas held himself in check. What had been an answer to prayer was turning into another disappointment. "Was this Martha's idea?"

"No, it was both of ours. We had to compromise and this was our solution." His gaze was stern. "If you and Faith can't work it out, then we'll find somebody else. But we want both of you for the job."

Silas rubbed his forehead with his callused fingers. Melvin wasn't giving him much of a choice here. And Silas couldn't afford to be emotional about the situation. "I'm willing," he said, barely able to say the words out loud. So much for not being emotional. "But I doubt she will be."

"Maybe she'll surprise you."

He let out a bitter chuckle. "Surprise? Faith doesn't know what that word means. She plans everything, down to the tiniest detail."

Melvin shrugged. "People change."

Silas was about to make another sarcastic comment, but held off. Change was possible. He ought to know.

He'd been forced to change. But Faith was different. She was predictable and liked it that way. He had to acknowledge he'd always been drawn to her steadfastness. Then he thought about Faith's grandfather's death. How her predictability had turned into inflexibility. Yes, she had changed too.

The door opened and Faith and Martha came in. Silas noticed Faith's lips were a little blue around the corners and Martha was visibly shaking. If he'd been thinking straight, he and Melvin should have gone outside and let the women stay in the house to talk. He started to take off his coat to give to Faith. But when she shot him a frigid look, he changed his mind. No, this wasn't going to work out. He was going to either lose this job or have to work with another carpenter. Faith wouldn't yield. That word wasn't even in her vocabulary.

Melvin moved to stand beside Martha. "Well?" he said, sounding hopeful.

She put her hand on Melvin's arm. "I think we should go." She looked at Faith and then at Silas. "You'll let us know tomorrow what you decide?"

Faith nodded.

"*Ya,*" Silas added.

"We'll see you tomorrow, then." Melvin opened the door, and he and Martha left.

Silas looked at Faith, waiting for her to talk. She pressed her teeth on her bottom lip, something she did when she was deep in thought. The gears were turning in her mind like they always did.

He turned away, that small gesture making him

think of the first time they kissed. He'd gotten a wild idea soon after they started dating that he would coax her out of her house in the middle of the night. She wasn't happy with him, but she had met him in her backyard. There wasn't even a sliver of moonlight, and she made sure to tell him all the reasons they shouldn't be out there and all the rules they were breaking. Then he had joked about her kissing him, and to his surprise she had obliged. From that moment on he was a goner.

He shoved the memory from his mind and whirled around. She was still thinking, tapping her finger against her chin. She was very deliberate, often annoyingly so. Like now. "So?" he said, unable to keep the impatience out of his tone.

Faith cut her gaze to him. "Is this how we're going to start our working relationship? With you snapping at me?"

He pushed his hat farther back on his head. "Sorry. You've made a decision, then?"

"*Ya*. I'm willing to set aside our differences to help Melvin and Martha." She lifted her chin. "Can you?"

"Done." Then he paused. This time it was his turn to be deliberate and thoughtful, something he wasn't used to. But they couldn't jump into this job and expect things to run seamlessly, not without talking about it first. "We should set some ground rules."

She tilted her head, looking at him suspiciously. "What kind of ground rules?"

"No dredging up the past."

Faith nodded. "I think that's fair."

"Number two, no criticizing of each other's work. Or how each other works."

A pause. "All right," she said, "although I don't see how constructive feedback can be considered criticism—"

Silas held up his hand. "See? That's exactly what I'm talking about. All we have to do is work together to make this kitchen the best it can be for our friends. We both have our own ways of doing things. Somehow we'll have to figure out how to make that work."

Faith opened her mouth as if to say something, then she closed it.

He shook his head and let out a sour chuckle. "You were going to say something about the past, weren't you?"

"*Nee.*" Her eyes shifted downward.

"You're an open book." Silas leveled his gaze on her face. "I know exactly what you're thinking." Why couldn't he stop looking at her? She was so pretty. More than pretty. He loved the light brown freckles that dotted her nose, the tops of her cheeks, and her chin. Her hair was a mix of light brown and blond, like the sun had gently kissed the strands. She was a few inches shorter than him, enough that he could lean his chin on top of her head with ease.

"You only *think* you know what I'm thinking." Her caramel-colored eyes lit with indignation. "And you always made assumptions."

"Ha!" Silas pointed his finger at her. "There you *geh*, bringing up the past."

Faith's eyes widened. "You tricked me."

"Tricked. Right."

She huffed and scowled at him. "Why don't we prepare a schedule of when we're going to meet, how we're going to work, what we're going to do, who's going to order supplies—"

"Wait a minute." The thought of every minute and detail being scheduled made his skin itch. "Let's take this one step at a time. How about we meet here tomorrow after supper instead? Then we can go over *yer* endless list of things we have to do."

"It's not an endless list and it's very important. You can't just show up here with tools and wood and make something."

"Actually you can. I've done it a lot, as you well know."

She folded her arms against her chest. "If we're going to do this together, then we need to do it according to a plan."

Silas took a step toward her. "*Yer* plan, I'm assuming?"

"Unless you have a plan, which would be a first in *yer* entire life."

He had to put a stop to this now or they would never get started on the kitchen, much less finish it. Doubts started creeping up again. "We'll come up with a plan together, one that will work for both of us."

She gave him a small nod. "Agreed."

"Then I'll see you tomorrow," Silas said.

Faith headed for the door. "Tomorrow it is." Then she left.

Silas took in the empty space. He removed his hat and rubbed the top of his head. They hadn't even started working and already they were arguing. *Lord, this will take a miracle.* But he had to make it work. He put his hat back on and turned off the gas lamp. As he left for home, he hoped God was still in the miracle-making business.

· · ·

When Faith got home, she didn't go directly into the house. Instead she went into her grandfather's wood-shop and slammed the door. She turned on the lantern, then slumped onto the wood bench in front of the long, sawdust-covered table and let out a long sigh.

All the good intentions in the world wouldn't help her and Silas come up with a way to collaborate. And she still couldn't stop wondering why he was willing to work with her, even though it was clear that it would be an uphill battle for both of them. Silas wasn't known for sticking around when things got difficult. He had to have another reason for wanting this job, other than his friendship with Melvin. Just like she had her own reasons for not giving up.

She rose and picked up a small plank of oak, then set it on the table. Maybe she should back out. She ran her hand across the top of the wood, careful not to press too hard so splinters wouldn't burrow under her skin. Her hands were already rough, probably rougher than a woman's should be. But she didn't care. She'd earned the calluses on her skin, spending hours work-ing and practicing her craft, first with her grandfather and then alone.

She had as much right to this job as Silas did.

Somehow she'd have to make this work, and she knew she couldn't do it on her own. "Lord, help me." Then she swallowed. "And Silas too. Help us work together without making each other crazy."

CHAPTER 5

The next evening Faith arrived at Martha and Melvin's new house well before the appointed meeting time with Silas. She had taken part of the day off and had stopped at Martha's to tell her about her and Silas's decision, saving Melvin and Martha another trip out there. She'd planned to do some quick measuring before Silas arrived. Yet right away, she noticed Silas's buggy was there. She frowned. He was never early. She renewed her determination. There was no reason she couldn't get the measurements she needed.

When she walked inside the kitchen, she stopped at the sight of Silas lying on his back on the plywood floor. His eyes were closed. He wasn't moving. He didn't even appear to be breathing.

Panic rushed through her, the image of her grandfather's collapse slamming into her with full speed. She knelt beside him. "Silas!" She touched his face, his chest, his arm. "Silas! Can you hear me?"

He opened one eye. "Of course I can hear you. You're screaming in *mei* ear."

Faith groaned and sat back, her heartbeat slowing while her irritation mounted. "I can't believe you'd scare me like that."

His lips lifted in a smile as he looked at her. "Nice to know you still care."

She sniffed. "I'd care about anyone I found lying in the middle of the floor." She scowled. "What are you doing, anyway?"

"Visualizing." He jumped up from the floor, dust coating his dark blue pants. "And waiting for Melvin and Martha to arrive."

"They're not coming." She stood and crossed her arms.

"Why not?"

"I informed Martha about our decision."

He cocked his head to the side. "I see. You did this without consulting me?"

"I already consulted you. We decided last night to work together. I thought I'd spare Martha and Melvin the trip here. They've been very busy with wedding plans, you know."

"I know. And it's nice that you thought of them. But did it cross *yer* mind that I might have wanted to talk to them? To get an idea of the type of cabinets and flooring they want?"

Faith waved her hand. "I already know."

"Martha told you?"

"*Nee.* She said to use *mei* judgment. She trusts me to pick out what she would want."

"Does Melvin get a say in any of this?" Silas asked. "Do I?"

"Of course you do. And I'm sure Martha and Melvin will talk about it—"

"Like they discussed who was building their kitchen?"

He had a point. "Do you think Melvin really cares that much about the kitchen cabinets?"

"Knowing Melvin, he just wants to make Martha happy."

"And I know what will make Martha happy."

"So I don't have any input? I just take orders from you?"

Faith pulled a measuring tape out of her bag. "I'll take any suggestions or visualizations you'd like to offer."

"How generous of you."

She shot him a hard look. "You know I can't stand sarcasm."

"And I don't like being dismissed." He took a step forward. "This is supposed to be a collaboration, Faith. That means we each contribute equally."

Once again she got the sense that Silas was different. They were both twenty-two, but she'd always felt older than him, mostly because he was more interested in having fun than taking life seriously. But now, with him gazing at her in absolute solemn determination, they were on equal ground. "I'm sorry," she found herself saying, and meaning it. "I didn't realize I was shutting you out."

His brow lifted. "An apology? Never thought I'd hear one from you."

"What's that supposed to mean?"

"*Nix.*" He heaved a sigh. "Now it's *mei* turn to be sorry. You know how *mei* mouth gets ahead of *mei* brain sometimes." He gave her a lopsided grin. "How about we discuss our ideas now? Get them all out in the open so we can develop a plan."

"You want a plan?"

"Honestly, *nee*. But I realize that planning is important, especially on a project this size. Plus I know you like to have things in order."

She'd expected to have to fight him on that. She reached in her bag and pulled out her sketchbook, then handed it to him.

Silas thumbed through it. "What kind of wood were you thinking about using?"

"Oak. *Grossdaadi* has a lot of it in his woodshop."

"Enough for all these cabinets?"

"*Ya*," she said. "As long as we don't make any mistakes."

Looking up from the book, he said, "So you don't have enough."

"I just said as long as we don't make mistakes—"

"Faith, we will make mistakes. It's inevitable."

"With proper planning and measuring, we won't."

He handed the book to her. "*Nee* one's perfect, Faith. Not even you." He walked to the center of the room and lay back down, gazing up at the ceiling.

"I knew it. You don't believe in me."

Silas folded his hands over his middle. "I never said that. What I said was you weren't perfect." He turned his head slightly toward her. "Which is true." With that he gazed up at the ceiling again. "Stop being so touchy."

"I'm not touchy."

"*Danki* for proving *mei* point." He lifted his hands and started tracing imaginary lines in the air.

Faith watched him for a moment, fascinated. In the two years they'd dated, she'd never seen him at work.

She'd seen the carpentry shop and projects he'd finished, but this was the first time she'd witnessed him visualizing. "Do you do this a lot?"

"Lie on the floor and draw in the air? *Nee.* Then again, I've never stocked a kitchen with cabinets." He closed his eyes and traced again.

Unable to resist, she lay down on the floor next to him and stared at the ceiling. "I don't get it," she said. "What are you looking at? Why are you doing this?" She flailed her arms in the air.

His hands covered her forearms. "You look like you're directing traffic," he said. "Close *yer* eyes."

"Silas, we don't have time for this."

"There's always time for imagination." He turned until their eyes met and their noses were nearly touching. "Carpentry isn't just cutting and nailing boards. There's an art to it."

Now he was sounding like her grandfather, which made her heart ache. A second, different kind of ache joined her grief. Being this close to Silas was activating butterflies in her stomach, a sensation she hadn't felt in a long time. She shouldn't be surprised. He'd been the only man who'd made her feel . . . giddy.

She didn't want to feel giddy. She didn't want to feel anything, especially about Silas. She pulled her arms away from him and scrambled to her feet. "Did you like *mei* ideas or not?" she said, brushing the dust from the skirt of her dress and refusing to look at him. Or to acknowledge the heat rising from her neck to her cheeks.

"I did." He sat up and spun around to face her, still sitting on the floor. "They're . . . adequate."

"Adequate?"

"That's not an insult, Faith. You sketched out some very utilitarian cabinets."

"Which is what Martha needs."

"True. But I think she'd like some with a little character."

Faith rolled her eyes. "You know we can't make fancy cabinets. She wouldn't want that anyway."

Silas stood and held out his hand. "May I?"

She hesitated, then handed him the sketchbook. He took a pencil from behind his ear and started drawing. Less than two minutes later he handed back the book.

Faith looked over what Silas had sketched out, and she had to admit she was impressed. He had taken her drawing and added details—he had drawn grooves in her plain doors to make a rectangle within each door. He added dark circles, and she realized those were knots on the wood. He also added lower cabinets with a mix of drawers and doors. It wasn't fancy, but it wasn't boring either. It was . . . inspired.

"Does it meet with *yer* approval?" he asked.

"*Ya,*" she said, studying his additions. "Martha will love this." She looked up at him. "You got all that from lying down on the floor?"

"Nah. I'd been thinking about that last night." He grinned. "I was just lying on the floor to see if you would join me. Which you did."

"Ooh!" She started to toss the sketchbook at him, then remembered it was hers. "You haven't changed one bit!"

"Is that what you wanted?" he asked, his grin fading away. "For me to change?"

She paused. "I . . . I don't know."

He stepped back from her. "Well, *gut* thing we're not together anymore. And once we're done with this kitchen, you won't have to be around me again."

"Silas—"

"I've got to get home. I'll be over tomorrow evening to look at that wood." His eyes narrowed. "I know you said we'll have enough, but I'll be the judge of that." He brushed past her and walked out the door.

Faith didn't move. She couldn't, not when she was tingling from the top of her *kapp* to the tips of her stockings. She hadn't expected this. Hadn't planned for it. But she couldn't deny she was more attracted to Silas than ever before. Somehow she would have to deal with it.

. . .

The next morning Silas woke up in a good mood, something that hadn't happened for a long time. The fact that he'd dreamed about Faith last night might have had something to do with it. A good dream, where they got along, enjoyed each other's company, and the sadness that seemed to always be in her clear caramel-colored eyes had disappeared.

He'd seen a bit of that sadness diminish when he was teasing her last night. When he'd heard the buggy approach Melvin's house, he'd peeked out the window and saw it was Faith . . . and decided to have a little fun. He wasn't surprised when curiosity got the best of her and she joined him on the floor. He'd anticipated that. For all of her stuffy, stiff-as-a-board ways, she was insatiably curious.

What he hadn't anticipated was how strong his attraction to her still was. That had worried him for a split second as their faces were close enough that all he had to do was lean forward a fraction of an inch to kiss her. And despite everything that had happened between them, how she had cut him to the core by breaking off their engagement, he had to stop himself from stealing a kiss. He couldn't let himself get that close to her again. Predictably she'd gotten up and destroyed the moment between them. A good thing, for both their sakes.

But none of that affected his dream last night or his good feelings this morning. He whistled as he walked into the kitchen. Maybe he'd make pancakes for *Mamm*'s breakfast. She'd made them at least once a week for him when he was little, and even when he was not so little. He smiled as he reached for the cast-iron skillet in the cabinet next to the stove.

"Tommy?"

Silas froze, the skillet heavy in his hand. He set it on top of the stove and forced a smile as he faced his mother. "*Nee, Mamm.* It's Silas. Do you want some pancakes?"

"You look like Tommy." *Mamm* went to Silas and gazed up at him. Then she put her hand against his cheek. He hadn't shaved yet, and he felt her fingers brush his whiskers as she spoke. "I've missed you, Tommy."

He swallowed as he took her hand in his and gently

moved it away. "I'm not Tommy, *Mamm*," he repeated, willing her to understand him. "I'm Silas. I'm *yer sohn*."

"*Mei sohn?* I have a *sohn?*"

Pain pierced his heart. He had no idea who Tommy was. *Daed* didn't know either. But when *Mamm* was in one of these states, she kept talking about him. "*Ya.* You have a *sohn*. And I love you very much." He kissed her cheek. "Now, how about I make us those pancakes?"

"Pancakes." She frowned. She was still wearing her nightgown, her grayish-brown hair in a messy braid down her back. "Pancakes," she repeated. "Do I like pancakes?"

"You like *yer* pancake recipe," he said, trying again to smile and lighten the mood, which was becoming harder to do the more disoriented she got. "I'm not so sure you'll like mine, but maybe you'll give them a try anyway."

She tilted her head, her eyes filled with confusion, then she nodded. "I'll try them, Tommy."

"There you are," *Daed* said as he came into the kitchen. He looked at Silas, asking him an all-too-familiar silent question. *Is she all right?* Silas gave a quick shake of his head and started toward the pantry to get ingredients for pancakes.

"Emma," *Daed* said, going to *Mamm*'s side. "You need to sit down. Silas is going to make us breakfast."

"He is?" She looked at *Daed*. "Oh, *ya*. He is. I didn't know Silas liked to cook."

And just like that, she was back to normal. "I'm learning to like it," he said, grabbing the flour and baking powder. He shut the pantry door. "I'm just not very *gut* at it."

Mamm started to get up. "I'll make the pancakes."

Silas met his *daed*'s gaze. They both knew that wouldn't be a good idea. Until her condition was stabilized, she was unpredictable. "Silas can do it," *Daed* said, sitting next to her. He took her hand. "He doesn't mind."

"Nope. I don't mind at all. Besides, it's *gut* for me to learn how to cook."

"*Yer* wife should be doing that for you," *Mamm* said. "Where is Faith, anyway?"

"Emma, Silas and Faith aren't married."

"Oh." *Mamm* looked at Silas. "That's right. But you were going to get married, *ya*?"

"*Ya*." Any good mood he'd had before had completely vanished. Cold reality set in. He had a little fun with Faith, but that wouldn't last. There was too much pain between them. Too many misunderstandings. Which made him more determined to finish Melvin's kitchen as soon as possible.

Daed quietly talked to *Mamm* as Silas made pancakes. They were a little tough because he'd stirred the batter too much, but they were edible. At least *Mamm* was eating this morning. Last night *Daed* said she wouldn't touch her supper.

"I'm tired," *Mamm* said, putting down her fork. "I want to *geh* to sleep."

Daed finished chewing and stood. "I'll be right back, Silas," he said as *Mamm* got up from her chair. "Don't open the shop until I get back."

Silas nodded, then started cleaning the kitchen while his father took care of his mother. He sighed, his heart feeling like an anvil was dangling from it.

Why Mamm, *Lord? Why does she have dementia?* It wasn't the first time he'd asked those questions, and it wouldn't be the last. He was an only child, and his parents had had him late in life. But the doctor said *Mamm* was on the young side to have such an advanced case. And when *Daed* had asked for the prognosis, the doctor refused to give one.

Since that time two months ago, Silas's world had been turned upside down. He knew it would never be the same again.

"She fell right asleep," *Daed* said when he came back. Silas had just finished washing the dishes.

"She didn't sleep last night?"

Daed shook his head. "Not much." He looked ready to collapse.

"Why don't we get some help?" Silas put his hand on his *daed*'s shoulder. "You don't have to do this alone. The doctor said there are people who can stay with her during the *daag*, even at night if we need them to."

"Nee." *Daed* shrugged Silas's hand off his shoulder. "We take care of our own."

"All right, then why don't we ask some of our neighbors and friends to help? I'm sure the older ladies in church—"

"I said *nee!*" *Daed* walked to the table and sat down. "I'm not ready for people to know about her. Not yet."

"They're already wondering." Silas sat down next to him. "I can't keep making excuses at church, and you can't keep sending people away when they stop by to visit her."

"I just thought . . . this new medicine, it's supposed

to help." *Daed* sat up straight. "It will help. We have to give it more time. Then she'll be back to her old self." He smiled, but the smile didn't reach his eyes. "You'll see, Silas. We'll have *yer mamm* back soon."

Silas felt a crack form in his soul. His father was in denial. "What if we don't?" he asked quietly.

His father looked at Silas, tears in his eyes. "Then it's God's will. And we'll have faith that He'll see us through." He stood and put his hand on Silas's shoulder. "I better check on her. Make sure she's still asleep."

Silas sank into his chair, then leaned forward and rubbed the stabbing pain in the back of his neck. While he believed God would get them through whatever happened with *Mamm*, that didn't mean he shouldn't be prepared. He let out a bitter laugh. Now he sounded like Faith. That was her motto. Be prepared. Have a plan. Stay in control. But Silas didn't have control over his mother's illness, or anything else. *God is in control.* The reminder gave him some comfort.

CHAPTER 6

Y ou're out of sorts."

Faith looked at Grace, who was standing next to her as they refilled the candy bins in the back of the store. She picked up a dipper full of black licorice drops and poured them into the plastic bin. "I'm fine." She glanced at her hand holding the dipper, aggravated that it was shaking. She'd been unnerved all day, not only because of her reaction to Silas yesterday when he left Martha's new house, but because she would see him again this evening. How did everything get so complicated? She thought the hardest part of working on the kitchen would be making the cabinets. She didn't imagine it would be fighting her feelings for Silas.

"The gumdrops *geh* in that bin," Grace said, tapping Faith on the arm, then pointing to the plastic container next to the black licorice.

Faith looked down and groaned. Now she had mixed up the colorful spice drops with black licorice pieces. Fortunately she was wearing clear plastic gloves, so she could reach in and fish out the gumdrops. The mistake wasn't a big deal, but her carelessness was uncharacteristic. She couldn't afford to be distracted while she was woodworking. That could cause an accident or injury. She let out a sigh as she pulled out two red gumdrops.

"Faith."

Grace's serious tone got Faith's attention. "What?"

"Something's bothering you. I know you're tired—"

"I'm not tired."

"You haven't gone to bed before one a.m. for the past four *daags*."

"Neither have you, since you've been keeping track."

"It's hard *not* to when you keep waking me up. It's *mei* room too." She closed the top of the butterscotch bin. "Maybe you should move out into the woodshop," she said, her tone filled with sarcasm. "You spend more time there than at home."

"Maybe I should."

"Faith, Grace." Mr. Furlong was walking toward them from the end of the aisle. His thick gray eyebrows flattened above square, brown glasses. "I can hear you bickering from the other side of the store. I don't know what you two are fighting about, but it will stop now."

Faith and Grace both nodded, neither of them saying anything. Mr. Furlong gave them one last warning look before walking away. Faith blew out a breath, relieved that since she and Grace had been speaking *Dietsch* at least Mr. Furlong and the Yankee customers hadn't understood their ridiculous argument. "Sorry," Faith said, closing the licorice bin and opening up the spice drop container beside it.

"I'm sorry too. I know you don't like to talk about

yer feelings much." Grace tied up the large bag of butterscotch pieces. "I just wanted to help."

"I know." Faith sighed, pausing before she dug the scoop into the gumdrops. "I promise, there's *nix* to talk about. And I promise I won't come in so late anymore. I shouldn't have been so thoughtless about waking you up."

"I appreciate it. After all, I need *mei* beauty sleep." Grace winked at her and walked away.

Faith smiled. Her sister never failed to make her feel better. She and Silas were similar in that way. She gripped the scoop again. Silas. What was she going to do about him?

After she finished filling up the candy bins, she took her afternoon break. She went outside and pulled out her sketchbook. But instead of drawing, she wrote out a schedule. If she did most of the cabinet building in her grandfather's woodshop, then she and Silas wouldn't have to work together. He was putting in the flooring, so he could focus on that while she made the cabinets. Then when he was done she could install the cabinets, which wouldn't take her more than a day or two. When she was finished, she had made sure she and Silas wouldn't see each other until the end of the month, except for tonight.

Satisfied, she put her sketchbook away and went back to work. The rest of the day went smoothly, and when she and Grace went home, they helped *Mamm* with supper while Charity and Patience were outside working with *Daed* as he tilled the garden. It wouldn't be long before they would start planting vegetables and flowers.

During supper, Faith glanced at the clock on the

kitchen wall. It was six thirty and Silas would be here soon. His house was within walking distance. She realized she needed to tell her parents he was coming over. "Silas is stopping by tonight," she said, then shoved a scoop of mashed potatoes into her mouth.

Mamm's brow rose so high it nearly touched her hairline. "He is?"

Faith had to hide a frown at the enthusiasm in her mother's voice. She glanced around the table and saw that her three sisters were looking at her with curious expressions. Only her father seemed more interested in food than Faith's announcement. She choked down the potatoes. "He's going to look at the wood in *Grossdaadi*'s woodshop."

That got her father's attention, as it always did when his father was brought up. "Why?"

She sighed inwardly. There was no reason to lie. "Because we're working on a project together."

"Oooh," Charity said.

Faith gave her a look. Since she was thirteen, Faith would excuse her immature teasing.

"Oooh," Patience and Grace added.

"It's not like that." Faith put down her fork.

"So you're helping Silas build something?" *Daed* said.

"That's nice of him to include you," *Mamm* added. "Especially after . . . well, you know."

"I'm not helping him." Faith crossed her arms over her chest, well aware she was not only losing patience but maturity. "We're working on the project together."

"What project is that?" *Daed* cut into his meat loaf with the side of his fork.

"We're making kitchen cabinets for Martha and Melvin. Together. Equal partners."

Daed scratched his head. "You don't know how to make cabinets."

This was what she was afraid of, that she'd have to defend herself. "I helped *Grossdaadi* refurbish Katherine Troyer's cabinets."

"That's not the same as building them."

"I've read up on how to make cabinets. And tables, chairs, rockers."

"Whose idea was this?" *Mamm* wiped the corner of her mouth with a napkin. "Surely not Silas's."

Faith explained with as few words as possible about Martha and Melvin hiring both her and Silas. "That's why he's coming over and we're picking out the wood."

"Sounds boring." Charity took a drink of milk.

"Or it could be romantic." Fourteen-year-old Patience put her chin in her hand. "You two might even get back together."

"That will *never* happen." Faith pushed away from the table, irritated that her face was heating as she thought about the jolt of attraction that had gone through her last night when she and Silas were together. "We're two different people."

"You're not as different as you think." Grace's voice could barely be heard above Charity and Patience's discussion of how they were sure the wedding would be back on within the next few months.

Faith looked at her, wondering if her sister knew something she didn't. Grace wasn't teasing. Instead she looked stern and serious, which was unusual for her. "I've got to *geh*," Faith said. "Silas will be here any minute."

"Oooh," Patience and Charity chimed.

"Will you stop that!"

"*Maed*," *Mamm* said. "That's enough." She looked at Faith. "After you and Silas are finished in the workshop, make sure you invite him inside for some cake and coffee."

"In other words, be polite," Grace said.

Faith gave her a quick nod and turned, snatching her sketchbook off the counter before walking out the kitchen door. She gulped the fresh evening air, breathing in the sweet, rich scent of mown grass and tilled earth from the garden patch to the left of the house. She didn't want to invite Silas in for cake and coffee, even though that would be the hospitable thing to do. All she wanted was for him to look at the wood, tell her she was right about having enough to make the cabinets, and leave after she gave him their schedule. She went to the woodshop and turned on the lantern.

She sat down on the bench and waited for Silas to appear. And waited. And waited. Then she paced back and forth, opening the door and checking outside. The sun had gone down, which meant she had been out here for nearly forty-five minutes. Where was he?

Frustration rose within her. She shouldn't be surprised that he was late. He had always been late when they were dating. She was a punctual person, and when he would show up half an hour after he said he'd pick her up for a singing or a ride in his buggy, she had to force herself not to lose her temper. He always had an excuse—he lost track of time, he had to work extra at the shop to get a project done because he hadn't realized how long it would take to finish, he'd fallen asleep on the couch. And she was expected to accept these excuses with a smile and forgiving spirit. Initially, she did. But then she got tired of it.

She waited a little longer, her anger growing stronger with each passing minute. Then she couldn't stand it anymore. She grabbed her flashlight, turned off the lantern, and headed for Silas's. He wasn't going to do this to her. They had a job to do, and if he couldn't be responsible enough to show up on time to pick out wood, how could she rely on him in the future? *I can't rely on him at all.* She knew that firsthand, and him proving that to her again cut her deeply.

• • •

"Tommy? Tommy? Why am I here, Tommy?"

Silas clenched his jaw and went to his mother's side. She was sitting on the couch, pulling on the skirt of her dress, looking scared and bewildered. "You're home, *Mamm*," he said, trying to take her hand.

She snatched it from him. "Who are you?" she said, backing away from him.

"I'm Silas," he said, for the tenth time in the past hour. He glanced at the front door. Where was his father? At supper *Daed* said he needed to take a walk. Silas understood why. *Daed* needed a break. *Mamm* had been agitated all day, and it had gotten worse when the sun went down. Now Silas wasn't only worried about his mother, but his father too.

"Silas? Where's Tommy?"

"I don't know," Silas said absently, glancing at the small clock on the mantel of their fireplace. *Daed* had given *Mamm* the clock as a twenty-fifth wedding anniversary present almost ten years ago. It was nearly eight thirty. He gritted his teeth. Faith would be furious with him for being so late, but it couldn't be helped. He couldn't leave his mother alone, not even to go find his father. "*Mamm*," he said, lowering his voice and speaking softly like he'd heard his father do. "It's bedtime. You must be tired."

"I'm not tired." She stood and walked away.

Silas followed her. She went into the kitchen and started throwing open drawers. Silas shut them behind her. The medicine wasn't working. This was the worst he'd seen her. "Tell me what you're looking for and I can find it for you."

"Spoons," she said, opening the drawer that held the silverware. She stared at it, then walked away.

"The spoons are right here." Silas grabbed a handful and showed them to her.

She pushed his hand away and sat down at the table. Then she stared straight ahead.

"Lord, please," Silas whispered, his voice cracking. "Please help her."

He heard a knock on the front door and froze. His mother didn't move, just gazed straight ahead with an empty expression. Should he answer the door? If his father were here, he would send whoever stopped by away, especially with *Mamm* being like this. Could Silas even leave her to answer the door? He decided to ignore it, even when the knocking grew louder. When it stopped, he breathed a sigh of relief and leaned against the table. *"Mamm?"*

She didn't move or say a word.

"If you think I'm going to put up with *yer* irresponsibility, think again Silas Graber!"

He spun around at the sound of Faith's shrill voice, then groaned. He didn't need this right now. "How did you get in?"

"Yer door is unlocked." She narrowed her gaze. "I knew you were ignoring me."

Silas went to her, hoping he could calm her down. She had a right to be mad, but unlike in the past, he hadn't not shown up out of carelessness. "Faith, it's not a *gut* time—"

"It never is, is it? You always have an excuse for going back on *yer* word. This is a job, Silas. One you said you would take seriously. I'm not going to be pushed aside or ignored because you can't be bothered to—"

"Tommy? Tommy?"

The fear in his mother's voice made him forget about Faith's tirade. He went to her side, about to tell her that he was Silas. Instead, he said, "I'm here."

"Oh, Tommy." She took his hand and put it against her cheek. "I've been looking everywhere for you." She glanced up at him, tears in her confused eyes. "I want to *geh* home."

"You are home." He couldn't stop the tears from spilling from his own eyes. "I wish you could understand that."

She jumped up from her chair and turned on him. "I want to *geh* home!"

"Silas," Faith said. "What's wrong with *yer mamm*?"

"*Geh* to the phone shanty and call an ambulance." He was in over his head. His father would be angry, but his mother needed a doctor. He expected Faith to give him a hard time, but she immediately dashed out the door.

He spent the rest of the time until the ambulance arrived alternately calming down his mother and trying to get her to see reality. She had a few lucid moments, but she was growing more agitated. Just as the ambulance pulled up, *Daed* walked in the door.

"What's going on?" he said, hurrying to *Mamm*. "Emma, talk to me."

But she had gone into another speechless state. Silas looked at his father. "She's got to *geh* to the hospital."

He nodded. "I'm sorry, *sohn*. I was walking and I got so tired. I sat down under the tree by the pond near the Troyers'. I guess I fell asleep."

"It's okay," Silas said as the paramedics arrived.

"We'll take it from here," a short, stocky woman said.

Silas stepped back and watched as the woman talked gently and quietly to *Mamm*, while the other paramedic, a tall, thin male, spoke with *Daed*. The female paramedic somehow convinced *Mamm* to go with her to the ambulance. "I'm riding with her," *Daed* said.

"I'll meet you at the hospital," Silas said.

But *Daed* shook his head. "Stay here, *sohn*. I'll take care of this."

"But—"

"I said stay here!"

Silas nodded, and it was only after the ambulance left with his parents inside that he remembered Faith was still there—and she had seen everything.

CHAPTER 7

Faith couldn't speak when Silas turned around and faced her. All she could do was stare at him, her heart breaking, not only for him but for his mother and father. Then the pain she saw in Silas's eyes spurred her to action. She went to him. "What happened?"

He brushed past her and walked to the kitchen without saying a word. Faith followed him. There were a few kitchen drawers open, and Silas went around and closed them. "Silas," she said, "is *yer mamm* all right?"

He whirled around and glared at Faith. "You saw her. Did she look all right? Did she act all right?" He shook his head. "*Geh* home, Faith."

But she wasn't budging, not after what she saw, and not when Silas was so distraught. She went to the stove where the percolator sat. "Let me make us some *kaffee*—"

"For once in *yer* life will you listen to me?" Silas shouted. "I don't want *kaffee*, and I don't want you here. Get . . . out." His chest heaved as he spoke, and his voice cracked on the last word.

His words hurt her, but she stood her ground. "I'm not leaving until I know you're okay."

"Then you're gonna be here a long time." He sagged

into a chair and his head fell into his hands. "Forget what you saw."

"I can't." She sat down next to him. "How long has she been like that?"

He shrugged. "It started a couple of months ago. She's on medication but"—he lifted his head, his eyes haunted—"you can see for *yerself* it doesn't work. She's actually gotten worse since she started taking it. She's got dementia . . . and there's *nee* cure."

"Oh, Silas."

"Don't." He shot up from the chair. "Don't you dare give me *yer* pity." He glared at her. "Now I know why *mei daed* didn't want any help. Didn't want to tell anyone. We don't need you feeling sorry for us."

"I don't." But it was a lie. She was still shaking a little bit from the shock of seeing Silas's sweet mother having a complete breakdown. She didn't know a lot about dementia, but she vaguely remembered that she hadn't seen much of his mother lately, and she wasn't in church at the last service. Faith had to admit she also hadn't paid much attention. Avoiding Silas had meant avoiding his parents too.

"I've got to get to the hospital," Silas said, storming out of the kitchen.

Faith followed him. "*Yer daed* said to stay here."

"I'm not going to leave him alone." Silas spun around in the middle of the living room, his shoulders slumped. "I'm not . . ."

She couldn't stand seeing him like this. She went and put her arms around him. "It will be okay, Silas."

He leaned his cheek against the top of her *kapp* but

didn't return her embrace. "*Nee*, it won't. She's only going to get worse, until we won't be able to take care of her." He sniffed. "I'm not sure we'll be able to take care of her anymore after tonight."

She stepped back and took his hands. "Listen to me, Silas Graber. You're not giving up. I won't let you. We're going to pray for her, and for *yer daed*."

His gaze met hers. "Don't you think I've been doing that?"

"Then we'll do it again. And we'll keep praying." She squeezed his hands, closed her eyes, and prayed.

. . .

Silas was so tired. Every bone in his body ached. His heart ached. His soul even ached. But there was something sweetly peaceful about Faith holding his hands while she prayed with absolute confidence for his mother.

Without thinking, he tightened his grip on her hands. He hadn't held her hand in months. He felt the rough skin, the calluses so similar to his own. For that brief moment while she prayed, he did believe everything would be okay. Then again, she always had that effect on him when they were together. She was calm. Steady. And deeply emotional, even though she tried to hide it.

"Amen." She let go of his hands and stepped away, then looked up at him and smiled.

He nearly melted inside. Her smile made her face shine like the sun on a cloudless summer day.

"Should I let Martha and Melvin know you can't work on the kitchen?" Her voice was soft and . . . hopeful?

It also broke his trance. "You'll what?"

The smile faded. "You can't possibly work on the kitchen when *yer* mother is so ill."

His mouth fell open. "Unbelievable."

"Silas, I'm trying to help you."

"You're helping *yerself*." He pointed at her. "I knew you were still mad at me about the past. I have *nee* idea why, though."

"*Nee* idea?" Her tone turned shrill, the way it usually did when she was ticked off. "I told you why I was angry."

"Because you can't count on me, *ya*, I remember." He leveled his gaze on her. "And now I know I can't count on you. You would use *mei mamm*, after seeing how sick she is, to make sure you get what you want. So you'll have all the money from the job *yerself*." When her eyes widened, he huffed. "Don't act like that's not what you're doing." He turned and stalked off, then spun around again. "You're a piece of work, you know that? A selfish, spoiled brat who only thinks of herself."

Her lower lip trembled, and he almost took the words back. But he couldn't. First she shattered his heart, breaking off their engagement with some lame excuse about how she couldn't handle his irresponsibility. Which wasn't completely inaccurate, but she didn't even give them a chance to work things out. Now she wanted the kitchen job all to herself. She'd get all the money—money he and his father needed. And to think he actually believed she cared about his parents . . . about him. He was such a fool.

Yet as she stood there looking shocked, her lips quivering and her eyes filling with tears, his heart ripped even more. Unable to face her, he turned his back. Seconds later he heard the front door slam shut.

He looked up at the ceiling. "You know what, Lord?" he said, shouting. "She can have the job. I'll figure some other way to pay the bills. I'll take care of it myself." He fell into a chair, tears flowing again. He was helpless to do anything. He couldn't fix his mother. He couldn't work with Faith. He couldn't run the carpentry shop by himself, and he couldn't do the kitchen job. She was right about that. Not when his mother was so unstable. Not when he was sure he was going to lose her sooner than he'd ever thought.

. . .

Faith felt numb on her way home from Silas's. How dare he accuse her of taking advantage of the awful situation with his mother? Couldn't he see she was being practical? That she was trying to ease his burden, one she didn't know about until tonight? Instead he took her offer all wrong. Called her selfish. How could he say that to her after she had prayed so fervently for his family?

Yes, she should be angry. But she felt nothing. Nee, *not nothing. I'm hurting.*

She went inside, not bothering to be quiet. It wasn't that late, even though everyone was already in bed.

When she got to her room, Grace was sitting on the edge of her bed, brushing out her hair. Faith sat down on her own bed, not saying anything.

"Faith?" Grace put down the hairbrush. "Did Silas come over? Did you two get into a fight?"

"He didn't come over. But we did get into a fight."

"What does that mean?"

Faith looked at Grace. "I can't talk about it." She rose from the bed to get her nightgown, still in pain from Silas's words, and worse, the expression of stark betrayal on his face. He really did believe she was selfish and spoiled. Had he always felt that way? If so, why had they dated in the first place? Why had he asked her to marry him? Why had he once told her he loved her?

"Faith," Grace said, coming behind her. "Did you *geh* see Silas?"

She nodded, unfolding her nightgown.

"Does this have something to do with his *mamm*?"

Faith whirled around. "What do you know about Emma?"

Grace's eyes filled with sadness. "I know she's sick. She was at the store a few weeks ago and she was acting strange. First she forgot why she was there, then she couldn't remember *mei* name. I told her who I was, but when she left she said, 'Good-bye, Faith.' I'm not the only one who's noticed she's been behaving a little off recently. And the past two weeks *nee* one has seen her, and Silas's *daed* won't let anyone stop by."

Faith frowned. "You knew all this?"

Grace nodded. "You would, too, if you paid attention." She stepped back. "I don't want to hurt *yer* feelings, because it looks like you and Silas went at it pretty hard, but you've spent so much time isolated from everyone since *Grossdaddi* died. Even when you're not in the woodshop, *yer* mind is there . . . or somewhere else." She ran her finger under her nose. "You're not the only one who lost someone. I miss him too. I know you were his favorite—"

"I wasn't his favorite."

"*Ya*, you were. We all knew that. And it was okay, just like we understood that his death was the hardest on you. But that doesn't give you the right to stay isolated from the rest of the world. You're being—"

"Selfish." The word hit her to the core. Silas was right. She was selfish. She'd been so wrapped up in her grief—and yes, her pride—that she hadn't even noticed what was going on in her own community. Then she remembered Silas had mentioned money. "*So you'll have all the money from the job* yerself." He had no idea she wasn't getting paid for making the cabinets. But now his desperation to have the job made sense. Undoubtedly the medical bills for his mother were mounting up.

Faith sank down on the bed, feeling horrible. "I'm a terrible person."

Grace settled beside her. "*Nee*, you're not. You're hurting, though. And in *yer* typical independent way, you're not letting anyone help you."

"He didn't want *mei* pity," she whispered, remembering something else Silas said. And she understood that. He wanted to be strong, to show everyone else he was strong. Like she had after her grandfather died.

She'd used his death as an excuse to push Silas away—
just like Silas had accused her of using his mother's
illness. "I have to apologize to him," she said. She
turned to Grace. "But I don't know how."

"You'll figure it out." Grace took her hand and
squeezed it. "But not tonight. Sleep on it. Maybe something will come to you in the morning."

They both got into bed and Grace turned out the
light. "*Danki*," Faith said as she turned on her side.
"And I'm sorry if I've been acting like a spoiled brat."

"You haven't." Grace yawned. "I don't know where
you got that idea."

Faith shut her eyes. *I do.*

CHAPTER 8

Silas's head popped up from the kitchen table as he heard the front door open. He blinked and looked down at his arms, which were folded in front of him. When had he fallen asleep? He stood as his father walked into the kitchen, his boots thudding heavily on the floor.

"Where's *Mamm*?" Silas said, going to his father.

Daed gave Silas a weary smile. "She's okay, *sohn*. She's still at the hospital." Then his smile grew. "They misdiagnosed her."

"What?"

"She doesn't have dementia."

Silas's brow furrowed. "But she's been forgetting things. And the hallucinations, and the combative behavior, and calling me Tommy . . . what else could it be?"

"Something with her thyroid." *Daed* sat down at the table. He pulled a scrap of paper out of the pocket of his pants. "Hashimoto's ence . . . encepho . . ." He handed the paper to Silas. "Here, you read it."

"Hashimoto's encephalopathy." Silas frowned. "What is it?"

"The way the doc explained it, her thyroid gland"—he pointed to the center of his neck, pressing his finger against his salt-and-pepper beard—"is acting up. It's a rare disease, but one that can be managed with medication. The right medication."

Silas joined him at the table. "So all those symptoms her other doctor thought were dementia were really from this?"

Tears welled in *Daed*'s eyes. "*Ya.*" He clasped his hands together and started to weep. "Silas, I wasn't ready to lose her. But I thought I would. And I thought I would be okay, knowing that if she died, it would be God's will." He wiped his eyes with a handkerchief. "I've been so scared."

"So have I." Silas swallowed around the lump in his throat. "She's been so sick the past few *daags*."

"Even that's a blessing. If we hadn't gotten her to the emergency room when we did, she could have gone into a coma. The doctors want to keep her for a couple of *daags* to make sure the thyroid medicine works, but they're sure it will. You did the right thing by calling for help." He looked down at the table. "I might . . . I might not have if I'd been here."

Silas wanted to say the opposite, but knew that wasn't true. His father had been so private, so insistent on dealing with *Mamm* his way. After Silas's fight with Faith, he understood. Yet that didn't mean they should have been fighting this alone. "I want to see her," he said.

"You will when she comes home. Right now they want her to rest. She hasn't slept well in *daags*. Neither have I." He got up and rolled his shoulders. "I feel like I could sleep for a month, now that I know she's going to be all right."

Silas nodded. "I'll take care of the shop," he said.

Daed put his hand on Silas's shoulder. "I know you will. You've proven *yourself* through all this, Silas. I underestimated you."

"I needed to grow up."

"And you have. I'm looking forward to joining you back at work, as soon as *yer mamm* is settled at home."

"That sounds great. But right now, you need to get some sleep."

His father nodded and left. Silas sank down onto the chair, bent his head, and prayed, giving thanks that his mother would be all right. When he finished, he realized he was starving. He had just started to fix himself some eggs when there was a tap on the back door of the kitchen. He peered through the window and frowned. What was Faith doing here?

• • •

At first Faith didn't think Silas would open the door. Not that she blamed him. For the first time she realized how much she had hurt him, not just by accusing him of being irresponsible but also by ending their relationship. Through the kitchen window she could see how tired he was. Even at this distance the dark shadows were evident under his eyes. He stared at her for a moment through the glass. Maybe this was a bad idea. Maybe she should turn around and go to work.

She was late as it was, but Grace said she would explain to Mr. Furlong why Faith was running late. Just as she was about to turn around, Silas moved and opened the door.

"Why are you here?" he asked in a flat tone.

"I wanted to know how *yer mamm* is doing . . . and how you're doing."

"She's fine." He leaned against the door, the tension in his face lessening a bit. "They had the wrong diagnosis. She's on new medication and after a couple of *daags* in the hospital she'll be able to come home. She should be back to normal soon enough."

"That's wonderful news." Faith smiled.

"It is." He glanced down at the floor, then back at her. "*Danki* for praying for her . . . for us."

"You're welcome." She threaded her fingers together. "Can I come in? We need to talk."

He nodded and opened the door wider. "I was just about to make breakfast. Do you want anything?"

"*Nee.*" She was about to sit down, then changed her mind. "Why don't I make you breakfast?"

Silas turned around, and she almost laughed at the shock on his face. "Seriously?"

"*Ya.* You look exhausted."

He nodded. "I am."

"Then let me fix you something to eat."

Without a moment's hesitation he nodded, then sat down at the kitchen table. She was able to find things in the tidy kitchen quickly, and soon she had coffee percolating and eggs and bacon frying on the stove. She poured a cup of coffee and added a little milk to it, remembering how Silas liked it. She turned to give it to him and saw that his head was down on the table. She set the mug down beside him, but he didn't stir. Something inside her broke free, and the love she used to feel for him surfaced. She touched his hair, brushing a thick, curly brown strand from his forehead.

Instantly he sat up, then looked up at her. "Sorry. Must have dozed off." Then he picked up the coffee mug and took a sip.

"Does it need more milk?"

He shook his head. "It's perfect."

"The eggs and bacon will be done soon." She started to walk away, then stopped when she felt his hand on her arm.

"Why are you doing this?" he asked, his eyes filled with confusion.

"Because I want to." She went back to the stove, surprised at how natural and easy things seemed between them. As if making breakfast for him was something she should have been doing all along. But when she slid the eggs onto his plate and placed three pieces of thick, crispy bacon beside them, a knot formed in her stomach. She'd come here with a purpose, and she couldn't put that off any longer.

"Here," she said, setting the plate in front of him. Then she sat down, not waiting for an invitation to join him. She folded her hands, staying silent until he finished praying.

When he was done, he opened his eyes and picked up his fork. "You're not eating?"

"I already had breakfast." Which was only half true.

She'd eaten part of a banana nut muffin, not having much of an appetite. It was hard to admit she was wrong, that she was sorry. It was difficult to swallow her pride, but she had to do it, for both her and Silas's sakes. "I didn't just come here to check on *yer mamm*. I came here to apologize."

Silas stopped mid-chew. "Really," he said, then swallowed a mouthful of eggs. "Two apologies in a week? That's got to be a record." Quickly he raised his hand. "Now I'm sorry. I shouldn't have said that."

"It's okay." She looked down at the table. "One of the reasons I can't stand sarcasm is that it always holds a bit of truth. In this case, a lot of truth."

"Faith, it's okay." He put down his fork and looked at her. "I appreciate *yer* apology."

"You don't even know what I'm apologizing for."

"Doesn't matter. The fact that you're here and we're talking without fighting . . ." He smiled. "I'll take it."

His smile reached all the way to her toes. He was so handsome. Charming, sweet, and creative. Now she knew he was loyal, and had been so devoted to his family that he hadn't betrayed their trust. Perhaps he always had been loyal and she'd been too self-absorbed to see it. "I shouldn't have broken up with you the way I did."

"Are you talking about the one-sentence letter you sent me?"

"Um, *ya*. That. And refusing to see you after. That was selfish of me."

He picked up a piece of bacon and took a bite. "*Geh on*," he said around the food.

"You're not going to make this easy on me, are you?"

"Should I?" His voice was soft. "You tore out *mei* heart, Faith. I wanted to marry you. To spend the rest of *mei* life with you. I deserved more than a letter and the silent treatment."

"I know." She started to tug on the string of her *kapp*. "I handled it wrong. I should have explained why I couldn't marry you. When *Grossdaadi* died, I was devastated. I also felt guilty."

"His death wasn't *yer* fault, Faith."

"But I could have helped him. If I'd been paying attention instead of being so focused on working in the woodshop, I would have heard him collapse." Tears stung her eyes as she looked at Silas. "He died right outside the door."

He took her hand and held it tight. "Faith, the aneurysm took him instantly. Even if you had heard him right away, there was *nix* you could have done."

Tears ran down her cheeks. "That doesn't make me feel any better. I miss him so much, Silas."

Silas turned his chair so he could face her. Then he took her other hand. "I know that now. And I wasn't there for you like I should have been. I was late for the funeral. Then I didn't come by *yer haus* until hours after."

"I needed you to be by *mei* side," she said, sniffling.

"And I should have been." He let go of her hands. "I don't have a *gut* excuse, other than I didn't take *yer* pain seriously. I was also a coward."

She looked at him. "What?"

"I've had a pretty easy life, one I've taken for granted.

Daed's business has always been *gut*, so we never wanted for anything. *Mamm* was always there for me. She and *Daed* had never been sick, and I never knew *mei* grandparents. They all died before I was born. I'd never lost anyone I loved. Until you left me. And even then, I didn't really understand how deep grief is . . . until I thought I would lose *Mamm*." He reached for her hand again. "So if anyone needs to apologize, it's me. What kind of husband would I have been if I couldn't be there for you when you needed me most?"

"Silas, I . . ." She didn't know how to respond. He'd said the perfect thing. The mature thing. "We both made mistakes," she finally admitted. "You're not the only one who had some growing up to do. So I wanted you to know—I'm not going to build the cabinets for Martha."

Silas frowned. "Why not?"

"Because I don't know what I'm doing. I have to be honest about that. I would slow down the process, and I know how much you need the money and the work. It's better that another carpenter work with you, one who is more experienced."

He shook his head. "We can work together. And you're not giving *yerself* enough credit."

"*Nee*, I've given myself too much. I've been prideful, Silas. I'm glad Martha has faith in me, but—"

"She's not the only one," he said, his eyes holding hers. "I know you have talent. The only thing you lack is experience."

His words gave her a warm feeling. "Which is why this isn't the right time for me to gain that experience.

So I'm going to tell Martha today to find another carpenter."

"Are you sure?"

"I'm sure. I can make something else for Martha and Melvin." She chuckled. "Maybe a bread box."

"Faith," Silas said, moving closer to her. "*Danki.*"

She couldn't stop looking into his eyes, and she saw something familiar in them. Love. But a different kind of love this time. One that was deeper. More mature. One that she strongly felt in return. When he leaned forward and kissed her, she didn't resist. Everything felt right—kissing him, giving up what she thought was her chance to prove herself, laying down her pride.

He pulled away from her and smiled again. "Wasn't sure you would let me do that."

"I'm glad you did."

"Tell you what. How about you help me with *mei* part of the kitchen job? I could use *yer* design and help with measuring, and you can keep me on schedule."

Excitement grew within her. She would be a part of the project after all. "I think I can do that."

"*Gut.* Because there's an added bonus in it for me."

"What's that?"

"We'll be together."

She put her arms around his neck and whispered in his ear, "That's a bonus for me too."

CHAPTER 9

Okay, both of you close *yer* eyes." Faith tried to stem her excitement as she led Martha into the finished kitchen, Melvin at her heels. When they were all in the middle of the room, she said, "Now you can open them."

"Oh, Faith." Martha looked around the kitchen, tears in her eyes. "This is perfect."

Melvin walked over to Silas, who was standing next to the gas stove on the opposite side of the room. He shook Silas's hand. "*Gut* job," he said, grinning.

"She seems to like it." Silas tilted his head toward Martha, who was turning around in the middle of the room.

"Here," Faith said. "Let me show you around." The kitchen was simple and utilitarian, like she initially designed. But Silas had added his artistic touch, not only using the oak wood from her grandfather's shop but also mixing different types of wood—cherry, maple, and some birch—to give the cabinets a unique look. The pantry was deep and had a sliding door instead of one that opened out. The stain was light oak, but the knots and character of the wood shone through. While Silas and another carpenter, Levi Beachy, had done most of the building, Faith had done a lot of the finishing work, mostly sanding and staining.

"Faith, I love it." Martha hugged her cousin. "Now that the rest of the *haus* is nearly finished, I can't wait to move in after the wedding."

Silas appeared at Faith's side. He looked down at her as Martha and Melvin continued to take in the kitchen, remarking on the flooring, which Silas had put in himself. Now that his father was able to work in the shop because his mother was better, Silas had had more time to devote to finishing the kitchen, which he completed as scheduled.

"We should probably *geh*," Silas said, leaning down and whispering in Faith's ear.

"*Ya*. I doubt they'll even know we're gone."

She and Silas told them good-bye. Martha and Melvin waved to them, and they left. A short while later while they were riding home, Faith expected Silas to take her to her house. Instead he took her to his home.

"Why are we here?" she asked.

"I want to show you something. *Geh* on in the *haus*. I'll be there in a minute."

While he put the buggy away, she walked inside. Over the past month she had spent a lot of time here, and she didn't feel the need to knock on the door. When she walked into the living room, she saw Emma sitting there, her knitting needles clacking with rapid speed. "Hi, Faith," she said, her smile sweet and calm.

She looked happy, and most of all, healthy. The thyroid medication had worked, and although she'd have to take it for the rest of her life, she would be okay. "Where's Silas?"

"Putting up the buggy." Faith sat down on the edge of the couch. "He said he had something to show me."

"Oh." Emma put down her knitting. "Can I get you something to drink?"

"*Nee*. I don't want to interrupt *yer* work."

"You're not. I was just sitting here . . . waiting."

But Faith didn't miss her small smile. "Do you know what Silas is going to show me?"

Emma picked up her knitting again. "You'll have to wait and see."

"Hmmph," Faith said.

After several minutes Silas came inside. He bent over and kissed his mother on the cheek. Faith smiled. Since her illness he hadn't been shy with showing his affection for her, even though it wasn't typically the Amish way.

Emma put her knitting in the basket beside her chair. "I'm heading for bed," she said. "*Yer* father is probably sound asleep by now. *Gute nacht*." She touched Faith on the shoulder as she passed by the couch and left the room.

"I'm so glad she's feeling well," Faith said when Silas sat down next to her.

"Me too."

"Did you ever ask her who Tommy was?"

"*Ya*." He sighed. "She has *nee* idea. She didn't know anyone named Tommy growing up. Her doctor said some hallucinations don't have an explanation." He angled his body toward Faith. "I don't want to talk about *Mamm* right now. I brought you here for another reason." He pulled a piece of paper out of his pocket and handed it to her.

She unfolded it. It was a sketch of a small house—a *dawdi* house, to be exact—attached to a larger house, which looked suspiciously like the Grabers' home. Faith looked at him. "Is this what I think it is?"

"*Ya*. I figure I'll need help building it. And I'd rather work with you than Levi anytime—not that he isn't a nice guy. He's just not as pretty as you are."

She blushed as she looked at the paper again. Unlike her neat drawings, this was a more abstract sketch than she was used to. "I don't understand, though. Why are you adding on a *dawdi haus* now?"

"Because where else will *Mamm* and *Daed* live after we're married?"

Faith's eyes widened. "Married?"

He moved from the couch to kneel in front of her. "*Ya*. Married. I want to marry you, Faith. I don't think I ever stopped wanting to be *yer* husband." He grew serious. "But don't answer right away. I want you to be sure. And if you say yes, I want you to mean it."

She glanced at the paper again. "Do you have a pencil?"

He frowned and stood up. "*Ya*." He went to the side table near his mother's rocking chair and pulled out the small drawer. He took out a pencil and handed it to her.

She took it from him and started writing on the paper. Silas sat down next to her, and when he tried to see what she was doing, she angled her body away from him. When she finished, she handed him the paper.

He looked down at what she'd written.

Yes, I will marry you. And yes, I mean it.

He let out a whoop, stood, and scooped her up in his arms, whirling her around the room. "But there's one thing I want to change," she said, when he put her down. "If it's okay with you."

"Anything. I trust *yer* judgment."

She beamed as she took the paper from his hand. How long she'd waited for someone other than her grandfather to have confidence in her abilities. Now the most important person in her life had given her his approval, even though she now realized she'd had it all along. "The bathroom needs to be over here." She drew an arrow from one side of the house to the other. "Oh, and I think *yer* parents need more than one window in the living room. If we lengthen this wall—"

He silenced her with a kiss, and she forgot all about the *dawdi haus* and carpentry. All she could think about was how much she loved him, and about the future they would build together.

DISCUSSION QUESTIONS

FOR *A CUP HALF FULL*

1. After the accident, Sarah fears that she can no longer be a good mother because she is in a wheelchair. Do you think that Sarah's worries are justified, or is Sarah's mother correct when she tells Sarah that all mothers are scared?

2. Who is the hero in this story? Sarah, for finally learning to accept her disability? Abram, for all he does to make a good life for Sarah? Saul, Sarah's father, for helping Abram financially? Mary, Sarah's mother, for calming Sarah's fears about motherhood? What about Brenda, a loyal friend to both Sarah and Abram? Or, are all of these people heroes in their own right, each one serving the Lord and each other?

3. If you woke up one day and couldn't walk, do you think you would go through the range of emotions that Sarah did? Could you eventually accept the hand God dealt you, or do you think you might stray from Him for a while, or maybe forever?

4. Sarah forms a bond with a duck she names Henry, both struggling to live a new and more challenging way of life. Have you ever had a pet that you connected to because of a shared set of circumstances?

5. What were your initial thoughts about Brenda? Did you think that she was flirting with Abram? And if so, did you feel bad later in the story when you realized that Brenda is a genuine person who is kind and loyal? Have you ever found yourself in a similar situation, judging a person before you really know him or her?

6. If you could "be" any one of the characters and rewrite the story to accommodate or illustrate their hidden emotions, who would you choose and why?

FOR *HOME SWEET HOME*

1. Mia went against her parents' wishes when she chose to marry Chace. Have you ever felt compelled to go against your family to do something you believed in?

2. The Allgyer family members were like guardian angels to the O'Conner family. Not only did they offer Chace, Mia, and Kaitlyn a safe home but they also showered them with friendship, food, and baby supplies. Why do you think Isaac and Vera decided to help Chace and his family?

3. Chace suffered with a verbally abusive foster father. Were you ever betrayed by a close friend or loved one? How did you come to grips with that betrayal? Were you able to forgive that person and move on? If so, where did you find the strength to forgive?

4. Mia realized by the end of the story that her home is wherever she, Chace, and Kaitlyn are. What do you think was the catalyst for Mia's change of heart?

5. Which character can you identify with the most?

Which character seemed to carry the most emotional stake in the story? Was it Mia or Chace?

6. Mia and Chace were down on their luck when they moved into the *daadihaus* on the Allgyers' farm. Think of a time when you felt lost and alone. Where did you find your strength? What Bible verses would help with this?

7. What do you think inspired Dr. Simpson to help Mia and Kaitlyn? Have you ever helped someone in need? If so, how did you feel after you helped that person?

8. By the end of the story, both Chace and Mia found solace through prayer, and they decided to find a church to attend. Think of a time when you found strength through prayer. Share this with the group.

9. What did you know about the Amish before reading this book? What did you learn?

FOR *A FLICKER OF HOPE*

1. Thomas questioned why God would allow their house to be destroyed when he and Noreen had already gone through multiple trials. Do you think God uses a negative experience or trials in life to bring you to a new level of faith? Have you gone through a trial where you didn't understand God's plan and were tempted to ask why? Did you understand later?

2. Noreen considered going to visit her relatives after the fire. Do you think she had a strong reason to go?

3. After the fire destroyed their house, the Amish members in the district pooled their resources to

help Thomas and Noreen. Do the members' actions remind you of anyone in the Bible? Can you think of Scripture verses that encourage believers to share?

4. The bishop gave Thomas some advice that changed his entire perspective on his relationship with Noreen. What did the bishop tell him?

5. Noreen and Thomas each blamed themselves for being the one who caused the fire. How do you think this affected the way they interacted with each other?

6. Was Thomas wrong to leave Noreen when she was in labor?

7. What do you think was the major cause of Thomas and Noreen's rocky marriage?

FOR *BUILDING FAITH*

1. Since the death of her grandfather, Faith has retreated into herself as a way to deal with her grief. How have you helped a loved one deal with grief?

2. Silas had a lot of growing up to do, and it took his mother's illness in order for him to mature. In what other ways does God use events to help us grow in our faith?

3. While Silas's issue was immaturity, Faith's was pride. Why is it so difficult to recognize pride in ourselves?

4. Faith has an unusual hobby for an Amish woman— carpentry. Do you have an unusual hobby/interest? What drew you to that particular hobby/interest?

5. What character qualities did you admire in Faith and Silas? Why?

ACKNOWLEDGMENTS

BETH WISEMAN

It is an honor to dedicate this story to Ann and Bill Rogers, champions of the Amish genre and delightful people. Through writing and reading Amish books, friendships have formed, ones I suspect will last lifetimes. Bill, you make me laugh out loud, and I don't do that nearly enough. Thank you for that. Ann, I've told you before—you have 'the light.' You can brighten a room with your presence and smile, which is such a gift to all of us.

People go to jobs they dislike on a regular basis. I know I'm blessed to be able to write stories that I hope entertain and inspire readers, while also glorifying God. I try not to take that for granted. Everything I am and do is a gift from God. But no book would make it to the shelf without a team of believers, so much thanks to my publisher, HarperCollins Christian Fiction; my fabulous friend and marketing assistant, Janet Murphy; my agent, Natasha Kern; my husband, Patrick; and my friends and family who have supported me from the beginning.

And it is always a delight to work with fellow authors in this collection—Kathleen Fuller, Ruth Reid, and Amy Clipston. Rock on, gals!

Amy Clipston

As always, I'm thankful for my loving family. Special thanks to Janet Pecorella for your friendship and encouragement. I'm grateful for my special Amish friend who patiently answers my endless stream of questions. You're a blessing in my life.

Thank you to Jamie Mendoza and the members of my awesome Bakery Bunch.

To my agent, Natasha Kern—I can't thank you enough for your guidance, advice, and friendship. You are a tremendous blessing in my life.

Thank you to my amazing editor, Becky Monds, for your friendship and guidance. I'm grateful to each and every person at HarperCollins Christian Publishing who helped make this book a reality.

Thank you also to editor Julee Schwarzburg for her guidance with the story. I always learn quite a bit about writing and polishing when we work together. Thank you for pushing me to become a better writer. I hope we can work together again in the future!

I'm grateful to editor Jean Bloom, who also helped me polish and refine the story. Jean, you are a master at connecting the dots and filling in the gaps. I'm so thankful that we can continue to work together!

Thank you most of all to God, for giving me the inspiration and the words to glorify You. I'm grateful and humbled You've chosen this path for me.

Ruth Reid

This book would not be possible without God walking me through the pages. God, You are my source of inspiration, and the reason I write. You have shown me over and over that all things are possible with You!

Thank you to my family for your love and support. My husband, Dan, for your expertise in construction. To my children, Lexie, Danny, and Sarah, who are always so supportive. I love you all.

Thank you to my awesome editors, Becky Philpott, Becky Monds, and Natalie Hanemann. Your insight and knowledge have helped me tremendously. I am so blessed to have the opportunity to work with each of you. It's an honor to have the ability to write for HarperCollins Christian Publishing. Daisy Hutton, you're wonderful! Kristen Golden, Jodi Hughes, Karli Jackson, and Kayleigh Hines, thank you all so much. I am so grateful God has placed you all in my life.

Thank you to my agent, Natasha Kern, for your advice and godly wisdom. Thank you for believing in me. I am so blessed that God led me to you!

Kathleen Fuller

A huge thank you to Becky Monds and Jean Bloom, for being the fabulous editors you are. As always, thank you, dear reader. It's a joy and a privilege to go on this writing journey with you.

ABOUT THE AUTHORS

BETH WISEMAN

Beth Wiseman is the award-winning and bestselling author of the Daughters of the Promise, Land of Canaan, and Amish Secrets series, as well as novellas that have been included in many bestselling collections such as *An Amish Year* and *An Amish Garden*.

Visit her online at BethWiseman.com
Facebook: AuthorBethWiseman
Twitter: @BethWiseman

AMY CLIPSTON

Amy Clipston is the award-winning and bestselling author of the Kauffman Amish Bakery, Hearts of Lancaster Grand Hotel, Amish Heirloom, and Amish Homestead series. Her novels have hit multiple bestseller lists including CBD, CBA, and ECPA. Amy holds a degree in communication from Virginia Wesleyan College and works full-time for the City of Charlotte, NC. Amy lives in North Carolina with her husband, two sons, and three spoiled rotten cats.

Visit her online at Amyclipston.com
Facebook: AmyClipstonBooks
Twitter: @AmyClipston

Ruth Reid

Ruth Reid is a CBA and ECPA bestselling author of the Heaven on Earth, the Amish Wonders, and the Amish Mercies series. She's a full-time pharmacist who lives in Florida with her husband and three children. When attending Ferris State University School of Pharmacy in Big Rapids, Michigan, she lived on the outskirts of an Amish community and had several occasions to visit the Amish farms. Her interest grew into love as she saw the beauty in living a simple life.

Visit Ruth online at RuthReid.com
Facebook: Author-Ruth-Reid
Twitter: @AuthorRuthReid

Kathleen Fuller

With over a million copies sold, Kathleen Fuller is the author of several bestselling novels, including the Hearts of Middlefield novels, the Middlefield Family novels, the Amish of Birch Creek series, and the Amish Letters series as well as a middle-grade Amish series, the Mysteries of Middlefield.

Visit her website at KathleenFuller.com
Instagram: kfstoryteller
Twitter: @TheKatJam
Facebook: WriterKathleenFuller